The
CLAIMANT

By Hollis Alpert

The Summer Lovers
Some Other Time
The Dreams and the Dreamers
For Immediate Release
The Barrymores
The Claimant

The
CLAIMANT

by Hollis Alpert

THE DIAL PRESS, INC.   NEW YORK   1968

For E. L. Doctorow

Part One

1: The letter from Hilde Kolisch came with the morning mail. Gloria brought it in, having placed it on top of a batch she had already opened. "I didn't open *that* one," she said. "It looked personal."

"Which one?"

"The blue envelope. The address is handwritten, and it has a German stamp."

"If it has a German stamp," I said, "it's probably business." I picked up the envelope and saw nothing familiar about the handwriting, but then I turned it over and saw Hilde's name.

I must have looked my surprise, for Gloria said, "You see, it *is* personal."

"I don't get personal mail at the office," I answered, a little nettled by her obvious wish to pry, "but since this is from a secret agent working for the Syrian government on a highly dangerous mission, you did the right thing."

"That's one of your jokes, isn't it, Mr. Becker?"

I noticed one of the buttons light up on my telephone and

gave Gloria a significant look. She retreated to the outer office to take the call, and I picked up the letter again, remembering. Hilde would be—what—thirty-seven or thirty-eight now? She had been about twenty when I had last seen her.

I slit the letter open and started to read it but was interrupted when Gloria buzzed me on the intercom to tell me it was Professor Marcus on the line.

"Tell him I'm tied up right now and I'll call him back."

"Okay," Gloria said, in a tone meant to let me know she was perfectly aware that the letter in the blue envelope had some special meaning for me.

Well, it did. Hilde Kolisch was an old, old girl friend from my days with the Army Occupation Forces in Germany after the war. She had made life both pleasant and complicated for me.

To be blunt about it, there I was, an American Army officer of Jewish family, making love to, sleeping furtively at night with, a German girl. And to make things worse she had once admitted to me that she had not thought much about or questioned the German treatment of Jews. At the time, this was a more shocking thing to hear than it would be now—for we have all learned a lot since. For myself, having so recently come across the terrible evidence, my tendency was to regard every German, young or old, as guilty of complicity, regardless of proof.

We both had our guilts, I suppose. And, although they didn't have the same base, they did somehow have a way of heightening our moments together, filling them with a moody kind of eroticism.

I was young, too, only twenty-four at the end of the war, and Hilde represented my first big affair with a woman. It was strange to be made to feel both manly and ashamed. Knowing who I was and what I was, I also knew that sooner or later my relationship with Hilde had to end. Eventually, while still stationed with the Army in Germany, I met Lottie, a young Jewish woman originally from Prague, who was found near the end of the war all but wasted away in Bergen-Belsen. She had regained her strength and a sad kind of beauty when I met her. To put it briefly for the moment, when the time came for me to leave for home I asked her to marry me; she accepted, and I took her with me.

I was of course not the only young American whose personal life was drastically affected by the war and its aftermath. But mine was irrevocably altered, and later it sometimes seemed to me that I still held on to the war. It became a kind of base from which I could orient myself. I had *believed* in it. And when I stared into the face of evil I had no doubt that I knew its nature. Stupidity, thoughtlessness, ignorance—these did not explain or mitigate.

Poor Hilde. Time and again I would make her the butt of my futile protest. "Yes, yes," she would mumble, perhaps only to placate me, "there is something wrong with the Germans." And I would shout, "With *you!*" She would weep and beg to be taken in my arms, and I would console her, saying, "*Liebchen, Liebchen,* it was nothing you could help. Forgive me, *Liebchen.*" And we would make love as though it were the only path out of the rottenness.

I walked through the ruins of many German cities, and bitterly I saw them as justice. Once I heard an accordion play at night among the stark remains of Frankfurt, and I was overwhelmed by the sick, sweet plaintiveness of the sound. Yet by day I was one of those attempting to make order out of the dust of destruction. Long afterward, in my dreams, I would walk again among those ruins, although they no longer existed, always seeing the same figure: a man, concentrated, patient, selecting with great care bricks of a relative wholeness from the mass of rubble. Did I dream that man into existence, or did I actually ever see him? As I write, I see him again. He brushes the ashes from the chosen bricks before putting them aside. The man is a German. Gray dirt has settled in the harsh lines of his face. He looks like death.

Hilde's hair was ash blond. Her eyes were the very same blue as the eyes of a Dresden doll. She was slender but wonderfully soft to the touch. She smiled often, and she was prettiest when she smiled. I met her when I was stationed in Höchst, a suburb of Frankfurt, in the legal department of a military government section. When I went into the Army I had precociously completed my first year at Columbia Law School and, as is common with this kind of precociousness, was third highest in my class. "Alfred Becker, the brilliant son," my mother would term me, half fondly, half ironically, for she was one of those who had left her own Jewishness behind her—and my father with it. Going into the Army at the age of twenty-one, I was assigned within a few months to the Judge Advocate Division and was made a second lieutenant after thirteen weeks of officer training. A month before the invasion of the Continent, I was sent to England, assigned to a corps headquarters staff. My own landing in France took place six weeks after the establishment of the beachheads, and thenceforth, until the end of hostilities, I was used mostly as a liaison officer. As an officer I had not accumulated enough of the necessary demobilization points to be sent home early, and I was reassigned to military government. I must admit that I didn't mind. I would have made the request to stay with the Army in Germany in any case. I was now Captain Becker, and it was pleasant to be an Army captain at the age of twenty-three, especially with the war over.

My close friend Captain Christopher French was enjoying

the peace even more than I. He was tied up with Gretel, the German translator in our section, and one day he told me that she could arrange for me to meet her girl friend, who, according to Gretel, was cute and pretty. "Maybe," I said. I was truly dubious about the propriety of such a meeting. The nonfraternization rules were still in effect, although hardly adhered to.

Chris and I were among six officers who shared the same billet—a house not far from the Farben Administration Building, commandeered for our offices. The street we lived on was called Nachtigallen Weg, "Nightingale Road." It seemed peculiarly ironic to me to be living on a street called Nightingale Road. My room in the house was comfortably middle-class, and whoever the owners were they never came around, for the whole street of equally comfortable houses was reserved for American Army officer billets. Just as well. They would have encountered a party almost every evening in the living room downstairs, and they wouldn't have liked the way their small Bechstein was banged upon by the young lieutenant from Detroit who considered himself equipped to play it. Since I drank little, I contributed my monthly liquor ration to the festivities, the sound of which drifted up frequently to my room on the upstairs floor. After a while, the din would cease; I would hear footsteps on the stairs; doors would close one after another, after whispers and giggles. It wasn't easy to concentrate on the law books I pored over to be better prepared for continuing law school when I got back home. And it was little consolation to tell myself that German girls only mingled with American officers to get immensely valuable cigarettes, soap, chocolate, and nylon stockings. I would go with Chris to the PX and buy my allotment of nylons for him, so he could give them to Gretel.

Finally, Gretel brought Hilde to the office, ostensibly to see if there was any work for her. "How'd you like her?" Chris asked me afterward. "Not bad," I said. Actually, I had fallen for her almost at once. She wasn't as flashily pretty as Gretel, but something about her got to me. Maybe it was the guilelessness of her expression, the ready smile. Or maybe it was the simple dress she wore, a little flowered garment of yellow cotton that had been washed again and again into a soft fadedness. She wore no stockings at all, and her odor was not of perfume but of soap—in itself a perfume of sorts for a German girl in those days. That same evening the four of us had our own party in the billet, using the dining room for our soirée, for the living room was noisily occupied, and the piano-playing lieutenant was practicing "That Old Black Magic" on the Bechstein. For some unknown reason, I had preserved two bottles of champagne from my liquor ration, and these I brought from my closet for the occasion. When the champagne was gone, Chris and Gretel went upstairs to his room, and Hilde and I were left to stare at each other. Her English was halting, but my German was adequate for conversational purposes. When the lieutenant at the Bechstein began singing "Lili Marlene" to his own accompaniment, I made a remark in German to the effect that we were hearing the nightingale of Nightingale Road. Hilde nodded and laughed, then stretched out her hand and clasped mine. Towering over her, I felt clumsy. "You have a room here?" she asked. I said that I did. "I will be your girl," she said. "Come." It was as simple as that, and nothing like it had ever happened to me before.

She was careful to explain to me before we made love that I was not her first lover. There had been someone before me, a German, a soldier who had been killed. Did I mind? I told her I didn't mind, but that wasn't true. I did mind making love to a girl who had been made love to by a German soldier. In a way, I fought the pleasure she gave me. But later, hardly had

I escorted her through the MP gate that supposedly blocked off Nightingale Road to all but American military personnel when I missed her and wanted to make love to her again. She came regularly to my billet after that. It became even easier when the MP guards were removed from the gate and German guards put there in their stead. A pack of cigarettes every few days, and Hilde could come and go as she pleased. I gave her the customary gifts. She refused them at first, but I told her that attitude was silly. I had little use for the PX supplies myself, and they cost me so little but were so valuable to her. She wouldn't take chocolate, though. She said she didn't want me to think she was a German girl who would do anything for a bar of chocolate. Once I obtained for her an ounce bottle of Guerlain perfume called *L'Heure Bleue*. "I will only use it," she said, quite overcome, "for the blue hours on Nightingale Road. For my man." During our love-making she would tell me she loved me. "You love me, yes?" she would ask, and I would refuse to answer, always remembering that she was a German girl who had loved a German soldier before me. And, when the time came to break up with her, many months later, I was as brusque about it as if I had hardly known her. I didn't tell her that I had met Lottie. I simply said that I was going to be shipped home soon and had some traveling to do first, that I had a lot of clearing up of office work to do before I left Germany and wanted to spend as much of my remaining time as possible helping out some Jewish refugees in a nearby DP camp. "There's no point in your coming here anymore," I said. "Besides, it's much better for you to try to find someone else. You see, it's for your own good as well as mine."

Hilde sat on the edge of the bed, which she had carefully made up, her shoulders drooping. This is how girls look, I remember telling myself, when they know you don't want them anymore. I was determined to be objective. I watched, almost abstractedly, as tears formed at the corners of her eyes and crept down her cheeks until they reached her lips and she brushed them away with the back of her hand. "But I could see you until you go," she said. "No point in it," I told her. "No point in it at all. I can't marry you. You need a man who will marry you. We have to face the facts."

"Facts," she said, "yes." Her face frozen, she slipped her feet into the shoes I had had shipped to me from New York. I took her by the arms and was about to kiss her good-by, but she turned her face away. At the door she gave me her hand, as though only formalities were allowable now. "I'll take you to the gate," I said. "No, please," she said, "I will go alone." Afterward, the German guard told me she had given him all the cigarettes in her handbag, three packs.

I thought I would feel relieved after she left, but I didn't. I was physically sick. I actually threw up. Then I went to Chris's room and talked to him about it. "What the hell else could I do?" I asked him. "I can't have two women here in Germany, one German, one Jewish."

"Why not?" Chris asked, gently twirling the brandy in his snifter.

"Because I'm seriously thinking of marrying Lottie. I'd feel a hell of a lot worse leaving her here in that DP camp, not knowing what would ever become of her."

"I thought she wanted to go to Palestine," Chris said. "You going to join a kibbutz with her?"

"She'll come to America," I said. "We've talked it all out."

"You really like the woman?" Chris asked. "Have you slept with her? I'd never marry a woman I hadn't tested out in the sack first. You wouldn't be letting your rabbinical idealism run away with you, would you?"

"Maybe," I said. "I'd bring the whole goddamned camp with me if I could."

Chris wasn't Jewish, but he understood. He had once handed some packs of K rations to some emaciated survivors of a camp he had found on the road. He had stopped his jeep to give them the cardboard packs, and one had ripped a pack open and stuffed some food into his mouth. The man had gone into cramps and convulsions and died in front of Chris's eyes. The K ration had been too rich for his shrunken stomach. Chris was my best man when I married Lottie in the improvised synagogue of the DP camp. And he brought along his entire month's ration of liquor—and that meant a lot to Chris—for the party we had afterward.

It was March of 1947 by the time I came back home, to New York City. I felt out of things at first, because no one wanted to talk about the war anymore. And Lottie felt strange, too. I thought the stores and shops, restaurants full of food, the theaters, the concerts at Carnegie Hall, the fat newspapers, and the fat new cars on the streets crowded with well-dressed people —that all this would be like a new world and a pleasant one to her. But she found no contact with it or couldn't make the contact. And since I had to devote a lot of time to completing the remainder of my work at law school (I was able to do it, by pushing hard, in a year and a half), there wasn't much I could do to help her out. I consoled her and myself with the thought that at least she was comfortable (if not in luxury) and secure and that it would eventually work out well—which it did in a sense. For my experience in Germany enabled me, immediately after passing my bar exams, to join a law office that specialized in the kind of case I was well equipped to handle. These involved claims to property in Germany and Austria by the dispossessed victims of Nazi anti-Semitism. Laws promulgated at first by the Allied Control Commission and then by the West German government pertaining to restitution and compensation swelled our office files with cases. In 1951 I was given a junior partnership in the firm; four years later I was made a senior partner, and I was able to give Lottie the luxuries she had never really requested of me.

I returned to Germany several times on business trips. But only once did I make the effort to look up Hilde. That was in 1953, when I was in Frankfurt and visited a former Army officer of my section who had found it to his advantage to remain on as a civilian lawyer. He had met Hilde through me, and he also knew Gretel. But both, he said, had moved elsewhere—or it seemed to him he had heard something to that effect. I was not exactly pining for a lost love, but I remembered how harshly I had said good-by to Hilde, and by then my feelings toward the Germans had softened slightly. After all, I now dealt with them on a business and official level, and I had developed a grudging respect for the new government's evident desire to do something about past evils through legal restitution. No government, to my knowledge, had ever before assumed that much responsibility for a previous government's actions. Any such step forward, I decided, was worth encouraging. I would have liked to have talked to Hilde again, but the trips were hurried, and there was never time to track her down.

In 1965, when I received that letter from Hilde, almost eighteen years since I had last seen her, I was with the same firm, and my name was third in a list of seven on the pebbled glass doors of our suite of offices in a building on East Forty-second Street. Our specialization had changed; we were experts now in setting up small corporations and foundations that could take advantage of new tax legislation. Lottie and I had remained together, but, to the sorrow of both of us, we had remained childless. She had had a miscarriage in 1950, and following upon it an operation that made further child-bearing impossible. We knew what to blame it on, but we didn't talk about it. Earlier we had thought of adopting a child from a DP camp in Germany, but by this time it was too late, and Lottie was against it anyway. The children, most of them, were in Israel, and the girl I had thought of adopting in 1947 had already been adopted—with my help—by a couple in Brooklyn. But I'll come to that. For the moment, I'll add only that Lottie held up that child's case as an example of why my adoption ideas were dangerous. I still handled restitution cases, even though they had thinned out considerably, and there were quasi-official agencies attempting to wind up the whole huge caseload. People seemed surprised when they learned that I still had a lot of restitution work; they had thought the thing was finished, that the Germans had paid up and that the books had been balanced, however lopsidedly. Wasn't it time to let them off the hook? They didn't know about the technicalities that could keep a case hanging for years, and, truthfully, if profit had been my aim, I don't think I would have bothered. I charged—the firm did, that is—only token fees that contributed little, if at all, to the wealth of the firm. Because I seemed to be the one most willing to handle those cases, they were usually shunted to me, and other law firms referred them to me, too. They were always headaches. So it was that every week or two some man or woman bearing the deep scars of the past entered the reception room of Dworkin, Jaffe, Becker, Pryor, Jackson, Steiner and Fineman, seeking the help I was undeniably equipped to give.

At the time Hilde's letter came I had one such case in progress that was more complicated than any of the others I had handled. In essence, sixty former slave laborers, banded together for legal purposes, were suing Zeller-Bricken Industrie for compensation. Jewish relief organizations had made a really extraordinary effort to round up the survivors of a group of three thousand sent to the Hanover plant of Zeller-Bricken, engaged then in the manufacture of guidance systems for V-1 and V-2 rockets. These Jews, marshaled out of concentration camps, could hardly have been expected to work willingly for the destruction of London and other British cities, yet the Zeller-Bricken firm took the position that the sparse group of survivors was not entitled to compensation. I had already cited precedents—Krupp and Telefunken, for instance—but some Zeller-Bricken underling had replied to me that the firm's present management was of a constitution quite different from that of the wartime directorate and could not be held responsible for the firm's previous "labor policies." I wondered if my correspondent appreciated the irony of the term he had used as much as I did.

In spite of literally world-scouring efforts, we had found less than a hundred survivors of those "labor policies," and some still had such vivid memories of their working conditions that the mere mention of Zeller-Bricken resulted in a cold refusal to have anything to do with our case. The sixty I represented had been convinced by myself and others, such as my good friend Elihu Grossman, that, first of all, they deserved more compensation than they would ever get and that, secondly, such cases had moral value. The more Germans who could be forced to admit to their inhuman acts during the Nazi years the better. Several of our victims informed us that they could do without the moral benefits but that the cash, in their severely straightened and often handicapped circumstances, would prove very helpful.

West German compensation laws, promulgated over a period of some fifteen years, had never required private industry to compensate its wartime workers, and this was why, being on slippery legal ground, I was inclined to stress morality—aside from believing in it myself. My arguments were not effective, but then we learned that Zeller-Bricken was negotiating with the United States Defense Department for contracts. A Washington contact of mine had informed me that it seemed likely that a contract would be awarded for the manufacture of electronic guidance equipment to be installed in jet fighters. Details of the nature of the equipment were, of course, top secret. With this knowledge in mind, I immediately drew up and sent off to Zeller-Bricken another demand for compensation. This time a reply was forthcoming to the effect that if I were to be in Berlin in the near future, members of the directorate would be willing to have a discussion with me.

Then something else came up. Elihu Grossman, president of the New York chapter of B'nai Jeshurat, and a prime mover, I might add, behind the effort to compensate those sixty victims, received an interesting report about two of Zeller-Bricken's present directors. These two had been with the firm in the old days and had been clearly Nazi. This knowledge, if accurate, could effectively counter the firm's best argument against paying up—that there was no connection between past and present managements. Elihu for the past two months had been prodding me to go to Berlin and check up on a Herr Roehling and a Herr Weisse, the two mentioned in the report to him, which had emanated from a usually trustworthy source, the Yad Vashem in Jerusalem.

Not only was Zeller-Bricken's headquarters in West Berlin, but the city was a storehouse of documents, to which Elihu knew I could gain access. I kept promising Elihu that I would go to Berlin soon, and I wrote my principal Zeller-Bricken correspondent, Kurt Hildebrandt, that I planned to visit his city shortly. He replied that he would be honored to meet with me if I cared to call on him. This politeness, of course, meant nothing. Firms of the size of Zeller-Bricken had a dozen Hildebrandts to deal with correspondents like me. I would, I hoped, bypass him. Once in Berlin, I would have my own means of checking on Herr Roehling and Herr Weisse.

Six weeks passed between that last exchange with Hildebrandt and Hilde's letter. Getting away from the New York office was never easy, and I had been putting off a couple of other matters, too, until I was free to leave.

The letter was written in careful English. Hilde had learned that I came now and then to Berlin, where she was now living. Such an odd coincidence. She did translating, like her friend Gretel—did I remember Gretel?—and had done work for one of the judges of the Restitution Court in Berlin. American lawyers sometimes dealt with the court, and so she had asked Judge Kimmel if, by chance, he had heard of me. Imagine! Judge Kimmel had told her he knew me well and had seen me less than a year before. From him she had obtained my office address in New York, and now she wrote after all this time hoping that I was well and happy and hoping, too, that the next time I came to Berlin I would give her the pleasure of a meeting. How well she remembered me. So much had happened, so many years had gone by. How pleasant it would be if I should come to Berlin and we could meet again and talk. If I could give her advance notice, that would be helpful. In any case, she included her telephone number.

Why had she written? There was nothing in the letter to show that she wanted some special favor from me. Nor did there seem to be any urgency in her desire to see me. And did

I want to see her again? I remembered a reunion of high-school classmates I had attended and how bored I had been—everyone looking older than his age, the girls turned into worried-looking housewives, the men balding and paunchy. None of us had had much to say to the others. "You look exactly the same," we all had lied. After eighteen years, what could Hilde and I have to say to each other? Perhaps it would be wise not to write back. Better to leave it alone, I told myself, and later if I should have the time, or feel in the mood, I could look her up. That would make it seem more casual. And, after all, I couldn't even tell her exactly when I would be in Germany, since I kept putting off my trip.

At the same time, it was hardly polite not to answer. I decided to write her a brief note. Delighted to hear from her, and pleased that she still remembered. Yes, I did get to Berlin on occasion, and if one should arise soon I would certainly hope to get in touch with her. I couldn't be more noncommittal than that.

I brought the sealed letter to Gloria and dropped it on her desk. "Send it airmail," I said, "and get me the Professor on the phone."

"I suppose your wife knows all about this," she said with heavy sarcasm.

"No, but you won't give me away," I said.

As it turned out, Professor Marcus' call also had to do with the trip I was supposed to be taking to Germany. He had heard from Elihu Grossman that I would be leaving soon, and he hoped I wouldn't forget what I had promised to do for him.

"No," I said, "I won't forget."

"When exactly are you going?"

"Soon, soon. There are things to finish up here first."

"And little Sarah Stein?"

Little Sarah Stein! She was over thirty, and still he called her "little Sarah Stein."

"Naturally I'll look into that, too," I told him. He didn't need to remind me.

Some of my clients seemed to assume, where those trips of mine were concerned, that Germany was a place approximately the size of Long Island, that one could get around the country in a matter of a couple of hours or so. If I was scheduled to be in Berlin, how easy it would be for me to hop over to Munich or Hamburg! Look up so-and-so in Tübingen, I would be told, and ask him about . . . From experience I knew I could spend a day and a half looking up someone in Tübingen, with a first-rate chance of discovering that he had long ago moved to Innsbruck. But for Sarah Stein I would go to Tübingen, if need be, and to Innsbruck, too, for her case was what I suppose could be called a matter of conscience.

While stationed in the Frankfurt area after the war, I had made it a practice to visit nearby DP camps. In one I'd met Lottie, in another the Professor. The children at these camps were mostly under six, but Sarah was an exception. The Professor, head of a committee at the camp near Kassel, had me visit with the shy, gawky thirteen-year-old girl who could only remember her first name. Her expression was haunted and frightened, her eyes stared darkly into space, although after her shyness wore away she would smile at us sweetly. "The others will find homes," the Professor told me. "But this one I worry about. She is already almost grown." I had written about her to an organization in New York, explaining that in some ways it was easier to place the smaller children whose parents would never return. Eventually a warm home was found for her with a childless Brooklyn couple. This was after Lottie and I had considered taking her ourselves. None of us could have known then the kind of woman she would become. Sarah remained shocked and frightened; kindness helped on the surface but not beneath. When she was sixteen she had to be put in a mental institution in Central Islip, where she remained for a year. The diagnosis: chronic schizophrenia. She would leave and then return again to the institution for a few months at a time. Now she lived in Brooklyn, placidly enough, on some sort of tranquilizer treatment. The thing was, her foster parents were getting old and feeble, their income was minuscule and had to be supplemented by Jewish welfare. Sarah herself couldn't work; in fact, it was remarkable that she was able to look after the needs of the old man and woman as well as she did.

The crux of her case in dealing with the German restitution people—from whom I had tried to get compensation for her—was the lack of proof that her present condition was a direct result of persecution in a concentration camp. How do you prove that? Well, I and others had tried. A doctor was even sent by the German consulate in New York to give a diagnosis. His diagnosis: inconclusive. Some avenues would have to be explored further in Germany, and I had made up my mind that one day I would do so.

But Sarah was not the main reason Professor Marcus had called. That was about the candelabrum he was attempting to trace. He had elected me to handle it, so to speak. I certainly wouldn't have gotten into it any other way.

By the end of that day—maybe it was Hilde's letter and the memories it stirred up, or the Professor's call, or the conjunction of both—I had set the date for the trip. All day long I thought of that time in Germany when I would by night make love to Hilde and by day interrogate Germans who wanted their homes back, such as they were, or who required clearance for the jobs that American military government was making available. I must say, it was hard to find a genuine Nazi, and how Hitler ever got his support from the German masses must have been due to miraculous circumstances. Some days I would beg off and make those trips to the DP camps, which proved to be an excellent exercise for putting things in perspective.

But it all came back vividly, in a warm glow of nostalgia, and by five o'clock I knew I would be taking a Monday morning flight, two and a half weeks away. In fact, I commissioned Gloria to make my reservation with Pan American, because they flew directly to Frankfurt, with only a short wait for the connecting flight to Berlin. I wouldn't have to hang around the Frankfurt airport. And, at dinner that evening, I informed Lottie that I would be making another of my trips to Germany.

"Again?" she said. "Couldn't they send someone else for a change?"

"It's the Zeller-Bricken case, and I'm the only one in the office who's been handling it."

"How boring to have to deal with those people."

She meant the Germans, and well could I understand her attitude. But there was hostility, too, toward me, as though a long day had fixed and amplified hidden grievances in her mind. Lately, there had been more and more of this hostility.

I'd talked about it once with a psychiatrist, explaining to him that I found it hard to exist in such an atmosphere. Not that I wanted to leave Lottie—I only wanted to find out how to live with her. I mentioned to him her irritability, perhaps caused by the insomnia she was prey to, and her frequent spells of depression.

The psychiatrist told me that Lottie was far from unique. There was hardly a survivor of the concentration camps who had not shown symptoms of what he termed the "Post-KZ syndrome." Lottie, in spite of the ease of her life with me now, was bound to have it, too. I must admit, it did help me to be able to understand my wife in those terms.

In a conciliatory tone, I said to Lottie: "I'm supposed to be an expert on things of that kind, and, while there's not much of a fee involved, the case could get some publicity, and the firm's view is that it wouldn't hurt to have it."

"I did not remember asking you if it was going to make you richer," Lottie said, as though I had accused her of asking that. "If you want to do something, do it, but don't think you have to make it sound practical to me."

"I was trying to say," I told her carefully, "that from the firm's point of view certain cases are lucrative and some bring status. Some of the partners are rich enough to afford status. Maybe it's for that reason they happen to think this case is important. As for me, I'm just as anxious to get Sarah Stein's case settled."

"Poor woman," Lottie said noncommittally.

But, if the winds had abated, the storm center remained. After so many years together it was still difficult for me to know just what it was that caused her more difficult moods. The psychiatrist had gone at length into the causes of the "Post-KZ syndrome." "It has been observed," he said, "—and, by the way, these studies are all rather recent—that among some survivors, the world is regarded with mistrust. You see, a human being cannot be subjected to a life in a concentration camp without profound repercussions in his subsequent life. Hostility and suspicion develop, and in some cases psychosis, although I am not saying *that* about your wife. No, she's relatively normal, I'd say. And you can take it as normal that someone who's been through as much as she has would quite naturally display certain attitudes toward other people, and this would include you. To the stranger—and if you weren't in a camp you are a stranger—these attitudes would seem like bitterness, or envy, or cynicism and quarrelsomeness. But it's only to be expected."

The psychiatrist had probably been right, but still Lottie was a puzzle to me.

During our first two years together in New York I hadn't worried too much about Lottie's moods. She would adjust, I thought, and it had to be expected that it would take time. And now and then she did say to me that it was like a miracle for her to know that she would eat well this day and the one following, that she had sweet-smelling soap to bathe with, and a comb. She'd show me her comb, and say: "You can't imagine what a luxury this is." "A simple comb?" "Oh yes, for two years I went without one." The security, I thought, was the important thing, and her periods of silence and gloominess came, I was sure, from the memories still so recent. She told me the apartment house we were in made her nervous, so I rented a large, cheerful apartment in another neighborhood—on Fifty-fifth Street, very close to the center of things. She perked up some after becoming pregnant, but a few months later she lost the child, and an operation was needed following that, after which the spells of depression came more frequently. I told her it was only natural for her to feel badly, but she said it wasn't just the loss of the baby. This city, this country, was not where she wanted to be. "If I had to choose between New York and Prague," she once told me, "I would choose Prague, and I don't give a damn that the communists have it now. The Nazis were worse, I assure you." But Prague was not where she wanted to be either. She realized, she said, that she thought of Prague only out of a kind of childish homesickness. "It was the other chance," she said. "The one I had and lost." And through the years reminders came now and then from Lottie that if it had not been for my coming along she would have made her life in Israel, that the exodus would sooner or later have taken her there, and that even the life in the barracks at Sodesheim now seemed in retrospect to have been worthwhile, for she had felt herself to be part of a community, a sense she lacked here in New York. These New York friends of mine—they talked business or civil rights, or prided themselves on their cultural status because they attended the theater and read the *New York Times* regularly. And what was there for her here? Bridge with dull women, and movies that were never any good, and entertaining people she had no interest in.

And what could I do or tell her, except that I for one was thankful she was where she was and comfortably off.

But was it only that? I hesitated to plunge much further, for that would have meant exploring the groundwork of our marriage, and I was unwilling to explore something to which I felt deeply committed. Although sometimes I wondered—doubted, perhaps—whether I tried enough. I had offered, for instance, to take her on those trips of mine to Germany, but she had never wanted to go. I might have been able to be more persuasive. On the other hand, she did go with me on a trip I took to Vienna, on condition we would fly from there for a visit to Israel, where we spent ten days at a damnably hot time of the year. But Lottie had professed to love every minute of it, including, even, the execrable food served us in a Tel Aviv hotel. Maybe she had hoped that, having once seen the country, I would be moved to live there. She tentatively suggested it, in fact, putting it on the basis that I could be a lot closer there to the kind of work I liked to do. But behind that suggestion lay an assumption that I resented. I had met it in other Jews from Europe—this assumption that a Jew was a Jew first and belonged to his country of origin secondarily. Lottie would remain suspiciously silent when I would tell her that I was an American, not first or second, but an American, as though what I'd said was tantamount to covering up my Jewishness, as though I might be secretly fearful of a new holocaust of the kind that had almost ended her existence. But I didn't put my resentment of her attitude into words; she had been through more than enough, and I couldn't add to her burden.

So now, seeing her unhappy, I said to her as I always did: "You could come along."

"No thank you," she said, as though I was being ridiculous to merely mention such a thing. "Just tell me what I'm supposed to do while you're gone."

"Whatever you want to do. Would you want to take a trip somewhere? You mentioned that you'd like to go to Bermuda. Only a couple of hours and you're there. Zelda was talking about going to Bermuda." Zelda was her bridge partner. "The two of you could go together."

"We can play bridge here," Lottie said.

"Well, I've got this business to do. I can't let it go much longer. If I don't go soon I might as well forget it."

"I wouldn't be surprised if you have some woman over there," Lottie said.

"No," I replied patiently, "I do not have some woman over there."

"You had a German girl once."

"That's right," I said. "I did, eighteen years ago, to be exact."

Something a little psychic there, I thought. Funny that she should bring up Hilde at just this time. And she had sounded a little jealous, which was strange for a woman who had stopped sleeping with her husband, who had kept her bedroom inviolate for more than two years.

"With all those trips you make," she said, "you must have seen her again."

"Who?"

"The German girl. The one you used to sleep with."

"No, I've never seen her again," I said.

"Then you admit you slept with her?"

"I don't like to talk about such things," I said. "It's unhealthy. I just don't see any use in discussing it."

"And I suppose," Lottie persisted, "it was not unhealthy to sleep with a German girl?"

"Let's get off the subject."

"What lice they were, those women they used as guards," Lottie said. "I cannot understand why you never mind going back to Germany. It seems extremely strange to me that someone who is Jewish——"

"I'd rather not talk about it," I said, more sharply than I should have.

Lottie subsided suddenly, and a distant, sad look came over her face. I felt the old ache for her, and I was at a loss to know exactly what it was compounded of—some kind of love, certainly, a love that had managed to persist in spite of the denial of her bed, her frequent physical complaints, her protracted spells of dark depression. As for desire, that was about gone.

"How about a movie?" I suggested. "There's a James Bond thing playing on Third Avenue."

"I'd rather stay at home," she said. "I'm tired."

I had a lot of the evening left to myself. Nothing very unusual for a marriage of eighteen years. I went to the James Bond movie by myself, and it helped to take my mind off things for awhile.

2: Professor Herman Marcus, once of the history faculty of the University of Weimar, and later a resident of Himmler's model ghetto, Theresienstadt, was a friend and client of mine. When he heard that the German government was recompensing persecutees for the loss of property and valuables, he attempted through an organization of Central European refugee Jews in New York to reclaim some items and, of course, after long, fretful correspondence, failed, because West Germany was offering money and not attempting to find lost objects. But Professor Marcus was not interested in money—even though he was able to scrape together only a most modest living for himself. He wanted his property, and that was why he came to me as a client. It was understood between us that when I had successfully fulfilled my mission in his behalf I would get my own recompense, and it was this understanding that gave him the right, he felt, to burden me with his problems.

"But this doesn't require a lawyer," I told him when he had

first come to me about the matter a year earlier. "You can go to a half a dozen organizations, describe the property, and they'll make a search."

"I can't handle all that red tape," he said, as he made himself comfortable in my office and smoked a thin Dutch cigar to its last inch. "You take the job and bill me at the end."

I realized that actually Professor Marcus was allowing me to share his dream. He dreamed he would someday, somehow, recover the religious objects seized (stolen, he said) from the synagogue of Erfurt, of which his father, late and lamented, had been the rabbi. Rabbi Marcus, age seventy-one, had been dragged from the synagogue during the historic Night of Crystal, had been stomped and beaten by exuberant members of the Hitler Youth, and had died of a heart attack before he could be ministered to further. During the looting the venerable Torah scroll, with its rare handles of intricately worked silver, had disappeared, along with—worst loss of all—the synagogue's candelabrum of gold and brass that had been handed down for twelve generations. On behalf of the Professor, I made a claim upon the German authorities and asked that a search be made. No record of any such objects was found. But the Professor was offered a decent sum of money in compensation.

"Absolutely not," said the Professor. The Germans were being lazy. They were ducking their responsibility. Granted that Torah scrolls were in almost all cases destroyed, that the silver handles had probably been melted down. But not a candelabrum so historic as the Erfurt Menorah. Such things didn't disappear. They were hoarded somewhere. Even the Nazis had known that religious antiquities had a value far beyond their weight in metal. "Besides," the Professor pointed out, "they respected gold. Look how they cracked open the jaws of fresh corpses to get hold of a few grams from their teeth fillings."

As he had grown older, the Professor had made it his sole mission to find the candelabrum and present it to a congregation he attended in Kew Gardens, one that he, along with other refugee German Jews, had helped to establish. There it was again, the continuity principle. My own notion was that the Professor wasn't merely trying to recover something—after all there were some quite handsome modern examples of candelabra being fashioned by genuine artists—but that he was attempting to build a bridge from the past to the present. I had often tried to make him accept the unlikelihood of finding what he was searching for. But that candelabrum lived, burned, in his mind, and therefore it existed.

Now, as soon as my air ticket for Berlin was delivered to me by Pan American, I called up the Professor.

"At last!" he said. "I will make a list of names for you."

"What names?"

"People who will guide you in your search."

"How much time do you think I'll spend there?" I asked, as usual made a little exasperated by his persistence. "Anyhow, we've already written to those names of yours."

"These are new names." The Professor was patient with me. "You see, I have been doing some letter writing of my own."

"Behind my back? What is it? Don't you think I work hard enough on your case?"

"I know you're busy," the Professor said. "You have lots of things on your mind. I can't ask that you should devote all your time to me."

But that was exactly what the old rascal would have asked if he had felt he had a chance of getting away with it.

"What are these other names?"

"Max Gerson, in Berlin, is one of them."

"And I suppose I should know who he is?"

"He once was an antique dealer," the Professor said, with a small, restrained note of triumph in his voice. "He was a specialist in religious objects during the thirties."

"What good will that do us? You need a specialist who is in contact with the market right now."

"See Gerson," the Professor said. "He's very interested in the problem. But I'll give you other names, too. When do you leave?"

"In a little over a week."

"Good, you shall have my list tomorrow. And you won't forget Sarah?"

"Of course I won't forget Sarah."

Where Sarah Stein was concerned there was more hope. Before I left for Germany, I managed to get out to Brooklyn, where she lived with the old people. I went there on a Saturday, after the conversation with Professor Marcus. Mrs. Mishkin immediately set the tea kettle on the gas flame, Mr. Mishkin wanted my opinion of the prospects of the New York Mets during the coming season, and Sarah gave me her sweet smile.

"How are things?" I asked her.

"The same."

Only that stare into some kind of blackness told you that a disturbance existed in her.

"I'm going to Germany next week," I told her. "This time I'm going to try to wind up that case of yours."

"Oh, wonderful," she said. "We need the money so badly."

"I know."

"Prices are so high for everything. Oranges. I wanted to buy some, but I was afraid to. Pop loves fresh oranges. Do you like the frozen kind?"

"So-so," I said.

"I wish I could work."

"The doctor doesn't want it," I said. "You're fine, but he doesn't want you to take a job."

"I can type," she said. "I saw ads in the paper. A typist can make eighty dollars a week."

"Did you ask the doctor about it?"

"No, but I think I will next time. You know I learned to type in the hospital."

"Yes," I said, "but typing for an employer can be a strain. I know. I terrorize my typist."

"Not you," she said seriously.

"Look," I said. "This trip I'm going to try to locate someone who was in that camp with you."

She had never been able to remember the name of the camp, but we had established with reasonable certainty, through the tracing service in Arolsen, that she had spent a minimum of six months in Reichenau, a camp near Innsbruck, and that her parents had in all likelihood perished at Ravensbruck. The West Germans had offered compensation for the loss of her parents, but (if a certain cynicism can be forigven) one doesn't get much for lost parents. The sum offered would have helped her very little, and that was why I held out for the larger amount, made possible through changes in the restitution laws. Not many are aware of how much lawyers like myself have to go through in the way of haggling with minor German bureaucrats. One might think it is their own money that is being given away. One German official actually said to me once, "All the Jews living in New York are rich. I don't see the necessity for giving them the money."

Blood money, it has been called—so much per dead Jew. The truth, as usual, seldom gets into the papers.

The psychiatrist who had been attending Sarah lately—Dr. Morganstern—told me that the root of her disturbance was sexual, in his opinion. By now a bulging folder on her case had developed, report after report. He read a few items to me, much of it sounding strange and garbled. "I think it definitely points," he said, "to her having been sexually violated as a little girl."

"In the camp you mean?"

"We can make a guess that if it happened, it happened when she was perhaps eleven or twelve."

"Germans?"

He shrugged.

"Would your opinion stand up legally."

"You know more about that than I do. I suppose one would need witnesses of some kind, because Sarah's certainly not going to tell you, or us. That's blocked out, and deep therapy hasn't done any good."

Finding witnesses was part of my business. The lists have accumulated over the years. At Arolsen alone they could tell you the names of some 60 or 70 percent of the people in dozens of camps. The inquiries about Sarah had been sent out to Israel, Yugoslavia, France, Argentina, wherever survivors of Reichenau now lived. Did anyone remember a small girl, name of Sarah Rembarsky, parentless? No one did.

She remembered very little at the time she was found by other refugees on a roadside near Bad Tölz—only that she had swept floors from dawn till dark in a dank underground factory near Innsbruck. Because she worked, she had survived. She couldn't remember her last name at first, and so a man in the refugee camp where she was placed had given her his name, Stein. When she finally remembered her own, it didn't seem to matter to her that she had another. Anyway, in those days names didn't count for very much. All anyone had to do to get one was to lift some papers from a corpse.

In spite of the negative result of that inquiry to Arolsen, I felt it should be possible to find someone who remembered Sarah. It happened all the time, but you never knew quite where or when. There were still a small, hardy corps of us who kept in touch with the past and with each other.

"Sarah," I said gently, fearful of probing too much, "have you remembered anything recently about Reichenau?"

"The camp?" she said, with a perplexed expression.

"We're trying to find someone who remembered you there, or whom you remember. Sometimes faces, names, come back in a flash."

"Yes, they do," she said. "Only a few days ago I thought of Christianne."

"Who?"

"A girl at the camp. She was nice. I missed her when she left."

I kept myself calm, but it was really extraordinary that suddenly a name, perhaps a face, had broken through. "Do you remember what she looked like—where she came from?"

"No. She was a nice girl, and very sad."

I did not press her further. A first name, I knew, could be of great help, especially a name that, as in this case, was not Jewish.

"Christianne," said Mrs. Mishkin, who had been listening. "That's not a Jewish name. What kind of person with a name like Christianne would be in a camp?"

"A political, maybe," I said, and took Mrs. Mishkin aside. "Remember it. Tell it to the doctor next time he sees Sarah. And if she says anything else about her, tell him that, too."

Then I telephoned Dr. Morganstern and told him that Sarah

had remembered a name. "I'm going to make a try at locating this Christianne when I'm in Germany. Would that be of help to you?"

"Possibly," the doctor said. "I'd like to know about the conditions Sarah faced and, of course, any incidents of the kind we talked about. I'm encouraged that she remembered something, at least. I'd like to try some drug therapy, and the more facts I have about that period of her life the better."

"I'll see what I can do," I promised him. "Do I take it that you're getting hopeful about Sarah?"

"I wouldn't want to go that far," he said with his usual professional guardedness. "With the drug treatments I have in mind, we might get her to remember more, but this doesn't necessarily indicate that an improvement in her condition would result. So far she has resisted deep analysis. If that resistance lessened—— But you realize I'm speculating."

"Yes," I said, "of course."

"But any facts you could obtain," he said, "would have material value for me. I mention this because I assume that ordinarily you would be interested only in the legal aspects—testimony, in other words."

"I get the message," I told him.

I happened to run into the Professor the Sunday before I left. We were both in attendance at the bimonthly meeting of the Wiener Group, an association of Jews of German ancestry, of which my father had once been a member. The organization had swelled after the influx of German Jews prior to and after World War II, and many of the members thought of themselves as representative of the intellectual traditions of their old homeland. My father had taken me to one of the Sunday meetings while I was still in my teens, probably in an attempt to acquaint me with what he regarded as his family tradition, even though he was a second-generation American Jew. But his grandfather had been a professor of law at Weimar University, and in the Wiener Group this gave him a certain distinction. I suppose it was one of the few places he did have any distinction, for, as he grew older, his law practice declined, and his principal absorption was chess, to which he devoted himself religiously. He was a dreamy man, my father, with the nature—if not the ability—of an artist, and, though he remarried after the divorce from my mother, I think he never quite recovered from the blow of her leaving him. After the war, having seen what I had seen, I made a point of joining the Wiener Group, and of this he was very proud. "He takes after his great grandfather, doesn't he?" he would say, time and again, to other members.

Younger members of the group were sparse, and maybe for that reason alone I was made warmly welcome. But there was also a kinship that came from the restitution work I did. At least two thirds of the membership received monthly pension checks from the West German government, and, for more than a few, this was about all they had to live on.

Since I was leaving for Germany the next day I asked Lottie if she wanted to attend the meeting with me. "Gottfried Geist is going to speak," I told her.

"And who is Gottfried Geist?"

"A German journalist, here under the auspices of the Goethe Society. He writes for some of the best German magazines."

"No thank you," she said. "I don't think he would have anything to say that would interest me much. Anyway, those old people who go to the meetings are such bores."

"Not when you get to talk to them," I said, but I didn't press the issue. "You don't mind if I go?"

"On your last day here?" She shrugged. "Do as you wish."

"Is there anything you wanted to do particularly?"

"At the last minute, now that you ask, I can't think of anything. But I do have a book to read, and I will listen to the afternoon concert on WQXR. I, too, can lead a cultural life, and right here at home."

She intended some kind of irony, I knew. It was always that way. When I proposed doing something with her that she didn't care to participate in, her refusal somehow managed to give me a little sting of guilt, the implication being that I would go ahead and do what I wanted to do anyway. A loyal wife, I thought rather bitterly, would want to go where her husband went. But I didn't say it, and maybe I should have.

I at once picked out the shaggy head of Professor Marcus among the fifty-odd who attended the meeting. He was cordial.

"When do you leave?" he asked, gripping my hand in his veined old ones. An odor of tobacco came from him.

"Tomorrow."

"You're all packed?"

He made it sound as though I was making a trip for which I had prepared for months and which would occupy me longer than that.

"Well, not quite," I said.

"You have my list of names?"

"Yes, and now all I need is a solid month to look them up." The irony was in reference to the seven names he had given me, with addresses that stretched from Düsseldorf to Vienna. Only Max Gerson, the expert on religious antiquities, was in West Berlin. The most authoritative name was that of Martin Silbermann, who lived in Vienna. Silbermann I did not know personally, but I had corresponded with him. He had helped me locate three of the former Zeller-Bricken victims.

"You must be certain to see Silbermann," the Professor advised.

"But I may not get to Vienna."

"Then you must call him. I have included his telephone number."

"Those I don't see I'll telephone or write to."

"They will give you leads," the Professor promised me.

"How about this Max Gerson?"

"An excellent man. He will help you."

"I'm going to need it," I said.

"And when you find the candelabrum," the Professor said, "as I know you will, offer any price. I have friends who will see that it is raised."

"Suppose someone wanted ten thousand dollars."

"In that case," he said, "you will understand why I chose such a good negotiator."

"Your compliments will get you nowhere," I told him. "Suppose we take a minute before the meeting starts and go through your list. Who is this Goldwurm in Düsseldorf, for instance?"

"He is the advertising solicitor for the *Allgemeine,* the German Jewish weekly published there."

"And how will he be able to help us?"

"He has good contacts."

"But what kind of contacts?"

"He knows people who know things."

"Yes," I said, patiently. "And this Guggenheimer in Frankfurt. Who is he?"

"He has been successful in locating property stolen by Nazis."

"Have you been in touch with him?"

"Oh, yes."

"And has he obtained results?"

"Not yet."

"Then what do we need him for?"

"If only to know where not to look."

"I see," I said, mentally eliminating trips to Hamburg and Frankfurt. "Well, I'll do my best for you. That's all I can promise."

"We are in good hands," the Professor said, as the meeting was called to order.

Herr Geist hailed from Munich, where he specialized in drama and music criticism. He also wrote articles of a more general cultural nature for magazines, and a few of these I had read. I knew him to be of the newer crop of German writers, for whom, as for many like him, the recent past of his country was an embarrassment, a historical lump difficult to swallow. His talk, delivered in High German rather than his native syllables, roamed over the flowering of West German democracy, politically, economically and culturally. He might have been better advised to avoid the subject of unification of the two Germanies, but bravely he spelled out its paramount importance to the German people. His audience grew restive. "Never mind about that," someone audibly growled.

Herr Geist was schooled enough to read the signals. He veered smoothly into a more appealing topic. "A notable regret," he said, "in the Federal Republic today, is the absence of large contributions to the cultural scene by the Jewish Germans."

He did not go into facts and figures as to how many Jews were available in Germany to make these contributions—some thirty or thirty-five thousand in all, and most of them of advanced years. But all those in the room were well enough aware of the situation to hang on his next words. "The thinking German misses this contribution," he went on, "which in the past has consisted of generous gifts of talent and knowledge, of healthful humor, of acute observation. They enriched our theater and made our films some of the best in the world. All this the Jewish element of the German population had provided us before the Nazi calamity. I do not speak for myself alone when I say that Germans of today would provide a warm welcome to those Jews of genius and intellect, should they choose to make Germany their home again."

"And what about Cohen, the tailor?" the man sitting next to me murmured in my ear.

However, there were others whose eyes grew moist at the prospect Geist was laying before them, even though they were too old to return now, to be able to contribute much of anything. But what Geist said made them remember. I saw Professor Marcus stare at Geist with a set expression. The Professor remembered, too, I gathered, and I guessed that he failed to remember his placid days at the University of Weimar, and remembered instead only the bleeding, battered face of his father, lying on the street outside the synagogue.

It was a nice thing, I realized, even a warm and generous thing, for this group to have Herr Geist as their honored guest —courtesy of the German embassy. But was it in the best of taste, at least for some of those here? However, in the question period that followed, Mark Abramovitz, honorary president of the Wiener Group, posed his own question—one that did not allow too much for Geist's feelings: Now that twenty years had elapsed since Hitler had thankfully shot himself to death, was this time enough for the Jewish survivors, for Jewish communities everywhere, to forget and forgive? Since it was customary at the meetings of the group for a question-asker to immediately answer his own question, Abramovitz gave it as his opinion that the time was much too soon, if not for himself altogether, then for the six million dead who would not wish to be forgotten so quickly. One must speak for those dead, he said, as well as for the living.

Abramovitz had hardly paused for breath when a voice from the audience was heard.

"Only the dead can forget," said Jonah Hirsch, who was employed by a Jewish relief group in the city. "The rest of us can only remember, not as a duty, but as a compulsion."

"Your question?" prompted Abramovitz, attempting to keep to the form of the discussion.

"My question is: How are the dead to awaken sufficiently to forgive?"

Abramovitz looked nonplussed and glanced at Geist, who rose to his feet. His country, he said, had made amends and would continue to make amends. Naturally there was no thought on the part of any responsible German of ever forgetting the magnitude of the crimes committed by a criminal segment led by a maniacal dictator; neither was it possible, on the other hand, or desirable, for the present generation to brood constantly on the past. He, for one, was happy to see new bonds of friendship and respect being forged between the Jewish people, the State of Israel, and the Federal Republic.

Mrs. Arenstein, an elderly widowed survivor, spoke up from the audience. "Words of that kind," she said, "we should accept at their face value. Pride is a lonely joy." She sat down, and Abramovitz neglected to ask her what her question was.

Joseph Mittelman raised his hand. He was a small, dapper businessman in his early forties. "I have a genuine question," he said, removing his heavy horn-rimmed glasses for emphasis. "Does Herr Geist feel that Germany is doing all in its power to amend the past by rooting out all those criminals of the Nazi bureaucracy from the social and political fabric of Germany?"

"That is a question of great complexity," Geist answered. But, as for the Federal Republic's desire that the ends of justice be served as completely as possible, he had only to cite the Auschwitz trials presently in progress, the special district attorney's office at Ludwigsburg created to centralize all cases pertaining to former Nazi criminals, and the debate going on in the Bundestag in Bonn concerning these matters.

The exchange of views, of accusations and rhetorical questions, made me uncomfortable. At the same time, I felt sympathy and a certain admiration for Geist. Fair was fair. He had come into the lion's den and was proving himself to be brave. But a battalion of Geists would have been needed to wade through the morass of mistrust prevalent in his audience. After two hours of discussion there were still no answers that satisfied more than a few, other than the fact of the discussion itself, as Mittelman implied to me at the conclusion of the session.

"Very good," he said, "I think we brought some issues out into the open. What is happening, by the way, on the Zeller-Bricken case?" He had been one of the forced laborers at the plant in Hanover but had refused to join the group seeking compensation.

"I'm leaving for Berlin tomorrow," I told him, "to have meetings with their representatives."

"You expect to extract the blood money, then?"

"You know as well as I do," I said, "that the victims have legal and moral reason to claim compensation."

"And the money they get will help them?"

"In several cases, certainly. More important, there is the precedent."

"Such as that murder can be compensated by the payment of cash?"

"I think it goes deeper than that," I said.

"For myself," Mittelman said, "I am only capable of seeing black and white. Where Zeller-Bricken is concerned I see only black."

I knew there was no point in quarreling with him. He was the only one of his family to have survived, and it was his youth and strength that had kept him alive. "I don't like to involve myself beyond the legal question," I said.

"Well, I wish you a good trip." Mittelman clapped me on the shoulder.

That evening, since it was a Sunday—a day on which Lottie did not like to prepare meals—we went out for dinner. "I'll keep in touch with you," I said. "And you know my address in Berlin—the Bristol-Kempinski. I should be back in two weeks, three at the latest."

"If I know you," she said, "you won't be in any hurry to return."

"I don't understand why you make remarks like that."

"You understand very well, but you won't admit it."

"Admit what?"

"That you're only interested in your own affairs."

"Lottie," I said. "What can I do that I'm not doing for you?"

"You can think of me occasionally."

"But, I do," I said. "What else did I marry you for, except to think of you and look after you?"

"You haven't mentioned love," she said. "It's interesting how you never mention love."

I glanced at her, as we sat side by side at the table. We were in a small French restaurant that I knew was one of her favorites. I could not in truth see Lottie as the handsome woman she had once been. The strong nose had become more prominent, the lips tighter, the skin less clear. Her eyes were her best feature, large, dark, and brooding. Did she mean love in the romantic sense?

"Is that my fault?" I asked in a low tone.

"What are you accusing me of?"

"I'm not accusing you," I said. "You're the one who closes your door at night."

"Much to your relief, I'm sure."

"That's your assumption. We could try harder, both of us," I said.

"And what does that mean exactly?" Her dark eyes turned harsh and suspicious.

"I wonder sometimes if we make enough of an effort. I don't speak only of closed doors, but of our attitudes. We've gone through a lot together, the two of us; we've stuck together. All this is a good sign for the future."

"The future," she said. "You go away for weeks at a time, and you're talking of a future. Don't you think I'll be lonely?"

"But I told you I would like you to come with me."

"You didn't say you *wanted* me; you said I could come."

"Say the word," I said, "and you'll be on the plane with me tomorrow."

"Not Germany," she said. "I don't want to go there."

"Where would you like to go? If you don't want to go by yourself, I'll make the time to go with you when I get back."

"You know where I'd like to go."

"Israel. Then go."

"I haven't the energy," she said. "It takes time to arrange a trip like that."

"I don't know what else I can say."

"Sometimes I think you'd like to say what you don't admit."

"And what is that?"

"You know what I'm talking about."

"No, I don't."

"You'd be just as happy if I weren't with you. Maybe happier."

"That's not true, not at all."

"I've seen the way you look at younger women."

"And how do I look at them?"

"If you don't mind my saying so, you look as though you would like to go to bed with them."

"Even if true," I said, "would that be so terrible?"

The fact was, I'd had a few adventures during the past six or seven years—or maybe misadventures would be more accurate. One had been Gloria's predecessor. The usual thing: she stayed late, I took her to dinner, taxied her home. . . . Well, was that so terrible? She had soft lips, a soft body, and I hadn't made love with Lottie for months. Was I so terrible? Was my record so bad? On the evidence, no, I decided. If my conscience wasn't exactly clear, it didn't hurt me very much, either. Lottie may have wondered if I'd had any lapses from our tacitly agreed upon celibacy, but she seldom probed any more than she did at this moment.

"Maybe you don't only look."

"Come now," I said, putting my arm around her shoulder. "Take it easy. A lot of this is self-pity, and it's not justified. The only one I feel like going to bed with is you."

I saw warmth come tentatively into her eyes.

"Then why don't you?" she asked huskily.

"Here, at the table?"

Her gaze shifted away from me, but she reached out and clutched my hand, almost clumsily, as though she was unused to the gesture.

"I don't know what gets into me sometimes," she said. "It's an anger that builds up in me, and it's not your fault. I'm sorry."

"I don't know what gets into both of us," I said.

Later, when we were home, and I was packing my bags for the morning flight, I passed her bedroom. She had retired early, and had turned off the light, but, contrary to her usual practice, she had left the door open. I went into her room, bent over her, and whispered: "Are you asleep?"

"No."

I undressed and got into the bed with her. She was not wearing a nightgown. I clasped her, and we made love, but there was no ardor in her body and consequently little in me. We went through the motions, mechanically, both of us pretending.

When I left her for my own room and my own bed, it was as though I was already in the taxi, on the way to Kennedy, so far were we removed from each other.

3: For a long time I remained awake in my bed at the Bristol-Kempinski on the Kurfürstendamm. It had been late at night when the plane had landed at Tempelhof, but my internal clock was still set at its accustomed six hours earlier, and I knew from past experience that it would take several days before it would grudgingly adjust to the time difference. I was prepared, however, with a small transistor radio, and this I tuned to a Berlin station that provided generous doses of Beethoven and Mozart throughout the night, with brief interruptions by a soothing female announcer who spoke of the weather and forthcoming cultural events on this side of the Wall. Eventually, toward dawn, I dozed off, only to be awakened by the jangling of the bedside telephone. I had neglected to inform the hotel switchboard that I was not to be disturbed. Who, after all, would be calling me so soon after arrival? Max Gerson, that was who. Was he speaking to Herr Alfred Becker of New York City?

"Yes," I said, "but what time is it?"

It was half-past nine. Gerson apologized for awakening me, but he was following Professor Marcus' instructions to contact me this morning at an early hour. Irritated as I was at being rudely shocked from sleep, I could only admire the Professor's thoroughness. Gerson went on to say that his time today was at my disposal if I wished to meet with him.

"I'll have to call you back," I said. "I'm not sure of my schedule yet."

Business came first, which is to say my business with the Zeller-Bricken people. I explained to Gerson that I had some contacts to make, and he assured me of his understanding. The Professor had written him, he added, that I had other matters to take care of in Berlin. There was a pause at the other end of the line, as though upon this brief acquaintance I might be tempted to take him into my confidence about what I was doing here. I promised him I'd call later in the day.

"I will give you my telephone number," he said.

"I have it, don't I?"

"What number do you have for me?"

That question required my getting out of bed, locating Professor Marcus' list of names in my packed briefcase and discovering, sure enough, that I had Gerson's correct eight-digit number. There was so much changing of telephone numbers these days in Berlin because of the new exchanges being added, he explained.

There was no point now in trying to get any more sleep. I showered, ordered breakfast in my room, and made two calls over coffee—the first to Kurt Hildebrandt of Zeller-Bricken, the second to Liz Schofield at the American Document Center. Herr Hildebrandt, I learned, would not be at his desk until two in the afternoon, but Liz Schofield I reached at once. Liz and I were old Army buddies, as well as compatriots and friends.

Because of her it was seldom necessary for me to unwind the State Department red tape that prevented all but officially approved people from visiting the center. "When are you coming out?" she asked, after we had exchanged our greetings.

"Around eleven-thirty?"

"The guard will have a pass for you," she promised.

I had met Liz during the time I was stationed with the Army at Höchst. She had been a WAC sergeant then, a good-looking slightly stout woman in her late twenties who found her Occupation duties vastly more exciting than life in the small Indiana town from which she came. She switched to civilian status in 1948 and was transferred to the American Zone in Berlin, where she became assistant file chief at the Document Center. There she stayed, moving up in grade, with only one six-month leave at home intervening, and evidently that was enough to convince her that West Berlin was where she preferred to be, this in spite of a jarring experience she had had some fifteen years ago.

She had met a smooth, handsome Berliner whose seductive ways were spiced with comforting talk of love, marriage, and children. He was a teacher at the secondary level, and he revealed to Liz that he was slightly worried about a Nazi party membership he had been forced to apply for, especially since he had failed to note this fact on his *Fragebogen* in 1948. He wouldn't dream of suggesting that Liz extract any documents bearing his name from the center at which she worked, but he thought it was only honest that he tell her about these things. Naturally Liz became curious. The files revealed that her lover had become a Nazi as early as 1936 and that he had risen to officer rank when he had joined the Wehrmacht in 1939. She further discovered that he had volunteered for work with a certain committee in the habit of entering homes and apartments to check on how faithfully their occupants were observing food-conservation regulations. These committee members were unpopular all through Germany, because they actually lifted the covers of pots on the stove to see what foods were being cooked. Her lover, in other words, had been an enthusiastic Nazi and seemed hardly fitted to teach democracy to young Germans. The knowledge made Liz quite sick: she began to get symptomatic asthma attacks and only got back to normal when she stopped seeing her German friend.

She had told me the whole story several years before. What she wanted to know from me, specifically, was whether she should have forwarded the information she had stumbled upon to either American or West German authorities. The legality was plain, I told her. She would have overstepped the bounds of her position had she done so without an official request. Ethically she had made herself crystal clear by giving up the relationship. "But the man is still teaching," she said.

"So are thousands of former Nazis, all enthusiastically espousing democracy."

In the succeeding years Liz had remained unmarried and childless, with an ingrained mistrust of the German men she met and with little chance for permanent relationships with the men of the changeable American colony in Berlin. She shared a comfortable house with another female State Department employee and had, over the years, developed a kind of grim affection for her files. Her eyes were remarkably sharp at detecting in the dry-as-dust and efficiently storaged documents degrees of culpability in the deeds of Hitler's regime.

It took twenty minutes by taxi to reach the center in a section called Wilmersdorf, a residential area of West Berlin on the edge of the Grunewald. The guard was a young German in American Army uniform, and he produced my pass as soon as

I gave my name. A typist, serving also as receptionist, led me through dimly lighted hallways to Liz's office. Her hair was more flecked with gray than the last time I had seen her, but her eyes behind gold-rimmed glasses were as brightly blue as ever and her complexion as pink.

She gave me a welcoming hug and asked me what mischief I was up to now.

"I'm checking on a couple of fellows," I said.

"Am I supposed to help you?"

"Oh, sure," I said. "Potentially this could involve the national interest—a case I'm handling—and we ought to know the kind of people we're dealing with."

"It has to do with restitution, I suppose."

"Naturally," I said.

"I must say, you're persistent," she said. "I've noticed a change lately in the kind of research the professors are doing here. 'Objective' is the word for it, I guess. Himmler and Bormann are now to be regarded as pawns in the process of history. I'm quoting a research fellow from the University of Illinois. And there's an Englishman who doesn't think Hitler was responsible for starting the war. Does that make any sense to you?"

"I've heard it before."

"Somehow I think we're different," she said a little wistfully. She referred to the two of us, I knew, meaning that we had shared a similar attitude back there at Höchst. "Who are you after this time?"

I mentioned their names, Weisse and Roehling. "Sound familiar?"

"No. Have they disappeared?"

"They're right out in the open," I said, "and high up, too. They work for Zeller-Bricken."

"We can look in the files," Liz said. "It's for your private knowledge?"

"Can't guarantee it," I told her. "Any public use of your information, though, would be cleared through the regular channels."

"Just checking," she said. "You know I trust you."

She took me down to the temperature-controlled storage vaults ,where, as we went from room to room, she headed unerringly to the relevant files: party membership, SS membership, the 1938 national census. From these alone we found out that both Roehling and Weisse had been party members. There was little further on Roehling, but Weisse's record was more extensive. At age twenty-nine, in 1940, he had worked for Zeller-Bricken, in the Hanover complex, as assistant manager of the transportation division, something that didn't signify much because forced-labor practices were not yet in effect. But then we turned up his SS application in 1942 and his membership card, dated February, 1943. His service with the SS was specified as "detached," which could have meant anything.

"Could we pin him down any more than that?" I asked Liz.

"There's a West German team going over the RSHA files," she said, "so they've been removed. You'd have to go to the Bonn people directly for that. You say he's with Zeller-Bricken now?"

"If my sources are correct."

"I'm a little surprised," she said. "Those armament firms are supposed to have been cleaned up."

"So much so," I said, "that Zeller-Bricken is now doing business with our Defense Department."

She looked a little worried. "I'm sure I would have remembered," she said, "if we'd had any request about him."

She led me to another room. Weisse, she discovered, had

also taken the trouble to have his racial stock profiled. His profile card, stamped and evaluated in 1941, certified him to be of the second Aryan category. "Pretty good," Liz said, with a certain irony. His family lines were shown to have been "pure" for more than a hundred years.

"What do you think?" I asked.

"Just between us? A genuine Nazi bastard."

"What about Roehling?"

"Let's look a little more."

Roehling, we learned, had joined the Hitler Youth at age fifteen, had become a leader at eighteen. He had excelled in horsemanship, and had become an Army reservist while pursuing his studies at a polytechnic institute in Hanover.

"Seems to be just another Nazi," she said, finally, about Roehling. "I could find you a million just like him."

"I'm sure there must be something else," I said. "Usually these Israeli sources are pretty accurate."

"Nothing more in here," she said with certainty.

"Anyway," I said, "I have enough to go on."

"With Weisse you've got a lot. What are you going to do with it?"

"It's going to stay in the back of my head," I told her.

"You wouldn't just drop a hint to someone that you know something, would you?"

"Maybe just a very small hint," I said.

We went back to her office, and on the way I told her about Sarah Stein's case, mentioning that Sarah had suddenly remembered the name of a girl or young woman: Christianne. "What would that mean to you?" I asked Liz.

"You're sure she was in the camp with her?"

"She distinctly remembers this Christianne being nice to her in the camp."

"She could have been one of the German guards," Liz said. "That sometimes happened. Or a political inmate. If Christianne was German and non-Jewish, she might have made indiscreet remarks or been a bad worker in the war effort."

"Or even an anti-Nazi," I said.

Liz made a face. "That was so rare. She'd have been shot. Let's see about this Reichenau camp." She took a large volume containing the camp listings from a shelf and leafed through it. She read the information aloud for my benefit. "Founded 1938, protective-custody camp for known and suspected communists, party deviationists, and, after 1942, housed alien labor forces. Total capacity, sixteen thousand. Commander, Sturmbannführer Hans Dittersdorf."

"What about Dittersdorf?" I asked.

"Three possibilities: hanged or shot, a jail term, or disappeared. Do you want me to find out?"

"Could you?"

"It wouldn't be difficult," she said. "As for Christianne, we can try the Arolsen Tracing Service. You could do that yourself, or do you want me to do it? I don't know why I'm being so helpful."

"Because I'm irresistible," I said.

"Talking about your irresistibility," Liz said, "how is Lottie?"

She had met Lottie only once, and that was in 1947, and yet she never failed to ask about her.

"Well," I said.

Liz gave me a keen glance. "Everything okay at home?"

"Good as can be expected."

Liz didn't push it. "When I have your information," she said, "I'll call you at your hotel. How long will you stay in Berlin?"

"Figure at least a week," I said.

"I'm sure I'll have something by then. Do I get to see you before you leave?"

"I hope to take you to a fine dinner and a beautiful concert." I knew she loved music.

"You don't have to," she said.

"But I want to."

Unaccountably, a sad look came on Liz's face. Maybe it was because we saw each other so seldom, and, whenever we did, it meant more time had passed, and the certainty of spinsterhood had become more inexorable. And how eager for experience she had been during that time at Höchst. If I hadn't been so involved with Hilde, and then with Lottie, I too might have been awarded her favors. But we never really know about those things; our moods of loneliness would have had to mesh exactly; and, as it was, we had remained friends.

After serving me thick black coffee with heavy cream and lumps of pale brown sugar, Max Gerson read to me from a packet of typewritten notes. He was a tall, stooped man in his sixties, who could read easily without his glasses but had to put them on to see well at distances of more than a yard. I had called him once I had set up an appointment with Kurt Hildebrandt for the next morning, and he had invited me to his apartment in a rehabilitated building off Neue Kantstrasse.

"The Erfurt Menorah," he began with a trace of pomposity. "The artistic style reflects the optimism of the rococo period. This candelabrum of seven branches was commissioned from a workman in Mainz in the year 1747 by the eminent Pieter Leschnitzer and his wife, Hansi, of the Jewish congregation of Rüdesheim, which is several kilometers from Mainz. The base was of brass, and the branches were of gold in a semibeaded design

The spikes, expressing a forceful spirituality, are in the shape of a Venetian dagger, indicating that the workman was itinerant rather than local. The menorah was handed down for two generations in the Leschnitzer family, a branch of which settled in Erfurt. A certain Otto Lischnitzer presented the menorah to the Erfurt congregation in 1802, three of the gold branches at that time having become loosened, and, in exchange, was given by the Erfurt congregation a more modern and serviceable silver menorah for home use."

"Very interesting," I said, "but does that information help us locate it?"

"We should know what it is we are searching for," Gerson said, with a mildly reproving glance. He returned to his notes. "The Lischnitzer-Erfurt Menorah was regarded, before its disappearance, as an artistic-historic relic of noted individuality. The unknown workman very likely was not Jewish himself, but his spiritual feeling was deep, and the use of gold, not common at that time, indicates the purity of his intention. The weight of the menorah, after its repair by the Erfurt synagogue, is given in the year 1840 as fourteen pounds, or roughly six kilos, and in the year 1879 as fifteen and a half pounds, indicating obviously some further repairs. The brass is of a yellowish coloring, and the gold is of a deeper, almost rose, shade. Its general impression is one of a mellowed, but striking, beauty. The menorah disappeared during the Crystal Night riots of 1938 and has not been seen since."

"And now," I said, "how do we find it?"

"You are pressed for time, Herr Becker?"

"Not so much today," I said, "but I certainly will be."

"The methods of finding such a lost antiquarian object," Gerson said, "are several."

"And most of them have been tried," I added.

— 54 —

"We could first of all," he went on, ignoring my interruption, "advertise in the various antiquarian journals. That would take a longer time than you are prepared to spend. If, by chance, the menorah now reposes in the East Zone of Germany or in the vaults of the Democratic People's Republic, we could make certain inquiries and obtain, possibly, the information positive or negative, but that would take more money than you are presumably prepared to pay."

"How much money?" I asked.

"Possibly four or five hundred Deutsche Marks, or, roughly, one hundred American dollars, preferably in American Express traveler's checks."

"Well," I said, "if you felt that would do any good, it would be worth it to me for the Professor's peace of mind."

"The Professor," Gerson said severely, "has informed me that he will reimburse you for all reasonable expenses you may incur."

"Yes," I said hastily. "The Professor has assured me of that."

"Do you think this a justified expense?"

"Do you?" I asked.

"Wait," he said. "We will explore further. There is the Liesnitzcher family, for one direction."

"You keep pronouncing the name differently," I said.

"For the reason that the spelling keeps changing. A German-Jewish family of such long lineage tends to change the spelling of its name through the various generations. The family of our dearly beloved Hitler was once known as Heidler, for instance."

"But that's not a Jewish name."

"There are several German-Jewish and Austrian-Jewish families by the name of Heidler," Gerson said, putting on his glasses to emphasize his surprise that I should be so ignorant.

"I would prefer to believe he was not one of us," I said.

Gerson shrugged.

"As far as I have been able to ascertain, the Leitschnitzer family intermarried with Christian-German stock, and became known during the period of the Third Reich as *Mischlinge* of the first and second degree. Many of the family members thus managed to survive much of the holocaust, although some were taken during the last few round-ups of Jews. I have discovered Lieschnitzers presently residing in Munich and also in a village near Salzburg in Austria."

"And how does *that* information help us?" I asked.

"The Lieschnitzers might well be interested in recovering the menorah that is so much a part of their family history."

"That's too much of a supposition," I said.

"It depends on how serious one were about locating the menorah. How serious are you, Herr Becker?"

"I'll return the question. How serious are *you*, Herr Gerson? What's your interest in this whole thing?"

Gerson removed his glasses and wiped them with a crumpled handkerchief. "Business, Herr Becker," he said. "And affection for Professor Marcus. Combine the two, and you have something that can be called dedication. Am I right?"

"In other words," I said, "there would have to be a finder's fee, successful or not."

"A modest fee, yes. Let me explain. I was once an antiquarian. My shop was in what is now East Berlin. It was looted, once, twice. The windows were broken. I took the hint and went out of business. I spent a year in a camp. My health is not good, but I do what I can to keep alive. And I have one of those small pensions you are familiar with. I take small assignments now and then, but I don't charge much. You see, I have a lot stored up here." He tapped his head. "And I make these notes." He indicated the sheaf of typewritten pages. "Those are my assets. I believe firmly in the principle that we have a right to recover what was once ours."

Somehow that broke the ice. We weren't so far apart in our ideas about the rights possessed by human beings. I explained to Gerson my own position. I had only so much time, I told him; I had an office to return to, a wife waiting at home; I owed obligations to my partners and had other obligations. And, frankly, I had great doubts the menorah would ever turn up. "Now, what would you do in my case?" I asked him.

"Do what you can," he said. "The Professor understands more than you think. But I would try those two possibilities: the East Zone, and the Lietschnitzer survivors. And I will write some letters for you."

"To whom?"

"To the Lietschnitzers and to some dealers in objects of this kind."

"Good enough," I said. "I'll commission you as my agent. Can two hundred dollars—in traveler's checks—get you started?"

"Certainly," he said.

I took out a booklet of traveler's checks and signed over two of the one-hundred-dollar denomination to Gerson. "By the way," I said. "What's the method you use to get information on the other side of the Wall?"

"Very simple," Gerson said. "I get in touch with a certain lawyer. Lawyers still practice privately there. You merely have to know whom to get in touch with."

"I should have known," I said. "We lawyers will do anything for a dollar."

We shook hands ceremoniously, and I left, after assurances from him that he would be contacting me very soon, hopefully with information. By that time I was beginning to share the Professor's faith that his candelabrum existed somewhere after all.

Every time I came to Berlin I was impressed anew with its conspiratorial atmosphere. Back at home I would tend to disbelieve and assume it all to be the product of Cold War imaginations and spy novelists, but once I came close to that ugly Wall and became aware again of the isolated status of the city's western part, I realized that conspiracy was not only necessary but part of almost everyone's daily life. There were the separated relatives, the presence of military missions instead of consulates, the fact that Berlin was, strictly speaking, not an integrated part of the Federal Republic, and such physical reminders as the separated underground systems of the S Bahn and the U Bahn and the Russians grimly guarding their War Memorial. The methods of maintaining contact and doing business were multifarious, and you came across them only when there was business to be done. I had no doubt at all that Gerson would quickly make his contacts. As he said, all it took was money—and not such enormous amounts either by New York standards.

Back at the Kempinski I had a drink at the bar, knowing that when I finished it I was going to try telephoning Hilde. I assumed that she worked until five or six and that it would take her a half-hour or so to get back to her apartment. When my watch said 6:45, I found a telephone in the lobby and gave the operator her number. The telephone was answered at once, as though Hilde had been sitting by it waiting for it to ring. Her voice was utterly familiar.

"This is Alfred Becker," I said, with perhaps too much formality.

"Oh, good, good," she said in German. "You are here in Berlin?"

"Here in Berlin," I said.

"And when may I see you?"

"Tonight?" I had nothing else to do with the evening.

"I will arrange it," she said. "I can meet you at nine o'clock."

"Or I can come there," I said.

"No, I will meet you. Where are you staying?"

"The Kempinski."

"I will be in the lobby of your hotel at nine o'clock," she said.

"For dinner?"

"That is not necessary."

"We'll make it for dinner," I said.

"It has been so long, Alf."

"Yes," I said, "it has."

"Will you recognize me?"

"Won't I?"

"I hope so. I have changed, maybe not too much, but I have changed."

"I'll be the tall fellow wearing the white carnation," I told her.

She laughed, but a trifle nervously. "I remember how you always made jokes," she said.

That was odd. I remembered myself as being all too serious.

4: I was in the lobby waiting, having written a letter to Lottie and given it to the desk clerk to mail. It was one of those letters in which you seem to be saying something but really say nothing. A good flight, arrival on time, weather in Berlin a little on the cold side. Talked to an odd little man called Gerson about the Professor's candelabrum; he seemed to think locating it was possible, but I was as little hopeful about that as before . . . and, should she change her mind about joining me, all she had to do was send me a cable and get on a plane. I knew, of course, that she would not come. I had omitted the information that I would be meeting Hilde, but that was for the sake of peace and diplomacy. Habit, more than anything else.

The lady in question hurried into the lobby at ten minutes past nine. She was hatless and wore a trim coat of brown suede. She had filled out and was slightly matronly looking, but I had no trouble recognizing her. I rose from my chair to greet her, and she took both my hands and studied my face. "But you are the same," she said.

"You're being kind," I said. "But you're as beautiful as ever."

"Oh, no," she said. "I weigh too much."

"It's not noticeable," I told her.

She laughed. "We are both being silly, aren't we? How could we expect to stay the same? Still, you look very nice. You haven't got big in the middle, and I don't see any gray in your hair."

"You have the same blonde hair," I said. "Exactly the same."

"It takes work to keep it that way. But you recognized me?"

"Of course."

"If you had met me on the street suddenly, would you have also recognized me?"

"Absolutely."

She took a deep breath of relief. "I worried that I would have to introduce myself to you. It's so good to see you, Alf. Wonderful, really wonderful. I almost don't believe it."

Her eyes now were not so softly blue as I remembered, and they were etched with lines at the corners. Her nose was a little more prominent, but since it was a small, straight nose, this didn't take away from the attractive impression she made— that of a pleasant, youngish German woman, neither a patrician nor a peasant. The chances were that if she had hurried by on a street in Berlin I would not have been able to single her out from the crowd. And it was needless to worry that she still bore resentment against me for leaving her as I did. It was another time. We were old friends meeting, and, as though to make this clear to me, she slipped her arm through mine, saying, "Where shall we go?"

"Can you think of a place for dinner?"

"Come with me," she said. "We'll go to Bernhard's Café. It's not far. We can walk."

Bernhard's was on the Kurfürstendamm, a few blocks away, and was a restaurant with four small rooms. It was less brightly lit, less crowded than most of the other cafés in the busy area. "A favorite place of mine," Hilde said. She must have come there often, for our waiter asked if she would take her usual special cocktail.

"You must have it, too," she said. "It has secret ingredients. No one but Bernhard's makes it."

On the way there we had asked questions of each other. Was I married still to the refugee woman? Did I have children? How many times had I come to Berlin?

"Perhaps six or seven times in the past ten years," I said. And it was my turn to ask. She had married, yes, but was divorced now. And she had a child, a boy of seven. She lived with her sister and the child in an apartment that was too small, but she was lucky anyway, for the apartment situation in Berlin was still very difficult.

"So," she said, "tell me about your wife, your Lottie. Was it better to marry her than me?"

Her eyes were fixed on mine, no sign of mirth in them.

"I can't win no matter how I answer that," I said.

"Just answer the truth."

"It was better for my conscience to marry her."

Hilde nodded approvingly. "That sounds truthful. And it leaves a little room for me—for my feelings."

"We ought not to talk about the day we said good-by, that is, if you don't mind my making the suggestion. I'll just say this—I think I was crude and possibly too young to know exactly what to do about you."

"Both of us," she said. "I learned more after you left. Maybe if I had been a little older——" She didn't finish that thought. Instead she smiled. "All right, we won't talk about that."

Hardly noticing it, we had both slipped into speaking German, even though her English was easy and much improved over when I had known her before. The cocktails the waiter brought were on the sweet side, a mixture of fruit brandies, I guessed.

"Do you like it?" she asked.

"Yes, very good."

"I always drink them here," she said. "Tell me. Did you sometimes, maybe just once, miss your little German fräulein?"

"I never thought of you as that."

"You never wrote me a letter. Why?"

"I was married."

"Oh," she said with mock surprise. "Such an honorable husband."

"Just keeping things straight," I said.

"Other Americans I have met don't appear to mind making things complicated."

"Then you've met some other Americans?"

"A few. Now and then. One in particular after you left. But so unimportant, now that I think of him. I'd almost forgotten him. But not you. I think it proves you were important in my life."

"You wrote me a letter," I said. "Why?"

"You mean, did I have some reason besides wanting to see you again?"

"I must admit, even that reason seems a little strange to me."

"Then you are not as sentimental as I am. Actually it was my sister who made me write to you."

"Your sister? I don't remember meeting her."

"You didn't. She was too little then. She was my baby sister and lived with my mother. When my mother died, I began to take care of her. Now she is grown and would like to go to America and find a job. I would be just as happy about it. She goes with a man who is not pleasant, and I would like her to be away from him. Anyway, you being such an important man, I thought you could help her get some work. She is a very good secretary. Her English is good. But it would be very strange for her going to New York all alone. I told her I had heard about you after all these years—from Judge Kimmel—and she said, why not write to you? So I did, and you are here."

"I'm sure I can help her," I said.

"Would it be much trouble for you?"

"Hardly any," I said. "I'd be glad to do it."

"Tell me more about you," she said. "I have this feeling that you are successful and rich. Are you?"

"A little bit successful," I admitted to her. "Not rich, but I suppose I belong to that prosperous middle class you hear about. That puts me in the nice position of not having to worry too much about money. But more important it allows me the luxury of doing what I like to do."

"So you like your work," Hilde said, nodding approvingly. "Judge Kimmel told me you cause this country a lot of trouble and that you take our money for your Jewish causes."

"Only legally and legitimately."

"He was not being serious. It was funny—I had this sudden intuition to ask him about you." She had taken intermittent work as a translator for the past several years, she explained. There were times when she needed the money; after they had separated, Hans, her former husband, sometimes forgot that he had a child to support. An agency had sent her to the Restitution Court, where Judge Kimmel gave her some documents to translate from English into German. She noticed that the documents were often the work of American lawyers, and that had made her think of me. "Somehow I felt sure you were now a lawyer," she said. And she had also guessed that since I had married Lottie "out of deep sympathy for the terrible things done to the Jews," as she put it, I might, after all, be handling cases like those that came before the Restitution Court. "Still and all, I was almost shocked with surprise when the judge said he knew you."

"It's odd," I said, "the reason you gave for my marriage."

"How is it odd?"

"You said I married her out of deep sympathy."

"But, for what other reason? You were in love with me. Oh, certainly, you must love your wife now, but then you loved me. Can you contradict that?"

I didn't answer. A sense of confusion came to me, and the years seemed to fall away to that previous time. I had never really admitted to myself that I had been in love with Hilde.

I stayed silent. I had not expected Hilde to come on as strong and fast as this, to bring it all back.

"Why won't you answer?" she goaded me.

Behind her willingness to talk about everything was nervousness, I guessed, and a frustration, too. And I realized, now, that it would have been a lot better to have faced at the time of my leaving her those questions she asked now. I had been brutal, and she had wanted explanations. In order to save her pride she had not asked for them.

"It's kind of funny to talk about this eighteen years later," I said finally.

"No, it's not. We have both grown older. You don't have to worry about hurting my feelings. They have been hurt enough."

"By me?"

"Yes, by you and others. But I hold nothing against anyone. I will admit I loved you. For me, it was a very nice thing to have loved you. I look at you now, and I see how it was possible. How lucky we are to have this occasion to talk to each other again."

"Yes," I said, "that is very lucky."

Had I loved her? And did it matter now if I told her I had loved her? Especially if, for whatever reason, it was so important to her?

"If you would rather not discuss it——" she said.

"Yes," I said, "certainly I loved you."

"You smile," she said. "Why do you smile?"

"Because, we weren't the only ones in that house making love."

"You're saying I was just your fräulein." The corners of her mouth sagged.

"No," I said hastily, annoyed to be put in this position, "I wasn't looking for a fräulein, not the kind you're talking about."

"But you never considered me for marriage. That wasn't nice for me, a young girl already spoiled because of something I could not help. You made me feel I had a disease."

"What disease?"

"Being German."

She was overstating what I felt, but she had a point.

"I was young, too," I said, "and I was spoiled by what I saw when I came into Germany."

"And you blamed me for it. You don't remember all the things you said to me, but I remember."

"Well, I wish you'd forget them, because if I said them they weren't true. You're a very good person, and that's always the way I've thought of you."

"So your feelings about the Germans are changed?"

I hesitated before answering, and she caught the hesitation. I saw a hint of bitterness in her smile. Here, in this warm restaurant, I was in the midst of Germans, and I was not uncomfortable. Eighteen years before, I could never have conceived myself in such an atmosphere. Had these people who were eating, talking and laughing become different from the way

I had once thought of them? Or was it I who had changed?

"So?" Hilde said.

"I want to give you an honest answer," I said. "First of all, I've met a lot of Germans, and I've talked with them and done business with them. A few have felt the same shock I felt. But I can't say I like them all. Still, I've learned a little more since we knew each other, and I make separations now. If we met for the first time today, I don't think your being German would affect me much. Do you see what I'm trying to say?"

"I think you are trying to give me my clearance," Hilde said.

"Consider yourself fully and finally cleared, and please accept the apologies I owe you."

"Good. We can talk as equals."

"Now you're making me feel guilty," I told her.

She held up her empty glass. "Please order me another drink, in honor of my great clearance. Meanwhile, I must visit a certain place for ladies."

She got up from the table, and I watched her as she moved away from me. A lot of her added weight had settled around her hips and bottom, so that she seemed to waddle slightly as she walked. Or maybe it was only a pronounced sway. Yet, she was still physically pleasing, even voluptuous, in the way a Rubens female was voluptuous. But the cute little Hilde of my memories was no more. While having these thoughts I was reminded of what Lottie had said to me before I had left, that I looked at women as though I wanted to go to bed with them. Was I again considering Hilde as a bedmate? Not really, I thought. It was more curiosity, not unmixed with a touch of sentimentality.

I had ordered her another drink, and the waiter had brought it by the time she returned. She had freshened her lipstick, done something to her hair.

"So," she said, "since we are speaking so frankly, I will tell you what happened after you left." She took a large sip of her drink, then ran her tongue over her lips. "There was this other American I met after you went home. "I think he was one of those who just wanted a fräulein, and I became one for him. I did what I did deliberately. I wanted to find out if I could hold a man. At first he didn't tell me he was married. Then I found out. He had two children and came from Cincinnati. Do you know Cincinnati?"

"Not well."

"This time I would not let him feel sure of me. Instead I would one time grant him what he wanted, and the next time I would be cold. I found out that such treatment of a man gave results. He would coax me to admit I loved him, and I would never give a definite answer. I would say 'maybe' or 'I don't know yet,' and I would tell him there was someone else I had loved—you—and it was not so easy to forget. The funny thing is, this was true. I was not so dishonest, after all. But, my dear Alfred, he became horribly jealous of you. He wanted to know everything we had done in bed together. He would beg me to tell him, and when I would tell him he would grow furious. Once he even beat me. I was black and blue for days. There was something strange about him sexually. For a man who was married and had children, he did not know much about love-making. He would not undress with the lights on, but at the same time he would make me walk around naked and stare at me. Sometimes I would do it, just to tease him. When it came time for him to leave for Cincinnati, he told me he loved me and wanted to marry me. His idea was that I was to come to America—he would help me emigrate—and he would find me an apartment in Cincinnati until he had obtained a divorce. Then he would marry me."

"Was he serious?"

"I think so. Does it make you a little bit jealous to hear about him?"

"A little bit," I said. But it wasn't of this woman sitting across from me that I was jealous, but of the girl she had been. And I was a little sickened by her story.

"The reason I tell you this," she said, "is a compliment in a funny way. Somehow, by comparing you with him I learned that you were a nicer and a better person than I thought you were when you kicked me out. It was not just his willingness to leave his wife and family for me. After all, I had teased him into it. He was mean and a little stupid. He did not like Jews. I slapped his face once for saying something nasty about Jews, and all at once he began to cry. I don't know why. He was a major, and he drank too much. I slapped his face for you."

She was leaning forward, her hands on the table, her face tense from the drama of the scene she had just played for my benefit. I had to glance away from her, because I was embarrassed. Major who? So many of those American faces that had inhabited the offices taken over from an I. G. Farben plant were hardly more than blanks in my memory. My immediate superior I remembered, and Chris, of course, but few of the others.

"Who was the major?" I asked her.

She looked disappointed. I had not complimented her on her fine display of racial tolerance.

"What does it matter? You didn't know him. He was new in Höchst. He had not been through the war. He had been sent over for the Occupation. We were not allowed to smoke cigarettes, because cigarettes were money, he said. Every week he would send home money orders to his wife. Sometimes I sold his cigarettes for him. That, too, made me compare him with you."

"Because I didn't? Well, Chris did the same thing, and it never bothered me. I just didn't feel like doing it, that's all."

"Because you would be taking Occupation marks from Germans."

"Maybe. Look, suppose we order something to eat."

She nodded, gloomily, as though eating didn't appeal to her much. She wanted to talk.

I called over the waiter and asked for menus. The cuisine in this restaurant was on the sophisticated side, a mingling of typical north German dishes with some French specialties. We both ordered filet steaks and salads and settled on a Baden rosé wine.

"I didn't kick you out," I said, referring to her earlier remark. "I explained——"

"Yes, you explained to me that unfortunately I was not a victim of a concentration camp and therefore was not worthy of you."

"I'm sure I didn't say anything like that." I knew, in fact, that I hadn't.

"Your friend Chris told me everything after you left. He explained to me that an American Jew brought up as comfortably as you, and especially in New York City, where there is not much anti-Semitism, would naturally suffer from guilt over the dirty work of the Nazis. It was new to you—and a great shock. When you met Lottie, he said, all your sympathies went to her, and they would be strong enough to overcome your love for me. And, also, he said, you were not the kind of man who could serve two mistresses."

I should have expected that Hilde would talk to Chris after I left. Hilde had obviously needed to rescue her pride, and Chris hadn't been bound to respect any confidences.

"I suppose this has to be talked out," I said, "but it really is pointless. We neither of us have the same attitudes now. Besides, you make too much of the Jewish thing. Chris is not Jewish, and he didn't marry Gretel."

"Your friend Chris was a little bit of a snob. Bringing home a German girl would not be socially approved. Do you see him these days?"

"He once looked me up years ago, but I haven't seen him since. He's in Denver, has some job in the city administration."

"Unlike you, he wrote many letters to his old German girl friend. He said he was hoping to pay a visit to Germany someday and would then see her again, but he never came. Gretel has a theory that he does not get enough love at home."

"Not if I know Chris," I said.

That made her smile, and we both relaxed. Hilde wondered if I still remembered some of the parties we had had, and she reminded me of one I had forgotten. Chris and I had borrowed two nurses' uniforms and dressed the two girls in them, and we had attended a dance at the officers' club in Frankfurt. No one had guessed that the girls were not American, and both were told that they were the prettiest nurses in the Army.

I asked about Gretel. She lived in Frankfurt, with her husband, who was a chemical engineer, and they had four children. Hilde's husband, I learned, also lived in Frankfurt and worked for an automobile agency. She seldom saw him. How did I live, she wanted to know.

I described the apartment, told her about a summer place I kept on Long Island and the boat I used for fishing. Hilde was worried about New York as a place to live, especially as her sister might be going there, and she had heard the city was filled with violence. It was not as bad as that, I said. She had an idea that Harlem was separated from the rest of New York by some kind of boundary—almost the same as a wall—and I explained it as best I could. Our steaks came, and neither of us managed to finish them. We did drink the whole bottle of wine, and as I relaxed more I tried to see the former Hilde in the face of the woman across from me. Every now and again it would be there—in the sound of her laugh, in a moment when her eyes would widen solemnly. But eighteen years had brought flabbiness to the face and some other kind of change that I wasn't, as yet, able to fathom. What I did know was that I felt hardly a trace of the old desire for her. The same thing had happened with Lottie, and still there were strong ties. Not so with Hilde.

Through the evening her manner had undergone a change. The resentments had lessened and she became coquettish, transparently so. How long would I be in Berlin? Would I have time to see her? Would it embarrass me as a married man to see my old German girl friend?

"Oh, hardly," I said. "Anyway, you're a *friend* now."

"Just a friend?" she asked, as though I had said something roguish.

"An old friend," I said. "The best kind. We can talk to each other and understand each other."

"How proper you have become," she said. "You don't remember how we acted with each other? All those nights in that bed of yours on Nachtigallen Weg?"

"I haven't forgotten the name of the street either."

"Nor the bed?"

"I remember the bed, too. I remember it very well. We used to hear the lieutenant banging away on the piano downstairs. Once I got up and shouted down the stairwell, 'For God's sake, stop the noise!' "

"And that time it was not the lieutenant, but a colonel who was playing," Hilde said, "and he yelled back that he was the highest ranking officer in the house and he would have you court-martialed if you spoke like that again. You came back to the room like a shot. I like to remember those things, the funny things, the good things. I had so little then, and it made love all the more important."

It was growing late, I noticed, and the restaurant—at least the room we were in—was almost empty. Three fat German men sat at a table in the corner trading stories, smoking cigars and chuckling. Two waiters stood patiently against the wall.

"Then you withdrew the love," Hilde said, removing her hand from mine and sitting back, staring at me almost accusingly. "So suddenly. I had had this dream, that you would somehow manage to stay with me, that time would pass and the war would be forgotten and that one day we would marry. Stupid of me, yes?"

"Look," I said mildly, "we were young."

"We are not so old now," Hilde said defiantly. "Tell me, did you never miss me?"

"Of course I did. But I was so busy. There were so many things to arrange. To be honest, I missed you more after a year or two had passed."

"Then your Lottie must have been a disappointment to you after me."

"No," I said. "I pretty much knew what life would be like with Lottie."

"In bed?"

"That's not the kind of thing I talk about," I said.

"Sooner or later that is what a man and a woman like to talk about," Hilde said, looking mischievous. "If you were a European man you would have been talking about it hours ago."

"Well, I'm not," I said, with a touch of irritation. "I'm an American businessman, here in Berlin on business."

"You behave as though I am about to seduce you," Hilde said, still looking mischievous. "Don't be nervous."

I was on the defensive now. I changed the subject.

"You haven't told me much about the man you married."

"I don't think much about *him*," she said with a shrug. "I went to a school in Frankfurt to take some English courses, and I met Hans in one of the classes." Hans, she said, weary of war and Occupation, had felt that Germans should make their own future and stop being forever dependent on Americans. She had approved of his pride. "Why do you get married? We thought it sensible. Also, as a married couple we had better chance for getting a decent place to live. There was not much room for me in my mother's flat, and she was only concerned about the return of my father, who was a prisoner in Russia. When he did come back he was very sick and died soon after. I married Hans. Then, later, I came to dislike that same pride I had liked so much in him before. Strange, isn't it?"

She was grateful to Hans, though, for bringing her to Berlin. This city she liked, even when it was still picking itself out of the ruins. They had come in 1953, when Hans took a job with an Opel automobile agency that also carried with it a small apartment. It was no longer a good marriage, Hilde said, and she would have left Hans if her mother had not suddenly died, leaving her with Annemarie to care for. In spite of the coldness she now felt for Hans, they continued to share the same bed in the crowded apartment, and one day she found herself pregnant. A year after the child was born, Hans was transferred back to Frankfurt, but she and Annemarie and the baby stayed in Berlin in the same apartment. Three years ago she had divorced Hans.

"What went wrong?" I asked, a little depressed by her colorless recital of facts.

She shrugged. "How can I put it? Hans had become dull,

full of habits—— But we should not talk of such unpleasant, dreary things."

"At least we're filling in our lives for each other," I said.

"But you tell me so little about yourself. I still have the feeling you are hiding something from me about Lottie, about your life with her. You do not have the look of a happy married man, Alf."

"Do you know a lot of happy marriages?" I asked.

"Very few. Most of them are arrangements."

"The reason I don't talk about mine," I said, "is that in a sense it is an arrangement, but a necessary one."

"You rescued a woman," Hilde said. "A rescuer cannot abandon the person he rescues. I am only guessing."

"It's more than that, a lot more."

"But you have no children."

"She couldn't have any. That's part of it, too."

"How sad," Hilde said. "It grows late. I suppose we should leave and let the waiters go home. And you look as though you need sleep. Or is it that I bore you?"

"Oh, no," I said hastily.

"But we will meet again. Will you call me?"

"Certainly."

"When?" she asked. "Tomorrow?"

"If that's all right with you." I wasn't very sure that I wanted to call her.

"Call me at six o'clock," she said. Her eyes were soft now, almost as soft as I had remembered them—the soft, sweet, blue eyes. We could take up again where we left off, I thought suddenly, wondering if she expected me to make the invitation. She gave me an odd, wistful little smile, as though, again, she was aware of what I was thinking.

"I'll take you home," I said.

"No, it's not necessary. I'll simply take a taxi. Come. We'll walk back to the Kempinski, and there are always taxis at the stand there."

We walked, and she took my arm, leaning close against me, almost snuggling.

"So nice to be with you," she murmured.

The chill air was refreshing. The traffic had died away on the Kurfürstendamm, and some of the cafés were already shuttered for the night. Together we crossed the wide stretch of the Wilhelmstrasse. Once the bombs had screeched down on this very spot. In these dark streets Jews had been pulled out of buildings.

I owed Hilde something, I thought, because she had been my first real introduction to the pleasures of love, freely given by a mistress. And, to be truthful, never equaled since. Was that all one got, just that first big opportunity? Lottie had tried to please me, for a while, and certainly I had tried to please her. But it was not the same. For Hilde had taken so naturally and completely to love, if only because she had nothing else to count on, to receive or give. On Nightingale Road there had been no sweet cry of the nightingale. Amidst the ruins a German and a Jew had made love. Perhaps, after all, it had been the right thing to do. And had it been the right thing to do to marry Lottie, to leave Hilde behind in the ruins? Hilde had used a phrase in the restaurant: *out of deep sympathy for the terrible things done to the Jews.* Was that the only reason for my deserting her?

A taxi, a black Mercedes, waited at the curb in front of the Kempinski. I opened the door of the car for her and bent, very likely out of old habit, to kiss her. Her lips opened and surprised me with their softness. "Good night, my darling," she whispered.

5: The DP camp at Sodesheim, where I met Lottie, was about thirty miles to the northeast of Frankfurt, and my first visit there was on a sodden day in February in 1947. Naomi Genauer, a WAC corporal in my section, had come across the camp where some eight hundred Jews were awaiting immigration visas or transportation to Palestine. "You ought to see the children there," she said, and one day we arranged to borrow a jeep from the motor pool to drive to the camp. Sodesheim was not reached by any of the main roads, and those we traveled over were badly rutted and for one stretch went through a tall, bleak pine forest. We also came across a few farm villages, with names I'd never heard of, that bore little evidence of the war's having disturbed them at all. The camp was at the edge of the small town and had once been a Wehrmacht barracks, and a sign on the iron-barred gates identified it now as Bet Harabeem. We drove into a courtyard and parked at an administration office staffed by UNRRA officials and members of the camp's central committee.

The secretary of that committee, a man of forty who looked

much older and had managed to survive the rigors of Buchenwald, was anxious to show us the way camp life was organized. He explained that it was administered along communal lines, much like a kibbutz in Palestine, and that most of the inhabitants hoped soon to reach "Eretz Israel," although there was a minority that had applied for visas to enter the United States, Argentina, and Great Britain. He proudly showed us a large kitchen in which both men and women tended stoves with steaming pots on them and neat rooms, each containing from four to six beds, and he gave us copies of the mimeographed weekly newspaper published in Yiddish and German. It was the nursery, however, that Naomi was especially anxious for me to see.

When I went into the large room with the bare wooden floor and freshly whitewashed walls—heavy with the smell of disinfectant—the children were sitting on the floor in a circle, and in the center of that circle was a young woman whose face was pale and whose eyes and hair seemed all the blacker by contrast. She was in the midst of telling a story in Hebrew to the children, who must have ranged in age from about three to eight. Whether or not they knew the language or understood the story, they gave the young woman their unwavering attention. That was my first sight of Lottie, and, while she gave Naomi only a swift nod and seemed to ignore me, I somehow knew that she was aware of my presence. When she had finished the story, Lottie led the children in the singing of Palestinian songs, and something about those clear, innocent voices brought a sting of tears to my eyes, perhaps because I knew by then that a million like them had been shoved into furnaces or tossed into burial pits. We had to write to everyone we knew at home, I told Naomi, and tell them about these children, not one of whom had parents.

The children were dismissed for their lunch, and I was introduced to Lottie. She gave me a crisp handshake and, in English, asked Naomi and me if we would have lunch with her. Were we taking food out of their mouths? Lottie laughed. It was our own C rations we would be eating, but with Jewish bread made in the camp kitchen.

She talked only about the children at that lunch, eaten in what looked like a typical army mess hall. Some had been found alive in concentration camps, others among groups of refugees who took care of them in lieu of their missing parents, and they had been gathered here until arrangements could be made for their proper care. "They will grow up in Palestine," Lottie said. "It will be their own country." She seemed very sure of this.

"What about you?" I asked.

"I will go there too," she answered. "I would have gone before, but I have the children to look after first."

I asked her if she too had been in a concentration camp, and she said that was something she preferred not to talk about. But I learned later that she had been in Bergen-Belsen and had done forced labor and that she had belonged to a Jewish underground in Prague before being caught by Nazis. The camp secretary told me that. Lottie told me more about her experiences later, but she never dwelt on them.

"I'd like to talk to you again," I told Lottie as we were leaving.

"Come any time," she said, and I noticed how warm her voice became, and the sparkle of interest in her dark eyes, as though I had suddenly awakened some feeling in her.

"You liked her, didn't you," Naomi said almost accusingly as we drove back, for she knew about Hilde.

"A striking, remarkable woman," I said. "Imagine having the strength to go through all that and to survive, and hope, and help others. That's what being a human being is all about."

"She's attractive, too," Naomi said.

"No doubt about that," I said.

And when I slept with Hilde that night in my billet I felt guilty. I got up to the camp again a week later, and this time I asked Lottie if I could bring her to Frankfurt for an evening. There were American movies there, and the food was excellent, and I could probably even arrange for her to spend the night in one of the scarce hotel rooms. Then I would return her to the camp in the morning. I saw again that same anticipatory sparkle in her eyes as she readily agreed. I lied to Hilde the night before I went to get Lottie for our date together; I told her I was to be the section duty officer until dawn of the day following and would not be at my billet. I would see her, I said, the night after tomorrow. Chris, by then, had somehow managed to obtain an old Opel in running condition, as well as the papers to fuel it from American Army pumps, and he lent it to me. I drove Lottie to Frankfurt, where I had a card for the main officers' mess there at SHAEF headquarters, and it happened to be a particularly good evening for food: thick porterhouse steaks, as I remember, were served for the main course by the German waiters. It was the best food she'd had in years, Lottie claimed, and she took an almost malicious delight in being waited upon by a tall young German. Afterward I took her to the officers' lounge, where we sipped brandy and decided to talk the evening away instead of seeing the movie.

She had been born in Prague, she said, and lived there with her parents until she was in her late teens and was already attending the university at the time of the German takeover. She had begun to specialize in social studies, but the almost immediate anti-Jewish measures ended that ambition, and sensing that things would only grow worse for Jews, she had left her home and lived clandestinely with a group of other Jewish former students in a cellar of an apartment house. With this group she plotted a means of getting out of the country and into Hungary, and once established there she hoped to bring out her parents too, and her young brother. Her eventual aim was for all of them to reach Palestine. "I was never a Zionist until then," she said. "But, then, to reach Palestine became my dream, as it was for most of the others in the group, some of whom belonged to a Zionist labor movement."

Then one day she learned that the apartment house in which her family lived had been cleansed of its Jews. Her parents and her brother were first transported to Theresienstadt, a ghetto set up specifically for Jews. Her father, a doctor, had merited this supposedly kind fate because of his professional status. She later learned that they had lived in Theresienstadt until 1942, when they were among the first to be shipped to Auschwitz. Since nothing more was ever heard of her parents or her brother, she assumed they had been gassed within a few hours of their arrival. By then, with three others of her group, Lottie obtained false papers and was doing farm work near a town called Komarno, very close to the Hungarian border. In 1943 she and her friends finally made a carefully planned attempt to cross the border late on a spring night. A Czech border patrol apprehended them. The two males of the group were shot almost at once at a local police station, and she and the other girl went through an ugly interrogation before being spared. She spent three months in a Slovakian prison, where some things happened that she preferred not to talk about, after which she was sent to the Skoda Works to labor fourteen hours a day. She had pretended not to be Jewish all this time, but when she came down with influenza an ardently Nazi doctor accused her of hiding her real identity—he could tell a Jewess when he saw one, he said—and she was reported and put in a transport leaving for Bergen-Belsen. When the British entered the camp, finally, her weight was down to ninety pounds. After regaining her strength in a hospital, she decided to cross over to the American Zone, because of the firm British attitude about denying her a visa to travel to Palestine.

I was filled with wonder that a woman of such sensitivity could live through so much and still manage to retain her spirit. I was proud of her, and proud of myself for feeling so close to her.

"There is no more to tell," she said in the officers' lounge. "It is of no interest now."

But I took her hand, and she allowed me to hold it for awhile until she gently, and almost shyly, withdrew it from my grasp. I think it was then that I decided to bring Lottie back with me to the United States, if she would agree to come. I hardly knew whether it was love I felt or a mixture of pity, sympathy, and admiration, but I told myself that the war, my service in the Occupation, my presence in the ruins of Germany, would finally take on real meaning if the upshot of it all was that Lottie would return with me. I was due to go home in May —my section was moving to Heidelberg, and its personnel would be drastically cut—and I realized I didn't have much time to declare my intentions.

And I would have to cut myself off from Hilde. Soon after came the night I said good-by to her. The next day I went back to the camp and took Lottie for a ride in Chris's Opel. I parked on the side of the road in the midst of the dank pine forest and asked her to marry me.

"Why?" she asked.

"Because it would be right for us to spend our lives together," I said.

"I'm not sure I love you," she said. "And I am not sure how you feel. You have never asked me to sleep with you."

"Out of respect," I said.

"And perhaps a German girl in Frankfurt, or Höchst, where you work."

"Yes, there was a girl," I said. "I've stopped seeing her."

"Because of me?"

"Yes, because of you."

We kissed in a strained, unsure way, and I held her firm, lean, work-hardened body. I told her how close I felt to her.

"So you think you love me?" she asked in her direct way.

"Yes, I think so."

"Not only because of all that I told you?"

"Not only that," I said.

A brooding expression came into her eyes. "But I would have to go to America."

"And would that be so terrible?"

"I would give up something. What about your parents? Do they know?"

"I'll write, but I know they'll approve and be happy."

"There is a man at the camp," she said. "My close friend Simon. I told him that if we reached Palestine we would marry. He loves me."

"Do you love him?"

"Love," she said, after hesitating a moment. She pronounced the word with a certain bitterness. "To love, one needs to believe in love. I am not sure that I do."

"Believe in it?"

She nodded. "I believe in much that Simon believes, so sometimes I think I love him."

"And me?"

"Sometimes I think I *could* love you," she said cautiously.

"I would not be here with you otherwise. I am attracted, certainly. Doesn't it matter to you that I am older?"

"A couple of years," I said. "No, it doesn't matter. What does matter is that I can give you a good life, and you need a good life."

"I will think about it," she said.

I thought about it too, but always in positive terms. Lottie, for me, was part of the rebuilding—of our lives and, in a way, of the world. My idealism, Chris called it, my Jewish need to be constructive. For Lottie, I must have had a certain glamour. I roared into the camp in a jeep, brought gifts, spoke of a land of plenty, wore the officer's uniform of the conqueror, and, at the same time, appeared to feel deeply and, above all, to understand what *she* felt. Simon spoke to her of sharing a new life; I spoke of giving her a new life. Simon was familiar to her; I was strange. She would be crazy to refuse me, her camp friends told her. Even Simon. She would have a hard life with him, he said, and she should have things easier for awhile.

When I saw her next at the camp, she had asked me once more if I was sure of my feelings, and confidently I said I was. Her eyes filled with tears, and I asked her why she wept, and she told me it was because she had decided to go with me. "That's a funny reason to cry," I said, and she smiled and almost angrily wiped the tears away. She had become infatuated with me, I was sure. We were married at the camp two weeks later, after I had obtained the necessary papers, and Chris helped me pull the strings that got her on the same ship I was on. We could not share a cabin, though, because the ship hadn't been converted back from its troopship accommodations, and I sometimes thought afterward that it was the ship—the enforced separation—that started us on the wrong path. The voyage was rough, she was seasick, she had only strangers around her, and unconsciously perhaps she put the blame on me. Her almost schoolgirlish falling-in-love was gone by the time we landed at the pier in Manhattan, frightened away by the enormity of the decision she had made. We managed our first night together only after arriving in New York, and I invested in a suite at the Savoy Plaza for the purpose. Making love was difficult for her—her sexuality had been muted for so long. But I was certain that her passion would grow stronger in time— that would be part of the inevitable healing process.

Out of deep sympathy for the terrible things done to the Jews. In April of 1945, two years before I met Lottie, I had seen the camp at Orhdruf and had written a letter to my father, which I had put into the third person so as to maintain as much objectivity as possible. I wrote:

"Alfred Becker became a Jew on April 12th, 1945. Up until that time this young American, a first lieutenant in the Army, had had, probably, less than the normal amount of consciousness of himself as a Jew, in spite of his father's having made the effort to introduce him to synagogue services and having provided him with a bar mitzvah at the age of thirteen. We might be able to ascribe his lack of Jewish consciousness to the divorce between his parents—which occurred when Alfred was fourteen, and to his moving from a suburb of New York to the city and thenceforth—perhaps by his mother's design—failing to maintain contact with old friends, family members, and the Jewish organizations to which his father had belonged. Nor did he go to family weddings and funerals, which might have had the effect of heightening his Jewish identity. Suffice it to say that Alfred Becker, upon being asked his religion for the Army records, put down the word 'None.' But on April 12th, Alfred

Becker came across his first concentration camp, and he saw the blood-spattered bodies of eighty-three Jews—some of whom may not have considered themselves Jews either—and he came to the conclusion that a Jew, no matter how little he identified himself as such, must claim his Jewish identity. For there is no other way to combat the evil that is anti-Jewish."

"So, Dad," I finished, "count your son as a member of your lodges and organizations, and make contributions on my behalf to your synagogue, and explain that I may be a little hazy about the religious thing, and tell them all I'm one of them. I'll write more about the camp later, so that you can let your friends know what their fine former German associates have been up to lately."

I was a liaison officer at the time with the Twentieth Corps, advancing westward that April in the direction of Weimar and Jena. The movement was rapid, and at headquarters we still believed in a German fiction called the Redoubt, which made us all wary of any imminent end to the war in Europe. And who knew then about an atomic bomb? Certainly not I. The corps had moved its headquarters to Gotha, and equipment was still being moved into the office building of an insurance company when I took a spell at the radio. A message I took down from the Fourth Armored Division reported the discovery of a small concentration camp that was later identified as Subsidiary Camp S–III, a satellite of Buchenwald. An estimate guessed at from five to ten thousand bodies buried in trenches in the field outside the camp. Only three of the inmates had been found alive. I decided the message was important enough to be shown to the G-3 officer, Colonel Pringle.

"Five thousand bodies?" the colonel said, studying the message. "Whose bodies, Becker?"

"A unit of the Fifteenth Cavalry entered the camp and released the inmates."

"Live ones, I presume."

"Yes sir," I said. "Three."

"Three thousand?"

"No sir, just three."

"You'd better go down there, Becker," the colonel said, scratching the unshaven stubble on his chin. "The chief will want to know about this. We have Orhdruf listed as a temporary field headquarters of the Wehrmacht high command—up until February, that is."

"Orhdruf's twenty miles from here," I told him.

"I know that, Becker. I'm going to need a report on the place for the chief, so get going. It's supposed to be all clear down that way, but take my jeep anyway."

That was considerate of the colonel, because his jeep had a machine gun mounted on its hood.

"Where we headed for, Lieutenant?" my driver, Stearns, asked me when I found him in the motor pool.

"Orhdruf," I said.

"What's that, sir?"

"It's a town," I told him. "We take the colonel's jeep and head south."

I picked out the road we would take on the map, and we rode through Thuringian fields that seemed to take on a new green in the bright spring sunlight. It was placid countryside, hardly a sign of life, not even an American vehicle to show what the corps' situation map had shown—that we were in captured territory. Stearns slowed the jeep only briefly when two young German soldiers sprang from behind a barn with their hands held stiff above their heads. I waved them to head back along the road to Gotha, for it wasn't my job to corral prisoners.

"Raus," Stearns yelled at them and the two Germans obediently trotted down the road. Ten minutes later we came to a crossroads with a sign that said *Nach Orhdruf*.

"What's that crazy smell?" Stearns asked, as we sighted the red tiled roofs of Orhdruf.

"Lime, I guess." I figured the lime had something to do with the bodies in the trenches.

From every house in the town fluttered white flags of surrender; the residents were taking no chances that Americans might think they were still fighting the war. We saw some American Army vehicles in the streets, inquired of a Third Army MP as to the whereabouts of the camp, and were directed to the other end of the town, where there was a dirt road on the right that would take us there. Stearns gunned the jeep up the steep grade of the dirt road. We came to a plateau and saw some armored vehicles, including those of the Fifteenth Cavalry, parked along a stretch of barbed-wire fencing.

"Want to see this, Stearns?" I asked.

"Yes sir," he said.

We went through a gate into a large yard of hardened dirt, and the first thing we saw was a group of bodies sprawled in the last attitudes. Blood had seeped over their miserable clothing, machine-gun bullets had crushed away parts of their heads and faces, bony fingers still clutched at the ground.

"Jesus," Stearns murmured.

I talked to two G.I.'s from the Fifteenth Cavalry and got their story. Their light tanks and half-tracks had nosed up the hill about six that morning after hearing some machine-gun fire. A cavalry sergeant who spoke Russian had learned from three Russian prisoners who had managed to stay alive that the SS guards had rounded up all the prisoners they could find, a group of eighty-three Jews being used as forced labor in a nearby factory, herded them into the center of the yard, and opened up machine guns on them. Many prisoners, however, had been evacuated a few days before on a forced march. The guards had then fled, neglecting to look under the beds in an empty barracks in which the three Russians had hidden themselves.

Stearns followed me as I went to the barracks at the end of the yard. They were all much the same: burlap sacks on the bare ground serving as beds, a fierce smell of excrement pervading what were hardly more than elongated huts, each holding, according to a sign in German posted at the doors, two hundred and twelve persons.

Stearns stopped holding his nose long enough to say: "Looks like they could have crowded in a couple more, Lieutenant."

I didn't answer. I jotted down some details on a scratch pad. One of the barracks advertised itself as a hospital, and its difference from the others was that it had a wooden floor and some partitions. In the dimness I stumbled across something, and saw that it was the leg of an emaciated body, lying naked on the floor. It was the thinnest body I had ever seen. I had not known that anyone could get that thin before dying. One outstretched arm, the left, revealed a blue number tattooed above the wrist. The number was B41387, and I wrote it on my scratch pad, with the thought that maybe I could identify this victim who had died of "natural" causes. (I did manage to identify him four months later. His name was Hirsh Feldstein, he was twenty-two at the time of his death, and he came from Moravia. There were no known survivors in his family, and so there had been no point in finding out who he had been.)

As we returned across the yard we saw a small group of G.I.'s surrounding a body on the ground. I hadn't seen that body there when we first crossed the yard, and so I looked into that, too. "What's up?" I asked one of the soldiers. He shrugged and nodded toward a cavalry sergeant engaged in talking to the three Russian prisoners, who couldn't have been captured long before, because their Red Army uniforms were still fairly clean.

I looked at the body, a striking sight, because this man was plump, whereas all the others were emaciated. I saw, too, that the blood on his head and neck was uncoagulated.

"Can you tell me about this, Sergeant?" I asked.

"Yes, sir," he said. "I've been speaking to these Russians here. This fellow on the ground was a prisoner, a German criminal who was a trustee in the camp. He beat up a lot of other prisoners and hung some up on hooks inside that building, and he ran off with the guards, but he came back when he saw us hand food to these Russians. I guess he felt he was entitled to some rescue treatment too. The Russians saw him, and they grabbed him. This fellow here stuck a piece of a bayonet in the back of his head." He pointed to a short man in the uniform of a Russian major.

"When did this happen?"

"Couple of minutes ago," the sergeant said.

That had been while we were in the hospital barracks. The Russian major kicked at the body with the toe of his boot. *"Gross,"* he said to us, shaking his head, *"zu gross."*

"He means," said the sergeant, "that this one had food while the others starved. The major was hiding the piece of bayonet to kill himself with, instead of letting them get him."

The Russian major said something else, in Russian, with a sorrowful expression on his wizened face.

"What's he saying?" I asked.

"He's complaining that the guy died too quickly. Anything we're supposed to do about this, sir?"

"Damned if I know," I said, and I turned away and walked with Stearns out of the camp.

I had Stearns stop when we got to the center of the town and, on an impulse, asked one of the civilians where the mayor lived. He pointed out a large house on the main street, which looked as though it had been recently painted. I got out of the jeep and banged on the front door. A woman with a white, frightened face peered out at me from a window. I knew enough German to ask if the mayor was inside. She nodded, and a few moments later he came out, a bald, stocky man in his mid-fifties. "I formally surrender to you this town," he started to say, probably about to ask for consideration for the inhabitants.

"The hell with your town," I said. "Tell me what you know of that camp up there on the hill."

"I know nothing," he replied.

"Nothing at all?"

"The SS were up there," he said. He had only learned an hour ago what was up there in the camp. It was a military matter and not his concern.

"Don't you think, as the mayor, you ought to look at it?"

"*Ja.*" But he said it more as a question.

"In the back of the jeep," I said. "Your wife too."

We drove back to the camp, and Stearns waited in the jeep while I toured them through what I had seen. At one point it looked as though the wife would not be able to continue walking, and she clutched the arm of her husband for support. The face of the mayor was set in a stiff, unchanging mold, and he would not meet my eyes. A half-hour later we deposited them at their house. The mayor waited by the side of the jeep, as though expecting some order from me.

"You did not know?" I asked.

"*Nein,*" he said. "*Nein.*"

"That's all," I said, and I told Stearns to head back to

Gotha. At headquarters I wrote out a report and gave it to the colonel, who glanced at it briefly and nodded. "We move in the morning," he said. "To Weimar."

"Taken?" I asked.

"Yes, just got inside, and now the radio is blasting away about a place called Buchenwald. What the hell kind of a country is this, anyway?" The colonel seemed genuinely puzzled.

I never did write that other letter to my father about Orhdruf, and I think the main reason I didn't was that another message came through late that evening. The mayor of Orhdruf and his wife had hanged themselves from a rafter in their cellar, and I mentally kicked myself for not having found out what had gone on inside their heads. Was I too a murderer, because I had made them go through the camp? After getting to know Hilde, I told her about the mayor and his wife and asked her what she thought the reason was for their suicides. "Pride," Hilde said. "Their pride was destroyed, in themselves, their town, Germany. It was too much for them. That was all they had left to live for, and it was taken away from them." She didn't say I had taken it away from them.

But there was something else that had come into my mind, as the mayor had stood numbly before me after I had told him to get out of the jeep. I had had the distinct feeling that he had recognized me as being Jewish, that he had taken me for such, and when the message came about the hanging the same thought returned. But I didn't mention that to Hilde. Nor that I had suddenly, perhaps irrationally, decided to recognize myself as Jewish, for it was as a Jew that I had suddenly appeared before the mayor of Orhdruf and his wife as their judgment. They may not have known too much about the camp, but they had known about the Jews.

Twenty years after that day I saw Orhdruf, I was in my

comfortable room at the Kempinski, attempting to fall asleep and still attempting to claim my identity, for Hilde's remark had brought the struggle back. Was there no way to explain to her, or to anyone, that by marrying Lottie I had hoped to become more Jewish?

6:

To: *Mr. Elihu Grossman*
President, New York Chapter
B'nai Jesurat
1107 Madison Avenue
New York City

"Dear Elihu,

"I met today with three of the Zeller-Bricken directors, the meeting having been arranged by Kurt Hildebrandt, the fellow with whom I had been doing most of the corresponding. As we had guessed, Hildebrandt turns out to be unimportant, just a sort of glorified secretary. I found him in the Berlin headquarters offices of Zeller-Bricken, located in one of those slablike new buildings on the Kaiserstrasse. Automatic elevators, receptionists with upswept hairdos sitting behind free-form desks—I could have been on Park Avenue. Hildebrandt explained that I was now to see some of the top brass (my phrase, not his) and took me to a small but impressive conference room, where the three gentlemen were already waiting with their documents spread out before them on the table. I got the impression this was just another business meeting for them. Hildebrandt looked disappointed that he wasn't to be included in the proceedings: you've seen his type at the consulate in New York, complete to dark pin-stripe suit, horn-rimmed glasses, lots of white teeth, and well-polished shoes.

"Now to the directors. The important one, or presiding one, of the three was Herr Conrad Isserstadt, who has the title of managing director. He reminded me of one of those German actors in old silent movies—slim, well-tailored in the London style, smooth-faced, slightly bald, almost handsome in an aristocratic way. He didn't wear a monacle, but he would have been absolutely perfect if he had.

"Herr Willi Durlevanger was rougher in appearance, dressed in tweeds, and smoked a pipe. Looked as though he had once been a factory foreman and had risen to his present position through the ranks. A hearty outward manner, but with a foxy expression around the eyes.

"And there, too, was Herr Oskar Weisse, our old friend. By the way, your information on him checks out to an extent. I can't reveal my sources, not even to you, old friend, but if we should ever have to make this whole thing public, I can get the same information through official channels. Roehling, I'm more dubious about. So far, no involvement. Weisse is stocky, is a little watery in the eyes, and drinks too much beer to judge by his red-veined face. A very friendly manner, at least toward me; he kept nodding his head and smiling at me to emphasize his good fellowship.

"I took notes and so can give you a faithful account of what took place. Isserstadt told me that he and the two others were delegated as a committee by the remainder of the board to discuss the matter with me and were empowered to make suitable recommendations to the board, although, as it turned out, he already had a recommendation *from* the board. I'll get to that. He said he first wanted to make it clear that our claim was not a legal one, in that the restitution laws of the West German government relating to such claims had already expired. I corrected him on this, citing certain exceptions. This was all fencing, of course, since legality is not going to determine the issue.

" 'You cite sixty claimants to compensation from the former Zeller-Bricken combine,' he said and wanted to know if this represented a firm limitation on the number of claimants.

"I said I could not guarantee that limitation, and furthermore, that the claims were being made on the *present* firm, since we did not make the distinction between the so-called old firm and the new.

" 'We *do* make the distinction,' Isserstadt said, dryly. 'However, the sum requested by you and a certain Elihu Grossman of New York City on behalf of the claimants is set at two million Deutsche Marks, half of the sum to be paid to the present claimants and the other half to be set aside for suitable use by an agreed upon international Jewish relief organization. But, Herr Becker, nowhere in these documents do I see any reference to the sustenance provided the Jewish workers by the former Zeller-Bricken combine.'

"Imagine, Elihu! He wanted some credit for the so-called food and shelter provided the workers. Naturally I pointed out to him that the sustenance he referred to amounted to nothing more than a slow starvation diet and that the shelter provided had no toilet facilities, no heat, and inadequate ventilation due to inhuman overcrowding. I said, 'I think we should rule out the term sustenance, since it never amounted to more than nine hundred calories a day, as attested to by our nutrition experts, and that was certainly insufficient to maintain life over any lengthy period of time.'

"Isserstadt answered that German citizens were hardly better off during those days, and so I said that I would concede his point if he could cite any cases of widespread starvation among the German populace during the final two years of the war. He dropped the subject at once.

"He next brought up the bombing raids, both American and British, that had badly damaged the fusing subdivision, where most of our victims labored, and said that many of the deaths among the Jewish workers were due to this circumstance.

"This I admitted, but I went on to say that the workers had been slaves, that none had owed any obligation to the Third Reich, and that they had been forced to submit to risks involving bomb blasts and fire storms. I thought I was doing pretty well up to now, but I was caught by surprise when Weisse entered the conversation. He seems to have some importance, because Isserstadt, though nominally his superior, immediately shut up.

" 'Naturally,' Weisse said, 'our firm is disturbed by what looks like a blot on its record, namely the alleged employment of forced labor, but have you taken into account the fact that many Jews, by means of this forced labor, were enabled to escape the fate decreed for the Jews as a race by the leaders of the Third Reich?'

"Naturally, Elihu, that thought had occurred to me, but I hardly had expected to hear it from a German and particularly from one with a record such as Weisse's. I had to shift immediately to the offensive.

" 'Herr Weisse,' I said, 'the people forced to work for Zeller-Bricken were already considered dead by those leaders, in that they were not thought of as human beings. They were temporarily useful objects from which a product—namely labor helpful to the German war effort—could be extracted, and once the product was extracted they were given the same treatment as, let's say, the rind of a squeezed-out grapefruit. And here we deal with intent. Was the intent of the forced labor to save their lives?'

"Weisse surprised me again. 'Herr Becker,' he said, 'I say to you that among a great many citizens of the Third Reich there was such an intent, and it operated under the most restrictive and dangerous of conditions.'

" 'Are you saying,' I asked, 'that you know of people at Zeller-Bricken who attempted to save Jewish lives?'

" 'Yes, I am saying that. I was one of those people.'

"There you see the cleverness of the board, Elihu. They were attempting to turn Weisse into one of their strong points, and that meant they knew he was vulnerable. I decided to play it as though I was not aware of the ploy.

" 'Perhaps you'd explain,' I said to Weisse.

" 'I held a position with the firm at the time,' he said, 'and was able to prevent the transport to concentration centers of several hundred of the Jewish workers.'

" 'How?'

" 'I would prefer if that were to be discussed privately between us.'

"That means that I will have a further meeting with Weisse alone, and be assured, I will keep you informed. Meanwhile, Isserstadt took over again and brought up a number of minor and niggling points before stating the firm's basic position, namely that the Zeller-Bricken combine had been completely reorganized in 1952, that it was now a firm of respected eminence, and that its present membership could not assume the responsibility for acts that had occurred during the period of Hitler's rule over Germany. Nevertheless, Zeller-Bricken wished to go on record that it bore the same sense of outrage and shock as all other segments of the West German business community in regard to the treatment of minorities. As a token of this they were prepared to offer the sum of one hundred thousand Deutsche Marks to a responsible Jewish relief organization, to be designated by us, with the concurrence of the American State Department, and with suitable expenses for my legal services.

"I told him the offer was entirely unsatisfactory.

" 'Then we are at an impasse, Herr Becker.'

"The moment had arrived, Elihu, which, as you know, always bothers me, because it puts me in the position of being a bargainer. However, it had to be done. I'll give you my exact words.

" 'Gentlemen,' I said, 'until now we have carefully kept from public knowledge our negotiations with you. But we are well aware of your contracts with the American Department of Defense, which, in effect, means that American taxpayers will be footing the bill. There is a climate of opinion existing in the United States that would not view these dealings between you and the Defense Department in a favorable light, mainly because the name of Zeller-Bricken bears a certain connotation. Nor are we sure that all former Nazi elements in the company have been expunged. In fact, we have what we regard as authentic information to the contrary. Our position is that you have the obligation to wipe your slate clean, to reimburse those whom you exploited. We think the claims of the survivors are legitimate and justified; other large German firms have settled such claims. We would feel duty bound, if you ignore the claims, to so state to the American public.'

" 'Blackmail, Herr Becker?' Durlevanger suddenly interjected.

" 'Time-honored custom,' I told him.

"Isserstadt, though, was more interested in that reference to the former Nazi elements in the firm. He wanted to know if I had referred to any specific member of the firm, other than Herr Weisse, who had freely admitted that he had been employed by the firm during the war years, but who had also stated that his activities where Jews were concerned had been benevolent in nature.

"I withheld Roehling's name for the time being, pending learning something about him. I told Isserstadt I'd be glad to provide him with exactly the information as it had been given to me. He merely had to make the request. That, he said, would have to be decided by the board as a whole, whether such alleged information would serve any useful purpose. The board, in fact, might easily feel that an attempt was being made to apply pressure in a situation that had to do with civilized feelings or, to use an American term, public relations.

"At this point, Elihu, I got a bit angry. We used to say just after the war that Germans needed to be shouted at a little before they'd get off their butt ends. I raised my voice and complained that these negotiations had stretched out over a period of more than a year, that neither I nor you could afford to devote our whole lives to what was after all a quite simple matter—compensation—and that all of us, including the members of the firm, would feel better if we could get it settled. If the answer was no, I wanted it to be a firm no, and then I could go home and report. But since already a small offer was being made to us by way of settlement, it seemed to me the firm was tacitly admitting the validity of monetary compensation for past injustices.

"Isserstadt decided it was time to conclude the meeting. My thoughts would be conveyed to the directorate as a whole, he assured me, and he would have some further word for me shortly. We all shook hands as though we were the best of friends. I noticed by my watch that the meeting had taken precisely fifty-nine minutes, and I suspect that our claims, which is to say the consideration of them, had been allotted no more than one hour by the board. One must admire this precision of the Germans, and I would say it speaks well for the quality of Zeller-Bricken products. At the moment I await further word from the board and, possibly, that call from Herr Weisse. Sorry I don't have more definite news for you, but that's the way it was left. Would you kindly make a copy of this letter and send it along to my secretary, Gloria, for my files? My best regards."

Weisse had telephoned the next morning. We had agreed to meet in late afternoon at the terrace café of the Hotel am Zoo on the Kurfürstendamm, and at five o'clock I was seated at a table behind the glass enclosure. I had ordered a fruit juice while waiting, but it was still untouched when a long gunmetal-gray Mercedes 600 pulled up at the curb in front of the glassed-in terrace. I saw Herr Weisse leaning out from the opened window of the rear of the limousine. He beckoned to me when he saw me at my table. I left a five-mark piece for the waiter and went outside. The chauffeur sprang into action and hurried to open the door of the car for me.

Herr Weisse held his hand out and shook mine. "Herr Becker," he said, "I thought it would be more comfortable and more private if we held our meeting in this car. It is not mine. It belongs to the company."

I got inside and sank into the soft gray leather seat beside

Weisse, who opened the glass partition separating the front from the rear seats and directed the driver to cruise about for half an hour. "The Wall," he said, "and the Grunewald." He turned to me. "We will have a nice tour of the city." Then he closed the partition. The outside sounds became muffled; I could barely hear the hum of the motor as the chauffeur moved along the Kurfürstendamm to the Budapester Strasse and then in the direction of the Brandenburg Gate.

"We are fitted with a bar, as you see," Weisse said. He opened up a folded mahogany table that, in the roomy interior, in no way interfered with our legs. The flesh of his fifty-four-year-old face was shinily pink, and only around his eyes were there little puffs of fat. His thinning light hair was turning gray. "We also have coffee and tea. Tell me what is your pleasure."

"Coffee," I said. The caffeine would help counteract the relaxing effect of this much too comfortable interior.

"We have an excellent brandy," he suggested.

"Coffee will do fine."

He poured the coffee from a thermos flask into a thick crystal glass, then chose a brandy for himself.

"Smoke?" he asked, offering me a cigar from a thin box. "Havana. You don't have them, I understand."

"No, thank you," I said.

"You don't mind if I———? We are air-conditioned."

"Not at all."

He clipped the end of his cigar and lit it. Having fulfilled his duties as host, he sank back in his seat. "Very well presented, your case," he said, with a nod of approval. "Very nicely done. Isserstadt looks smart, but he is a little empty up here." He tapped the side of his head. "I told him the hundred thousand marks would never go down with your people."

"You're suggesting that the firm should agree to our proposal?"

We were traveling through the Tiergarten now, along the broad Strasse des 17. Juni. Twilight was descending on the city, and there were few pedestrians.

"The question is more complicated than that, Herr Becker," Weisse said, sipping his brandy. "You must, for the moment at least, examine it from the company point of view. We pay such a sum, a half-million of your dollars, and we admit guilt. Such things get around. Everyone knows that the Krupp firm paid, that Telefunken and Siemens made a settlement."

"In your case," I said, "a fast settlement would be the most private method. Since certain records do exist, a long delay could bring your firm considerable unfavorable publicity."

"Perhaps. At any rate, it is something to talk about. I will assume that, between us, there is no point in not admitting some facts of my background."

"Correct," I said.

"But you do not know all of it, I assure you."

"Undoubtedly so."

"With that proviso, I will tell you this: I was a captain of the SS. You know that much."

I nodded.

"I was also, at the end of the war, one of the few available people with the requisite experience to assist my firm in reestablishing itself. You undoubtedly are acquainted with the unfortunate postwar situation, particularly as it applied to German industry."

"I was here," I said, "and so I naturally wonder how you happened to be cleared by American or British authorities. Were you cleared?"

"Fully," Weisse said. He drew in deeply on his cigar and

let loose a cloud. It could almost be seen being sucked into the vents by the efficient air conditioning. "I might say, in fact, that there was intervention on a high level to make certain that I was cleared without prejudice of any kind."

"Really?" I met his eyes, which were almost twinkling with good fellowship.

"You are surprised, I see. The investigation determined that there was no culpability on my part—or, for that matter, on the firm's part—in any category of the crimes against humanity by the Nazi government. The clearance was given me as early as 1947. I had been interned, in a camp near Linz, with our SS field-unit officers. At that time I was with the Waffen SS."

"You would have been picked up by Third Army forces," I said.

"Exactly so."

"You admitted to them you were with the SS?"

"I was not one of those who attempted to remove the little tattoo under here." Weisse indicated a spot just under his left armpit. "It is still here. I also admitted to my interrogators that I had *personally* requested the use of Jewish forced labor at the Zeller-Bricken Hanover plant. Now why would I admit that? What do you think?"

"I am listening."

"Nor am I one of those who professed not to know what was going on. I knew. I also knew that where precision work was concerned the Jews could provide a high degree of ability and skill. Humanitarian aspects aside, did it not make excellent sense to use them?"

"They worked for their lives—or so you mentioned at the meeting."

"No," he said abruptly. "Ah, the Wall." He had glanced out his window. We were traveling along it, in the direction of the Potsdamer Platz, which was on the Eastern side. I caught a glimpse of Checkpoint Charlie and the no-man's land between. "Terrible thing, is it not? But to return to the subject. I merely used that as an argument. Even Himmler saw the light eventually. I never knew that strange gentleman, by the way. The administration was very complicated."

I wondered. He had tossed that last bit out gratuitously.

"You see, Herr Becker, like many others who did not approve of the regime, who were in fact repelled by its excesses, I came to the realization that it would be more constructive to appear to be working with it. This is not impossible, you will admit."

"I've known of cases," I said.

"I like very much that you are well informed," he said approvingly. "You can understand how, in my position, it made good politics to join the SS."

I let myself reveal a touch of impatience as I asked, "But why, Herr Weisse, is it necessary for us to meet in private like this?"

"More coffee?" he asked.

"No thanks."

He poured himself more brandy and took an appreciative sip.

"Herr Becker. The facts are these. In 1943 I became a member of the SS. I was advised to do so. My firm had entered a period of critical labor shortages, and the plants had the necessity of working at the top of their capacities, due to the nature of the equipment they provided the armed forces. In spite of our priorities, we could not meet our commitments, and this had come to the attention of Hitler himself. He was most interested in the Zeller-Bricken guidance systems for German rocketry. Radar installations were being increasingly bombed;

this called for constant replenishment from Zeller-Bricken, not to mention Siemens. On the instructions of an officer of the firm I applied for SS membership, and specifically for a commission. Naturally, because of my background, I would be well suited for RSHA duties. You yourself know that the only additional sources of labor—the foreign labor, the so-called antisocial elements—were completely under the control of the SS administration."

"Very few of whom," I said, "have ever been called to account."

"Herr Becker," he said, holding out his hands in an appealing gesture. "That kind of responsibility is perhaps a good deal less legal than moral. Many connections must be proven before you can make a man with a typewriter, sitting in an office, a killer. Especially the underlings. They are told what to do; they do it. It is my earnest opinion that the responsibility for the actions we all abhor must lie directly at the feet of maybe half a dozen men at most. Half a dozen—no more. Must you then punish all of Germany?"

"I'll agree," I said, "that it's not our business to go into those matters. Right now, I have a job to do. I'm interested only in what way you can assist in its completion."

"Let me conclude," he said. "I, personally, had no reason to dislike Jews. In fact, a doctor friend of mine had returned from the Russian area of operations with truly disgusting stories about what was happening to Jews. I was as shocked as he was. But, unlike the doctor, I was in a position to do something positive. With my SS commission came my appointment as Zeller-Bricken's labor-recruitment officer. It all fitted together. I put a request through channels for four thousand Jewish workers. I was granted three-fourths of that number. What I could not foresee was the strictness of their supervision by SS personnel.

My hands were tied. You understand? I am being completely frank with you."

"But you haven't told me why."

"My dear Herr Becker, let us admit between us that you are threatening the use of certain pressure tactics in order to win your case against Zeller-Bricken. This means, to be precise, that you will acquaint the world with certain facts about my long-past associations. The world, I assure you, will pay little attention. *Der Spiegel* will print a paragraph, the *Frankfurter Rund-scheit* will publish a small editorial, the majority of the German press will protest the attack against the integrity of our industry. More of the same, they will say. It is enough already; it is too much. Germans are tired of the smell of dead cats being dug up. They turn their noses away. Nevertheless, because of the contracts with the American Department of Defense, Zeller-Bricken may well be forced to accept my resignation. I will give it to them. That is all. Then what happens to your case?"

"Are you suggesting I make some kind of deal?"

Darkness had settled over West Berlin. The chauffeur took the soundless vehicle through the quiet streets and avenues of Grunewald. Here was a part of Berlin that had survived the bombings almost intact. The villas and mansions were guarded by iron gates, enclosed by hedges. In these houses one could imagine settling into a comfortable, untroubled existence. The air from the surrounding woods was fresh. The lights shining through draperied windows bespoke a leisured warmth.

Herr Weisse spoke again, after a pause. "A friendly arrangement, perhaps. Naturally it is to my personal interest to avoid embarrassment. I have fruitful years ahead of me. I have no wish to retire. And, Herr Becker, I sense that you are not altogether anxious to make your items of fact public."

"What kind of arrangement?"

"I will be your friend at Zeller-Bricken. I will do all I can to push the figure mentioned to you to a higher level."

"Can you push it to a half-million dollars?"

"Two million marks! I must be honest with you—that sum is impossible."

"Then this discussion is pointless. Would you ask your chauffeur to drive me back to the Kurfürstendamm?"

With two thick fingers of his right hand, Weisse drummed on the lacquered surface of the drawn-out table top. Then, as though noticing he was giving away his feelings of perturbation, he abruptly stopped drumming.

"Let us face facts, Herr Becker. I am in a position to help you, personally, and also your clients."

I pretended to overlook his implication of a bribe. "I'm just here doing a job," I said. "I have other work to do, also, and I'd like to get back to it as soon as possible."

"You put me in a bad position," he said.

"My case is not directed against you," I said. "I'm here as a representative. If it wasn't me, it would be someone else taking exactly the same position."

"You see," he said, pursuing his own reasoning, "I, personally, would like to take your clients' side. But I also belong to Zeller-Bricken. I am the man in the middle." He drummed again on the table top for a few seconds. "All right, I will do everything I can. I cannot promise, though, the results you hope for."

"Nor can I."

He nodded resignedly, and tapped on the window separating us from the chauffeur. "To the Kurfürstendamm," he ordered when the man opened the glass slightly. He turned to me. "You wish to go to your hotel?"

I nodded.

Weisse again tapped on the window and ordered the chauffeur to take me to the Kempinski. From his wallet he drew a card and handed it to me. "In the event you wish to contact me," he said. "I would deem it a pleasure, by the way, if we could meet again for a chat, for social purposes only. We should know each other better."

"If there happens to be time," I said vaguely.

"Yes, you should meet my wife and my daughter. They both enjoy meeting Americans. You are Jewish, by the way?"

"Yes."

"So pleasant to have Jewish people in Berlin again. One misses their spirit."

I smiled a little.

"Sincerely," Weisse said, as the car halted in front of the entrance to the Kurfürstendamm on Meinekestrasse, "if I can help you in any way, kindly feel free to call on me. My daughter, by the way, is a fashion designer. She could assist you with any shopping you might wish to do."

"Thank you," I said.

His hand was already held out as I opened the door, and I shook it before stepping from the car. No reason, I felt, not to be civilized.

I checked at the lobby desk for messages. There were two. Gerson had called again, and so had Liz. In my room I decided to let business go until the next day, so I telephoned Hilde as I had promised to do.

"Yes, my darling," she said, recognizing my voice immediately. "You are to come here to dinner. We have cooked for you."

"We?"

"The two of us—Annemarie and I. We have stuffed a goose and obtained a lovely wine."

"You shouldn't have taken the trouble," I said. "I'll be glad to take you both out."

"No, no," she said. "Can you come in an hour? Annemarie is anxious to meet you. I am dying to see you again. You can relax here better. I am sure you had a busy day."

"Yes," I said, "quite busy. And I still have a little work to do."

"What time can you come, then?"

"Seven-thirty, maybe eight."

"Good, we will have dinner at eight. I will expect you."

Before I left I wanted to write Elihu a letter about my meeting with Weisse while it was still fresh in my mind. I wrote him on hotel stationery, first summarizing the conversation and then adding:

"Obviously, we can make the assumption that Weisse is definitely worried about this case of ours. But I'm not yet certain whether this is a personal matter with him or whether it extends to the entire directorate. Note his apologia. He asks us to believe not only that he was free of all criminal taint, but that he was actually attempting to be a benefactor of Jewish humanity. Do you believe it? Of course not, and I share with you a total suspicion of his truthfulness. At the same time, our court system (we're not in court, I realize) demands that we provide the defendant with the benefit of the doubt. Frankly, we have not yet *proven* Weisse's guilt. The records we have seen tell us only so much. They leave open the question of motive—and Weisse, I am sure, has very cleverly taken advantage of this loophole. It is almost as though he is aware, and has been, of the structure of our plan. I wouldn't put it past him to have done some research. He has also opened up the possibility of a friendly relationship between the two of us. Why? What has he to gain by this? All this, you may be sure, Elihu, I will attempt to explore.

"I feel hampered, still, by the lack of direct evidence. He did, after all, manage to get shipped to his plants three thousand victims who would surely have perished in concentration camps otherwise. Some came right from the maw of Auschwitz. And some survived. Our sixty clients are, ironically, part of the proof of his contention.

"For the moment, then, I would counsel going slow on making public any revelations about Weisse or Roehling. The latter personage evidently feels secure, for he has made no effort to contact me or put in any kind of defense. Doesn't all this give you the definite feeling that they are staying right with us, matching us step for step? I do not mean to give the impression that there is something conspiratorial going on. Let us instead ascribe this to that admirable German efficiency we have all heard about.

"As soon as anything else develops, you will hear from me."

7: Hilde lived in Wilmersdorf on a street not far from the Hohenzollern Platz. I could have walked, but it was late by the time I mailed my letter to Elihu, and I was sped to the address by a taxi. The buildings on the block were almost all that kind of blank, gray-façaded structure so predominant in Berlin, dating from the early and mid-fifties when the city was frenetically rebuilding. No elevator being provided, I walked up the four flights of stairs and rang Hilde's bell.

"I have put little Hans to bed," she told me, after a greeting that included a mutual kissing of cheeks, "but you must say hello to him—otherwise he will not sleep."

The apartment was furnished in a mixture of solid old pieces and the modern styles seen in Berlin shopwindows. The lamps were large and flamboyant, the coffee table was made of thick green glass on a gilded base, and the sofa I sat down on was covered with a nubbly pepper-and-salt fabric. I got up immediately when Annemarie came into the living room from the kitchen. She was taller and slimmer than Hilde but had similar light hair and blue eyes. It seemed to me that there was more curiosity than friendliness in her greeting. "Herr Becker," she said, "I have heard all about you, for a long time now." She was in her early twenties and had an experienced look about the eyes. I could think of a lot of New York businessmen who would have been happy to employ her as a secretary on the basis of looks alone.

Hilde ushered me into a small bedroom, where a solid little boy of six or seven lay in bed, his covers tossed aside. He, too, was blond. When I gave him my hand to shake he grabbed it and wanted to engage in a wrestling match. Hilde quieted him with a stern warning that all lights would be turned off if he did not immediately desist and go to sleep. Meeting Hilde's child gave me a slightly queasy feeling, almost as if he were partly my own, and I was relieved to leave the bedroom for the living room again. Hilde handed me a whisky and soda without asking and sat with me on the sofa. "Dinner is almost ready," she said. "Annemarie has done most of the cooking. How did your business go?"

"Well enough, I suppose."

"Your restitution cases?"

"Yes."

"It sounds so important," she sighed. "Always what you were doing seemed so important to me. I see Americans in Berlin now, and I still think they are hurrying around and changing our lives."

"One of these days soon," I said, "and it will all be forgotten."

"And you won't return to Germany?"

"Probably not. I haven't been coming on pleasure trips."

"And what do you feel about Germans and Germany now? The same?"

"You mean as before?"

She nodded.

"The most honest answer would be to say I'm confused."

"How so?"

"I admire a lot, I approve—but grudgingly—and I still see traits that bother me."

"Do you want to change us entirely?"

"No."

"And would you marry a German woman now?"

"If I were unmarried?"

"Of course I mean that. I know that you are very well married." She smiled.

"Let's just say that if I were ever to marry a German woman it would cause problems in my life. You see, because of the work I do, I naturally associate with many who have definite feelings about Germans."

"They would regard you as a traitor?"

"I don't honestly know," I said. "It might be difficult for the woman," I said. "By that I mean she might run into some prejudice or fixed attitudes."

"And all that is not over yet," Hilde said, as though she had just been made aware of the fact. "Annemarie!" she called.

"*Ja!*"

"Tell us when the goose is ready for the table."

"Only a moment," Annemarie called back from the kitchen.

A few minutes later we were seated at a round table in the dining part of the kitchen. I opened the bottle of chilled Rhine wine, tasted it, pronounced it excellent, but refused, on the grounds of lack of experience, to carve.

"She is a wonderful cook, don't you think?" Hilde asked, after we had tasted and judged the goose.

I agreed, and Annemarie took our compliments with composure. I knew I was being studied by her. She had little to say at first, while Hilde filled the conversational gaps with chatter about how lucky they were to have this flat, small as it was, and about Annemarie's secretarial excellences. Unfortunately, she added, Annemarie spent too many hours at discothèques. If she wanted to live and work in New York she ought to be spending more time perfecting her English.

"Do you think my English is so bad?" Annemarie asked me, speaking in English.

"No, it's very good," I said.

"It is her spelling," Hilde said in German.

"Spell *parliamentarian*," I said to Annemarie.

Annemarie spelled the word haltingly and left out one letter, an "a." I corrected her and suggested she try *constitutional*. She got that one correct.

"She'll do all right," I said.

"Will I be able to find a job, do you think?"

"I'm sure of it. But what will you do without her?" I asked Hilde.

"I have little Hans."

Annemarie gave a short laugh. "And also a friend who wishes to marry her."

"You didn't tell me about that," I said.

"Naturally, I keep a few secrets," Hilde said.

From the sharp glance she directed at Annemarie, I gathered that she had decided now was definitely not the time to divulge them.

Annemarie only smiled. "She still dreams of you," she said. "She always hoped that one day you would come back to her."

"Annemarie!" Hilde was upset.

"Neither of us," I said, "ever quite got over it."

Annemarie gave me an amused stare; it was as though she was our superior in knowledge and experience.

"So why did you never do anything about it?" she asked.

"You have come here many times. You could have found my sister. And I was the one who made her write to you. Otherwise, she would never have written."

"This is not something we should talk about," Hilde said, her tone anguished.

"I'm inclined to agree," I said.

"How silly," Annemarie said. "We should always speak of things that concern us. I have no patience with people who hide their thoughts and feelings. If I fell in love with you this moment I would tell you. What you two should do, while there is still time, is make love with each other," Annemarie went on.

I glanced at Hilde, but now her head was turned away from me.

"Why?" I asked.

"Have you thought of how little time each of you has left?"

"Look," I protested, "neither of us is *that* old."

"Old enough," Annemarie said. "You should do something about it before it is too late. If I felt about you as Hilde does, I would arrange for us to make love."

"He has a wife," Hilde said.

"Who doesn't have a wife?" Annemarie said. "Three-quarters of the men who ask to make love with me have wives. Do you love your wife, Mr. Becker?"

"Of course."

"Do you only make love with her?"

"Now we're getting into the area of my secrets," I said.

"Pay no attention to Annemarie," Hilde said to me. "She has too much mischief in her."

"But," Annemarie said, "it is very important that you know who I am, and how I think, before you do me a favor. Otherwise, a friend of yours might blame you for recommending me as a secretary."

"She is of a different generation from us," Hilde said, by way of explanation for her sister's conversation.

"What is so surprising about what I say?" Annemarie asked.

"The frankness surprises me," I said.

"And do Americans always lie to each other?"

"Come now," Hilde said. "No more of that talk. Alfred, how is your work in Berlin?"

I told them something of it, and was particularly vague about my researches concerning Weisse. Annemarie's expression was so neutral as I talked that I had no way of guessing how she viewed my work. We went back to the living room for coffee and dessert of berries and cream. Hilde sat beside me, while Annemarie curled up her trim, leggy body in a large chair across from us. We talked about Chris and Gretel, about the days at Höchst, and the nights too, for there was no purpose in being anything but frank in front of Annemarie.

"It strikes me," Annemarie said after awhile, "that you both miss those days. Aren't you ashamed of yourselves now?"

"Please don't answer her," Hilde begged me.

"I just want to say," I said in answer to Annemarie, "that I'm not ashamed of myself."

"I know your reasons for that," Annemarie said. "Hilde has told me all about your refugee wife. That, of course, is highly admirable."

"And I don't agree with that, either," I said.

"It seems to me," Annemarie said, "that you are a simple man who is afraid to be simple. Don't take it as an insult. I like people who are simple. But it would be so much easier for us to talk if you were not always judging what you say before you say it. Perhaps it's that you are a lawyer."

She stretched her legs, got up, and went to a shelf on which lay her pocketbook. She opened the pocketbook, took out a set of keys, and placed them on the glass top of the coffee table directly in front of Hilde and me.

"Those keys," Annemarie said, "are to the apartment of a friend of mine, a young woman who is willing to leave her apartment and spend the night here."

"Annemarie!" Hilde screamed at her sister, her face flushed a deep pink.

"You can use them or not," Annemarie said to us, pretending to stifle a yawn.

There were two keys on a ring. They seemed huge. One, obviously, was for a lobby door, the other for the door to a flat. I took Hilde's hand and patted the back of it.

"I know how embarrassed you must feel," I told her.

But she wasn't completely embarrassed, I noticed. In fact, she had an expectant, eager-to-please smile.

Annemarie ran her hand along her hair and kept studying me, as though my reactions were now of interest to her.

"I'll have another drink," I said carefully, "and then I'd better be going."

8:   Max Gerson did not wait for me to telephone him. Promptly at nine the telephone rang in my hotel room, and I recognized his gruff voice. "I was about to call you," I told him in mild apology.

"I also have many things to do," he said. "But your matter first. Negative results in the East."

"So soon?"

"The official lists were consulted, I assure you, and no record exists there of the candelabrum. This does not rule out its presence there somewhere, but I would regard it as unlikely, since all such treasures in the possession of the Reichsbank—which, as you know, fell into Russian hands—would by now have been catalogued. Meanwhile, I have located some members of the Lietschnitzer family and have addressed them letters of inquiry. I should hear very soon."

"I can't very well wait around Berlin until you do," I said.

"But you go elsewhere in Germany?"

"Very likely."

"Then I can contact you wherever you are."

"I suppose you can," I said grudgingly, bothered that I would have to keep Gerson apprised of my movements on the slim chance that he might unearth some slight clue to the whereabouts of the candelabrum. Still and all, I had promised the Professor that I would do everything I could to fulfill his mission. "I'll let you know when I leave," I told Gerson, "and tell you where you can reach me."

The porter, at my request, sent up a selection of morning papers and, with them, my mail. One of the letters was from Gloria, who had a list of queries for me. She left the most important item for last: "Your wife called and asked me to make out for her a check for fifteen hundred dollars. She said she needed the money for a trip she was taking, but she didn't say where she would be going. I suppose it's all right, isn't it? Giving out the money, I mean? Please excuse my asking, but I didn't expect to have to arrange for that much. Had to have Mr. Pryor give her a cashier's check."

Gloria had been left with explicit instructions to provide my wife with whatever cash she might need, but I could understand her puzzlement, since Lottie had never requested anything like that amount before. Fifteen hundred dollars? That could take someone a lot of places and for a considerable length of time. Whenever Lottie left me in the dark about her plans I grew apprehensive, and the feeling came now. She ought to have written. Each day since I'd been here I had written her a letter—kept open the channels of communication, so to speak. That was the least we could do for each other. On an impulse, I wrote out a cable and left it at the lobby desk for transmission: NO WORD FROM YOU PLEASE WRITE LOVE.

I called Liz, using the telephone in the lobby. She, at least, had solid information for me. "I tried to reach you yesterday," she said. "I think we have located that mysterious Christianne of yours. In fact, we have located two Christiannes."

"Both were at the camp?"

"Yes, Arolsen happens to have the Reichenau lists. Christianne Eggeling now Ludwig, age fifty-six. I can give you her Munich address. The other is Christianne Macklenburg, no present address, her age would be approximately thirty-six, originally from Salzburg but presently living in Vienna. No address available, but you should be able to trace that fairly easily. I'd suggest you telephone Frau Ludwig, or write her. If she's the one, you can forget the other. Do you want me to type all this out and mail it to you?"

"Please," I said. "But what about Sturmbannführer Dittersdorf?"

"No help to you, I'm afraid. I called Ludwigsburg on that. The U.S. Seventh Army found the camp and took Dittersdorf into custody. He made an attempt to escape and was shot. End of Dittersdorf. Naturally, Ludwigsburg wanted to know why I was after the information, so I thought it best to tell them. They know of you, it turns out, and a Herr Langsehn there would like to talk to you."

"Why?"

"He didn't say. He'll be in touch with you at the Kempinski. You certainly have enough to keep you busy here."

"Thanks to you," I said. "We'll have that dinner together soon."

"You always say that."

"Really," I told her.

"Okay, I'll be waiting, palpitating."

I took down the address of Christianne Ludwig and got the telephone operator at the hotel to see what she could do about finding a number to call. In a matter of no more than fifteen minutes I had Christianne Ludwig on the line. Her voice was tired, and suspicious, too. I explained to her that I was an American lawyer handling a compensation case and asked her if she could remember a little girl, about twelve years of age, whose name was Sarah, and who had been an inmate of the Reichenau camp in 1944 and 1945. "She was a Jewish girl," I added.

"How did you know I was in the camp?"

I explained that she had been traced through Arolsen.

"I have forgotten it all now."

"Everything, everyone?"

"Yes, it was a mistake. I never should have been there. I am a good German. I always was."

"If I came to see you," I said, "maybe we could talk about it."

Her voice grew shrill. "Why should I have been taken away?" she asked. "I worked in a factory. I was sick one day and did not report it, and the next day I was taken."

"But there were others with you. This little girl—she is a woman now—she remembers a Christianne who was kind to her. Were you that woman?"

"Kind?" she said. "No one was kind in that camp. We had numbers, not names."

"This girl remembered a Christianne," I said stubbornly.

"The singer, probably. There was a Christianne with a fine voice. The commandant had her sing for him. That one I remember. She took the easy way, if you know what I mean."

"No, I don't."

"It is not for me to talk about it. I do not remember your little Jewish girl."

"Thank you," I said. "I'm sorry to trouble you."

"No trouble."

I hung up, and asked the hotel operator to check the Vienna telephone book for a Christianne Macklenburg. She reported back that there was none. "Try information," I suggested. Information had no number for that name either. It looked as though I'd have to make a trip to Vienna. I knew I'd have to go somewhere, and I was just as glad it was there. A girl who sang for Sturmbannführer Hans Dittersdorf and took the easy way—I could guess what it meant. And, if my hunch was reliable, she would remember Sarah.

Two communications that seemed to be at odds with each other came in the mail the next day. One was a formal note from Isserstadt of the Zeller-Bricken board, who regretted to inform me that the directorate, which had convened in a special meeting, had voted against my proposal but had agreed to a doubling of the original offer. The matter was now being turned over to the firm of Asmodis and Steglitz, legal counsel for Zeller-Bricken, which would be pleased to handle any further clarifications of the situation that might be necessary. Herr Steglitz had been apprised of my presence in Berlin, and it was suggested that I contact him. This development was hardly surprising to me. I had expected a stall, and lawyers were experts at stalling. The other communication was an invitation to the annual Berlin-Futura Ball being held the following evening at the Charlottenburg Palace. Someone had written across the bottom of the embossed card, "Sent at the suggestion of Oskar Weisse." A way of Weisse's telling me, I guessed, that avenues of mutual interest remained to be explored.

I called Liz again. "Your dinner date is going to be sooner than you thought. Are you free tomorrow evening? We'll have dinner and then go to a big party." I told her about the ball and Weisse's instigation of the invitation.

"Sounds like fun," she said, and we arranged that I would pick her up for dinner.

"These affairs are always formal, you know," she warned me.

"And I always bring my dinner jacket," I assured her.

At first I had thought of asking Hilde, but I knew I would feel more comfortable with Liz, mainly because she was an American.

Another interesting development of that day was a telephone call from Ludwigsburg. Herr Langsehn wished to speak with me, I was informed by the hotel operator. Herr Langsehn's voice was briskly pleasant. "We are informed," he said, "that you are here working on some negotiations with the firm of Zeller-Bricken. Is that correct?"

"Correct," I said.

"We are interested in this case."

"Why?"

"It is not a matter to speak about on the telephone, Herr Becker, but, if it would be agreeable to you, a member of our staff will contact you at your hotel. When could you see him?"

"Tomorrow morning," I suggested.

"Good. His name is Zimmer. You will hear from him. I hope myself to meet you one day soon, but unfortunately I am tied up here at Ludwigsburg."

"As a matter of fact," I said, "I had thought of paying you people a visit."

"I had rather thought you might. Speak to Herr Zimmer about it."

It took me several minutes of reflection to get that telephone call into its proper context. Ludwigsburg was the town where all matters pertaining to the location and prosecution of Nazi criminals were centralized. In fact, the office there was called the *Zentralstelle,* meaning "Central Office." This office maintained a liaison contact with the Yad Vashem in Jerusalem, and it was certainly likely that the Yad Vashem had made inquiries of the Zentralstelle about any criminal dossiers in their possession on Weisse and Roehling. This in itself would have been enough to awaken Ludwigsburg's interest in the two. In addition, Ludwigsburg was well aware of my own associations, and Liz would have apprised them of my presence in Berlin. But they were making the assumption, I realized, that I was here not as much on a compensation case as on the exposure of two former Nazis. They probably wanted to know what I had on Weisse and Roehling; on the other hand I wanted to know what *they* had, if anything.

Zimmer telephoned the next morning.

"I'll meet you at the Terrace Café of this hotel in half an hour," I told him. "I'll leave word where I'm sitting."

On the way there I stopped at the desk; to my relief I found a letter from Lottie.

It had been raining earlier that morning, but now sun brightened the café tables and chairs, a pattern of pinks and oranges. A pretty young waitress in a pink uniform brought me a bottled orange juice. I ordered a plain omelette and then opened Lottie's letter.

"I have such a good chance for a trip to Israel, and I am taking it. It is a Hadassah tour, at a special rate, sixteen days altogether. I leave on Thursday." (Today was Friday, which meant she had already arrived there.) "Maybe you could meet me in Israel. I enclose my itinerary, with the hotels we are booked into. The ladies will be a bore, I know, but I feel sure I can manage to get away from them from time to time. This is a good season for visiting Israel—not too hot—and with you busy in Europe I have not much else to do with myself. I will write to you again from Israel. So far I have received two letters from you but they do not tell me much. I send my love to you."

What had gotten into her? She was not usually so impulsive—a reaction maybe to what she assumed was my neglect of her?

My omelette arrived simultaneously with Herr Zimmer, whose black hair was combed smoothly back and whose liquid brown eyes made him seem more Latin than Germanic. He looked about forty, and his suit needed pressing.

"You'll join me for breakfast?"

"Just coffee," he said, looking my waitress over appreciatively. She was something to look at—slim-waisted, full in the bosom, a fine-featured face.

"Not bad," I said after the girl had left us.

"This café has the best in Berlin," he said. "I have studied the situation."

"Back home," I said, "a girl like that would be smoking cigarettes on television."

"I do not understand."

I explained to him about how pretty girls in the United States sold cigarettes, beer, and automobiles on television.

He gave a quizzical nod of his head, as though the information confirmed an impression he had of America. He pulled a thick wallet of reptile skin from his jacket pocket, extracted a card and handed it to me. The card, imbedded in clear plastic, identified him as Sergeant Gerhard Zimmer, of the Stuttgart central police, detached for temporary duty with the Zentralstelle of Ludwigsburg. I handed the card back with a smile.

"You can come to the point," I said. "I assume we understand each other."

"Entirely?" he asked. "By the way, I speak English, if you prefer."

No necessity for that, I told him. I also said that I assumed we were both interested in certain gentlemen connected with a certain firm, and therefore it would not require mentioning their names in this, after all, rather public place.

"Agreed," he said. "But please understand that I have not the authority to handle this matter with any finality. I am, in a sense, the emissary of a gentleman who recently contacted you on the telephone."

"I understand."

"Good. The request we make then is that you do not make public such information as you possess about the subject we mentioned a moment ago."

"You'd have to tell me the reason before I could agree."

"The subject is under investigation by my office, and we could possibly be of assistance to you," he said.

"How?"

"That would be a matter you would have to take up with my superior."

"At the main office, you mean?"

"It would be best," he said.

"Are you suggesting I go there?"

He nodded. "We would be pleased to provide you with transportation."

"Is your honest opinion that it would be worth my while to make the trip?"

"I think so, yes."

"In other words, I give you something, and you give me something."

"It could work out like that."

He looked uncomfortable, as though he was transgressing

the boundaries of his authority. He was an investigator, not a decision maker.

"So," I said, "all you're here for is to ask that I make the trip?"

"And to assist you with arrangements."

"All right," I said. "I'll do it, but I'm not sure of when exactly I'll be able to leave. How will I find you meanwhile?"

"Miss Schofield can always find me."

"What does she have to do with this?"

"We are acquainted," he said.

Yes, I thought, he was probably spending a lot of his time using her files. He stood up and offered me his hand.

"Good day," he said, and threaded his way through the tables to the door. The last I saw of him was when he crossed the Kurfürstendamm to the other side. I'd have to wait until at least one o'clock before telephoning Elihu in New York, because it would be too much of an imposition to awaken him before seven in the morning, his time. First, I telephoned Herr Steglitz to arrange an appointment with him later in the afternoon. He would see me at three, he said.

While waiting to speak with Elihu I filled some of the time by writing Lottie a letter, telling her I was pleased about her trip but that it looked as though I would be too occupied with my business here to meet her while she was in Israel. I'd be sure to let her know, though, if the opportunity came up. So far, I wrote her, I was meeting only complications and no solutions, but maybe things would clear up soon. I addressed the letter to her at the Dan Carmel Hotel in Haifa, after checking her itinerary. She would arrive at the Dan Carmel in three days' time. I remembered we had stayed there once. From the hotel gardens, bright with sunlight, we had gazed out over the roofs of houses on the slopes of the city to the shimmering blue of the harbor crescent, and Lottie had said how happy she would be to stay there. "You mean, live here?" I had asked. And she had said, in her abrupt way, "Why not? What do we have that is so necessary to us in New York?" I had not answered her, really. All I had said was: "It *is* beautiful." And, though I felt some kinship with Israel, I knew I could never have the feeling for the country that Lottie had. "You are a tourist," Lottie had said, turning away from the splendid view. For her now this trip would almost be like going home.

Elihu's voice reached me in a rising and falling pattern of sound. He could hear me clearly. For a moment, he said, he thought I was calling from New York.

"Are you awake?" I asked.

"Yes," he said, "but my wife is cursing you from under the blankets."

"Kiss her for me. Do you hear me well?"

"I hear you."

"You have to do something for me. One of the fish may be bigger than we thought. You know who I'm talking about?"

"The same one?"

"Yes. Get someone to the Columbia University Law Library. They have the Nuremberg documents, the mimeographed stuff."

"What's wrong with the Forty-second Street Library?" Elihu asked.

"They don't have complete files. Who will you send?"

"He has to be a lawyer?"

"Yes."

"My son studies law—will he do?"

"If he is brighter than his father, certainly. Have you got a pencil and paper?"

"Wait a minute." Elihu's voice came back. "Right."

"Take down these code designations. They all apply to the

mimeographed documents of the trials, and your son—what's his name, Leo?—Leo will understand them. They are: NG, NI, NDKW. Got those? If references to the Z-B combine turn up—anything at all, but especially names of personnel—I want photocopies made and sent to me here."

"What's it all for?"

"Our fish may be criminally involved. If so, this will change our policy. Nothing, in that case, should reach the papers. I repeat: *nothing*."

"I hope you know what you're doing."

"The idea is to apply maximum force on Z-B at the critical moment. My suspicion right now is that they have been let off the hook for some reason. If they are faced with an action by their own people, I would think they would want to make some public gesture."

"How will you find out?"

"I have made a contact. But I need every bit of information we can get. Something else—ask Leo to go to the YIVO Institute on Fifth Avenue. They're in the Seventies. Tell Leo to see Arthur Goldstein there. He has a file on RHSA Administration personnel. See if any interesting names turn up. Understand?"

"I read you," Elihu said.

"Mail anything Leo finds to me at the Kempinski here. If I should leave temporarily, I'll see that they hold mail for me. That's all for now. This call is costing me a fortune."

"But you haven't said how we are doing."

"I don't know yet. Meanwhile they've put up twenty new buildings since I got here, and the sun is shining for a change."

"Well, you sound cheerful," Elihu said.

"So long for now." I hung up, knowing that Elihu would not waste any time. I mentally kicked myself for not having been more thorough in researching Weisse and Roehling beforehand. I had depended too much on Liz's sources, figuring she would have it all. I sat in a chair in my hotel room aware that something tangible, yet elusive, was escaping me. Why wouldn't she have it all? What was it that Ludwigsburg had? A document, maybe? Something from the locked files at Alexandria? There was something funny going on, but I couldn't put it all together. And somehow I lacked the necessary patience. I wrote Gloria a note, however, telling her it looked as though I would have to remain over here longer than I'd thought.

Karl Steglitz was tall, wore horn-rimmed glasses, and could not have been more than thirty-five. His office was near the Englischer Garten in a small professional building with a gleaming new façade. From the looks of their suite, the latest in reddish mahogany furniture and stuffed black-leather chairs and sofas, the firm of Amodis and Steglitz was dignified and wealthy. Steglitz' private office was lined with legal works.

After a brisk handshake, he got immediately to business. "I have been empowered," he said, "to arrange for a payment of two hundred thousand marks to your clients or to such a fund as directed by you. This offer, I might add, strikes me as being generous." He spoke in English.

"Why so?" I asked.

"You don't think so?"

"No, as a matter of fact, it strikes me as being extremely ungenerous."

"But you have no case," he said, his eyes seeming to bulge from behind his glasses.

"And how have you managed to determine that?" I asked.

"I can answer that very simply. You see, I have taken the

trouble to acquaint myself thoroughly with the federal legislation in the field of compensation to victims of Nazi persecution, plus all subsequent revisions and addenda."

"Have you memorized all that?" I asked. "Or are you reading to me?"

He removed his glasses and cleaned them with a starched white handkerchief, avoiding a glance at his desk. "I find that only Article Five, Section D, relates in any form or manner to your claim against Zeller-Bricken, and even in that case, its applicability lapsed in 1962. You are three years late, my dear Herr Becker."

"I suppose you know about the Ordinance of July 6, 1956, also," I said.

"Certainly," he said, "particularly as it pertains to inheritability, but since the claims have been made not on behalf of survivors of victims, but rather on behalf of the so-called victims themselves, neither, then, does this ordinance apply in your case."

"You went to a lot of trouble to find out what is beside the point," I told him.

"You don't make yourself clear," Steglitz said.

"If you will read our brief carefully you will see that it does make clear the nonapplicability of existing legal standards. I will restipulate that for you now. There are extra- or supra-legal standards to be applied here; they have to do with sovereign states or governments. Zeller-Bricken is dealing through quasi-German government auspices with an arm of the United States government. As a public trust, it is required that all dealings with German firms be deemed morally appropriate."

Steglitz leaned back in his chair. "I was not aware of any such requirement."

"You can easily be made aware," I told him.

"So now you wish to deal in threats," he said.

"A very strange procedure for a lawyer, of course," I said. "No, it's not a threat. But in certain cases, publicity can be used as an enforcing weapon. Zeller-Bricken at this time might be highly vulnerable to certain types of publicity. Now what I'm saying here is that only in the last resort would we submit our case to the court of public opinion. We might win or lose. But we would have completed our moral obligation."

I had unsettled Steglitz. He cleared his nostrils with two brief snorts and played around with some papers on his desk. "We have made an offer," he said. "No one denies you the right of making a counteroffer."

"Counteroffer, hell!" I said. "Our claim stands: the full amount. We're not bargaining with you. What kind of offer do you think you've made anyway? One-tenth of the amount asked! I believe you called it highly generous."

"What kind of time limit do you place on the negotiations?" he asked.

"I can't decide that on my own. Mr. Elihu Grossman of New York City is the official representative of the victims' group and would be in a position to advise me. Until now he has requested that the negotiations be continued without publicity."

"Mr. Grossman, of B'nai Jeshurat," Steglitz said, glancing at a sheaf of papers on his desk. "But his name is not on the list of victims."

"He is a fair, honest, and concerned gentleman who has been empowered by the victims to make decisions on their behalf."

"And does he stand to profit by any arrangements made with Zeller-Bricken?"

"In no way whatever."

"Then why does he concern himself about this?" There was a thin smile on his lips. What else but business would concern an American Jew named Elihu Grossman? He had no gift for charm, this Steglitz, and he was plainly of the type that caused American visitors to claim that the Germans were arrogant, smug, and self-satisfied.

"Let me ask you a question," I said. "How would you feel if most of your kinsmen were liquidated by gas or bullets—innocent people every one of them, by the way—and the remainder worked to death?"

Steglitz grimaced and said, "This is rhetoric. I only wondered if your Mr. Grossman had a commercial interest in this case."

"Mr. Grossman," I said, "had the extraordinary good fortune to leave your country before he, too, could be liquidated. He did, indeed, lose whatever wealth he had managed to accumulate, and this he was very happy to relinquish. His sense of obligation is toward those who went through what he would have gone through had he stayed here."

Steglitz sighed. "I can only repeat the offer. I will be in further contact, of course, with Herr Isserstadt, of the Zeller-Bricken board. If there is news, I will contact you. Is that agreeable?"

"I will probably contact you first," I told him.

We shook hands, and he ushered me through the door, walked solicitously with me to the door of the anteroom, and gave me a comradely wave as I left. Maybe he thought he had stalled me. On the other hand, maybe he knew that I was stalling him, too.

I was about to leave my room for an early dinner with Liz before taking her to the Charlottenburg Palace, when the telephone rang. "You have been neglecting me," Hilde said, with a note of reproach in her voice. "Has Annemarie frightened you away from me?"

"No, nothing like that. I've been busy."

"And tonight? What do you do tonight?"

"I'm tied up, Hilde. I'm attending a function with an American friend of mine. A professional thing."

"No explanations needed," she said quickly. "I only thought you would have a little time left over for me."

"Can you meet me for a drink tomorrow?"

"Are you sure you want to see me?"

"I'm anxious to," I said, with more politeness than sincerity. "Suppose we meet at Kranzler's around six tomorrow evening."

"Yes, good, I will be there. What is this function tonight?"

"The Berlin-Futura at the Charlottenburg."

"Oh," she said, "that is for very important people."

"It was actually a business acquaintance who invited me," I hedged. "I was hoping to ask you, but since it is quite possible I will meet people who know me—do you understand?"

"Yes," she said. "I understand, of course. We will meet tomorrow, then."

But there was disappointment and regret in her voice. All this, I thought, was like trying to make a dead fire flare up into flame. There were all too few sparks left in the embers. I was made suddenly aware of my forty-four years.

Liz somehow sensed that I was not in the best of moods. We sat in Kottler's, a small restaurant on Motzstrasse that specialized in Swabian dishes and featured an accordionist and zither player and a decor of dark-stained oak.

"Something the matter?" she asked.

"No," I said, "but I'm annoyed at having spent a week here with nothing much to show for it."

"You're closing in on Christianne," Liz said.

"You did that, not me. I'm more bothered about the other thing. I don't like my jobs to be complicated. I'm not even sure now exactly what's going on. You didn't tell me that a friend of yours called Zimmer has been looking in your files."

"The man from Ludwigsburg? They're always digging into the files. There's a thing going on about Himmler's administrative headquarters." A sudden look of comprehension came on her face. "You mean Weisse?"

"Could be. Weisse hasn't really denied it. Of course, he was one of the *good* Germans, jamming the machinery from within."

"But if he admits it, that proves your case, doesn't it."

"It changes it," I said. "I think it does, anyway. I don't want to blackmail them into giving us what we want. If we show the connection between the past and present administrations, that ought to be enough. But if Weisse and/or Roehling is being looked into by Ludwigsburg, that's a lot more serious. We haven't claimed anyone was a war criminal, not the real hardcore kind. And if Weisse were exposed publicly, by Germans, that could even give Z-B an out. They could cry foul and say they were hoodwinked by him all along."

"But what could they find about Weisse that we haven't found?"

"Well, he did ship those Jews to Hanover. He admits it himself, except he says it was in the interest of keeping them alive. There are a few cases of high-level Germans who did make some sort of effort of that kind, but they're rare. The odds are so much against Weisse's telling the truth that they aren't really odds. And the Ludwigsburg investigation substantiates the supposition. Okay, Weisse shipped them there. Z-B asks for Jews, and Weisse gets them, using his SS connection. But what else did he do? The Germans don't drag anyone into court unless they've got a case, and this kind of case requires documents. Well, Ludwigsburg has to have something to go on before they look for more. What?"

"I just run the files," Liz said.

I had ordered us a bottle of richly red Spatburgunder, and when the waiter filled our glasses Liz and I clinked them to nothing in particular.

"Funny," Liz said, reminiscently, "how we both joined the Army and saw Germany. I don't exactly feel at home here, but I don't feel at home in America, either. Not anymore. How do you feel about being involved with Germans?"

"Insane," I said. "They're a maddening people. They can be so damned correct, the soul of honesty, they love dogs and flowers, they cry at the movies, and if someone tells them to smash a baby's head against the wall they smash it. Not any longer, maybe, but only eighteen years ago they were still doing that. These days they're sentimental about Jews, but can you trust it? Meanwhile, to make it all crazier, there's something important to the world going on here."

"You mean they're getting rich and fat again?"

"No, I mean they're trying on something vaguely termed democracy for size. I can't honestly remember another nation in history that has done as much to make up for the past. Maybe it's just good business. But, by God, when I make out a claim correctly and fill in all the blank spaces and get them stamped in a dozen places, they pay up. It'll cost them billions before it's through. But what do they *feel?* Remorse? Guilt? Ten years ago I would have said they didn't feel a damn thing. Today, I'm not so sure. Here and there it's getting through to them. Oh, sure, there are still some nuts around who are openly anti-

Semitic. But we have the same type at home, too. They're by definition disgusting, to themselves, too. But just suppose that they can behave like people again, that what the Germans are trying to do works, that they can behave like people again, and all in a relatively few years' time. It gives me some hope. Not much, but a little."

"You're suggesting we ought to forget the past?"

"Absolutely not. Let's remember it as long as possible. I know some people, Jews and non-Jews, who won't buy a Volkswagen or a Mercedes or a German tape recorder. They won't be caught dead helping the German economy. I have one friend who won't even *listen* to Elisabeth Schwarzkopf. This boycott idea can work both ways. You may feel noble or righteous, but you're not proving anything."

"I, for one," Liz said, "don't put much trust in Germans. Maybe I've been around those nasty files too long."

"Talking about untrustworthy Germans, if you meet Weisse tonight," I said, "look him over and let me know what your woman's intuition says."

"My woman's intuition," she said, her smile rueful, "hasn't always proved trustworthy."

9: If it was Weisse's purpose to have me meet him at the Charlottenburg Palace, he evidently had nothing to conceal, for the main-floor interior was already crowded with several hundred guests by the time Liz and I arrived. And more kept coming; in taxis, private cars, chauffeured limousines. The palace, very nearly restored to its prewar splendor, blazed with light, even from rooms that still remained to be completed. "Fantastic, isn't it?" Liz commented. "I can remember when this place was a mess of ruins."

"You're willing to give these people some credit, then."

"For the way they've rebuilt things—yes," she said.

We simply wandered where most of the crowd—all in evening dress—wandered, into the imposing garden salon, an oval room of impressive and high-ceilinged dimensions that projected a curving expanse of windows into the palace gardens. A battalion of waiters in special uniforms of white jackets and striped trousers threaded their way through the throng, offering champagne from trays. Liz gazed around with experienced eyes. "Everyone who is anyone is here," she said. When I asked who in particular, she said that senators from Bonn, members of the city administration, representatives of military missions were all out in force. Some she recognized. To these I was introduced by her, and the brief chats were all the same: "Really a splendid occasion." "Quite a party." "Very significant for Berlin." "A magnificent job of restoration." Handshakes all around and we moved on, nowhere in particular, merely, it seemed, to see if we recognized other people. We must have been there nearly an hour, the crowd having grown considerably thicker, before I caught sight of Weisse.

He stood in a group near one of the large windows that looked out on the garden, flanked by two women, one his own age, the other much younger and, even at a distance, attractive enough to be glanced at twice. Weisse had already noticed me, I realized, for he gave me a nod and, excusing himself from the group he was talking to, moved toward me, the women following.

He pressed my hand warmly with both of his. "Herr Becker," he said, "it is good to see you here."

"Miss Elizabeth Schofield," I said, "Herr Weisse. Miss Schofield lives in Berlin."

He gave no sign that Liz's name was familiar and immediately presented what turned out to be his family.

"My wife, Frau Irmgard Weisse," he said, "and my daughter, Fräulein Elizabeth Weisse, of whom I have already spoken to you."

I shook hands with both. So slim, so cooly exquisite was Fräulein Weisse that it hardly seemed possible she was the offspring of the stout Herr Weisse and his almost equally stout wife, who immediately made much of the fact that her daughter and my friend bore the same first name.

Weisse hoped I was enjoying myself at this event, which, he said, with some tendentiousness, "is so important in the life of this city. It demonstrates that we are moving courageously into the future. They must take notice on the other side of the Wall."

"How?" Liz asked.

"They have their representatives here," Weisse said, "you may be sure of that. They miss nothing."

"Have you seen the model of the city of tomorrow?" Fräulein Weisse asked me, in polite, noncommittal tones.

I had seen it in the entranceway—a model, under glass, showing West Berlin as it might look one day, with blocks of rectangular buildings, malls, broad boulevards, elevated roadways, and, of course, such surviving edifices as this very palace as monuments of the past. It was hardly a dream city, but it did look efficient, and very neat.

"I've seen it," I said. "Do you like your future home?"

Fräulein Weisse's only comment was a shrug.

"And what do you do in Berlin?" Frau Weisse asked Liz.

"I'm at the Document Center," Liz said.

"Oh, I see." Frau Weisse pursed her lips, perhaps not sure of what the Document Center was.

I glanced at Weisse. His eyes were veiled. And, suddenly, I found myself meeting the eyes of Fräulein Weisse, whom I had surprised as she studied me. They were violet eyes, or that was their color in the glow cast by the candles in their wall holders. I saw that her hair was almost coal black and that she wore it pulled tightly to her head, a style in contrast to the prevailing upswept coiffures of most of the women who were here. She was taller than her mother, nearly as tall as her father, and she might have been of an age anywhere between twenty-five and thirty. Her dress was simple, but elegant, of a cream-colored satin that fitted closely, and whose thin straps left most of her shoulders bare. I remembered that Weisse had said his daughter was a fashion designer.

"Is that your own design?" I asked.

She appeared disconcerted for a moment. "My dress?" she asked.

"Yes."

"Well, yes," she said. "It has been made for me."

I felt vaguely chastised for asking.

"And I understand you are here on business," she said to me.

"Yes."

"You are business acquaintances?" she asked, indicating Liz in her glance. Or possibly lovers, her manner also seemed to say.

"In a manner of speaking, only. We once worked together years ago, but now we are friends."

"Ah, I see."

"I love your dress," Liz told her. "It's stunning."

"Oh, thank you."

Suddenly, Herr Weisse grabbed my hand, pumped it twice, then shook Liz's. "Excuse me," he said, abruptly, and his wife obediently followed him as he moved away. But Fräulein Weisse remained with us. Was it Liz's presence here that had made Weisse retreat, I wondered.

"Fräulein Weisse designs fashions," I explained to Liz, unnecessarily, for she had heard me ask about the dress.

"Yes, I know," Liz said.

"I am actually a consultant," Fräulein Weisse said, "for one of the big stores here. I do not do as much designing as I used to. My father has told me that perhaps I might be of help to you if you are doing some shopping here for your wife." Her eyes strayed toward Liz with another hint of speculation and came back to me.

"Well, I hadn't planned to do much——"

"Well, for heaven's sake, Alfred," Liz broke in, "she can help *me*."

"Oh, certainly," Fräulein Weisse said soberly. "And there are certain discounts I have that you can take advantage of, if you wish."

"Very kind of you," I said.

Fräulein Weisse opened a tiny, beaded evening bag and handed me a card. "This is my business address and number. Please call on me at any time."

From behind me a voice boomed out. "Alfred Becker!"

I turned and saw Judge Kimmel, and we greeted each other like the old friends we were. He was a white-haired little man who wore pince-nez.

"And what are you doing in Berlin? Something that has not to do with me, for a change?"

"Not at the moment, but I'll be getting to you sooner or later," I said. I introduced him to Liz, whose name was familiar to him, and to Fräulein Weisse.

"This man," the judge told the women, "is a menace to us. He takes our money away from us."

Fräulein Weisse gave me a solemn gaze.

"From my point of view," I said, "he very generously gives money away."

"Come with me for a moment," the judge said to me, grasping my elbow. "There are friends of yours here. You must say hello to them. Will you ladies excuse us briefly?"

Liz nodded, and Fräulein Weisse looked remote.

The judge guided me away through the crowd and, when

we were far enough away from the others, said, "Now tell me what you are really doing here. You haven't any business with me on this trip, so it must be something bigger." Presumably, he didn't want me to meet anyone after all.

"I'm representing a claim against Zeller-Bricken," I said.

"I suspected it," he said. "I was talking recently with one of your State Department people, and the matter came up. It seems the firm is perfectly clean."

"Really?" I said. "I'm not so sure."

"According to him—the man from your State Department— the matter had been looked into, and Z-B was found to be highly respectable. I give you this for what it's worth."

"Who was this man?" I asked.

"Oh, some assistant to an under-secretary. I shouldn't give away confidences."

"Well, I won't give away confidences, but we think we do have a case."

"I see, I see," the judge said. "Very interesting. I won't ask anything more. Those ladies . . . I know Fräulein Schofield slightly, but Fräulein Weisse—does she happen to be the daughter of the Z-B Weisse?"

"Correct."

"Then you are on friendly terms with him?"

"In a manner of speaking," I said.

"I used to know Weisse," the judge said. "A remarkable fellow. An acrobat, you might say."

"You mean, he always manages to land on his feet?"

"Yes, exactly that. But I will allow you to go back to your ladies now. You must be sure to pay me a visit before you leave Berlin. There are some new clarifications of the most recent amendments of the restitution laws. I would like very much to discuss them with you."

The Claimant

I promised to call on him at the Restitution Court on Rauch-strasse and returned to where I had left Liz and Fräulein Weisse. Liz was alone. Fräulein Weisse had excused herself, she said. "So what does your woman's intuition tell you about Weisse?" I asked her.

"Nothing really," Liz said. "Only that he seems very sure of himself. As for his daughter, I think she likes you."

"What gave you that impression?"

"She obviously wanted to be more helpful to you than to me. It was also the way she looked at you, as though she were anxious to make an impression. You could do a lot worse in Berlin, you know."

"Thanks," I said. "But what concerns me is that Weisse had absolutely nothing to say to me, unless by saying nothing he was saying something."

"Maybe he was only telling you that he's not the least worried by what you're up to," Liz suggested.

"I don't know, I don't know," I said. "He *did* invite me here, or at least arrange to have me invited."

"Well, the least we could do," Liz said, "is drink some more of that very good champagne."

I tracked down a waiter, seized two glasses of champagne from his tray, and was heading back toward Liz when I found myself face to face with Fräulein Weisse. "Oh, Herr Becker," she said, with no trace of a smile on her face, "you must excuse me for leaving like that, but I saw an old friend. The thought has come to me—perhaps we should make an appointment now?"

"For what?" I asked.

"The shopping. I am very anxious that you should see some of our better places. Would sometime tomorrow do?"

I felt a little stupid, because I couldn't remember that I had agreed to accept her earlier invitation. "Well," I began, "to-morrow——"

She interrupted me. "Tomorrow will be excellent. It will perhaps be more convenient if I call at your hotel at, say, three o'clock?"

"That would be very kind of you," I said. It was difficult not to be aware that a woman of considerable beauty seemed to be anxious to make an appointment with me. There was always something I could shop for, I supposed.

"Three o'clock, then?" she asked.

"Yes."

"Good. We will meet." She held out her hand, and I took it. It was slim, finely boned, and soft. I didn't see her again until after midnight, when the crowd had thinned out. She was dancing with a tall man who wore glasses and had a shock of thick blond hair.

"If you'd like to ask her," Liz said, noticing my gaze, "go ahead."

"No, I want to whirl you around," I told her.

A few minutes later we happened to brush past Fräulein Weisse and her partner. She turned her head slightly and met my eyes, and for the first time allowed a faint smile to part her lips. "I'm sure she wants you to ask her," Liz murmured.

"I'm not dancing with the enemy," I said.

"That's your own assumption," Liz said. "How would you know for sure?"

We left the palace shortly after. Liz insisted that since we were going in opposite directions it only made sense to go home separately, so I hailed a taxi for her.

On the way back to the Kempinski, I thought about Fräulein Weisse's eagerness to make a shopping appointment with me, knowing there had to be a reason for it. I decided that it must have something to do with Weisse's policy of friendliness toward me. He had arranged to have me invited to the palace. He had seen to it that I met his daughter. She had seen to it that I would meet her the next day. Did they hope that she would be able to persuade me to soften my demands or give them up altogether? Maybe so, I thought; but somehow I couldn't imagine Weisse would be that obvious.

I stopped at the concierge's desk in the lobby of the hotel for my key and was handed a message. Max Gerson again. Please call at once. Since it was past one in the morning I'd have to disobey him. He would call at nine anyway.

Before I went to bed, I racked my brains making out a shopping list. Lottie, of course, would be highly insulted if I brought her gifts from Germany, so I decided instead to shop for something pretty for Gloria and for two lady cousins of mine in New York. And something for Hilde. It occurred to me that a gift was in order for Hilde. But exactly what was appropriate for an old girl friend I had neglected for eighteen years? It seemed that I could use Fräulein Weisse's advice, after all.

10: "We are getting results," Max Gerson said portentously the next morning as he led me into his dusty, book- and object-crowded living room. "I have received an important letter. The Professor, I think, will be encouraged."

"You mean, you've located the candelabrum?"

"Not as yet. But we now know someone else besides the Professor believes the candelabrum still exists. That is something, yes?" He peered at me as though to make certain I was the same person who had visited him previously.

I suppressed my skepticism and merely pointed out that it would be something, yes, if the one he spoke of had a certain authority for backing up the belief. "Also," I said, "we are going on the assumption that the candelabrum has not been destroyed and therefore is bound to be somewhere. Where? That's the question, I would assume."

Gerson sighed. "Will you smoke?" he asked me, holding out a package of Astor filtered cigarettes.

"Thanks, no."

"You are a man of simple logic combined with an impatient nature, Mr. Becker. We are searching for an object that has been lost for twenty-seven years. War and catastrophe have happened in the meanwhile. Overnight results cannot be expected. In addition, the fortuitous circumstance must be encountered. I have such a circumstance, a letter."

He glanced significantly at a letter, still in its envelope, on the large, discolored brass tray he used as a coffee table and catchall. "Would you care to read it?" he asked.

"Who's it from?"

Gerson picked up the letter as though it had great value and handed it to me. "From Eva Lietschnitzer," he said, "of the Austrian branch of the family I have already mentioned to you. She was good enough to reply to my letter of inquiry promptly. You can read the German handwriting?"

"I believe so."

The handwriting was small and cramped, but clear enough for me to be able to make out the words. The writer desired Herr Gerson to know that the Erfurt Menorah, once in the possession of her ancestors, was of deep concern to her, and for some time she had been making inquiries in an attempt to establish its whereabouts. The results had been negative, so far, but she had recently come across an interesting fact. "A few months ago," she wrote, "I made one of my infrequent visits to Vienna, where I am in touch with art dealers and antiquarians, who know of my interest in acquiring the Erfurt Menorah. One of these mentioned to me that the price of such objects has soared in recent years, due to the renewed interest in similar antiquities on the part of collectors. He could not account for this interest, himself, because the collectors he dealt with were non-Jewish. It was naturally advisable for him to keep a list of any such antiquities being sought by collectors, among which was the Erfurt Menorah. However, he had not received a request for the Erfurt Menorah for at least a year, a fact that has made him suspect the menorah is now off the market. My dear Herr Gerson, you can imagine how this news has excited me. It is for me a proof that the menorah exists and is now in someone's hands. I feel it in my old bones. Unfortunately, I no longer have the energy to make the necessary researches." But, she suggested, if the gentleman Herr Gerson represented would be willing to pay a visit to her in her home not far from Salzburg, she, in turn, would provide him with what information she possessed.

"An interesting letter," I said to Gerson, "but it leaves us exactly nowhere."

"It leaves you in Vienna," Gerson said, "where avenues will open up for you. Take my word for it."

"Salzburg," I said, "then Vienna, then God knows where. How am I supposed to find the time?"

"You are not at the North Pole, Mr. Becker," Gerson said. "Vienna is a few hours' air time. If you prefer, you may commission me to make the trip."

"Well, as it happens," I said a little grudgingly, "I have something else to do in Vienna, but I hadn't counted on a side trip to Salzburg."

"Another few hours—what does it matter? The Professor would expect you to do it for him."

"Oh, I'm sure of that," I agreed.

"Good," Gerson said. "I will immediately write Eva Lietschnitzer and inform her of your coming. When will you go?"

"In a couple of days, maybe."

"Wonderful. I feel we are closing in on the menorah. Will you allow me to serve you some coffee?"

"Yes," I said, "and a map of Austria. This letter was sent from Seefeld. Where is it exactly?"

"On the Attersee," Gerson said, "perhaps thirty kilometers from Salzburg. Beautiful country. You'll enjoy the trip."

I nodded dubiously. "Look," I said, "you've been going to some extra trouble for me. I owe you something, don't I?"

Gerson coughed and wiped his glasses. "Two hundred marks, I think," he said delicately, "will adequately take care of the matter."

Fräulein Weisse was presumably precise about keeping her appointments. As the second hand of my watch swept past the numeral twelve at three o'clock, she came briskly into the lobby of the Kempinski, immaculate in a suit of dark brown wool and a gauzy scarf of lavender that protected her neck from the brisk weather outside, her dark hair shining and perfectly in place. She headed toward me without hesitation, as though she had known where I would be sitting, and gave me her hand, gloved in tan kid, as I rose to meet her. She did not smile, and this made her direct gaze into my eyes a little startling.

"You have made a list of what you would like to buy?" she asked me.

"Not exactly," I said, "but I have a few ideas."

"Do not make up your mind yet," she advised. "I will take you some places first. I have my car outside."

The car was a dark green Porsche and looked new. The bucket seats were of black leather. I noticed she handled the five-speed gear shift like an expert, as she shot the car into reverse, then low, and second.

"There is a place on the Bismarckstrasse," she said, "not far from the new Opera House. I will take you there first."

She swung us into the Kurfürstendamm, slammed into third

gear, jockeyed through two cars in what she considered her path, turned north on the wide Leibnizstrasse, then headed west on Bismarckstrasse. "You have been busy today?" she asked.

"Yes," I said, "but not as busy as I would be back in New York."

"Yes, I can understand that," she said. "You have your life there. We are not too much part of your life here in Berlin." Abruptly she down-shifted and slid the car into the curb. "Here we are."

We were in front of a shop featuring ladies' apparel. The name "Erika Kreuzner" was lettered on one of the windows.

"I take you here first," she said, "because this shop features my designs. I do not do much, but what I do goes here. If you should select anything, pay no attention to the price tag. I will arrange that." This she told me as she locked the doors of the car.

"The trouble is," I said, "I don't know what I'm looking for."

But she was already leading the way into the shop. Cries of delight from two saleswomen. From the rear of the large shop a woman of middle years came trotting to Fräulein Weisse. "Lisabett," she cried, "what a great joy to see you." They embraced and shook hands.

"I have brought you a customer," Fräulein Weisse said. "Frau Kreuzner, Herr Becker from New York."

Both my hands were grasped and shaken. Would I have coffee first? I declined, thanking her for the courtesy. For the next half-hour I was shown blouses, skirts, sweaters, dresses, the newest in mini-skirts, nightgowns, negligees, beach robes. When a design was by Fräulein Weisse, Frau Kreuzner flourished it before my eyes, remarking on the color, the fabric, the artistry of the styling.

"Very nice," I kept saying, "very nice."

To my unpracticed eye, Fräulein Weisse's styles in blouses, skirts, and dresses did have some distinction. They were pleasingly feminine—I knew that much.

"I'd like a blouse for my secretary," I said finally. "Something she would not find in New York."

"This one, I think," Fräulein Weisse said judiciously. She went behind a counter, opened a cabinet, and brought forth a plaid blouse of muted colors. "You see," she said, "this is made from a very delicate hand-printed cotton. It will be suitable for the late spring and summer. Only this shop carries this particular print."

"Exquisite," Frau Kreuzner breathed.

"She will not find anything like this in New York," Fräulein Weisse assured me.

"I'll take your word for it," I said, and I described Gloria's size.

Instructions were issued. The blouse was to be carefully wrapped and sent to my hotel. The price, I learned, was piddling.

"Have you thought of what you would like for your wife?" Fräulein Weisse asked me.

"We'll let that go for now," I said.

"The suede coats here are very nice," Fräulein Weisse assured me.

"No," I said. "She has a suede coat."

"Gloves?" suggested Frau Kreuzner. "We have some beautiful gloves."

It was hardly possible to explain that my wife would be insulted if I brought her something from Berlin. I said: "You see, she's on a trip herself and will be doing her own shopping."

"Oh, I see," Frau Kreuzner said. But she didn't see. One

thing in particular she did not see was why I would be on one trip and my wife on another. I could see the question in her eyes.

Fräulein Weisse only gave me a cool, veiled glance and continued to be politely helpful. At last we left the apparel shop and were in her car again. "Is your purchase satisfactory?" she asked, as she switched the motor on.

I said, "But I don't know why you're doing this."

"You don't?"

She turned the motor off and faced me. "But my father, Herr Weisse, told me you would understand."

"Understand *what?*"

"That in view of the delicate situation involving both of you, it would be better if you talked with me instead of him."

It was as though a light blazed before me. She was the negotiator!

"You see," Fräulein Weisse said, "he has explained your situation to me. He is anxious to be of as much help to you as possible. But it would not seem proper if he were to meet with you, except casually."

"And so as my friendly shopping assistant and acquaintance——"

"Precisely," she said.

"Forgive me for being blunt," I said, "but when do we talk? I mean, about what we're supposed to talk about."

"Today, if you like. I live not far away, on Schillerstrasse. Would you care to go there?"

"If it's within the rules."

"The rules?"

"You're making them," I said.

"We'll go to my flat, then," she said.

"But we haven't completed the shopping," I said.

"Oh?" She cocked her head a little to one side and gave me her level gaze, almost a stare.

"There is a woman I know here in Berlin," I said. "We are old friends. I would like to give her a gift before I leave. But I'm not sure of what it ought to be."

"You can tell me a little more perhaps?"

"Something for old times' sake," I said. "Something personal, and yet not too——"

"Something," she cut in, "that will not make her assume what you do not want her to assume."

"Yes, that's the idea."

"Jewelry, of the right type, might be suitable. A watch that she would wear on a chain. She might like that, as a sort of keepsake. On the other hand, earrings, or some sort of brace-let——"

"The watch sounds fine," I said.

"It is growing a little late," she said, glancing at her own watch. "I suggest we have our talk, and tomorrow, if you have the time, I can meet you again."

"You're most kind," I said.

"Not at all." She started the motor again and rocked me back with the briskness of her acceleration. The apartment house she stopped at on Schillerstrasse was new, modern, and had squarish balconies jutting out from each of the seven floor levels. I followed her through a long, narrow entranceway to an elevator, an automatic one that carried us upward silently.

"Gifts are difficult, I know," she said conversationally. "They can go wrong so easily if not chosen with sensibility and taste. Yet they are important. That say what words often cannot say."

"Both generally give me trouble," I admitted, for which I received an impersonal smile.

We emerged from the elevator at the sixth floor. Fräulein Weisse extracted a key from her handbag and opened her apartment door. Inside I noticed large, colorful French posters of the 1890's against the severe white of the walls. The oval rug was white, too, and revealed the high polish of the dark wood floor. Filmy white curtains seemed to flutter down the windows. The two armchairs and the couch had plain black coverings, and the only signs of Fräulein Weisse's profession were an unassuming work table near the door to another room—her bedroom, I guessed—and the French and American, as well as German, fashion magazines on a glass-topped coffee table. Not much doubt about it: this was the apartment of a serious, tasteful, yet very feminine, person.

"Sit down," she directed, "and I will bring you a drink. Gin, or would you prefer Scotch?"

"Scotch, thank you."

Elihu, I thought, you won't mind my having a drink with the enemy.

She soon returned from her kitchen with a tray holding a bottle of Johnny Walker, two glasses, a bowl of ice, and a siphon bottle of sparkling water. She had taken off the jacket to her suit, and this revealed her blouse of lavender jersey, which matched her scarf and looked original enough to be of her own design. Her firm and graceful arms were revealed, too.

"Please mix your own," she said, seating herself in the vacant chair.

When I was about to mix hers, too, she insisted on doing it herself, pouring in a small amount of the Johnny Walker, and splashing a few bursts of the sparkling water over it. No ice, though.

"To your negotiations," she said, with a certain reserve, and lifted her glass slightly.

I still wasn't sure whether or not she possessed a sense of humor, nor did I have any idea of what her own attitude was toward the mission her father had given her. Best, I thought, to assume she was completely tied in with him.

"This is a most pleasant place for a discussion," I said tentatively.

"My father," she said, almost conversationally, "is a man of complexities. I don't mind that. Like so many Germans of his generation, he has a past. It pains him, I know, and in a way it pains me. He has always tried to care for me well, and I respect him for that. But, Herr Becker, I would appreciate it if you would not assume too quickly that I have any sympathy for his past. I am being clear, I hope."

"We're to be frank?"

"Please," she said.

"I assume you're saying you realize your father was a Nazi."

"Certainly," she said. "Who wasn't?"

"But you're willing to help him now?"

"Why not? It was a long time ago. He is certainly no Nazi now. He does valuable work for his company and is well accepted even among your American officials. Besides, he is my father, and he has asked this favor of me."

"But what favor? I was given to understand he had nothing else to offer us."

"We are coming to business now. All right, since you are probably in something of a hurry——" She overrode my polite gesture of denial. "So I will tell you what my father has discussed with me. He would first of all ask you that you have patience for a while longer."

"But for what reason?"

"He thinks it would be to your advantage—that is, to the advantage of your people. I quite understand that you are not working here for your personal gain."

"Even so," I said, "it boils down to a matter of money. The suit we have going against your father's firm specifies the amount quite clearly."

"You were offered two hundred thousand marks?"

"Yes, a settlement amounting to one-tenth of the claim."

"My father," she said, "is quite convinced that his firm will offer you a larger sum."

"Did he mention a figure?"

"Yes, five hundred thousand marks."

"That's already a considerable increase," I said.

"Yes, but getting his firm to offer this amount will require a little time. He cannot guarantee that it will happen overnight."

"It doesn't matter," I said. "It's not enough, anyway."

"I see." She studied me with her level gaze, as though wondering just how difficult I was going to be.

"The thing is," I told her, "I'm not empowered to accept a lower figure."

"Usually," she said, "in this kind of discussion, one party goes up a little and the other comes down a little. You have remained stationary."

She had no smile on her face, but I was now fairly certain that she did have a sense of humor.

"Can't help myself," I said.

"But you could contact your people, and perhaps they would give you a lower figure."

"Your father, in other words, would like to know what lower figure we might be willing to accept."

"Yes, that would interest him, I am sure."

"There isn't a lower figure," I said carefully. "We ask for

two million marks, a half-million American dollars. The amount is both reasonable and just."

She stared into my eyes again, as though to make sure that I was being completely honest with her.

On a hunch, I said: "Don't *you* think it is reasonable and just?"

Her shoulders seemed to droop slightly, and her face grew troubled. "It is not fair of you to ask me that, Herr Becker," she said, her voice firm.

"Not in the spirit of the negotiations?"

"Please let us not joke," she said, her tone almost a rebuke.

You were the one who started it, I thought, but I kept myself from saying it aloud.

"Fräulein Weisse," I did say, "I am not an obstinate man, and I am also not a bargainer. And your hospitality is appreciated——" I was about to get up, when she stopped me by suddenly holding out her hand. Her eyes, which now struck me as darkly blue—perhaps because of the fading light—smoldered.

"You are not bargaining my father's position, which is his life—you are not bargaining that?"

"It may seem so," I said, "but it is not the case. Your father asked you to have this discussion with me, and I, much as I have enjoyed it, did not ask for it. There is nothing to bargain. We stated certain facts about your father; this helps us make our case. Otherwise, we would not be concerned about him at all."

"Unless, of course, he also happened to be regarded by your people as some kind of criminal."

"You said it—I didn't."

"Would you be kind enough to tell me who are these people you represent?"

"They are Jews," I said. "They are Jews in their forties, fifties, and sixties."

"Have you met them all?"

"Some of them."

"And they claim my father did something to them, something criminal?"

"None of them has ever seen your father, I would guess," I said. "His name wouldn't mean anything to most of them, and I doubt there's a single one who would charge your father with being a criminal."

"Then why is he being investigated?" she asked.

"By me?"

"Yes, by you and others. It must mean they think he has done something criminal."

I made sure to look blank. If Weisse knew he was being investigated by Ludwigsburg, if he had told his daughter, then it was not only me he was concerned about.

"The only investigating I've done," I said, "is in records that are available to any college student, if he can show a good reason for looking at them. What other investigations are you talking about?"

"He is being observed, Herr Becker, by a man from the German police."

"How can you be sure of that?"

"My father claims to know. What disturbs him is that he thinks it is because of the very help he gave to your people during the war."

"My people?"

"You are a Jew, are you not?"

"Yes, I am a Jew."

"Then they are your people, are they not?"

"Yes," I said, "they are my people. And the help your father gave them killed most of them, I regret to say."

"I do not believe that," she said flatly and without indignation.

"Look," I said. "I don't want to disturb you, Fräulein Weisse, and I certainly don't want to become involved in something that must bring on certain emotions. I understand that you, as a daughter, love and are loyal to your father. So I think we shouldn't talk about this any more. Your father has made an offer through you. I've already answered that the offer cannot be accepted."

I put my glass down on the little table. The clinking sound it made seemed loud and harsh.

"You must go now?"

I wasn't certain, but she had sounded vaguely regretful.

"I have no appointment until six," I said. "But I don't think I ought to take up more of your time. You know where to reach me."

"But we are to have an appointment tomorrow?"

"You want to keep it?"

"Of course."

"Well, you're being very kind."

"You continue to say that," she said. "But you are someone I feel sympathetic toward. You feel sympathetic toward me, also, I think."

"Yes," I admitted. "I like you."

For the first time, her lips widened into a genuine smile. Her eyes, amused now, turned soft. She was utterly beautiful.

Hell, I thought glumly, I could fall in love with her.

11: We talked for at least an hour longer. It was almost by tacit agreement that we stopped talking about her father and about the matter that had brought me to Berlin. My curiosity about her had grown, and having admitted to her that I liked her, I now felt free to ask her questions. She answered them freely. As she told me about herself, I had a tangible sense of our drawing closer to each other, although we still remained at the same distance in our chairs. She forgot to offer me another drink, and I didn't really want one. The conversation alone made me heady. She wanted to know about me, too. I told her that I was married. "Naturally," Elizabeth murmured, and I wasn't sure how much irony she intended. I also told her about my past affair with Hilde and my present meeting with her. "I have no interest in her now," I said quickly. Elizabeth nodded understandingly. I looked at my watch finally and said it was time to leave. I had arranged to meet Hilde at Kranzler's, I explained.

"Yes, you must go," she said. "I have kept you too long."
I stood up.

"We'll meet tomorrow," she said, "yes?"

"When?"

"Any time. You tell me." She sounded oddly submissive.

"Twelve," I said. "I'll call for you here."

"You must take my telephone number."

I wrote it down, but I would have remembered it anyway.
She stood indecisively near the door to the hallway. "Alfred——" she said, as if she were trying out the name experimentally. She looked frail at that moment, easily crushable. I wanted to gather her into my arms, but I held back. This is one hell of a way to do business, I thought. One does not take one's negotiator into one's arms because the opportunity is there. Besides, I'd had a lot of practice over the years keeping control over myself—excepting those few lapses, of course.

Was it my doing or Elizabeth's? Her eyes, which had been averted from mine, now regarded me again with a tentative expression. She held out her hand in an almost involuntary way. I took it, and something ouside of me seemed to be drawing her toward me. But she came without resistance. And it happened. She was close against me. Her head came only to my chin. Her hair was faintly perfumed. I bent and found her lips. They were available, and very soft. I tried not to think at all, and I can't say for exactly how long that kiss lasted. Maybe it was only for a few seconds; it might have been much longer than that. We were both a little out of breath when it ended.

"You must admit," she said, "this is quite strange."

We grinned at each other, relieved at the breaking of the moment's tension, its embarrassment to both of us. Then, more boldly this time, I kissed her again, and it was now obviously admitted between us that something had happened, that the chemical reaction had occurred. I still couldn't think, only that at Kranzler's Hilde would be waiting for me, and how was I to get around that?

"I could call at Kranzler's and leave a message," I suggested, knowing that I did not want to leave just yet and that Elizabeth was fully as reluctant about having me go.

"No," she said, with a firm shake of her head. "That would not be correct. There is tomorrow. We have agreed to meet. We will have a chance to sleep and know how we feel in the morning. Perhaps we will realize that we have made a mistake."

"Have we?"

"I don't know. I am very mixed up. I am not always so mixed up, but now my head is not clear. You are confusing me."

"You didn't expect me to kiss you?"

"One expects it," she said, with a shrug, "often, and from many men. It is a question of whether one wants to avoid it. I did not with you. I do not yet know why."

"Are you supposed to report this kind of thing to your father?"

She looked genuinely shocked. "He doesn't control me, and certainly he does not dictate my feelings. You think I am some kind of Mata Hari?"

"No," I said. "I don't have that kind of imagination. I only wondered how fully you would describe our meeting today."

"I will tell him what he is concerned about, the business he asked me to discuss. He is not so interested in you as you might think."

"You mean you're only to get me off his back for awhile."

"I don't pretend to read his mind," she said. "He asked for a little assistance, and I gave it to him. My father is a very busy man, and he has a lot on his mind. I do think, though, that you are very interested in him. I am not sure why this is so, because

he is not the firm—he is only a part of it. Is there some problem in your mind about him?"

"Right now," I said, "I suggest we forget about your
father."

I wanted to kiss her again, but she stopped me this time.
Her hand against my chest was surprisingly firm.

"You have a few minutes," she said. "Let us talk for a
little."

But I saw her eyes were shining, and I knew I had not been
rejected. She brought me another drink, and we sat together on
her couch, her shoulder touching mine. "Since you have a wife,"
she said, as though it was time to be practical, "I think I
should know something. Do you go around kissing women like
this often?"

"Very seldom."

"But you are not a very faithful husband?"

"Considering everything," I said, "I am a remarkably faithful husband, but now and then I choose to feel that I have a
certain amount of freedom. What I am most careful about is
that I do not hurt Lottie."

"Your wife is not well?"

"She has reason to be sensitive, and very easily hurt, and I
do have the desire to protect her. Maybe I'm not making myself
clear, but for your own understanding, I should tell you that
she was in concentration camps and that she was in very bad
shape when found. She was the only one left out of her family."

A look of pain came on Elizabeth's face.

"How dreadful," she said, "how sad."

"But she is better now, and in many ways has recovered
fully. You can't expect that she would be a completely whole
person."

"We must be careful," Elizabeth said, almost primly, "not

to kiss again, certainly not in the way you kissed me at the door. Why did you do it?"

"Feelings," I said.

"I don't mind being friends," Elizabeth said, "because I like you so much. You are a secure kind of person. By that I mean that you give a woman—me, at least—a feeling of trust. If it were not for your wife, I might have considered love-making with you. I mean that, if you had left, when we were at the door, I would have thought about the prospect of making love with you."

"And now?"

"That is out of the question."

But she had made it a question, and it was in both of our minds—that thought, that fantasy.

"The least we can do," I said, "is be honest with each other."

"I thought it was noticeable that I am being honest."

"It is," I assured her.

"In the interests of honesty," Elizabeth said, "I should tell you that I am twenty-eight years old and that I take the position that I can do as I please until the day I have promised someone otherwise, and that I have managed to fall in love a few times, and that others have loved me. But I have insisted on my independence, I assure you."

"You give that impression."

"But I am a woman, with woman's feelings, and they can be aroused, particularly when I like someone very much—as I do you."

"You're asking me to be careful?"

"I am depending on it."

"That's a terrible responsibility," I said with a sigh.

"If you intend to try to seduce me," she said, "I would wish that you inform me in advance."

"I'm not intending it," I said. "What happened there happened. Usually I'm more cautious."

"I would hope so," she chided me. But I noticed that her eyes were shining.

"It is just as well that we only remain good friends," she said. She took my wrist and looked at my watch. "It is time for you to leave, I think."

"Yes," I agreed.

It was close to six, and I was going to be late as it was. We went to the door together, my arm about her shoulder, and this time I contented myself with kissing her cheek.

When I left her building I found that a light mist had begun to fall. I was hatless and should have sought a taxi, but I walked instead to Kranzler's, knowing it would make me even later. I was possessed by feelings that had been dormant for a long time, and the city seemed different to me now. The mist softened the harsh lines of the streets; buildings, so few of them truly handsome, seemed iridescent. Sixteen years, I thought. She was sixteen years younger than I, and this alone required me to judge my way carefully.

I saw Hilde from the street, seated at a table on the terrace behind the glass partition. I walked in, entering the uncomfortable warmth of the infrared heating system.

"You are late," Hilde said, with an obvious attempt to fix a smile on her troubled face. I removed my Burberry and folded it over the back of one of the empty chairs. I had been on business, I told her, and had gotten delayed, and there had been no empty cabs on the Kurfürstendamm.

"What has been happening to you?" she asked. "You seem so busy."

"I'm trying to get things wrapped up here."

"You'll be leaving Berlin soon?"

"Yes, but I'll have to be coming back again."

I saw that she had ordered one of Kranzler's ice-cream concoctions.

"Wouldn't you like a drink?" I asked.

"Perhaps a little later."

"I'll have one."

I ordered a Scotch and soda from the waiter who was standing at my shoulder.

Hilde wanted to know where I would be going and what I would be doing. I outlined the Vienna trip for her and told her of the woman who lived near Salzburg, but I did not mention Ludwigsburg.

"So fascinating," Hilde said, almost enviously.

"I'm trying to finish it," I said. "I've been involved in these things for a long time. One of these days they must end."

"In some ways you have changed, Alfred," she remarked. "But in other ways you have changed very little. But you have changed toward me. That much I can see."

"We're not really the same people anymore."

She sat back, with a resigned expression on her face.

"You wish to tell me something," she said.

"What?"

"That I am no longer suitable for you, that I am not the young Hilde who pleased you so long ago. But I am not asking anything from you, Alfred."

"I didn't think you were."

"And I will apologize to you now for my sister's behavior of the other evening."

"No apology needed," I said. "None at all. She was joking. I knew that."

"You'll still help her?"

"Certainly. She's a pleasant girl, very lively, a little un-orthodox. I like her."

"More than me, perhaps?"

"Oh, no," I said. "We are old friends."

"Old friends," Hilde said mockingly. "Alfred, it would have been so easy for you. I don't mind your being married. Why do you wish not to have me?"

"Too many complications," I said. "I couldn't offer you anything."

"You don't have to offer me anything. I could help you. I could help you with your work."

I sat silent. The waiter had brought me my drink, and I sipped at it.

"I am German," she said. "That is still the obstacle for you. You will always have a resentment against me. It would not be possible for you to love a German woman."

I had nothing to say. She was wrong, but I didn't want to tell her that she was wrong. Sitting with her, at this very mo-ment, I was in love with a German woman. Unless, like a sud-den brief fever, it would pass away in a day or so.

"What you do not understand," Hilde said, "is that between the German and the Jew there is an attraction. A strange thing to say, I realize."

"Very strange," I said.

"The German man, you know, fears this attraction in his women. He knows about it, I assure you. The Jewish man offers his women what the German cannot offer them."

"I don't know why I don't want to talk about that," I said, "but I don't want to."

Hilde drew back from me as though I might have been

about to slap her. "All right," she said with a resigned nod of her head. "I can see that you have not much interest in talking to me this evening."

I made an effort to apologize, to say that there were some things I felt were too complicated to discuss, but Hilde's expression remained frozen.

"It doesn't matter," she said, "because I do not have much time at this moment, anyway. I must meet someone." She added, as a kind of studied afterthought, "I must meet someone who is an old, dear friend of mine. You wouldn't know him, of course. There are, my dear Alfred, other people in my not-so-young life."

"I understand," I said.

"I hope you had not made plans for this evening concerning me."

"No, I didn't have much in mind."

"Good, then," she said. "I will be on my way."

"Would you like me to find you a taxi?"

"No, I will take the U Bahn. It goes right there. You see, we have an entrance right in front of us."

The steps leading to the U Bahn were just a few yards away. Hilde gathered up her gloves and her handbag. "Please telephone me before you leave Berlin," she said curtly.

"Of course I will." I rose and saw that my drink was hardly touched.

"No, stay," she said. "It's not necessary to be so polite."

"I hope we'll see each other again, Hilde."

"Shall we?" She took a step away from the table, then turned back to face me, her face distinctly flushed. "It could have been very nice between us, Alfred, but something has spoiled it for us."

I said, as easily as I could, "It hasn't been spoiled for me,

Hilde. It has been wonderful to see you again—a great pleasure for me."

"*Auf Wiedersehen, Alfred,*" she said, and left me. I sat down again at the table, regretting that she felt hurt but not really sorry that she had gone. I wasn't equipped to handle her feelings anymore, and civility alone wasn't going to do any good. Besides that, my own warm impulses were already headed firmly in another direction.

While I dawdled, two women of middle age came along and asked me if I minded sharing my table. Kranzler's ground-floor terrace had grown crowded, and I was occupying a table with four chairs. "Please do," I said in English, upon which they took me for a tourist and, after a "*Danke schön,*" proceeded to ignore me. I listened to their talk, not really curious, but there wasn't much else to do. Hilde's leaving had created a void in my evening. The women were planning trips in June but weren't yet sure of exactly where they would head for. One of them had her mind set on Yugoslavia, but her husband was against it. He had been a young soldier there during the war, and he doubted that Yugoslavs would have any love for Germans, even now. Both women agreed this attitude was quite old-fashioned. Tourists, after all, brought good German marks with them, a currency more solid than the dollar or the pound. With this, they gave me a quick glance, but I pretended not to have heard or understood. They were well embarked on comparing their impressions of Rome, where both had been the previous summer, when I paid my bill and left the café.

The mist had lifted. I walked back toward the Kempinski, stopping now and then to examine the glass-enclosed display cases in the middle of the sidewalk, with their showings of cameras, watches, costume jewelry, and other goods that would attract the tourist. Passing a women's apparel shop, I looked at the styles and thought of how exciting it would be to see Elizabeth again. Need I wait until tomorrow?

In my room at the hotel, impatience got the better of me, and I picked up the telephone with the idea of asking her out to dinner. But I received no answer. She was gone already, and it occurred to me how much I did not know about her. Suppose I weren't married, I thought—would I have come on stronger than I had? Or would I have exhibited more caution? Perhaps more than I'd realized, I was in the habit of using Lottie as an anchor, not so much against physical unfaithfulness, as against wandering too far into unknown and dangerous emotional areas. Elizabeth was all too dangerous, and I warned myself that I'd better be careful.

As an aid to maintaining objectivity, I wrote a note to Elihu, informing him that Zeller-Bricken had upped the offer somewhat, but not substantially, and that it had been done through Weisse, who now appeared to be the principal bargainer. "I am not yet sure," I wrote, "whether Weisse is bargaining for himself or his firm, but I am inclined toward the former assumption, since he has asked his daughter—a quite nice and attractive person, by the way—to serve as a medium of communication between us. Actually, I prefer the arrangement. Things are developing slowly, but let us hope they will speed up."

After mailing the letter, I went in to the Grill Bar of the Kempinski and had a drink at the minuscule bar in the corner of the room. Two Americans sat on the stools next to me, and one of them, a man of about my own age, with a reddish complexion and balding hair, began talking to me at once. He and his friend, he said, had been doing some business in Frankfurt, and had decided to take a look at Berlin before returning home. He handed me his card. His name was Kenneth Sloane, and he was from Dayton, Ohio. He was in the machine-tools business.

I was introduced to his friend, Bob Johnson, from Cleveland, who was a lawyer. I was a lawyer, too, I said. That made us friends. We had dinner together in the Grill Bar, and Kenneth —who soon had me calling him Ken—wondered if I knew much about Berlin's night life. They had been to Resi's, the place with the telephones at each table, the night before and had found it disappointing. "Just a water show," Bob Johnson said sourly, "with some tired old bags sitting at the tables and calling us up."

After dinner I took them to the Alabama Saloon, which had its touristy aspects but was at least lively. The Alabama was a new, low-ceilinged place, run by a young Rumanian with ambitions of building a nightclub and hotel empire, who had created a discothèque atmosphere of informality and noisy jazz. He employed girls who ran bars in each of the three rooms, and who, when not working behind the bars, sat on stools cadging drinks and were available as dancing partners. The walls were decorated with film posters, and the tables, with long benches instead of chairs, were always crowded.

"This is more like it," Ken said, after he had paid a two-mark fee for checking his raincoat.

The girls on the loose were, most of them, fairly pretty. They were good dancers, too. After we had been seated at a table near the dancing place, I caught sight of a familiar face on the dance floor. It was Annemarie Kolisch. Her tall, slim body, encased in a shimmering sheathlike dress that ended above her knees, undulated and twisted. The boy she danced with had handsome Negroid features of a pale tan coloring. He was no more than nineteen, and there wasn't much doubt that he was the product of an affair between a Negro Occupation G.I. and a German girl. Was this the man Hilde had worried about, or was Annemarie a professional here?

Annemarie caught sight of me a few moments after we were seated, gave me a surprised look, and when the four teen-age musicians had stopped playing, left her partner and came over to me.

"You were supposed to be with my sister," she said.

"She had to leave early," I said.

I introduced her to my two companions, who were fervently delighted to meet her. They invited her to sit with us, and she promptly accepted.

"What are you doing here?" she asked me.

"We're exploring Berlin night life," I said.

"This is as good a place as any," she said. She was interested in my two companions, I saw, and when the music began assaulting the room again, Kenneth asked her to dance. He had a hard time keeping up with her, but he was obviously enjoying himself.

"You seem to know this town pretty well," Bob said.

I explained that I had been coming here long enough to know the city fairly well on the surface, but that was all. "A true Berliner," I said, "is something else again."

"That girl," Bob said. "Would she maybe be available for the night?"

"That's what I mean," I said. "I haven't the faintest idea. She could be, and, on the other hand, she probably isn't."

"We could ask her," Bob said.

"I'd rather not be here when you do," I said. I was beginning to be bored.

When Kenneth came back with Annemarie, I made my excuses. Annemarie looked disappointed, but she did not leave the table.

"So long, pal," Bob said as I left.

When I was back at the hotel I called Elizabeth again. Still no answer. I went to bed, but it took me a long time to go to sleep.

The next day was clear and mild. I had breakfast at the Terrace Café of the Kempinski, which, with its oranges and pinks bright and shining, was more cheerful than ever. My friends of the night before were breakfasting there too, and gave me comradely waves. Bob made a thumbs-down gesture, his way of telling me they'd had no luck.

"Sit down, join us," Kenneth said.

I had no reason to refuse, so I sat with them and ordered my usual orange juice, eggs, and coffee.

"That friend of yours, Annemarie," Kenneth said, "she got mad as hell. Hope it doesn't put you out."

They had taken turns dancing with her, Bob said, and she had seemed to be having a hell of a lot of fun. Between numbers, she had drunk a considerable amount of brandy and told them that she would be coming to New York soon. She had gotten them to talk about Dayton and Cleveland and had also inquired into their marital states. "Couldn't lie to her, could we?" Bob asked plaintively. "Why the hell should it matter to her, anyway?"

"I told her we had a suite here together," Kenneth went on. "I suggested we have some drinks in the suite where we would be more comfortable. She was polite, said no thank you."

"I said there might be a little something in it for her," Bob said. "That was when she got mad at us. Just got up, stalked away, and the next thing we knew she was gone. Left the place. Now, why the hell was she being so friendly with us if she wasn't after anything?"

"She probably liked you," I said. "You hurt her feelings."

"Well, hell, she knew we were married and just out for a good time," Bob said. "I don't get these girls at all."

"You ever made out with her?" Kenneth asked me with a keen glance.

"No."

"Have you tried?"

"Couldn't very well," I said. "I know her sister. An old friend from my Army days."

"I'll be damned," Bob said. "You should have told us that."

They were leaving that afternoon, on the Pan Am flight that stopped at Hamburg and went on directly to New York. They thanked me for having shown them something of the town. You had to hand it to the Germans, they said. Built this whole place up out of a heap of ruins.

After they left, I found myself wondering about Annemarie. She might be going to the Alabama just to enjoy herself. Never, I was sure, would she have agreed to go with those two Americans, if only because they might have reported back to me. Whatever curiosity I had, I was fairly sure it wasn't going to be satisfied, for the only way to find out anything about Annemarie was to find out for myself. Ready to expect disappointment from Elizabeth, I vaguely considered the possibility of Annemarie as someone to help me forget her. "Act your age, if not your sense," my mother used to say to me as a boy. She wouldn't say it to me now, but the advice held true.

By noon I had managed to retrieve my relatively sedate forty-four-year-old self as I turned into Schillerstrasse. But, as soon as I noticed Elizabeth's green Porsche parked at the curb in front of her balconied building, I was aware not only of a pang of anticipation but of a sense of excitement and energy. Forty-four years was not so old, relatively speaking. I got into the automatic elevator and rose to her floor. Taking a deep breath, I rang her bell.

Only the faintest of smiles crossed her composed face as she said, "Come in." She gave me her hand in greeting. "I'll be ready in a minute." Her black dress of a fine wool material was simple but clung to her body and emphasized its gracefulness. I followed the waft of her perfume inside. It was not the same as yesterday's—perhaps she changed her perfume with her mood.

She left me in her sitting room while she busied herself in her bedroom. "Now we are ready," she said, re-emerging wearing an outer coat of gray cashmere. "We are to find a gift for your friend. Yes? I know of a place."

"I thought I'd ask you to lunch, too," I said tentatively.

"Lunch?" She hesitated, considering. "I had made an appointment for a little later. An old friend from my days at the *Hochschule*. But you could join us if you liked."

"I wouldn't want to be in the way."

"No, it is nothing like that, nothing private. I think, really, that Ulrich would enjoy meeting you. But I must telephone him first and tell him we will be three. He is sensitive, you see."

I didn't see what he would be sensitive about unless he were jealously in love with Elizabeth, and that I could well understand, but she didn't explain further. She made the call in her bedroom, and I heard her telling her friend, "You will be interested in this man. He is an American. I think you would enjoy talking to each other. He is quite intelligent, an important person. Good-by, my dear."

She came out from the bedroom again and said, "Let us go."

I caught hold of her arm as she was about to open the door. She moved toward me, submissive, but with eyes that showed doubt.

She said, as I held her, "We must speak about this. I don't know if this is right for us."

"I don't either."

"Because of that," she said, "I would not answer the telephone last evening."

"So you knew I tried to reach you."

"Yes, I did know, and I was afraid to talk to you."

"Why?"

"I was afraid that I would ask you here."

"That wasn't why I called," I said. "I was alone for dinner, and I thought if you happened to be alone——"

"Even so," she said, "I would have asked you to come here."

"In that case, I would have come," I said, confident again.

"Yes, you are very polite," she said, mocking me. "Well, we must talk about it."

"When?" I asked. "We'll be having lunch with your friend."

"There will be time, I think."

In the car, she headed toward the Breitscheid Platz, with the Kaiser Wilhelm Church in its middle, and turned into the wide, busy Tauentzienstrasse. A few blocks later she turned off into the center of Charlottenburg and stopped in a side street lined with small shops. "Here," she said, "is a very nice jewelry store. We will find something for your Hilde."

The elderly man who was alone in the shop was Jewish. I would have known, even if his name had not been Herr Gruenfeld, and his look at me also contained a hint of recognition. He knew Elizabeth well and seemed to regard her as a good customer. But I wondered: Would she have taken me here if I had not happened to be Jewish?

She explained to him that I needed a gift for a lady, and he brought out small trays on which were watches, bracelets, lockets, and pins of odd shapes. I chose a small watch of gold, with tiny sapphires in place of numerals. Elizabeth insisted on choosing the delicately linked chain to go with it. The price, slightly more than a hundred dollars in marks, was much less than it would have been in New York.

"It's not too much money?" she asked me.

"No."

"Put it in a little case," she instructed Herr Gruenfeld. "We will make our own wrapping for it."

In the car again, she said, "Now we have done our duty toward your old love, and someday you may do the same for me."

"I hope not for the same reason," I said.

"We will go meet my friend Ulrich," she said. "This restaurant, where we will meet, is not fancy, but the food is good. You must insist on paying the bill, please. Ulrich will try to pay it, but he has not much money." Her friend, she explained, was the same age as she but was still a student. "He has been taking degrees in literature."

She retraced our route to the Breitscheid Platz, took the Kurfürstendamm this time, and entered another small street not far from the Savignyplatz. The restaurant was small and dim. It had only seven or eight tables and was run by an Italian who was married to a Berliner. The cuisine was Italian, she had told me. Ulrich was waiting for us, a tall thin man who looked younger than twenty-eight. He sprang to his feet with alacrity, appeared to be delighted to meet me, and gave Elizabeth a fervent kiss on her smooth cheek.

Whatever hesitancy or strangeness that might ordinarily have been present between Ulrich and myself was quickly dissipated by Elizabeth, who told her friend that I was a frequent visitor to Berlin, that he need not attempt to speak his miserable English with me, since I spoke German well, and that I was a lawyer who specialized in redressing the wrongs done to the Jews during Nazi times.

"Has he met your father?" Ulrich asked her, a question obviously meant to be mischievous. He knew something about Weisse, I saw.

"Yes, they are business acquaintances," she said, noncommittally.

She asked the wife of the Italian owner for menus, told her we would have a bottle of her best red wine, and pointed out the best dishes to me. I had a sense of reassurance from being in the restaurant; it was so much like a place we might have gone to in New York. And the veal dishes we chose, when they came, were hardly different from the kind an American-Italian restaurant would have served. She had a way of doing everything right, I thought, almost as though she were clever enough to know exactly what would make me feel most comfortable and at home.

Ulrich studied at the Free University. Had I visited it? Not lately, I told him, but I had given a lecture there a few years ago.

"Yes, on what subject?"

"International aspects of restitution."

"You believe in it?" he asked.

"Restitution? As a legal fact, certainly."

"But in terms of its moral significance?"

"You must not take Ulrich too seriously," Elizabeth interjected. "He is first of all a socialist, he is secondly a deep cynic, and thirdly he has a great mistrust of any German over the age of thirty."

"And," Ulrich added, "as soon as I am thirty-one I will mistrust myself. You know, at the university, some of my friends have a saying about the restitution program. They say one hundred marks equals one dead Jew."

"Some of my friends say it, too," I told him.

"Then you agree it has no meaning?"

"I would say that it has more than one meaning. There is an action involved, a commitment, and there are results. Unfortunately, you can't ask or expect that dead Jews be brought to life again. Nothing gets around that fact, and I can understand how it can lead to hopelessness."

Ulrich nodded. I suddenly noticed that one side of his face hardly moved when he spoke, as though the nerves on that side were dead, and having noticed that much, I saw a pale scar near his cheekbone; it must have come from a childhood wound. The bombings? "But," he said, "it would take something of a miracle to solve the problem."

"What problem?" I asked.

"The final solution of the German question," he said.

"Oh, Ulrich," Elizabeth protested, "every now and then you become boring."

"But our friend here," he said insistently, "must be concerned with this. How can he face us otherwise? How can we face him?"

"I don't think you're talking about the German question," I broke in. "You're talking about the history of brutality, which rose to a peak in Germany at a certain time."

"You clarify very politely," Ulrich said. I saw that only one side of his face could smile. "But I am nevertheless concerned about German brutality, and you must admit that my people (I do not regard them proudly) have at least demonstrated a modern mastery of the art."

"But it is not as simple as all that," I said. "I assume you have read your history."

"Yes," Ulrich said, "I have read it carefully, and it has confirmed my worst suspicions. Notice the deceit and trickery, the lack of morality that characterized our first attempt at democracy during the years of the Weimar Republic. People say now: Ah, we were democratic once, before Hitler came along to spoil everything. But is this really so? While treaties and agreements were being made at Genoa and Locarno and London, all the time the military was rearming and hiding this fact from the control commissions. While speaking peace, even among the top political leaders there were those wishing, hoping, planning revenge on France. True, there were some Germans who made the attempt to behave honorably, but most of the time it was double talk." A flush came to his face as he gained excitement from his own words.

"It was only one more step," he went on, "from the cynicism of the Weimar years to the complete abandonment of morality by Hitler and his supporters, who included the important majority of Germans. We will exclude the little people, who did not know how to think at all. Our vaunted education did not, after all, extend far into the masses. Does not this say something about the Germans, who, as a group, a community, a nation, were invariably moved by the most cold-blooded of self-interest? Conspiracy comes naturally to the Germans, I am sad to admit, for otherwise how could so many have believed in the nonsensical conspiracy set forth in the Protocols of Zion, a fictitious document that was accepted more readily in Germany than in Russia, its country of origin. Some of our very best people, the most loyal and moral, were those Germans of Jewish descent, and these during the Weimar years were reviled and in some cases murdered. I offer you Foreign Minister Rathenau as an example. So, I tell you, the ground for Hitler was very fertile and well prepared. Now we speak of those twelve years of the Third Reich as an exception, something divorced from the more rational context of German history, but I do not believe this to be so."

Elizabeth glanced at me. I saw disturbance in her eyes, and also pride in her friend's eloquence.

"I'll tell you why Germans believed so thoroughly in the conspiracy of so-called international Jewry," Ulrich said. "Because they saw in this the mirror of their own nature. They transposed the German into the Jew, and felt themselves cleansed thereby—a simple and satisfying act of transference. This is why I say there is a German question. And this is why I would warn those outside not to trust us. We are not yet trained to stand by what we say; and what we say and what we do are out of self-interest only. So, we compensate those we have harmed, knowing we will get something far more valuable in return—the trust we do not deserve. The political forces are democratic now, but this is because Germans gain so much by being so. Militarism would be idiotic at this point in their history, because the forces on each side of them—you and the Russians—are atomic, and even the German will subside if he is threatened with more force than he can possibly cope with. It is a little sad that there is a wall between this part of Berlin and the other, but I feel deep down that it is not such a bad idea. Anything that forces Germans to be peaceful is a good idea."

"Do you include yourself among these Germans?" Elizabeth asked him suddenly.

"I am not sure," Ulrich said. "But you see, I have already retreated. I stay in school, I study, I talk, I argue, but I do not participate in this new and American-sponsored Germany. Nor do I include you, my dear Lisabett, because you are all too innocent and such a good soul. We, both of us, belong to a pleasant but basically useless minority. On the other side, we both must admit to having parents of the kind we would not trust if they were not our parents."

"And what does that mean?" she asked.

"I will speak for my own father, not yours. I know my father to be a convinced anti-Semite. In this he has not changed one bit, though he does keep his voice much lower, and after all, there are so few Jews he can see to attack. He was a Nazi party member, and he still speaks of those good days before the war. With all that, he is not such a bad fellow—he is good to my mother, and he sends me an allowance, out of guilt perhaps that he did not protect me sufficiently from the bombings when I was a child, but he sends the money willingly. He thinks now that Hitler was a little crazy, but it took time for him to swallow that pill. What do we do with his generation? Naturally, being German, we let them lead us. You see what I mean?"

"You are part of a generation too," Elizabeth said. "Why don't you do something?"

"Maybe," he said, with a quizzical expression, "because I think there are others more deserving of my great abilities than Germans. More seriously, though, I would rather go to Africa or to another undeveloped place. I am inclined to be literary, and I could write about their problems. Don't you agree that would be a better course for me?" He had turned in my direction now.

"Not necessarily," I said. "Speaking personally, I'd prefer you to exercise your conscience in your own country. Retreat— into the mind, or to some other country—isn't much of an answer for the questions you raised."

"Excellently spoken," Ulrich said. "I applaud you for your

American dynamism. I will take the hint and speak not again until I have *done* something."

"Ulrich," Elizabeth said, "you are not being very polite."

"Lise," he said, "on the contrary, I very much enjoy speaking to your friend. More than that, I can see that you like him, and that in itself gives him a good reference."

I wondered if I detected a slight note of jealousy in his words.

Elizabeth behaved as though she too had noticed this, for she quickly said, "And if you keep talking like that, I will make it clear that I do not like you."

Ulrich smiled, seemingly secure in his knowledge of their long relationship. They could afford to be biting with each other.

When our lunch was over, he insisted that I take his address and telephone number and said he would regard it as an honor if I would look him up whenever I was in Berlin. As Elizabeth had forewarned me, he made a strenuous effort to pay the luncheon bill and looked saddened when I prevailed.

"I will drive you back to the university," she told him.

That meant, I assumed, that our afternoon was over. My time was up. Outside the restaurant, Elizabeth held out her hand to me. "Call me," she said.

"When?" I asked.

"When you feel like it," she answered, with so much coolness that the words seemed more of a dismissal than an invitation.

I said good-by and strode away from them. The Kempinski was about ten blocks away, and I walked the whole distance, so mystified about Elizabeth's behavior during those last moments that I was hardly aware that the sun was warmer than at any time since I'd been in Berlin. More people were out, taking advantage of the sparkling afternoon, their coats had been shed, lovers walked on the Kurfürstendamm with their arms around each other's waists. When you feel like it, Elizabeth had said. Why not take the invitation at its face value?

I found no mail for me at the lobby desk of the hotel. At the newsstand, the international editions of the New York papers hadn't come in yet. I took a couple of Berlin papers instead and went up to my room. I feel like it, I said to myself at twenty minutes past three.

I picked up the telephone and asked the operator to try Elizabeth's number.

"Alfred," I heard her say accusingly and almost at once over the phone line. "Why did you wait so long to call? I have been back here for fifteen minutes!"

Part Two

12: "I have something I must do later in the evening," Elizabeth said on the telephone, "but if you would like to meet for a drink in a little while, that is, if it is not too soon——" It was not too soon at all. I met her at Wagenknecht on the Olivaer Platz at five. When I walked in, she was already seated at a table in the warm, coffee-odorous interior and had decided that instead of a drink she would prefer coffee and some of the Berliner cakes, since she would probably have to forego dinner.

"I must explain to you why I might have seemed a little rude when I left you earlier," she said. "Ulrich is so curious about me, and he is always suspecting some deep involvement with anyone I bring to meet him, and so to protect you from any of his false assumptions——"

"False?" I said.

"Well, after all, you are only a visitor in Berlin, and after you are gone he will say something like, 'What happened to that good friend of yours?' implying that some little fling had occurred and now I was to be left alone, pining away. You see, he builds these fantasies about me."

"Jealousy, maybe," I said.

"Perhaps so, but we went through all that long ago. Ulrich and I are close, but he is not the man for me. It's hard to explain, I think, about someone I have known as long as Ulrich."

"It's not hard to understand his fondness for you," I said.

"You say nice things." She smiled. "He is intense, as you must have noticed, and he speaks his mind, and sometimes he tries to do things about what he thinks."

"Who are you seeing later?" I asked. "I hope you'll forgive my curiosity."

"I am flattered that you are curious," she said. "But it is not very important—a favor, actually, for Ulrich. I must deliver a message for him."

"I see," I said, but I didn't.

She munched at a cake and smiled at me. "I'm afraid, if I tell you, you will think I am only some kind of conspirator. You see, I must go to East Berlin."

"But can you?"

"The passport is no problem for me. I have two, one as a Berliner, one from the Federal Republic. As a West German I can go there with as little trouble as you can. I simply leave the West Berlin passport at home and use the other. There are many here in Berlin who can do that."

"And you go often?"

"No, not often."

"Well, why don't I go with you?"

"You mean, to protect me? How sweet of you, Alfred, but I think it would be a bore for you. You must have more interesting things to do."

"I can't think of any," I said.

"Then, certainly, you can accompany me. I would enjoy that very much. But if we go we should leave quite soon, because after eight o'clock the checkpoint will be closed from this side, and to avoid spending the night there we must return by midnight. You're sure you want to go?"

"Absolutely."

"How nice," she said. She lowered her voice. "Since you will come with me, I will tell you the little secret. Ulrich, who does not have a Bonn passport, wishes me to contact a friend of his on the other side, a student at Humboldt University. They are attempting to arrange some kind of conference on the French political philosophers of the nineteenth century. They are presently canvassing to see how many would like to attend such a conference, and then they will find a way to propose the meeting more or less officially. I am the courier, that is all. It is quite safe, I assure you."

"And how will you do the contacting?"

"You will see," she said. "Don't worry yourself about it. But, you must have gathered, from the way Ulrich talked at lunch, that he has at least a certain sympathy for the other side. He believes in a form of socialism, but what it is exactly I'm afraid I am too dense to understand. How do you react to Ulrich?"

"Favorably," I said.

"Does that mean you like him?"

"I think it does."

"He is a nice young man," she said, "but a hopeless idealist and a hopeless cynic all at the same time."

"Do you tell your father about these trips you make?"

Elizabeth shrugged. "It doesn't concern him, and what doesn't concern him I seldom tell him. He is a very busy man, as you know. Perhaps you even know more about him than I do."

I wondered, briefly, if the last was meant as an invitation to tell her what I knew, and she seemed to sense my thought, for she said, "Let us make a bargain between us that we don't talk any more about my father than is necessary."

"Only when we negotiate," I said.

"But you told me it was hopeless to negotiate!"

"You could decide to meet my conditions."

"We shall see," she said. "Perhaps I shall be able to persuade him."

"Him?"

"Yes, the man we are not to talk about. However, you may tell me as much as you like about yourself. For instance, why no children for a man of your age and station?"

"That would involve talking about Lottie," I said.

"I don't mind—if you wish to talk about her."

"No, I don't think I do. Not now, anyway."

"But certainly you realize she is a barrier between us. I am not sure I am all that broadminded, even though I am not prejudiced, necessarily, against a man who is married. It depends on the circumstances. I notice you did not want me to select anything for your wife while shopping."

"She has *her* prejudices, you see?"

"Yes, I see," Elizabeth said. "But don't you share them?" Her look was candidly questioning, and I hesitated.

"I don't see how you can lump all people together," I said carefully, "or any one group of people."

"Such as Germans?"

"Yes, or Jews."

"There are so many things I would like to talk about with you," she said. "I hope we will have the time."

"But if there is to be a barrier between us——"

"Oh, as friends, certainly not," she said with spirit.

"And only as friends?"

"But there is no other choice for us." She hesitated. "Isn't that so?"

"I think we've already crossed over the line," I said.

"Of what?"

"Friendship."

"Then we must retreat," she said.

"No kissing you?" I said.

"On the cheek, perhaps," she said judiciously. "As the French do. Friendly gestures are quite permissible."

"Thank you."

"Now shall we take our little trip to the land of the German communists?" she asked.

We took her car as far as a parking place opposite the Bahnhof am Zoo, the large station where the U Bahn lines converged along with the trains that went through the corridors. Elizabeth told me she preferred this egress to East Berlin because the formalities at the Friedrichstrasse Station—the one U Bahn stop as the train traversed East Berlin before re-entering the Western zones—were less time-consuming. The ride was brief, too, no more than ten minutes. Passport control held us up another fifteen minutes, and after the ceremony of changing our West German marks into East German marks was completed, we were free of the surveillance of the Vopos with their slung machine pistols.

Although I had visited East Berlin before, I was not altogether prepared for the seeming emptiness of what had once been the most teeming area of the old Berlin. Three taxis waited at a stand outside the Friedrichstrasse Station, all relatively ancient Russian cars.

"Where do we go?" I asked Elizabeth.

"To the club for artists."

"And what happens there?"

"We will meet a few people and talk for a little while."

We got into the taxi at the head of the stand and Elizabeth told the driver to take us to an address on Johannisstrasse, which turned out to be within a mile of the station. The building we stopped in front of was four stories high and unprepossessing from the outside. Inside, however, there were traces of shabby elegance—wood-paneled walls and a marble staircase that wound upward to the second floor, our destination. We had stopped on the ground floor for the inspection of a card that Elizabeth took from her handbag and gave to a woman seated at a table in the foyer.

"My credentials as an artist," Elizabeth explained to me as we took the stairs. "I am known here, you see."

The rooms on the floor above were furnished comfortably; one was a sitting room, another a reading room in which several of the club members read newspapers and magazines, and a third a lounge with several tables and a bar. Elizabeth led me to the bar, where we sat on imitation leather stools with chrome legs. A bartender asked us our wishes, and I ordered brandy for both of us at Elizabeth's suggestion. The bottle the bartender poured from identified the brandy as Czechoslovakian, and it had a pleasant fruity flavor.

Very soon we were joined at the bar by a couple Elizabeth introduced as Herr and Frau Beckmann. They were happy to see her again, they said, and happy to meet me. I was a friend of hers from New York, Elizabeth told them. I learned that Herr Beckmann worked as a state architect, and that Inge, his wife, was employed as a film editor by the state-controlled cinema studio in East Berlin. They were both civilized, polite, and free of overt propagandistic purpose, although they admitted this club was maintained principally for the Western contacts it provided. Was I a writer, a film director, an architect, a musician? Inge Beckmann asked me. None of those, I told her. Well, she said, if I had been, and my presence in West Berlin had been noticed, I might well have found an invitation to come here in my box at the hotel. "We are very interested in knowing people and exchanging views with them," she said. "The Wall has its purposes, of course, but we must find ways of maintaining contact with those who are colleagues in our professions." Her plump face was friendly.

"Fräulein Weisse is one of these colleagues, then?"

"Certainly," Inge Beckmann said. "She is always welcome here. Now tell me about what goes on in New York."

While I tried to give her some understanding of the atmosphere in New York, we were quietly joined by another, a tall young man with blond hair who was introduced to me as Klaus Wassman. He sat next to Elizabeth at the bar, and they were soon engaged in a murmured conversation. There was nothing very clandestine about their meeting, I realized; the bartender, if he were some kind of agent of the state, could easily have listened to what the two were saying.

We stayed at the bar for about an hour, after which there were formal handshakes all around, and I was invited by the Beckmanns to be a visitor at the club at any future time I happened to be in East Berlin. Herr Beckmann insisted that I take his card; it would be all I needed to gain entrance.

Outside, in the darkness of Johannisstrasse, I said: "They were certainly hospitable enough. Did you accomplish your mission?"

"Oh, yes. There was nothing unusual about it. The purpose of the club is more than social, I'm sure you realized. The evening is still a little young. Is there anything you would want to do while you're here?"

"Is there much to do?"

"There is a new state nightclub on the Karl Marx Allee I've heard about."

"Let's try it."

As we descended the stairs of Haus Warschau I heard the sound of a band. A headwaiter took our admission tickets and led us through three large rooms separated by grillwork panels to a table in a dim corner. Most of the other tables were occupied, and a few couples danced to a tune that struck me as several years out of date, although I couldn't recognize it. Little lamps on each table shed pools of light; otherwise no effort had been made to provide a decorative scheme.

When a young waitress, flushed and perspiring, handed us a bill of fare, I saw that the food and drink were inexpensive, well within the means of the ordinary worker.

"Does this convince you that you should be a communist?" Elizabeth asked.

"Not quite, but there's something to be said for it."

"I must tell you," she said, "that when I do a favor for Ulrich, it does not mean that I always agree with him completely."

"I didn't think so."

"He is not a communist, but he thinks it important that cultural contacts be maintained as much as possible. I rather agree with that. What are your views?"

"I'm a typical liberal capitalist," I said.

"Then you are prejudiced."

She had put me on the defensive, something I had not expected. "Not as much as you might think," I said. "I don't buy too much of this Cold War business. But I am repelled by the idea of anyone regimenting my thoughts and activities."

"And you like to move about, I see. So do I. But these people are Germans, too, and I can't help feeling some sympathy for them. When I am here, I can't help being aware of how much our lives are affected by decisions taken on the highest levels. That bothers me, but to be truthful, I don't know what to do about it."

"You can carry a message," I said.

"You make fun of me," she said, "but it would do no harm if all of us carried messages to other people."

The waitress came back to us, and we ordered brandy from her and also a plate of sausages, because we were both hungry.

"I believe," Elizabeth said, "that it could be included in our definition of friendship for you to ask me to dance. As I remember, you do dance."

"Would you dance with me?" I asked.

"I would be very pleased," Elizabeth said.

The song being played now by the eight-piece orchestra was a brassy version of "Prisoner of Love," and it carried me right back to my days in the Army. "The last time I danced to this music," I told Elizabeth, "was at an Officers' Club dance at Fort Meade, Maryland."

"And how long ago was that?" she asked, nestling her shiny dark head against my shoulder.

"More than twenty years ago."

"And who was the girl you danced with?"

"A girl from Baltimore who was stolen away from me by a lieutenant colonel."

"Were you sad about that?"

"No, because I immediately stole another girl away from a captain who was drunk."

"Did you know many girls before you were married?"

"No."

"Is that why you hold me so close now?"

"I can't help myself. Are you uncomfortable?"

"No, I am very comfortable," she said, "and it gives me a guilty conscience."

"The brandy has helped me with mine."

"Then you must be careful not to drink any more."

"All right," I said.

"And you must be careful not to flirt with me."

"I'm doing my best."

But there was no denying the sense of excitement I felt. It was inexcusable, but the attraction was there, given strangeness at this moment because I was so out of my element. The blare of the band was tinny, the young German couples who brushed against us as they made the most of this brief chance to escape from the bleakness of their daily lives were alien to me on more than one score, and yet I too was allowing myself to dream impossibly. From the sheer relaxation of her body against mine I knew that Elizabeth had also let down her guard. With a brassy flourish the music came to a halt, and we drew apart.

"Well, that was nice," she said.

We left the place soon after. Elizabeth had suggested we ask the head waiter to summon a taxi for us, and he agreed to do so readily and, just as readily, accepted the tip I gave him. We waited only a few minutes outside Haus Warschau until the taxi, with its white-checker identifying strip, pulled up at the curb. "Bahnhof Friedrichstrasse," I told the elderly driver, and he nodded.

As we traversed the length of the wide avenue I glimpsed the Hotel Berolina, the most imposing of the new hotels in East Berlin; the International, a cinema theater; and apartment houses with bright slabs of Meissen porcelain set into their façades.

"They are trying hard, you see," Elizabeth said. "They also

have their ideas of the Berlin of the future. This was the worst-bombed quarter of Berlin during the war, and there was nothing to do but build it over. So this grandeur has replaced old, ugly tenements."

"As some people say about New York, it's a nice place to visit, but I wouldn't want to live here."

"And the other side of the Wall?" she asked lightly.

"That would depend on my capacity to forget."

"Berliners are trained to forget," she said. "It is the only way for them."

"Were you here during the bombings?" I asked.

"Only close to the end. My mother had sent me away to live on a farm, near Ergau, south of Leipzig. It was very pleasant there. I was taught to ride a horse by the farmer's son, and I had enough food and a place to sleep. But then the war drew closer, and we heard the Russians were approaching. That was supposed to be something very bad. My mother came from Berlin—there were still trains running—and took me away with her. We got to the outskirts of Berlin, and we heard that Berlin would soon be under attack. Somehow my mother obtained a bicycle—I suppose she paid a large sum for it—and she pedaled us toward the west. I remember sleeping at night in dark cellars, and I could hear planes overhead and bombings in the distance. We were in a town called Wittstock when some dusty British tanks rolled in. They were followed by British soldiers, who gave us some cans of food. It was not so bad. I was not old enough to know that for Germans this was the last disaster. I remember, we had been in a cellar with a woman who was some kind of official, and when the soldiers came I saw her take a pin off her blouse and throw it into a sewer. It was her Nazi party pin, and that was the first time I realized that to be a Nazi was a bad thing. I asked my mother if my father, who was then in the south with an Army unit, would also throw away his badges, and she told me I was never to ask that again or to mention my father to anyone."

She paused, because we had reached the Bahnhof. I paid the driver, and we entered the station.

"You mentioned Ergau," I said. "I remember passing through Ergau in a jeep."

"Even if I had seen you," she said wryly, "I doubt that I would have been much impressed at that age. Are you trying to suggest that our destinies are intertwined?"

"Just slightly so."

"More than slightly," she said, impulsively taking my hand. "I like you very much."

I felt ridiculously pleased by her saying that.

Customs and passport control did not take us long at this hour—eleven o'clock—but it was a twenty-minute wait until our train came. Once inside the car, we were almost tangibly back in the atmosphere of West Berlin. We disembarked at the Bahnhof am Zoo, and walked to where the Porsche had been parked.

"It's still fairly early," I remarked. I wasn't anxious to leave her.

"There is always another day," she said. "How long will you stay in Berlin?"

"Not much longer. I've got to go on to Munich and Salzburg, but I'll be coming back when I finish up in those places."

"And how long after that will you stay?"

"I suppose it will depend on some answers provided by your father."

"I might be able to extend the negotiations," she said. "That is to say, if you would modify your position."

"You certainly tempt me," I told her. "But I must keep my personal feelings separate."

"Yes, of course," she said. "I was only joking. I will drive you to your hotel."

A few minutes later she stopped the car at the curb of the Kempinski.

"Well," she said, holding out her hand. "It has been very pleasant."

I put my hand on her shoulder, and she moved toward me. "You mustn't kiss me," she said, but I kissed her, hard and long.

When she drew away, she took a deep breath and asked, "Why do you do this?"

"I can't seem to help it," I said.

She gave me a long stare, as though absorbed in speculation about me. Then, suddenly, she turned the starter key. The roar of the motor seemed very loud. "Alfred, I am taking you to my place," she said with decision. "I don't want to leave you yet."

We made love that night, both of us hungry for it, and with no shame or embarrassment. She confessed that she had known it was going to happen while we were dancing at the Haus Warschau and that she had also known that she was going to have to be the one to make it possible because, as she put it, "You are not very good at seducing. I like you for that. If you feel that you must never see me again, now that it has happened, you must not hesitate to tell me so. But please let me know. Don't just disappear."

"I won't disappear," I said.

A tinge of light was in the eastern sky as I left her apartment house and walked back to the Kempinski. The perfume of her body was with me in my bed, and even as I slept I was somehow aware of her compliant loveliness, as though she haunted me still.

It was close to noon when I awoke, and of course, it was only to be expected that I would find a letter from Lottie when

I checked at the desk in the lobby. I was also handed a letter from Elihu, sent special delivery from New York.

I read Lottie's letter first, expecting that I would be subjected to an attack of conscience. But no such thing happened. It was as though Lottie and Elizabeth were completely separate in my existence, the one not having anything to do with the other. Unfortunately, that state of euphoric objectivity could not be expected to be other than temporary, I was well aware. Meanwhile, I felt confident that I would be able to handle things. Just keep everyone and everything in proper place and perspective, I told myself.

Lottie had mailed her letter from the Dan Hotel in Tel Aviv, and her mood, as far as I could judge, was good. The tour had carried her this far, some of her companions had turned out to be quite nice, the weather was close to ideal. But the best thing of all was that she had looked up a few of her old friends from the camp at Sodesheim who were now long settled in Israel, and she had been greeted like a long-lost sister. "I broke down and cried," she wrote. "I couldn't help myself. They are urging me to break away from the tour, so I can visit with them a little longer, and I may do this. Could you not meet me here? I am sure these old friends will welcome you, too, for they remember you from our wedding."

That got to me. I felt the first twinge.

The remainder of the letter was more typically Lottie. The stomach trouble that had bothered her for the first few days of her trip—had she mentioned it in her previous letter?—had improved, and she supposed it had been caused by the change of food and water from what she had been accustomed to. "Of course, you with your suspicions will think it was psychosomatic, but I am happy to assure you this is not so. I saw a doctor in

Haifa who told me the symptoms were clearly gastrointestinal.
He gave me medicines, and soon the upset went away. So you
see? This warm, dry climate has given me more energy than I
have had in years. It is strange how it agrees with me so well.
I hope your work goes speedily and that you may find the time
to come here."

Another twinge. I knew if I found free time I would want
to devote it to Elizabeth. Still and all, I came away from that
letter relatively unscathed.

The envelope from Elihu contained material, however, that
was more disturbing to my peace of mind, for, in addition to
Elihu's brief note there was a summary on Oskar Weisse prepared by Leo. Although it contained little that was new, I was
nevertheless reminded that it was part of my purpose here to
uncover as many details about Weisse as possible. Leo's thorough search through the relevant Nuremberg documents had
turned up not a single reference to him, and only one to the firm
of Zeller-Bricken. That last had to do with what we already
knew, that Z-B was listed among those German firms having
employed slave labor during the Second World War. "No record of prosecution," Leo reported. That much we also knew.
Leo had next gone to see Arthur Goldstein at the YIVO Institute, and Goldstein, coincidentally, had just happened to have
received a new and fuller listing from the Yad Vashem archives
in Jerusalem of RHSA personnel, Amt II B. "This was a sub-
bureau," Leo explained unnecessarily, "in the Office for Administrative and Economic Questions." Here Weisse's name did
turn up as O. Weisse, Hauptman. "This new set of records,"
Leo wrote, "has one other mention of a Weisse, no first name,
but also with the rank of Hauptman. This Weisse is listed on
the staff of Amt VI C, but Goldstein has no way of knowing if
the two are the same, and regards it as unlikely that Weisse

would have belonged to more than one bureau. Sloppily, Leo had neglected to tell me just what Amt VI C stood for, and I wasn't sure myself. I had not prowled around sufficiently among the intricate byways of Himmler's Berlin headquarters.

But it had to be checked out, and I wasted no time in calling Liz at the Documents Center. "What did Amt VI C have to do with?" I asked her.

"Espionage," she told me promptly. "It's a little tricky, that office, because it was not Gestapo, and it operated separately from the Abwehr—Army intelligence. Prior to the invasion of the Soviet Union, the office operated in zones of Russian influence; afterward, it branched off into the Arab countries."

"You're terrific," I complimented her.

"May I ask why you ask?"

"Well, we've come across a Weisse in that bureau, except it hardly figures. It's never been suggested that he was an intelligence agent."

"Could be another Weisse," she said.

"Do your SS records show any other Weisse?"

"Not to my knowledge," Liz answered, "but I can check again. But why would that change anything, if there were two Weisses or just one Weisse? He could have been switched around, couldn't he?"

"It would change things," I said, "if our Weisse had been in the Amt VI C office *prior* to his Zeller-Bricken connection. His whole story would go up in blue smoke, don't you see? He'd be of the hard-core garden variety of SS Nazi, and his firm wouldn't have a leg to stand on where he's concerned. Do you think you might be able to check that Amt VI C Weisse out a little further."

"I can try," Liz said, "but I'm afraid it's all getting a little too complicated for my simple mind."

"If we can find the truth," I said, "you'll be amazed how simple it can all be."

"All right," she said, "I'll take your word for it. What about that pretty daughter of his? Did she take you shopping?"

"Yes," I said carefully.

"And did she find you beautiful things?"

"Very nice," I said.

"Did you find out why she was so agreeable?"

"Far as I can tell," I said, "she was merely being hospitable."

"Are you sure she's German?" Liz asked.

"Now, now," I told her. "You must avoid these national stereotypes."

"I can see she's already softened you up," she said tartly. "If her father does turn out to have been a spy you'd better watch out."

Another uncomfortable thought. But the barriers had come down between Elizabeth and me, and a lot more is revealed in a soft bed than the naked flesh. Elizabeth was, above all, honest. I felt it; I knew it.

In fact, it was the other way around. Was I?

Like a persistent reminder of my obligations, a call came from Max Gerson.

"When do you leave Berlin?" he asked. "Today or tomorrow?"

"What makes you think I'm leaving today or tomorrow?"

"I assumed so, especially since Frau Lietschnitzer is expecting you to visit her. I have had a further note from her containing her telephone number. She wishes you to call when you arrive in Salzburg, and she will give you exact directions from there. Will you take down the number?"

I jotted it down.

"You will be back in Berlin after you finish your trip?"

"I expect so."

"If Frau Lietschnitzer cannot direct you to the menorah, I will have some further leads for you."

"What?" I nearly shouted the word at him.

"These are only distant possibilities," he said soothingly. "We would only follow them up if the Salzburg direction proves inaccurate."

"Shouldn't I know about them first?"

"It would only complicate your search," he said. "One thing at a time."

"I can't spend my whole life at this," I reminded him.

"I understand, Herr Becker. But searching for precious objects of the type of the menorah takes time and patience. Your American methods of hurry and efficiency are not always effective for this."

"Herr Gerson," I said, "blessings upon you. I will get in touch with you when I'm back."

There was a flaw in his logic, I decided: I was to hurry and see Frau Lietschnitzer in the hope of finding the menorah, but I was also to have patience in pursuing the same end.

But I did get busy after his call, and made arrangements for my departure. I decided I'd leave the next day, head for Stuttgart first, which was the closest large city to Ludwigsburg, and from there go to Munich, because I had the nagging feeling I ought to check out the Christianne I had talked to on the telephone. After all, I had that address, and I didn't have the address of the other woman. While in my efficient mood, I also put in a call to Herr Langsehn in Ludwigsburg and made an appointment to see him the following afternoon. Then I went to a travel agency and made some fairly precise arrangements, including reserving the car I would rent in Munich, because the drive from there to Salzburg and Vienna was a scenic one, and on autobahns almost all the way. I booked my hotels, too.

Very good. Now I could write Elihu and tell him that I was proceeding as I had indicated to him when I had called him. Leo's work had been fine, I also wrote, and might turn out to be significant, depending on what I learned at Ludwigsburg. I communicated to him, too, the fact that Weisse had raised the ante through an intermediary, but that I had refused to bargain. That was all. I couldn't mention anything about Elizabeth. I felt badly about that, because Elihu was someone in whom I would ordinarily confide. But not this. Elizabeth was strictly private.

I still had some unfinished business in Berlin, the gift for Hilde. Everything, it seemed, was conspiring to keep my thoughts focused on Elizabeth. Hardly more than forty-eight hours ago we had gone to that little shop together. It seemed incredible, but when we had picked out the watch for Hilde we had not yet made love. I debated whether to have the watch sent to Hilde or present it in person. That depended, certainly, on whether I would have dinner with Elizabeth. I hadn't said I would call her that same day, but I did.

"Oh," she said, with what sounded like genuine sorrow, "but I have arranged to have dinner with friends of my mother this evening. I have seen so little of her lately, and there is this little dinner she expressly had me invited to."

"It was just an impulse," I apologized.

"Tomorrow evening instead?"

"Tomorrow I leave," I told her. "The arrangements have all been made."

"How terrible," she moaned. "How terrible. You will call me before you go?"

"Yes," I said, "when I wake up in the morning. Unless it would be too early——"

"No, no, call. Be sure to call. Have you missed me?"

"It's only five hours since I saw you."

"But I have already missed you so much," she said, "that I ache. I literally ache."

"So do I," I said.

"I kiss you," she told me.

Well, then, I thought, I would have a farewell dinner with Hilde, if she would see me. She was in when I called and, before I could tell her I wanted to invite her to have dinner with me, she made a hasty apology for her abruptness that evening at Kranzler's. I pretended that nothing had happened and explained that I would be leaving Berlin the next day and wanted to see her before I went. "Not a Last Supper, I hope," she said, making what was not a very good joke.

"No, I expect to be back in Berlin."

I suggested a very good and small restaurant called the Ritz. She was pleased and said she would meet me there at eight. The headwaiter, whom I had called beforehand, had prepared us a table with tall candles and a bowl of flowers. After he had opened a bottle of wine for us and I had tasted and approved it, I presented Hilde with the gift. She was almost shy about accepting the small box but exclaimed with delight when she saw what was inside. "I will wear it always," she said, "and think of you." She made another bad joke about how in the old days it would have come from the PX. The dinner, after that, seemed interminable. There was less than ever for us to say to each other. The old relationship had lost its hold. As if she too knew this, she turned the desultory talk to Annemarie. "She told me she saw you at the Alabama Saloon." Hilde hesitated and then brought out what must have been on her mind throughout the dinner. "I don't like her to go to that place," she said. "It's not a good place for her."

"Why?"

"I am ashamed to say it, but she meets men there. Alfred, that is why I wanted you to help her find work in New York. It is too easy for her here, and not good for her. Do you know what I mean?"

"I suppose I can guess. Does she take money?"

Hilde nodded, looking miserable. "I didn't want to tell you, but I must."

"I told you I'd help her."

"You will still do it, now that you know about her?"

"No reason not to."

She sighed in relief. "Oh, that is good of you. I was afraid you would be—how should I say it?—very moral?"

"Don't worry about it. I'll find her a job in a nice place."

And that was why she had really written me, I thought. She had feared her sister was turning into a whore. I was more depressed than ever. That was a fine thing for me to be doing, I thought, giving references for a German girl who hung around bars and picked up men. Well, I would go through with it and hope for the best.

I must have looked a little doubtful, for Hilde asked, "What are you thinking?"

"Oh, just how capable any individual is for judging another person."

"You have been in Germany for only a short time, and already you sound like a German," Hilde said.

I resented the remark, but I didn't say so.

13:   The next morning I telephoned Elizabeth on awakening. Though her voice was sleepy, she was alert enough to ask exactly when I would be returning to Berlin. I told her a week at the latest. "And it could be sooner," I added.

"And where do you go first?"

I decided to lie. I said I would be flying directly to Munich.

"You will call me from there?"

I promised I would and felt like a betrayer. But I could not tell her that I would be in Ludwigsburg—not yet. Certainly I would tell her one day. I lied again through omission rather than commission when I scribbled a hasty note to Lottie before leaving for Tempelhof, addressing it to the King David Hotel in Jerusalem (her next stop according to her tour schedule). It contained the usual trivialities, although I had been strongly tempted to break through my trepidation and dishonesty. "But I can't hurt her that much," I thought. More, the act of telling her was tantamount to casting her adrift—and myself. Perhaps it was that latter possibility I feared the most. My image of myself, my total identity, was involved. Naturally, I thought, I must lie, or at least avoid the truth. When I checked out of the Kempinski, I handed the letter to the desk clerk and asked him to mail it for me.

By noon, I was in Stuttgart. Herr Langsehn had promised me I would be met at the air terminal, and, sure enough, a tall young German was stationed at the exit gate, facing the emerging passengers, with a card that read "Herr Becker."

"I am to take you to Ludwigsburg," he announced to me formally, after I told him I was the one he was looking for. I checked my bags first and took the time to reconfirm my reservation on the five o'clock flight for Munich. It seemed terribly important that I be there in time to make an evening call to Elizabeth.

My driver turned out to be a law student who was spending six months at the Ludwigsburg Zentralstelle training in investigative procedures. His English was so halting, and he turned to me so often as he drove the small Opel through the hillside vineyards on the outskirts of Stuttgart, that I suggested we speak in German instead. I wanted him to keep his eyes on the road, which was crowded with traffic. Stuttgart, during its frantic rebuilding and its rise as an industrial center, had not yet managed to solve its road-traffic dilemmas.

"I have studied English for six years," he told me, his tone slightly hurt. "Is it not so good?"

"It's fine," I said, "and it will be better with more practice." I asked him his name, which turned out to be Hermann Mueller. He was fair-haired, blue-eyed, and had a querulous manner that came from some unexpressed dissatisfaction within himself. Or perhaps it was only that I was an American who spoke German somewhat better than he spoke English.

"You were born in Germany?" he asked.

"No. My father's family was German, and I spent time here after the war and picked it up. I mean," I added, "my father's family was German-Jewish."

He registered that remark without comment, but I knew that in his mind it meant that I was Jewish, and not German-Jewish, by descent. On the other hand, I did not regard myself as German-Jewish either.

"Why do you visit the Zentralstelle?" he asked me, but with doubt in his voice that he should have asked the question at all.

"Just to have a talk with Herr Langsehn on a private matter," I said.

"I could guess," he said more boldly.

"But it wouldn't be a good idea."

"I understand," he assured me.

We spent the remaining time during the fifteen-mile trip discussing the relative merits of American and German automobiles, a subject in which he appeared to be vastly interested. Ludwigsburg was north of Stuttgart and was on the tourist route mainly because of its prize attraction, the Ludwigsburger Schloss, a huge baroque palace, and because it was near Marbach, where Schiller had been born. Like many towns that had been bombed and reconstructed, its streets were wide and planted with young trees. The Lankestrasse, on which the Zentralstelle was located, was in a residential section. Hardly a likely location for a prison, for that was what Number 28 Lankestrasse turned out to be. An ordinary door in a high, gray concrete wall led to an interior and another far heavier door with a small grill opening in it. Mueller explained to the guard through this gate that I had official business with Herr Langsehn, and after examining a list on which my name appeared, he let me inside. Mueller shook hands with me and left. Another guard took me through a long corridor to the office of Herr Langsehn, explaining that the left side of the building was administrative, while the right wing was given over entirely to prison quarters. "Who is kept here?" I asked.

"War criminals," he said succinctly. Killers of Jews, in other words.

I knew that some had been here for years, waiting for trial while the cases against them were being completed. I also knew that if the Zentralstelle ever moved against Weisse, he could be interned here if it were thought necessary, and Elizabeth, too, would be visiting Ludwigsburg.

The door we stopped at had a wooden plaque that identified this as the office of Assistant States Attorney Bertel Langsehn, of the Central Office, State Judicial Authorities. Quite discreet, really. Anyone not well initiated in the terminology of West German bureaucracy would not have been aware that the plaque identified Langsehn as a member of the administrative headquarters expressly set up in 1958 by Bonn to focus its efforts to extirpate the murderous Nazi past. Little publicity ever came to Ludwigsburg, except when East Germany would broadcast an embarrassing announcement to the effect that an official in the Zentralstelle had his own Nazi past, for which, so it was claimed, he should be accountable. Yet I knew the office was doing a job; there would have been no Auschwitz trial at Frankfurt otherwise.

The guard opened the door for me and then left me to a middle-aged secretary who rose from her desk quickly, asked me to wait, *bitte,* for only a moment, and went through a double door to the larger office occupied by Langsehn himself. Then, with a smile similar to that of a nurse ushering in a patient to see a doctor, she indicated that I should enter. Langsehn, a portly little man of about forty, with pink cheeks and pale round eyes, was standing behind his desk, delicately holding a cigarette. "I am honored, Herr Becker," he said, "that you pay us a visit." He stuck out a chubby hand, and I shook it. "You speak German, of course?"

"Well enough, I hope."

"Come sit over here." He led me to the one other large object of furniture in the room besides his desk, a square oak table around which were three straight-backed oak chairs. From one of the two narrow windows I looked out on Lankestrasse, where I could see, still parked near a slender tree, the Opel that had brought me here.

"You see," he said, as though it was necessary to explain, "we did not at first know precisely who you were. My apologies. Because, you see, I had already heard of you from Justice Kimmel, with whom I am acquainted."

"I should make the judge my publicity agent," I said.

"Ah, yes, I see. Yes, he speaks of you kindly. We maintain a friendly liaison. Those who claim restitution can sometimes be of service to us. But you certainly know what we do here?"

"I have a general idea."

"Here is a little something that will make it more clear." He handed me a pamphlet that outlined, I saw, the functions of the Central Office. "And while you read I will see that you are provided with—coffee? Tea?"

"Coffee, if you don't mind."

He gave two claps of his hands, and the secretary came in. Would I take cream and sugar? she wanted to know. By the time I had finished reading most of what was in the pamphlet, she was back with a tray on which was chinaware of heavy white porcelain, a white porcelain coffeepot, and some crisp thin cakes. Some of the words of the pamphlet stayed with me:

. . . the Ludwigsburg Center has pieced together no fewer than five hundred and forty complexes, each encompassing one or more participants who are known by name, and with a criminal dossier prepared in the case of everyone. Certainly the German courts will have to deal with many of these in the years to come. . . . A Complex can be considered as having to do with one instance, one of those many places of horror where human beings were tortured and killed, and also the organizations set up to commit such mass murder. . . .

"So, you see," Langsehn said, pouring a stream of rich black coffee into my cup, "we do a lot of work here. You might say that the trials at Frankfurt are some of our handiwork. You, as a lawyer yourself, can understand the difficulties in preparing such a complicated case. We had those fellows right here, in our own prison wing, and I may say to you with confidence that we expect most of them back. You take how many lumps of sugar?"

"Two," I said.

Delicately handling the sugar tongs he plunked two lumps into my cup.

"Cream?"

"Please."

He poured the cream, then took the chair opposite me, leaning his elbows on the table so as to let me know we were to be informal, if not downright casual. "I am sure you are aware, Herr Becker, that your interest in Oskar Weisse interests us here. We had already been in touch with Justice Kimmel about the matter of the survivors of the Zeller-Bricken camp—we will be polite and call it a labor camp—on the chance that the name of this Oskar Weisse would already have turned up among his papers."

"Also," I said, taking a guess, "he might have been able to

make some inquiries among American officials in Berlin as to Weisse's, let us say, political health."

"Excellent, Herr Becker," Langsehn said, nodding almost happily. "We understand one another."

"And I hope you also understand," I said, "that I don't make it my personal business to be an avenger."

"But on the other hand," he said, his round eyes measuring me soberly, "you would certainly like to see justice done when criminality is indicated."

"No reservations about that," I said. "Now, if you'll tell me why you've asked me here——"

"In the hope you will tell us what you know."

"Certainly, I'll tell you what our case is based on," I said.

"Please do."

As clearly as I could, I explained to Langsehn, who nodded his head with each point I made, that my own concern was not necessarily with bringing to justice either Roehling or Weisse, even assuming criminal behavior on their part, but rather with proving a continuing connection between past and present management at Zeller-Bricken. Having proved that much, we could then go on to claim liability on the part of the company. "Weisse enters into this particularly," I said, "because of the existence of records that show his membership in the SS and his previous connection with the company. Naturally, the more we know about his involvement in the transport of Jewish labor and the administrative arrangement for this labor, and also about the involvement of other Zeller-Bricken managerial personnel in these and similar activities, the stronger our case becomes. This is not a court matter, as you can see. The weapon we do have is publicity."

"And this I have asked you not to use," Langsehn said, with an apologetic smile. "May I ask what your records are?"

"What is available at the Document Center in Berlin, plus some odds and ends, as, for instance, a memorandum that presumably came from the Yad Vashem in Jerusalem."

"Not a record of a conversation with Herr Weisse himself?"

"Is that what you're after?"

"It could help."

I shook my head. "Suppose, then, you tell me what *you* have."

"I have your word that this is to be kept in strictest confidence?"

"If you insist."

"I fear I must, for the moment."

Good, I thought, for then I cannot possibly tell Elizabeth.

Langsehn clapped his hands again, and in came the secretary, this time carrying a file envelope plainly marked, in black letters, WEISSE.

"Does she read your mind?" I asked.

"Let us put it another way—we have the same mind."

He brought out several papers from the envelope and placed them in a neat pile before him on the table. Most of the documents, I saw, were facsimiles.

"Now," said Langsehn. "Here we have the name of O. Weisse on this large and inclusive list of administrative personnel at the RHSA headquarters in Berlin. I assume this is not news to you?"

"No."

"But you will also note his name, with rank, on this list— a fairly complete one—of the Economics and Administration Office of the Supreme Headquarters, SS, referred to in the American procedure at Nuremberg as B II 1."

"I happen to have that bit of information too," I said.

He looked surprised.

"YIVO in New York," I added.

"Yes," he said, dryly, "their thoroughness is well known to me. There is a saying of mine well known to my secretary: If Alexandria won't provide it, ask YIVO. To go on—I assume you are not interested in such papers as birth certificate, educational record, first date of party membership, birth certificate of wife, birth certificate of daughter————"

"Is that Elizabeth Weisse?" I asked.

"Yes, why?"

"I've met her."

"She is of no interest to us, nor the wife. Family testimony would automatically be ruled out. We checked both, as a matter of course, and our guess is they know less about Weisse than we do."

I took a deep breath, cautiously.

"To go on—his record of racial purity, membership card in the SS, record of employment and positions held with Zeller-Bricken, and, a more interesting little item, this indication of service during the period April, 1940, to June, 1941, with Amt VI C, SS—but no indication of official rank or position."

"Are you sure it's the same Weisse?"

"See for yourself."

I saw that what he handed me was a paymaster's receipt, with Weisse's office and section stamped on it. Oskar Weisse, no rank or serial number, had received and signed for the sum of four hundred seventy marks for a period of four weeks' employment during June and July, 1940.

"But he was employed by Zeller-Bricken during that period," I said.

"Admitted, certainly," Lengsehn said. "So now we put one and one together. Amt VI C, SS, was an intelligence apparatus. Weisse was an agent for this particular apparatus, while ostensibly an employee of Zeller-Bricken. We may assume he traveled for Z-B through the Eastern European countries on business, while also picking up information. Most necessary, wouldn't you say, in view of the approaching attack on the Soviet Union?"

"But that doesn't make him a criminal," I said. "Not anymore."

"Other than the SS connection, and there could be an element of perjury as well. But an interesting fellow this Weisse, don't you think?"

"Extremely. But I still don't see what you've got on him."

"Not this letter, for instance?"

He handed me a photocopy of a letter written on Zeller-Bricken stationary, and addressed to Oskar Weisse, Hauptmann, SS, RHSA, Berlin. The writer wished to acknowledge the usefulness of Hauptmann Weisse's suggestion to the firm of Zeller-Bricken. He agreed that three thousand workers would be of great value in these critical times, assuming that the SS would take the responsibility of providing quarters, and that it was agreeable to him, furthermore, that these workers be Jews in good health and capable of heavy work. The letter had been signed by Willi Roehling, Hanover Plant Manager, just below the typed *Heil Hitler!* A file clerk had dutifully recorded the date of receipt of the letter and the date of filing: January 7, 1943.

"Do you have the original of this?" I asked.

"The original is in the possession of the Berlin investigative team, which works separately from this office."

"Nevertheless, if the statute of limitations is approved in the Bundestag, you wouldn't have a case. You're going to be confined pretty much to cases of murder. Furnishing Jewish slaves to a business firm isn't automatically construed as———"

"It is just that point that interests me," Langsehn said, interrupting. "Now we have here this memorandum from Weisse to Roehling. Suppose you read it for yourself."

The memorandum was dated January 18, 1943: "In reply to your question as to the sum required for the labor services of Jewish concentration-camp inmates, I must stress the reasonableness of the Administration Section's request in this matter. It is based on precise statistical information. Previous experience has proven that you may expect an average life expectancy, assuming good health, of nine months. Wages have been fixed, for Zeller-Bricken, at an average of seven marks per week, which I can assure you, is a good figure. For this we provide transportation and an original issue of clothing. We allow you a deduction of .7 mark per week per laborer for food and clothing purchased by you. Any burial costs will be assumed by this office. I hope this clears up the matter satisfactorily for you. *Heil Hitler!*" The memorandum bore the initials O. W. in ink and the typed names of Roehling and Weisse.

"But this isn't an original document either," I said.

"A member of the investigative team found it among the files examined at the Cologne archives. These files have now been catalogued, and if necessary we can obtain the original document."

"Does this prove murder? I couldn't get a conviction on it."

"We would have to forge another link or two."

"Such as?"

"Awareness on the part of Weisse of a certain order sent to the Economics and Administration Office of the SS in September of 1942."

"Concerning," I said, " 'The Delivery of A-Social Elements to the Reichsführer SS to Be Worked to Death.' "

"Exactly quoted," Langsehn said, nodding. "As you see,

there was no mincing of words. The conference during which this order was drafted, you undoubtedly know, took place on September 14, 1942, at Himmler's field command post at Zhito-mir. Present were such fine people as Thierack, Rothenberger, Streckenbach, a certain Lieutenant Colonel Bender of the Judge Advocate's Office—to give the order the stamp of legality, nat-urally—and two other unnamed witnesses to the proceedings. This office has reason to believe that Weisse was present at the Zhitomir conference."

"If you can prove that, you have your case," I said. "Prior knowledge."

"It is our understanding," said Langsehn, "that a document with the full names of those present at the Zhitomir conference is in your files in Alexandria. Neither Berlin nor this office has been able to obtain the release of the document or a facsimile from Alexandria. 'Not locatable,' is the word we get. Frankly, I had hoped that you would have knowledge of the document or access to it."

"How did you learn of it yourself?"

"The information came out of thin air—an anonymous let-ter addressed to this office. The writer claims that he was on a document-collecting team working for your own Occupation forces in 1947, that he had come across this list in a secret memorandum, and that because of its importance he had com-mitted it to memory."

"There was one other unnamed person present."

"Yes, the chap died recently, a minor official in the Bonn Ministry of Defense. From his service records we were able to ascertain that he could easily have been at Zhitomir at that time. Now you understand our interest in Weisse. To put it bluntly, can you help us?"

"You're only interested in Weisse—why not Roehling?"

"No prior knowledge," Langsehn said. "Nothing provable in any case. Like all the others, he will claim innocence of any intention to eliminate the workers. He would be believed—the usual thing, a cog in the wheel, orders from above—— The statute of limitations protects him against a less major charge. But with Weisse—the SS connection, and the list, if we can get it——"

"Not really my kind of work," I said. "I'd have to think about it."

"But we are giving you here the absolute proof that you need for your own case."

"But you said I'm not to make use of it."

"If you were to judiciously mention a few facts to someone at Zeller-Bricken, I might not object."

"And you'd alarm your quarry."

"He is certainly alarmed enough already," Langsehn said.

"May I think about it?" I asked. "I'll tell you this, frankly—I don't like the idea of spying around for you."

"One little list," said Langsehn. "Or, since you know Weisse, an admission from him that he was present at Zhitomir. He, of course, would not have to know that we have forged a few other links in the chain."

"And then I'd have to testify, wouldn't I?"

"Would you find that an imposition?"

"It depends," I said, "on how it adds up in my mind."

"Herr Becker," Langsehn said. "You are certainly aware of how many of those Jewish slaves perished at the camp provided by the SS for their quarters at the Z-B plant in Hanover."

"Nearly eighteen hundred," I said.

"And how many were transported to Buchenwald and Dachau between December of 1944 and the end of the war."

"The remainder."

"And how many have survived."

"There are seventy-one presently alive," I said, "if our search is correct, of which I represent sixty."

"I would think, then, that you would not mind doing this little thing for us."

"I said I would think about it."

"Good. Now, suppose I take you on a little tour of our own files and archives before you leave. You will see true German bureaucracy and efficiency, I assure you."

I looked at my watch. There was still an hour and a half remaining before I had to be at the airport. Langsehn assured me that a driver would be provided me at any time I wanted one. "You stay in Stuttgart?" he asked.

"No, I'm due in Munich this evening."

"And how long will you remain in Germany?"

"A week or two, I'd imagine."

"Good, we may have the opportunity for another talk before you leave." He led me through gray, antiseptic-smelling corridors to show me his files. They were indeed efficiently catalogued. "You know of the debate going on at the Bundestag," Langsehn said, "about the extension of the statute of limitations on Nazi crimes. If there is no extension, much of this labor will have been wasted."

"There's no statute of limitations on murder," I said.

"No," Langsehn said, and he gave me a catlike smile.

14: The Lufthansa Caravelle seemed to arch its back as i climbed steeply on its course toward Munich. From my windov seat I looked at the wooded Swabian highlands receding as th declining sun cast long, forbidding shadows. Something gnawe at the back of my mind. The passenger in the seat ahea handed me the pilot's courtesy route map, with our flight pat marked, our altitude and flying time noted. The air corridor through East Germany were marked too, and although we wer now flying over West German territory only it occurred to m that the Berlin-Frankfurt corridor I had traveled earlier in th day had taken me almost directly over the town of Orhdru. On an April day, just about twenty years ago, I had travele in a jeep and had seen the sign: *Nach Orhdruf.*

Bony fingers had clutched at the blood-spattered earth c the compound. Machine-gun bullets had ripped into thos emaciated, starved, work-weakened Jews. Twenty years. I ha done something, perhaps not very much, but something. Ac complishment hadn't been the purpose—just not forgettin

I'd had enough doubts about the worth of it all as time had flowed on and by. I still had them. The dead couldn't be brought back, and there was a limit to the help that could be given the living. But I'd tried. I had not been entirely unfaithful. To Lottie, yes, but not to the identity I had claimed on that April day.

Langsehn had been clever. He wanted me on his side, and he had known how to go about getting me there. He had drawn the kind of legalistic, circumstantial case beloved of lawyers, and in doing so he had changed the nature of my own case. Zeller-Bricken could now be accused of much more than harboring two former Nazis. The charges had become far more grave. For, if Langsehn managed to build and prove *his* case, Roehling and Weisse were involved in a far more serious category, that of "crimes with the result of death." So, Langsehn had offered me a deal: the use of those far graver charges in return for a certain amount of collaboration.

He had assumed that while preparing the case on behalf of the Zeller-Bricken slaves I had gone through the available and pertinent material. I had. But I had overlooked the conference at Zhitomir, having seen no connection. It simply hadn't occurred to me that either Weisse or Roehling was in any way associated with the top hierarchy.

For the Zhitomir conference had involved only the top. I had enough knowledge of the history of the time to know that the original "extermination by work" concept had originated in the busy mind of Goebbels. In mid-September of 1942, as I remembered it, Goebbels had conferred in Berlin with Justice Minister Thierack and suggested that the until-then haphazard use of "Jewish and other antisocial elements of the population" could be streamlined into a policy beneficial to the Third Reich. Thierack had then gone to Martin Bormann for Hitler's approval. Granted. A few days later Thierack had flown to

Himmler's field command post at Zhitomir. The "action squad rons" by then had shot around a million Jews, and speedier means of extermination were already being employed at six major killing centers. During a five-and-a-half-hour conference Himmler had been made to see the value of the "extermination by work" concept. Not only would the limited use of semi skilled and skilled Jewish labor aid the German war effort, but payments for their services could help swell the coffers of Su preme SS Headquarters, never averse to bureaucratic enrichment

Agreement was reached, an order prepared. And—if Lang sehn's supposition was correct—if Weisse had indeed been present at the conference he would have instantly seen the use fulness of the order to the firm with which he was associated Zeller-Bricken, and thus his alibi now could fly out the window of his limousine for all it was worth. I remembered how plaus ible they had all been when I questioned them during my period with the Occupation forces. "Don't blame me. Blame Hitler." These days they were going further. "Yes, we admit those ter rible exterminations. Others did them, of course. Not us. But look at what was done to the innocents of Dresden. The great est fire bombing of history. The English pilots, too, took or ders." Always overlooked, when these arguments were made was the fact that Germany was mobilized on a total war foot ing. Everyone worked for the war effort, including the innocent of Dresden, a long-decayed cultural center, but also a railway center, and a place with plenty of factories. Besides, they had brought the whirlwind on themselves.

Now what about the top brass at Zeller-Bricken? I could assume that they knew something about Weisse and Roehling But I could also assume that they knew about that legislation pending in the Bundestag that could place a statute of limita tions on war crimes. Besides, Weisse had long ago been cleared by American Occupation authorities. Obviously, the firm felt its position to be safe. Furthermore, the American Department of Defense had tacitly admitted the firm's lack of former Nazi connections by entering into negotiations. Why, then, should I be a trouble maker? Because I had once seen bony fingers clutching at red-stained earth. Because I had also seen the emaciated body of a dead Jew whose name had turned out to be Hirsh Feldstein, and whose bone-thin arm had borne a tattooed number: B41387.

It was close to seven by the time I checked into the Bayerischer Hof in Munich. There had been enough light left for me to recognize the twin towers and cupolas of the Frauenkirche, but much had happened to the Promenadeplatz since I had last been in the city. Munich had grown solidly handsome and in many ways was now a far more agreeable city than Berlin. Here there was no Wall to remind one of fearsome possibilities. Everything thrived, and no hotel lobby anywhere was larger and more cosmopolitan than the lobby of the Bayerischer Hof. I told a man at the inquiry desk that I was expecting a rented car to be delivered to me in the morning, and in a matter of a minute or two he had arranged for it to be placed in the hotel's garage to await my pleasure.

The room I was escorted to was twice the size of the one I'd had at the Kempinski in Berlin. The telephone on the mahogany shelf at the bedside immediately beckoned me.

A few minutes later Elizabeth's voice came through the receiver.

"It's Alfred," I said. "I'm at the Bayerischer Hof in Munich."

"I have been sitting and sitting by this telephone," she said. "I have been forced to talk with people I do not want to talk with—all for the privilege of hearing your masculine voice."

"I've been pretty busy," I said evasively.

"And what have you been doing with yourself?"

"I've had to look up someone. It took time."

"You sound funny, Alfred," Elizabeth said.

"What do you mean?"

"Usually you are more direct. You tell me what is in your head. But now I have the feeling you are hiding something. Have you met another woman already?"

"No." My laugh sounded uncomfortable, even to me.

"There is something wrong, Alfred. What is it?"

"Nothing," I said. "I've only been missing you."

"Do I make you nervous?"

"No."

"But you sound nervous. Perhaps you don't want me to come to Munich."

"What did you say?"

"I said, perhaps you don't want me to come to Munich."

"You'd come?"

"Yes, if I were sure you wanted to see me."

"Yes, I'm sure."

"You see, I have suddenly decided it is absolutely necessary for me to see the new fashion collections in Munich. Do you think there is room for me at the Bayerischer Hof?"

"I wasn't planning to stay beyond tomorrow."

"Then you don't want me to come?"

"Yes," I said, "come. Hurry. When will you be here?"

"I can get a plane from Tempelhof in the morning. It will stop at Frankfurt. I take another plane for Munich. Three hours in all. So, I could be at the Munich airport by ten o'clock. The flight number is Lufthansa 412."

"I'll be waiting for you," I said.

"At the airport?"

"Yes."

"Do you still love me, Alfred?"

"Yes."

"I will see you in the morning. Good-by, Alfred. And you will tell me why you sound so funny."

"All right."

"Then there is something?"

"We'll talk tomorrow," I said.

After I put back the receiver I thought: It will be settled somehow tomorrow. *It will end, or it will change.* But something was going to have to happen.

That evening I wrote Elihu a letter. I ordered dinner to be served in my room, and, after it was brought, I used hotel stationery. One way to assure that personal considerations will not affect business dealings is to close off the possibility. Therefore I laid the whole Weisse matter out for Elihu, knowing that he could always act independently of me.

"Dear Elihu: I write this from Munich, after a visit to Ludwigsburg earlier in the day. The trip was worthwhile as it turned out, since further revelations have resulted. . . ." I outlined the gist of my talk with Herr Langsehn. "My guess is," I went on, "that the list referred to by Langsehn exists somewhere, for otherwise we would not have known that those more important persons had attended. On the negative side, however, is the fact that Weisse has obviously felt himself to be safe from such an incriminating circumstance. You, as well as I, know that in many bureaus of the Supreme SS Headquarters in Berlin, at the time of the German collapse, files and papers were put to the fire. In addition, false identity documents were issued to administrative personnel most likely to be seized and prosecuted by the Allies. Weisse never assumed any such false identity.

Either he was not aware that such a list as that of the Zhitomir conference would ever come to light, or he assumed that all such documents had been burned.

"A further point: anonymous communications such as that received by Langsehn tend to have a pretty good reliability average. I remember once talking with Judge Kimmel about this. I had asked him why Germans so often betrayed other Germans whose Nazi connections had not been known. Sometimes, he said, it was business rivalry. Sometimes it was conscience. Or it could be jealousy. Tarnished German pride enters into it, too.

"So, let us assume there is a list. How do we get hold of it? Notice the term used by Alexandria: *Not locatable.* This interests me. It is officialese that could have more than one meaning. If Alexandria does have the list, I doubt whether you, for one, could obtain it. They've closed the door on us all too often in the past. But I will give you one possibility. Graham Heckler, at the State Department—he is a third assistant secretary in the office for European affairs—is a good friend of mine, from Army days. He just might be able to open the door. I hesitate to ask this of him as a personal favor, but at least you could see him and talk to him about it through the use of my name. Do what you think is proper and best.

"Meanwhile, however, we have a good deal to go on, and it is possible that when I return to Berlin I can throw a little more of a scare into the Zeller-Bricken people. But bear in mind that we are now holding a hot potato in our hands. Ludwigsburg undoubtedly would like to use the Weisse case for its value as an example. This could obtain for them the additional investigative personnel they are lacking at present. But if Zeller-Bricken is branded before we conclude our own negotiations, our case would be of little importance to them, for they'd have a much bigger thing to fight. I have given my word to Langsehn that we will avoid the publicity route for the time being, and he is agreeable to our using the information in the Weisse file for our own purposes. But what I do not like is his asking us to be virtually his agents. I want you to make the decision, whether to go after the document or to have me go further and worm the information from Weisse himself. So put your head to work and figure out what we ought to do. I should be back in Berlin in a week, and you can contact me at the Kempinski."

I gave the letter to the desk clerk in the lobby, specified that it be sent air mail special delivery, and reserved a room for Elizabeth for the next day. The reservations clerk was brisk but agreeable. "There is a room vacant next to yours," he informed me. "I can put Fräulein Weisse there."

"Very good," I said, and the clerk smiled discreetly.

At nine the next morning, I called the desk to see if my car had arrived. It was in the garage, I was told, and it would be brought to the hotel entrance at once. It was necessary only to provide the clerk with the information on my American driver's license. The car was a Mercedes 190, low-powered but comfortable. I found my way to the airport easily enough; it was to the east of the city, and the way was well marked. I had given myself a half-hour for the trip but made it in twenty minutes. After leaving the car in the parking area, I still had time to wait before Elizabeth's plane touched down. I was at the gate when she came through, wearing a coat of red wool with a small collar of sable, and she rushed into my arms.

"You look exquisite," I said, "and you smell delicious."

"It is a mysterious perfume that is supposed to charm you out of your senses."

"Hardly necessary," I said.

Her bag arrived in a few minutes, and I led her to the Mercedes.

"You have your own car?"

"Rented," I said.

"How wonderful. It is like being on vacation."

We were familiar with each other, and yet we each felt a sense of strangeness. I knew so little of her, she of me. We shared only the relative freedom of my time in Germany.

"If I ever marry," she remarked, as I started the car, "I will never let my husband travel alone."

"Why not?"

"We are demonstrating the possibilities."

"I do have a little work to do today," I said.

"Are you allowed to tell me about it?"

"No secret," I said. I told her about Sarah Stein, and the need to find a woman whose name was Christianne. There was only a slight chance that the Munich Christianne was the one I was seeking, but I had to look her up to make sure.

"Am I allowed to come with you?"

"I'd consider it a privilege."

"And," she said, "if this is your woman, then you would not have to go to Vienna."

"Maybe not," I said, "but I do have to go to Salzburg."

"But that isn't far."

"No, it's not far."

"It would be pleasant to see Salzburg," Elizabeth said. "What do you do there?"

I told her about Frau Lietschnitzer and the Professor's candelabrum.

"That sounds so interesting," she said. "I like it better than your work in Berlin."

"I do too," I admitted. "But I would probably not be in Germany at all if it weren't for that case."

"Oh, it is all so mixed up," she said, tensing slightly as I applied the brakes when a car in front of me suddenly slowed down. "Forgive me," she said. "It is because I drive myself so much."

"Would you like to drive?"

"No, I prefer to be in your hands."

I glanced at her, and as she smiled I saw the gleam in her eyes.

"Work first," she murmured. "Now tell me why you sounded odd on the telephone last night."

"I'm going to have to be honest," I said.

"Yes," she said softly, "it would be better."

"Yesterday," I said, keeping my eyes fixed on the road ahead, "I went to the town of Ludwigsburg, where the Zentralstelle is located. You know of it?"

"A little, yes."

"They have some information that has to do with the Zeller-Bricken case."

"Did any of it have to do with my father?"

"I'm afraid some of it did."

"And you will use it?"

"I don't know."

"Is my father in trouble?"

"He may be."

"And what you are thinking is that it would not be very honest, or nice, not to make use of the information, since you are involved with me."

"You're putting it well," I said. "You know how badly all this makes me feel."

She gave a deep sigh.

"What is it you want to tell me?" she asked.

"I don't want to be unfair to you."

"But you are already unfair."

"How?"

"You are married."

"You're saying that makes me unfair to two people."

"I remove myself," she said. "I asked for it."

"If you want to stop it now," I said, "I won't argue or object. I'd only accept."

"Do you ask me to be disloyal to my father?"

"No."

"What do you ask of me?"

"For now," I said, "only what you feel."

"Feelings——" she said, brushing her hand across her eyes as though they were tired.

We had reached the hotel, and the doorman opened the door on her side. I told him we would be using the car again shortly, and he promised to have it kept nearby. I carried Elizabeth's bag into the lobby myself, and, after she had registered, a bellhop insisted on carrying it to the room. He scurried about, turning on a lamp, a light in the bathroom, and I hastily gave him a few marks, after which he left.

"Where is your room?" Elizabeth asked.

"Next door."

"Very thoughtful."

"The clerk's idea," I said.

"I see."

She sat on the bed without removing her coat, and her eyes were downcast.

"I am beginning to think I should not be here," she said.

"It's as you want it to be," I said.

"I am an independent woman," she said, "but I was brought up to respect and obey my father."

"Are you obeying him now?"

"No."

I had a feeling of heaviness in my chest.

"What do you want to do?" I asked.

"Tell me what can happen to my father."

"Maybe nothing."

"And maybe?"

"A trial."

"And it would ruin him?"

"It could."

"And you would help?"

I thought before answering, but having gone as far as this I had to go further. "It's barely possible that I would have to. I would not do it by choice."

"And it would be terrible for me and my mother as well."

I didn't answer.

"You frighten me," she said. "You really frighten me."

"I love you," I said.

"Have you thought that I would tell him what you have just told to me?"

I nodded.

"You are asking me not to tell him?"

"Elizabeth," I said, "he knows already, I am sure."

"He has only told me he has been followed around by a man from the police, but he does not know for what reason."

"If he doesn't know the reason," I said, "he has nothing to fear."

"But you know the reason?"

"Yes."

"I think I hate you," she said.

"I can take you back to the airport."

She remained seated on the bed, her palms clasped.

"You didn't expect any of this?" I asked. "But you knew why I was in Berlin. I didn't come for my health. I came to do a job."

"And an American must always do his job."

"It's not an exclusively American characteristic," I shot at her.

"I knew there was something wrong," she said, "when I spoke to you on the telephone. I should not have come. Something warned me not to come."

I sat down on the bed beside her and put my arm around her shoulders. She did not protest, but her body remained unyielding.

"Let us go see this Christianne woman," I said. "We'll talk of it some more."

"What else is there to talk of, other than of how you have taken advantage of me?"

"If you were to remain with me," I said, "I would talk to Lottie."

"Your wife? About what?"

"About you."

She turned and gave me a level gaze.

"And you would hope," she said, "that she would be generous and say, 'You are free; go back to your German fräulein.' But if she were not generous——"

"I have my own obligations," I said.

"At least you are showing that you want to be honest."

"I think so."

"But that is not very much."

"What would you have me do?"

"Forget about this case—not because it will destroy my father, but because it will destroy us."

"I can't do that."

"I don't understand how you can love someone and still make that person suffer."

"I can try to explain it to you."

"You have explained too much already. We have both made a mistake. I think we must stop it now. Would you find out for me when is the next air connection for Berlin?" I saw the fixed determination on her face.

"All right," I said.

I picked up the telephone and asked for information. There were planes leaving at one in the afternoon, and also at three and five.

"Please find out if there is room for one on the one o'clock flight," I said, "and, if so, make a reservation for Fräulein Elizabeth Weisse. And, call me back in her room."

The information came a few minutes later. Fräulein Weisse had been booked on the one o'clock flight.

"It's nearly eleven-thirty," I said. "We should be leaving for the airport in a few minutes. Would you like something? Coffee? A drink at the bar?"

"No, thank you," Elizabeth said, standing up and then moving toward the window. She gazed out. "I am taking you away from your business as it is." A harder edge had come to her voice. "But I forget. How stupid of me. I *am* part of your business."

"That's unfair of you," I said.

"Sorry. I won't bother you anymore. I will take my own taxi to the air terminal."

Sunlight, flooding in through the window, made her dark

hair gleam. She was beautiful, and also untouchable. I would have gone to her, but she would have frozen up, I knew.

"No reason why I shouldn't drive you there," I said. "I have plenty of time."

"Thank you, but I would really prefer to go alone."

"We ought to talk this out," I said. "It's only a mess if we let it be a mess."

"And messes are stupid, Alfred. Neither of us should tolerate them. We must be very clear about what we do."

"You're saying good-by?"

"Yes, I am quite sure that is what I am saying, Alfred. Good-by."

"Now?"

"Why not?" she said with a shrug.

It was hard for me to believe she meant it. She had turned against me so abruptly. She was willful, captious, and cruel, I decided. I had trusted her too much. She had once said it was time to retreat, and we hadn't retreated. Now, for me, it was time. I'd get badly hurt, otherwise.

"Good-by, Elizabeth," I said. "I'm sorry."

"For what?" she said, but it wasn't a question. We had reached the point where we were both standing on our dignity.

She was still looking out the window as I left her room.

I knew I had to keep busy. I went immediately to the lobby and asked at the porter's desk for a street map of Munich. The attendant asked if he could help me, and I said I had to get to Winzerstrasse 17. "Yes," he said, "here it is," and he circled the spot on the map with a pencil. "It will take ten or fifteen minutes by taxi." I told him I had a car and would drive there and he marked out the route for me through a maze of streets. Even so, I had trouble. I took the Luisenstrasse instead of

Schleissheimerstrasse, and when I realized I was heading away from my destination I simply stopped dead, and cars behind me came to a halt, too, and horns blared angrily.

"What is the matter with you," a driver asked in German, as he pulled beside me.

"I'm a stranger here," I said, speaking deliberately in English. "I'm sorry I made a mistake."

He glared at me and drove off.

Winzerstrasse, when I found it, had the look of the old Munich, which meant it had escaped heavy bomb damage. The houses were of dark red brick and had entranceways that led into small courtyards. Number 17 was perhaps the shabbiest of them all, and the arched entranceway was narrow, grimy, and smelled of cooking odors. A board listed the tenants. Ludwig was the D apartment, on the ground floor. I circled the courtyard, planted with a few bushes that were more gray than green, until I found D and pressed a bell button. Nearly a minute went by before the door opened and a young man confronted me. "What do you want?" he asked me suspiciously.

"I'm looking for a Frau Ludwig," I told him. "Christianne Ludwig. I'm an American lawyer, and I would like to ask her a question or two. It won't take long. I called some days ago from Berlin."

"I am her son," he said, with more than a trace of insolence. "You can ask me."

"I'd like to see her, if I may."

"Wait here," he said, and leaving the door only slightly open he went back inside. It was a full five minutes before he returned. "You can come in," he said. "But she has already told you everything she knows."

"I'd just like to ask another question or two."

He pulled a cigarette from a pack, put it between his lips,

and lit it before taking me inside. The room we entered was small, and I saw that it was a workroom. Frau Ludwig was at a sewing machine and seemed to be stitching floral designs on a sweater. A pile of sweaters was on a table near her.

"This is the American," the young man said to his mother, who was already peering at me over her shoulder.

Reluctantly, she stopped the sewing machine, rose heavily, and came toward me. She was stout and short, and wore glasses with heavy lenses through which her eyes appeared to be large and bulbous. Her hair was gray.

"*Guten Tag,*" she said with a show of politeness. "How can I help you?"

"I'm sorry to disturb you," I said, "but I have been working for a long time on a difficult investigation, for someone in need of help."

"The Jewish girl you asked about."

"Yes."

"I told you, I don't remember the Jewish girl."

"But there must have been many."

"Yes, many."

"I have a picture of the girl," I said. "Sarah. It was taken in a DP camp, late in 1945. Will you look at the picture?"

"*Bitte,*" she said

I had the snapshot in a pocket of a small notebook folder. It showed a small, frail girl of twelve or thirteen with somber, haunted eyes and stringy hair that hardly reached her ears. The dress she wore was too long for her. In the snapshot, Sarah stood in an attitude of beseeching bewilderment. The Professor had taken the picture, and he had shown it to me before introducing me to Sarah at the camp.

Frau Ludwig studied the picture, holding it close to the thick lenses of her glasses. She shook her head.

"You've never seen her?"

"I couldn't say for sure. She looks—like the others."

"There were a lot of these young girls at the camp?"

"They were workers. They came from all over. I too worked."

"It was an underground factory Sarah worked in," I said, "near Innsbruck, we think."

"What year?"

"From 1944 until the end of the war. She was found on a roadside near Bad Tölz, with others. She is not well, now. There was mental damage done. Can you tell me something about the camp?"

The son spoke suddenly, his words an angry burst. "You should not ask a question like that. Not of a German! Do you think we are insensitive?"

"I ask only for my client," I said.

"Then ask the client," he said.

"She has very little memory," I said.

"Be quiet, Erich," Frau Ludwig commanded. "It was a bad place. It must be admitted it was a bad place. It was—you must understand, Herr——"

"Becker."

"Herr Becker, you must understand that the girls were young. The commandant liked girls."

"Do you mean he had his private brothel?"

Frau Ludwig's son gave me a look of daggers, as though I were attacking the high reputation of himself and his country and implying that his mother was a whore, in addition.

"There was one barracks," she said, "that was better and cleaner than the others. We knew the girls who were put there were whores. Some went willingly, because of the food. Others —I don't know. We used to fear that we would be taken there.

But they left the German girls alone, unless they asked to stay in the barracks. I did not ask. There was this little Austrian, also named Christianne. She sang very well. She was in that barracks, and sometimes she sang at the commandant's quarters. We all knew she was a whore. She was in my barracks, at first; like me, she had been accused of being derelict at her work. Our punishment was severe. We could not understand. We were not——"

"Jews," I said.

"Yes, Jews."

"One day Christianne told us she did not intend to starve. And the next day she left our barracks."

"Do you remember the commandant's name?"

She shook her head.

"Is it your business to investigate war crimes?" the son asked me, bitterly.

"No."

"Then why do you ask her the name of the commandant?"

"Because I happen to know it," I said. "It doesn't matter. He's been dead a long time. Shot."

"By you Americans, I presume."

"He attempted to escape after being captured. He was shot then."

"I don't remember his name," Frau Ludwig said wearily.

"Was it Dittersdorf?"

Frau Ludwig nodded. "Yes, I recognize that. It was Dittersdorf. A tall man, with a heavy face. He was a kind of degenerate. His wife too."

"His wife?"

"Yes, we heard that she liked to be there when he would bring a girl to his house."

"All this is sickening," the son said.

"I'm sorry, but it could be helpful," I said. "Your mother must be receiving a pension for her sufferings. This girl can't receive her pension until we know what happened to her in the camp."

"I don't remember the girl Sarah," Frau Ludwig said.

"You want her to say she does?" the son asked.

"No, not if it isn't true. But I might want to make out a statement of what she has told so far, and she could sign it and have it notarized. There would be a fee for that, of course."

"What kind of fee?"

"One hundred marks."

"She will do it," the son said abruptly.

"Is there anything else you can tell me?" I asked Frau Ludwig. "The names of others who were in the camp, for instance. That particular barracks."

"The barracks was one of three that were closest to the gate," she said, "and also closest to the guards' barracks."

"I mean," I said, "anyone who was *in* that particular barracks."

"Most are dead," she said. "You know that."

"All right," I said. "I'll have the statement sent to you from my law offices in New York. The fee will be sent with it."

"Tell me," the son said, "—this girl was Jewish. Why is she entitled to a German pension?"

"Your government made the rules," I said. "I only follow them. Thank you for your time."

The son led me back to the apartment entrance and gave me a firm, correct handshake, as at the conclusion of a business deal. I heard the sound of the sewing machine starting up. She was a proper German. I doubted that she would ever have concerned herself about the little Sarah. Meanwhile, there was another Christianne, perhaps in Vienna.

15: "No," the clerk at the reservations desk said, "Fräulein Weisse has not checked out. I am positive." He looked positive, for didn't all the evidence point to his being correct? There had been no notification from Fräulein Weisse, her key was not in her box, and the porter had not been informed to have her luggage brought down. Was she leaving today, by chance?

"I don't know," I said. "I don't know her plans."

I had stopped at the desk to pay any charges she may have incurred, but there was only a small bill for a lunch sent to her room—an omelette, coffee, and a demi-liter of wine.

"It would be simple to check her room," the desk clerk said, with his hand already hovering over the telephone.

"No," I said. "I'll call her myself."

But I didn't call. She may only have decided to take a later plane, I thought in the elevator. I passed by her door and put the key in the lock of my own.

I still had no appetite for lunch, although it was nearly two in the afternoon. My intention had been to return to the hotel, pack, and leave immediately in the car for Salzburg, which was, at most, a three-hour trip by autobahn. But this intention was interrupted by a knock on my door. I attempted to remain composed as I opened it, but I was overwhelmed by feelings of relief and what must have been sheer happiness when I saw Elizabeth.

"Alfred," she exclaimed in a kind of wail, "we did not say a proper good-by!" She came into my arms and nestled her dark head against my shoulder. "I didn't want you to leave." She had begun to sob. "When I begin to love, it is not easy to stop. Not so suddenly. What am I to do?"

"You stayed," I said. "That's the important thing."

"What have you been doing all this time?" she asked me. "I waited and waited for the sound of the key in your door. Why didn't you knock at my room first?"

"I knew you were there," I said. "Pride, maybe."

"So silly," she said, holding me, as though for support. "Have you eaten?"

"Not yet."

"Are you *very* hungry?"

"Hardly at all."

"Good."

The bed was there, large and inviting. We drew the drapes and closed the blinds. In the dimness, she insisted that I be the one to undress her. We clung together between the sheets, and I was filled with love and with the pride of possession of her lithe responsive body. "I do love you, Alfred," she whispered fiercely. "I do love you."

Afterward we walked to the Odeonsplatz and had food and a bottle of wine at the Hofgarten Café, typically dark and German and half empty at this hour of the afternoon.

"I must tell you," she said, "I must make a confession to you." She looked into the clear depths of the Pfalz wine in her glass. "I telephoned my father. I told him what I had learned from you. Does that make you angry?"

"It's done," I said.

"But he was not alarmed," she said. "He told me it was all a misunderstanding and that it would be cleared up soon."

"Is that why you stayed in Munich?"

"I would have waited for you in any case," she said. "But if my father knows and is not alarmed, it cannot be so bad for him, can it?"

"As a lawyer," I said, "I know they can't prosecute on what they have now. But if they should find more, it would be a different matter."

"If that ever happened, would it change your feelings for me?"

"Does that worry you?"

"Yes, I think so."

"But we can't erase him from our lives, you realize."

"I must live my own life," she said, setting her lips stubbornly. "But I would hate it if I were caught in the middle between the two of you. Who must I follow? It would be expected of me—wouldn't it—that I defend him as much as am capable?"

"What do your feelings tell you?" I asked.

She gave a little shudder. "Right now—it is terrible of me to admit this to you—they say to follow you. How can I love my father and say that?"

"You do love him?"

"I don't know. Habits are strong. Oh Alfred, I wish we could run away somewhere and forget all this." Hastily she added, "No, I don't really mean that."

"Did he say anything about your meeting me here in Munich?"

"I told him only that we had happened to meet coincidentally, in the lobby of the hotel. He thinks I am here on my fashion work."

"So you're not being completely honest with him."

"That would be nothing new," she said dryly. "I am curious about something. Do you do what you do because it is your profession, or——" She seemed to be considering the choice of her next words.

"Or?"

"Or because you are Jewish?"

"I'll have to think before I answer," I said. "Does it bother you that I'm Jewish?"

She shook her head soberly. "No, it only makes you more intriguing to me. You see, you say you are Jewish, but neither of us believes in this matter of race, and you do not seem religious, and you act very much like an American, and you also speak German quite well."

"*Quite* well?"

"Well enough," she said judiciously. "But your accent is as though you had been born in the middle of a river between Germany and some other country. You don't mind my saying that?"

"I'm happy," I said, "as long as you understand me."

"But you haven't answered my question," she said.

"Because I would have to tell you about my whole life," I said. "The answer should be simple, but it isn't. Have you known many other Jews?"

"Not many. Berlin doesn't have many. People say it would be better for Berlin if there were more Jews."

"And how many say that?"

"Not many," she admitted, with a smile that was a little apologetic. "My father introduced a young American-Jewish Army officer to me once. It was perhaps ten years ago. He invited him to dinner, mentioning that he was some kind of associate, and this man—he was a captain, I think—made some complimentary remarks to me. I thought he was very nice."

"Let's have our coffee in Schwabing," I said.

We took a taxi there and found an espresso place on Leopoldstrasse. We sipped our coffee, watching some young bearded artists trying to sell the paintings they'd hung between the trees along the pavement.

"Did you go out with the captain?" I asked her, feeling a little jealous in advance.

"He never asked me."

"But you would have."

"Why not?"

"I want to be the first American-Jewish Army officer in your life," I said.

"For that, you are the first," she assured me. "Tell me about what it was like for you in Germany during the war."

I told her a little of my duties, and I told her, too, of finding Orhdruf, but I didn't tell her about the suicides of the burgomaster and his wife.

"It is hard to imagine such places existed," she said. "You must have hated all Germans."

"At first," I said. "But later my feelings became mixed up, and I didn't know what or whom to hate."

"Your German girl friend," she said, as though reminding me.

"Yes, Hilde. But, you see, she couldn't have hurt a fly. Nor could you."

"Don't compare me to Hilde," she said pettishly. "I too can be jealous. I am *not* your first German girl friend."

"My favorite one, though."

"You are being sincere?"

"Absolutely."

"Now I feel like walking a little more," she said.

I paid for the coffee, and we went out into the strolling throng. They were mostly young people; they laughed, it seemed to me, too strenuously, and if they had had too much beer they were inclined to jostle and to forget to apologize. Some stared at Elizabeth, and I knew it was because she was beautiful. We examined some of the paintings on the sidewalks, and Elizabeth said that they made her eyes hurt, and since we were so near the Englischer Garten and the Haus der Kunst, why not go and see some good paintings? There was only a half-hour left until closing time at the museum, but we paid the admission anyway and walked through galleries lined with impressionist paintings.

"We should also see the Rubenses at the Pinakothek," Elizabeth said, "the most and the best anywhere."

But there wasn't time for that. We took a taxi instead back to the Bayerischer Hof, where I inquired about theaters and operas for the evening. The ballet company was performing at the Theater am Gärtnerplatz this week, and the porter was able to arrange for tickets for that evening. Elizabeth was pleased. She said that the ballet company had a good young designer and she had wanted to see his costumes and decor.

With time for a drink and a quick dinner, we went into the hotel's grill room.

"Tomorrow you leave for Austria," Elizabeth said after the waiter had brought Camparis.

"Looks like it," I said.

"And after that?"

"Berlin again."

"And?"

"New York, it looks like."

"You said earlier you would talk to your wife."

"Yes."

"Do you still intend to talk to her?"

"It depends on you."

"In what way?"

"On what you feel, on what you want."

She put her fingers to my lips. "Don't talk like that," she said. "Don't say any more. Anything of that kind is too far away. We must enjoy the moment. I think that is all we have, for now."

"Maybe more."

"But we must not talk about it. I know you so little, so little about you. You told me about a concentration camp and how it made you react. I want to see one."

"Thank God, there aren't any," I said.

"Yes," she said, "there is Dachau. It is a museum now. I want to go there with you. Would you take me before you leave for Salzburg?"

"You're sure you want to go there? It won't be pleasant."

"I know. But I want to see it."

Dachau was a Munich suburb, no more than twelve miles from the city. I had been at the camp not long after its liberation and remembered reaching the place by jeep along a road that led through wide, flat, empty fields.

"I can take you there in the morning," I said. "If you're sure."

"I must see it," she said, "so I can understand more about you."

We went to the Theater am Gärtnerplatz that evening, and, as Elizabeth had promised, the costuming and decor were striking. The dancers performed an eerie modern ballet that told a story of an old cleaning woman come to clean the stage of a theater after the performance was over. As she worked, from the shadows emerged the ghosts of ancient performers in ancient plays, brought to life by the memories. Finally, with a swish of the old woman's mop, the ghosts vanished. If it were only that easy, I thought.

The night was mild when we emerged from the theater. We took a taxi to the Schwabing quarter, and wandered again through sidewalk exhibits and crowds of young people. We tried one of the Schwabing nightclubs called Tabu, which turned out to be dark and depressing, and then visited another called Jazz-Keller, where we listened briefly to some loud rock 'n' roll music.

"All this," said Elizabeth, as we left the place, "is for people younger than we are."

"Younger than I am," I corrected her.

"Somehow," she said, "I missed becoming part of this generation. Born too soon. I prefer yours."

We slept the night in my room, and were very close and very content.

The town of Dachau was not hard to find, but the camp was another matter. The empty fields that I remembered were now dotted with houses and manufacturing plants, and some had been turned into pastured farm land with tall white silos and huge black horses pulling plows. Finally, an attendant at a gas station put us on the right route, and we came to the gates of the camp, which now had a large parking area for visitors. Already two buses had arrived, and parties of tourists—Germans

—were being escorted through the main barracks, which was the museum.

"Was it so clean and well kept?" Elizabeth asked, at first sight of the barracks.

"Very likely," I said, "except for the interiors of the barracks where the prisoners were kept. What you see now is all officers' and guards' barracks, but there were once rows and rows of prisoner blocks, some built of wood and others of brick and cement, and electrified barbed wire stretched on and on." Some of those barracks were now being reconstructed, we saw, as we stood in the main compound. Neatly lettered signs directed visitors to the main museum, to the crematorium, to the memorial chapel. Elizabeth gazed about her, seeming to try to understand what this place had been twenty years before. Poplar trees grew now where the barbed-wire fence had been, and the main building, which had been the camp headquarters, was painted white, as was a replica of one of the watchtowers. It was all very clean and antiseptic now, and our feet crunched on clean crushed bits of stone and granite.

Inside, the exhibits were mainly of pictures and texts. Elizabeth whispered the words of the captions, translating them into English, as though she didn't want the other visitors to hear. " 'The post stood two and a half meters,' " she read. " ' The prisoners were put to hang on it for hours. Loops were fastened to the tops of the posts; through the loop a chain ran with handcuffs attached. The prisoner was made to climb on a stool, his hands were put behind his back with the handcuffs attached. He was then pulled up and the stool kicked out from under his feet . . .' But——" She turned to me. "It does not say what this punishment was for. Do you know, Alfred?"

"I suppose I do. Trifles, if anything at all. A few seconds

late for a roll call, maybe. But mostly it was at the caprice of the guards. But are you sure you want to see this?"

"Yes," she said. "I must."

A party of Bavarian tourists clattered by us, most of them women on the elderly side. The sound of their heels reverberated on the wooden boards, for the converted barracks was low and narrow and was partitioned into small rooms.

" 'Whippings,' " Elizabeth murmured, " 'administered on a special design of whipping block——' A special design! 'Usually twenty-five strokes with an ox-hide whip.' Who made that rule?"

"Higher up in Berlin," I said. "There were the so-called legal punishments and the illegal. The illegal were not forbidden; it merely meant they were thought up by the individual guard, according to his imagination."

The pictures of the forlorn faces of the inmates were not much different from those we had seen before; they had been publicized enough. What caught our attention more were the documents, photostated and blown up to poster size.

We read one of these together, a copy of a medical examination sheet. A camp doctor had been painstaking in his reporting. "On the left buttock there were extensive blue-black weals, which were swollen and festering. The right buttock contained holes the size of a man's fist, so that grafting was necessary. Apart from this the right kidney is injured, so it will have to be removed. Urine is bloody."

The unlucky patient's name was or had been E. Schmidt, age 37.

"A German," Elizabeth said.

"And the doctor, too," I said.

"It was from the whipping?" she said.

I nodded.

Near us three women from one of the tourist parties peered at a picture of a dead body, its fists clenched, lying near barbed wire. They spoke in low tones to each other. I didn't catch the words, but Elizabeth did.

"Did you hear what one said?" she asked me.

"No."

"She said they had suffered, too, during the war." I couldn't tell if there was a note of irony in Elizabeth's voice.

She studied a blown-up photostat that had to do with gold fillings and gold teeth. It was a report sent to the Reichsführer SS, Berlin. The writer of the report told of the quota of fifty kilograms of gold for dental treatment having been filled. He begged for confirmation that all further gold collected could be handed over directly to the appropriate agency of the Reichsbank."

I felt rather than saw Elizabeth stiffen. She clutched my hand.

"What is it?" I asked. "I'd better take you out of here."

"No," she said. "No. Do you see the name signed to that report?"

"Yes. Otto Hipke, SS Obersturmbannführer."

"I must tell you," she said. "There was an Otto Hipke who was a friend of my father's. He used to play with me when I was a little girl. Could it be the same one?"

"Could it?" I asked.

"He has been dead a long time," she said. "My father would know, wouldn't he? And how he died?"

"Will you ask him?"

"Perhaps," she said, setting her lips tightly.

She insisted on going through all the rooms, seeing all the exhibits of agony, torture, and inhumanity. "I knew about some of this," she remarked at one point, "but not about all of it.

Naturally, this was never spoken about at home. My father must have known, then."

"I'm afraid so," I said.

Later we were again out in the fresh air, in the thin sunshine. A wind was blowing from the south, from the mountain regions. We could barely make out their outlines in the far distance.

"Now the crematorium," she said firmly. "The sign says that way."

We passed a memorial, and Elizabeth insisted on stopping to read the inscriptions. We learned that the memorial was called the International Monument and was built on the former roll-call square of the camp. "They lined up here by the thousands," she said, "and stood for hours in all sorts of weather, in their thin clothing. You know about that."

"Yes."

The surviving ex-inmates and their relatives had paid for the monument and also, we guessed, for the fresh flowers laid against it now.

"Not everyone has forgotten," she said.

Not far away was another memorial, this one built to the memory of the Jews who had died in the camp. The plaque was in three languages: German, French, and English. Carved in the stone, in bas-relief, was a seven-branched candelabrum, and I thought of the Professor and was glad that when I left the camp I would be headed next for Salzburg. I must get on with it, I thought.

Not far from the memorials were the two crematoria, one a smaller and older model that had proved insufficient for the demands made upon it, the other a more modern plant with four ovens, each containing an iron stretcher twelve inches wide. Flower beds were planted outside the buildings; trees cast their shade. If it were not for the high, stark chimneys, one might have never known their purpose.

The gas chamber had never been used. It had been built toward the end of the war, and the inmates had sabotaged its construction. Meanwhile, those who were to be gassed were put in vans and taken to a nearby gas chamber at Hartsheim. The Hartsheim chamber had served as a model for the Auschwitz installations. I wasn't going to tell Elizabeth about that, but she asked me, "Where were they gassed?"

I told her.

"And here they were tortured," she said, "and starved, and hanged, and shot."

"This was the first camp," I said. "Everything was tried out here."

"And I was alive when it happened," she said. "The medical experiments, too?"

"Yes. Mostly on Jews."

"Some came from Zeller-Bricken?"

"Quite likely," I said, "when they were no longer useful."

"I understand a little better," she said.

"What?"

"Why you do what you do."

I felt vaguely dissatisfied with her remark, but I didn't quite know why. Again we were out in the open air. "We've seen enough," I said. "Let's get away from here." She was silent.

"Look," I said, "there were people from the town of Dachau who risked their lives to push food through the fences."

"I am glad I am not from Dachau."

She clutched my hand tightly as we walked back to where I had left the rented Mercedes.

"If I knew," she said, "if I felt my father knew of this, or had anything to do with it, I would not care."

"Care about what?"

"If he were hanged," she said.

I saw tears welling in her eyes.

In the car, she turned to me and said, "I don't want to go back just yet. Will you let me drive with you to Salzburg?"

"Of course," I said.

"I couldn't leave you now," she said. "I must be with some-one whom I know is a good person. Do you understand? All those in the camps—they were the good people. The ones on the outside——"

"Some were decent people, and some weren't," I said.

We had packed our bags that morning, and they were in the trunk of the car now. Instead of driving Elizabeth to the air-port, we got onto the autobahn and headed for Salzburg. Eliza-beth nestled against me as I drove.

"Is it important that you find the Professor's candelabrum?" she asked me.

"It's a kind of crazy business," I said, "and ordinarily I wouldn't do such a thing, but I've known the Professor for a long time, you see, and I know it's important to him."

"I like that answer," she said.

By autobahn it was a pleasant trip to Salzburg. The more we drove, the closer we came to mountains, and they loomed against a blue sky scattered with clouds. We stopped for gas at a station just before the Austrian border, and Elizabeth asked if she could drive for awhile. I had kept the speed at a rela-tively stodgy 100 kilometers an hour, but she pushed the car to its limit. As we sped along, I mentally translated kilometers into miles per hour and noticed she was keeping the needle at about eighty-five.

"I hope the tires are good," I said.

"The car is almost new," she chided me. "Don't be nervous. I always drive this way."

"In a Porsche," I said.

She shrugged, as though to say that automobiles were meant to go fast. We made remarkable time to Salzburg, and Elizabeth, who knew her way around the town better than I, found the hotel, the Bristol, with ease. I had booked only one room and was a day late, but my room had been held for me, and they were able to give another to Elizabeth.

"Only one night?" she asked me, as she filled out the reservation card.

"I think so," I said, wondering if she intended to go on with me to Vienna, also.

Once in my room, I put in a call immediately to Frau Lietschnitzer in Seefeld. Conscience—I had wasted a day—not wasted it really, but spent it—and Elizabeth was with me, and that was pure luxury.

16: I had remembered Salzburg only as I had seen it during the early postwar days, when it had bustled with Army trucks and jeeps, and the drabness of neglect had covered its charm. Now it gleamed, and it had grown, too. The Bristol was a relatively new hotel. The Goldener Hirsch, where we had our dinner, looked as though it was cared for like a precious antique, and the food lived up to its guidebook promise. We wandered the town until late in the night, pausing in front of baroque church façades, climbing the tortuous path that led to the Festung Hohensalzburg, the castle fortress that dominated the left bank of the Salzbach, as though we were on a hasty vacation and had to see as much as possible before traveling on. Elizabeth had agreed to keep me company as far as Vienna, where she would take a plane back to Berlin, by way of Frankfurt. "Some day," I told Elizabeth, "we'll come here again and take our time." She gave me an oblique glance, as though wondering exactly how I'd arrange to keep that promise.

We had our breakfast in the cozy coffee room of the Bristol and left the hotel at ten. This gave us an hour to reach the home of Frau Lietschnitzer, on the shore of the Attersee, between Seewalchen and Weyregge, two of the villages that dotted the banks of the long, narrow lake. I drove, taking the autobahn as far as St. Georgan and passing the blue, inviting expanse of the Mondsee on the way.

"I like the way you do business," Elizabeth remarked, as she took in the vistas of water, fields, forests and the hovering slopes of the Styrian Alps. The skies were clear, and it was a sunshine-filled morning that took the sting from the briskness of the April weather.

We were in a happy mood, for we still had most of a day ahead of us before Elizabeth would take her plane.

The Attersee I had seen before, too. The Corps Headquarters, before its dissolution, had gotten as far as Reid, a small town between Linz and Gmunden at the head of the Attersee, and I remembered a day in late May when I had commandeered a jeep thinking I might visit Berchtesgaden and, instead, had come across the lake, seemingly forgotten and undisturbed by the war that had just ended. I had stopped at a small wooden jetty, where I had opened a can of C rations and drunk in thoughts of peace for the first time in a long while.

The lake shore was as somnolent as I remembered it. We passed two other cars. On the land side of the road, at a gravel driveway between thick hedges, a sign said LIETSCHNITZER. When we turned in, we saw a solid old house, square in shape, three stories high, set in an area of perhaps half an acre. Tall pines shaded the house, which was of stone and painted a pastel pink. A Volkswagen was parked in the driveway, and I parked the Mercedes next to it.

A flight of half a dozen steps led to the entrance. On the

door was a polished brass knocker. I knocked twice, and a bell jangled inside. An elderly woman opened the door and stared at us impassively.

"Frau Lietschnitzer?" I asked.

"Come in, please," the woman said with a nod.

We were escorted into a drawing room and invited to seat ourselves. The woman left, and a few minutes later Frau Lietschnitzer slowly entered. She inclined her head in a semblance of a bow. I introduced myself and explained that Fräulein Weisse, a friend, was traveling with me as far as Vienna.

Frau Lietschnitzer examined Elizabeth with more care than she gave me. Her hair was pure white, and she had small, black eyes set deeply in a lined face of leathery brown.

"How pretty you are," she said to Elizabeth.

Elizabeth thanked her with formality.

The room had a floor of fruitwood polished to a high shine and was dotted with several small rugs. There were two settees, chairs of various sizes and degrees of comfort, and a low table of polished ebony. Frau Lietschnitzer lit a floor lamp, although it was hardly necessary, since the three tall windows filled the room with daylight.

"It is good of you to come all this way," she said to me. "I hope I will be able to give you the help you need. You will have coffee, of course."

She used an old-fashioned bell pull to call her servant, the woman who had admitted us.

"My guests will have coffee."

Frau Lietschnitzer took a position on one of the settees and suggested that we take chairs near her. She lit a cigarette, explaining that she was a cigarette addict and that it was much too late to worry about smoker's diseases. She had a few other complaints that required her more immediate attention. "As I wrote Herr Gerson," she said, "I have not been well lately. Now, let us talk over the matter of the Erfurt Menorah. Kindly explain your claim to it."

Elizabeth was silent but attentive as I told Frau Lietschnitzer about Professor Marcus, the history of his family, his dedication to the rediscovery of the candelabrum that had graced his father's synagogue, and his employment of me as his agent.

"Is it so valuable, then, that you would give so much of your time to this search?" she asked.

"Monetarily?"

"I know its monetary value," she said dryly, in her guttural voice. "I refer to your own interests. You are obviously a busy man, an American. I would expect you are Jewish."

"Yes," I said.

"And you?" she asked, turning to Elizabeth.

"No, I am German," Elizabeth said.

"I am part Jewish and part German," Frau Lietschnitzer said, as though it was necessary to explain. "I am lucky to be alive."

"I realize," Elizabeth said in a low tone.

"My family has a long history," she went on, "and since it has always been a Jewish family, I have considered myself Jewish. I explain this to you so that you will understand my own interest in the menorah. It had once belonged to my family, and it was a member of my family that bestowed the menorah as a gift upon the Erfurt Synagogue, in the year 1802."

I nodded.

"You know all this?" she asked.

"Yes, I am acquainted with its history," I said.

"And what do you do exactly, Herr Becker?"

"I'm a lawyer," I said, "in New York."

"And is it the menorah that has brought you over here?"

"That, and some other matters. I manage to make fairly frequent trips to Germany."

"Your family is German?"

"My grandfather, who came to the United States, was German. German-Jewish, that is."

"Yes, we must make the distinction," Frau Lietschnitzer said, and her voice grated, like sticks crackling in a bonfire. "But, it must be settled who exactly has the largest claim to the menorah, assuming it can be located. And, should it be located, it will undoubtedly cost money to obtain it. Who pays the money, Herr Becker?"

"I hadn't gotten to quite that point," I said. "I'll confess that I have strong doubts that it exists."

"Oh, it exists, Herr Becker. I am sure of that."

"If so," I said, "I can undoubtedly arrange for the necessary financing—for its ransom."

"A well-chosen word," Frau Lietschnitzer said, with a nod and a semblance of a smile. "Since it was stolen—and under the most disgraceful circumstances. 'Pillaged' would perhaps be the correct word. But please understand," she turned to Elizabeth, "I do not blame the Germans. An insanity occurred. It is like a relative going insane and committing unheard-of acts. You do not blame the relative because you know he is insane."

"I blame the Germans," Elizabeth said in a flat voice. "And I blame all those who would try to excuse the Germans for what they did. You do not have to be careful with me, Frau Lietschnitzer."

"The insanity is hidden now," Frau Lietschnitzer said softly, almost in a mumble. "But I see the coffee has arrived."

The servant set a tray on the ebony table and was dismissed by Frau Lietschnitzer, who, with an arthritic effort, poured out coffee and handed each of us a filled cup on its saucer. The cups were of thin, fluted china with a floral design. They might have been taken from a case in a museum.

"Now," she said, leaning back against the settee, and even this movement was made with an effort, "as to the question of ownership, or custody. You will admit that as one of the last surviving Lietschnitzers I have the prior claim."

"Legally?"

"Well, what is your legal opinion, Herr Becker?"

"I'm afraid no one has a prior claim, except its present owner. When the gift was made by your ancestor his ownership rights ceased, unless you have a document attesting to certain privileges in perpetuity. It is a matter, too, that can't be decided by the West German government. The place of theft was Erfurt, which is East Germany. As for the East German government, I suspect it would claim for itself the custody of the menorah. It was for this reason that I had inquiries made in the Eastern Zone, to see if, by chance, it was in a government repository."

"And how legal is Professor Marcus' claim?"

"Exactly as invalid as yours," I said.

"Then it is a matter of sentiment, is it not?"

"That's just about it."

Frau Lietschnitzer now addressed Elizabeth. "And who, my dear, would you say has the prior claim?"

"As a matter of sentiment?"

"Yes, of course."

"Forgive me," Elizabeth said, "but I would place myself on the side of the Professor. It was in his father's custody—or rather the synagogue presided over by his father—and, spiritually, the Professor wishes to—to re-establish that synagogue in his new country. I can see how greatly valuable the candelabrum would be for this purpose."

"How well put!" Frau Lietschnitzer exclaimed. She looked with pride from one to the other of us.

I, too, had thought it nicely put. I had explained the situation to Elizabeth, but not at all in that way.

"I bow to your superior judgment," Frau Lietschnitzer said to Elizabeth. "I forgo my claim in favor of Professor Marcus."

"Now," I said with a smile, "all we have to do is find the candelabrum."

"Yes," the old woman said, "we will discuss that at lunch. But first I must show you over the house. Those Lietschnitzer possessions I was able to recover after the war—with the kind help of Austrian and German officials, prodded a bit, perhaps, by American authorities—are mostly gathered here. It was our summer place for more than a hundred years. The other houses——Well, no matter. They are gone. And what would one do with them?"

The lunch was a plain one, served on a glassed-in sun veranda that overlooked the Attersee. The servant, who was also the cook, had prepared a soggy schnitzel, vegetables that lacked salt, and a sugary tart that was all but tasteless. Frau Lietschnitzer hardly touched her food. Elizabeth and I pretended to find it delicious.

I was given the list of art and antiquities dealers she had already contacted in Vienna. In particular, I was to look up Gustav Horst on the Ringstrasse. A more promising list was one made up of the names of more than fifty Viennese collectors who were known to have an interest in antiquities of a Jewish nature. "I have written to seven of these—their names have a checkmark placed next to them—but with negative results. Yet, I feel certain the menorah is either in Vienna or is held by someone with Viennese connections. Herr Horst assures me it is most remarkable that no one, except myself, has inquired as to its availability in the last year."

"Could mean something," I said.

"It could mean only one thing," she corrected me. "That someone has it. One other fact. In Vienna now there is a virtual cult for the collecting of Jewish art objects."

"The Jewish people of Vienna?" I asked.

"There are hardly enough Jewish people of Vienna to make up a cult," Frau Lietschnitzer said. "I refer to the Viennese. It is a way they have of showing how their hearts bled over what happened. Or perhaps I am unkind. Perhaps they do truly appreciate Jewish art and are anxious to acknowledge how much the Jews contributed to the culture of their city."

Elizabeth looked her disbelief.

"I understand," Frau Lietschnitzer said, "that the Viennese would like now to have some Jews to improve their theater and relieve the dullness of their newspapers. But we must not be unkind. *They* suffered, too."

I was reminded of the remark made by the woman in the museum at Dachau.

"It will not be an easy task," she warned me. "You must get into houses. Perhaps the one who has it will not want to give it up. And, when you find it, you must not hesitate to make a large enough offer. The money can be found. I myself will make a contribution. I have written you this check."

She handed it to me. It was made out to my name, drawn on the Erste Österreichische Sparkasse, for the sum of twenty-five thousand Austrian schillings—approximately a thousand dollars.

"You're trusting me with this?"

"Why not? You had enough trust in me to come all this way."

I folded the check and placed it in my wallet.

"Let us hope," I said, lifting my wine glass, "that it will be required."

The wine, of some local vintage, was too young and not very good. I began to suspect that Frau Lietschnitzer had dug deep into her resources to make out that check.

Elizabeth and I left immediately following lunch, explaining that we had to be on our way to Vienna, a good four hours away. At the door, Frau Lietschnitzer kissed Elizabeth on the cheek and thanked us for our visit. "I wish you well," she said, and added, with a look of knowledge in her bright black eyes, "I wish both of you well."

She was at the door, looking out over the tranquil blue Attersee as we drove off.

We drove steadily, by autobahn, until we reached the airport. It was easy enough to get a place for Elizabeth on a six o'clock Lufthansa flight for Frankfurt, from where there was an eight o'clock Air France connection for Berlin. We had some time left, which we spent together. She accompanied me as I made arrangements to turn over the car; I had decided I'd be best off using taxis in the city, and I could get back easily enough from the airport by taxi, too. We had a half-hour until her flight was to be called, so we had a drink together in the bar of the modern, glassy new airport, our table allowing us a view of the planes landing and taking off. We held hands. We had talked little on the trip from the Attersee to Vienna, aware that each kilometer we drove was bringing us nearer to the time we'd have to part.

"How long will you stay here?" she asked.

"I don't know. Not more than a few days. I'll try to wind things up and get back to Berlin."

"And will you call all those collectors and antique dealers?"

"I'll do all I can," I said.

"And you won't waste Frau Lietschnitzer's schillings?"

"You mean on an imitation?"

"Yes, I was thinking that," she said. "If someone knows how badly you want it, one could be easily made. Don't you think?"

"I'll be careful," I said. "I'll have it authenticated. Except, I'm afraid we're talking about a phantom candelabrum."

"No," she said, "I believe Frau Lietschnitzer. She is a woman who knows a lot, more than you'd think. The money was not just a gesture."

"Everyone has been talking me into thinking I'll find it," I said. "And now you."

"I would like to think it could be found," she said. "Will you let me know if you find it?"

"Of course I will," I said. "I'll be back in Berlin."

"Alfred," she said, gripping my hand more tightly than before, "you must not think you must come back to me. Do you understand?"

"Not quite," I said.

"What I mean is: you will think about all that has happened after I have gone, and you will have those second thoughts, which are the worst and also the best thoughts. You will have second thoughts about me, and who I am, and maybe you will feel you have committed yourself to something you should not have. You are not committed to anything concerning me—that is what I want you to realize. All this has happened, yes. Also, it is all that needs to happen. Do you understand what I am saying?"

"Not altogether," I said.

"Alfred," she said, almost chiding me. "You will begin to

think about your wife again, and you will feel sorrow about her, and your love for her will return. If that happens, don't feel you owe me anything. I have known all along the risk in what I have been doing. I accepted it, and I am not ashamed. And I am not asking for more. Now you understand me, I am sure."

"Yes," I said, "but you don't have to be all that damned big about it. I'm not sure I'll have any second thoughts."

"No," she said, clutching my hand tightly, "it is important that we leave each other now as though we might never see each other again. Except that you must promise to inform me about the candelabrum. But then you must feel free to resume your life as it has to be. I don't count on anything from you."

"But you're entitled to something from me. Is this your way of saying good-by again?"

"It is not the same kind of good-by. Why do you make me spell it out for you?"

"I don't like our good-bys," I said.

"Nor do I. But this is a good-by with love. We both know that. It has been wonderful for me. For you also?"

I didn't answer but bent down and kissed her cheek.

"That is the proper kind of kiss for us," she said. "You remember we agreed on that?"

"And on the same night we broke the agreement."

"It was already the next day."

"Technically speaking only."

"You shame me," she said, but she did not look ashamed. "But really, Alfred, let us be sensible. I am going back to Berlin, where I will do my work, and make up for the time I stole. I will keep you from my mind as much as possible."

"I'd rather you thought about me."

"Do not fear," she said, taking my palm and holding it against her cheek. "As for my father——"

We stared at each other.

"Do what you must do," she said.

I wasn't to think of her, she meant. I wasn't to feel bound to her in any way.

"If he were to make an offer," I said, "that would be acceptable to the people involved, I don't see why I could not simply accept it and close out the case."

"Who knows? We might meet to negotiate once again," Elizabeth said with a tight smile.

"I am not a judge," I said. "And I am not a policeman."

"You are saying that now. You could change your mind. But I will talk to my father."

"I didn't come," I said, "expecting to get in it this far."

"I understand," she said. "I will keep on trying to understand."

Over the public-address system, a pleasant female announcer called the number of Elizabeth's flight. Passengers were to proceed to Gate 4. The flight call was repeated in French and English.

"I'll walk you there," I said.

I walked her to the gate, and we stood among the throng of passengers. She made me bend closer to her face, and she whispered in my ear: "You are free. There are pretty girls in Vienna. Remember that you are free."

"That's going a little far," I said.

The serious expression of her face turned into a smile that was bewitching.

"I know," she agreed. "That is to make you realize how noble I am."

The passengers were moving through the gate. Elizabeth kissed me quickly and showed the attendant her ticket. She gave me a wave, almost casually, and went through. I saw her step on the bus that took the passengers to the plane. I saw her again through the window of the bus, but she didn't appear to be looking at me. She looked, instead, exactly as serious and impersonal as on the evening I had first seen her. Then I lost sight of her as the bus moved off. I turned away, feeling a hollow sensation in my chest, and walked back through the terminal building alone.

Part Three

17: "You must be certain to see Silbermann," the Professor had said in New York not so long ago, and now that I was in Vienna I was glad to obey the injunction. With Silbermann I would, at least, be on fairly solid ground, for he dealt in realities, in written words, in documents stamped with a date, in old newspaper clippings. Over the years he had spent his time and energies assembling and making patterns out of what were not unlike gigantic jigsaw puzzles. I knew about his work, because in my field it was important to know about it. And he had proven himself to me by locating three of my sixty Zeller-Bricken claimants.

So I sat at a table in the Europa Café Kärntnerstrasse, near the Neuer Market Platz, with a *Kaffee mit Schlag* and a *Gugelhupf* before me, as Silbermann had specified, waiting for the man to appear. He was understandably cautious about meeting people. No overt attempt had ever been made on his life, but he had been followed menacingly a few times. For he was a tracer, a hunter, and unlike a few others who had gotten some attention merely by claiming they had ferreted out old Nazis Silbermann had had results. He had tracked down several.

In fact, the Viennese newspaper I looked through whil waiting, the *Oesterreicher Tageblatt,* had a small news iter about him. Through his researches, an officer of the Linz polic force had been identified as a former guard at the Theriesen stadt ghetto and had temporarily been suspended from hi duties until a formal investigation could be made. An editoria writer in the paper was not happy about this development. "Th exposure of such petty figures," he wrote, "after the passage o so many years can only result in a tarnishing and cheapenin of the present-day national image. These people unearthed b Silbermann have long been punished by their consciences, i indeed they are guilty. Add up Silbermann's illustrious recor and one finds that actual convictions of past crimes have totale only three, with a sum total of eight years' imprisonment fo those concerned. What then does Silbermann prove? Only tha young Austrians were conscripted by the Nazis and force sometimes into unpleasant duties. Meanwhile, Silbermann gain the publicity he so evidently desires—and at the expense of th public pocketbook."

The last was a reference to the fact that Silbermann ha been granted a stipend by the Austrian Commission for the In vestigation of Wartime Crimes. It was not enough to keep hin solvent, and it was customary for those organizations who use his services to make contributions to his office, which he calle the Austrian Refugee Location Bureau. Actually, his curren work was the location of Nazis. He kept files. I had heard the were a maze that only he or his wife was able to unravel.

I hadn't gotten to him right away when I had called the number given me by the Professor. First I was told I had calle a wrong number, then I was asked who I was (it was a woman

his wife presumably, who had spoken to me), and then I was
informed that Silbermann might possibly get in touch with me.
I counted on his curiosity about me and, sure enough, I didn't
have to wait long in my room before the telephone rang. He
made me recite, like a litany, the names of my law partners, and
only then did he agree to meet me. The café he had chosen was
busy and had large windows. He could observe me before coming inside.

When he did arrive I was startled. I had expected to see,
from my own vantage point, someone hanging around outside.
But no—he simply marched in, seated himself across from me
and said in English, with a heavy accent, "How do you do,
Mr. Becker?"

A trifle annoyed by the rigmarole, I said: "How do you
know I am Mr. Becker?"

But no smile came to his face. This was not a joking matter
to him. "It is my business to know," he said shortly, then beckoned the waiter and ordered himself tea.

"Not coffee, in Vienna?" I asked.

"No, it is too damned strong," he said. "Bad for the nerves
and the digestion. I see your own cup hasn't been touched."

"I just had breakfast," I said.

"Mr. Becker," he said, "I am a busy man. Why do you wish
to see me?"

"I suppose Professor Marcus has written you," I said.

He looked at me in surprise. "The candlestick? Does the
fool still expect to find it?"

"You've answered one of my questions," I said.

He had thinning sandy hair and a mottled complexion, and
he breathed heavily. I wondered if he had a heart condition.
He had gone through enough. Three years in a concentration
camp, an escape from a transport bound for Birkenau, many

months of hiding out in Polish forests and villages, and the discovery at the end that he was the only surviving member of his entire family. His long dedication to his present work was understandable.

His tea was brought, and he dropped in a lump of sugar and stirred. Then he looked around the café, examining each face in turn, as though a Gestapo agent might be on the prowl.

"If I had to make a guess," he said, "I would have guessed that you wished to see me about a certain electronics corporation that has on its board of directors a gentleman called Weisse."

"How did you know that?"

"You forget I found three of the workers for you."

"I didn't forget it."

"Who do you think provided your Mr. Elihu Grossman with the information about those two Nazis on the board?"

"Grossman told me it came from Israel."

"Certainly," he said. "I tell them, and they pass on the information. So it comes from Israel and not from me."

"Do you care?" I asked.

"The credit?" His eyebrows raised in irritation. "No one wants credit for what he does? Recognition is not required? How could I do my work if no one knew I was doing it? Who would ever talk to me?"

Obviously, the staccato series of questions needed no answers. Silbermann's anger was easily aroused. He had been crusading for a long time, and the longer he crusaded the more he demanded justification of his efforts—from others and from himself. If his name did not appear in the papers for a time soon enough a new revelation was forthcoming from him. And, true enough—as the editorial in the newspaper had complained—the revelation usually involved a minor figure in the

murder hierarchy. What made him more interesting to newspaper reporters, who never failed to get a story if they managed
to interview him, was his pinpointing of the whereabouts of
missing Nazis. Was Bormann alive? Absolutely, he would insist, and he would then give what were purported to be the
arch-criminal's movements in recent years. Not that he had ever
actually caught a Bormann or a Mengele, but he gave the impression of being an implacable pursuer. There were a few
others like Silbermann: In Belgium, Hans Gruss was the head
of a small society of hunters; in Haifa, Leonid Kossoff made
several flamboyant statements a year that invariably failed to
check out. (When every other hunter knew that Eichmann was
in Argentina, Kossoff placed him in Abyssinia.) Nevertheless,
Silbermann had value. "He doesn't find many people," Elihu
once told me, in discussing him, "but he keeps the issue alive;
he reminds Germans, Austrians, and brutes everywhere, that
their guilt feelings are phony. He'll find a murderer, and the
punishment maybe will be a suspended sentence. But it makes
a comment."

"Who tipped you off about Roehling and Weisse?" I asked
Silbermann now.

"I have my correspondents," he said with an owlish look.
"You'd be surprised, the people who write to me."

"That's why you need the publicity?"

"Who said anything about needing publicity?" He eyed me
suspiciously.

"I just happened to notice they were complaining about
you in the local papers."

"The Austrians," he said. "The worst of the killers and
the most hypocritical about the past. Don't trust them, my
friend."

"I'm careful about whom I trust," I assured him, but I had a slight twinge of guilt about Elizabeth. Surely Silbermann would not approve of my friendship with her.

"This Weisse," he said, "I'm interested in him."

"In what way?"

"He'd be a nice big fish to catch."

"So Ludwigsburg thinks, too."

"They do? They have a case?"

I shook my head. "They're looking into his record. A lot of inferences would have to be drawn, but it's just possible it's in your area." I wondered if I was telling this to Silbermann just to prove to myself that a relationship with Weisse's daughter wasn't going to affect my normal behavior. No, I told myself, I would be saying this to Silbermann if I'd never met Elizabeth.

"He was in the SS administrative offices, I know that much," Silbermann said. "What else is there?"

"He could have been at Zhitomir."

"Any record of that?"

"Just an informant's say-so. Ludwigsburg thinks there's a list somewhere."

"If you're asking if I have it, I don't."

"Just wondered," I said.

"What did he do?"

"He admits arranging the transport of Jews to a Zeller-Bricken plant in Hanover as laborers. But if he knew about the work-to-death plans formulated at Zhitomir, that would involve complicity."

"You'll never prove it," Silbermann said with a shake of his head.

"Why not?"

"They won't let you."

"Who's they?"

"You'll find out, my friend. When you get into that area, you get into the real conspiracy."

"Which is what?"

"Silence."

"But Ludwigsburg is working on it."

"Ludwigsburg is working on six hundred thousand cases. And how many will come to court? A few dozen, a hundred at most. Have you turned into a hunter yourself suddenly?"

"No," I said. "Weisse figures in my case, so I want to know as much as I can learn about him."

"He's too slippery," Silbermann said. "The only ones you can catch are the brutes and the sadists, because most of them are stupid, and they're all frightened. I go after the ones who don't sleep well at night. The ones who planned it all, who worked out the details—they're safe."

"Maybe not."

"Watch and see," he said. "I've been in this business a long time. So you came to see me about Weisse?"

"Actually," I said, "I'm trying to locate a woman."

"A Nazi?"

"No, I need her testimony for a case." I told him about Sarah Stein, and the woman whose name was Christianne. "If I'm on the right track, I'm looking for a Christianne Macklenburg, last known to be in Vienna."

"Well," he said, "let's make like Sherlock Holmes. No present address means that she is married, or that she is dead, or that she has left Vienna, or that she is a whore."

"Why a whore?"

"She'd take a professional name. Why do you come to me about this?"

"I thought you might provide a shortcut."

"You're prepared to make a small contribution to the or
ganization?"

"Your organization?"

"That's right. I have expenses, I maintain an office. Doesn'
Elihu Grossman realize that it takes money to do my work
Even the Austrians are more generous than you Americans.'

"I'll tell him when I see him. Meanwhile, I'll see that you'r
paid a fee."

"Not a fee," he corrected me, "a contribution. I do no
charge fees or draw a salary."

"How do you live then?"

"I take expenses."

He didn't smile, so I didn't smile.

"How long will you be here?" he asked.

"Not long."

"I will be in touch with you. Stay well. I must leave now.'
Just as he was rising, he said, matter-of-factly, "If I am fol
lowed when I leave here, kindly telephone me at the sam
number you used earlier."

I spent the afternoon in antique shops. I visited four in all
One shop owner had heard vaguely of the Erfurt Menorah bu
had no idea of what it was or how it could be located. Two
others tried to interest me in some old candelabra they had
for sale. The fourth shop, which was run by Gustav Horst, a
thin, stooped man of about sixty, was filled with bric-a-brac
lamps, china, and silver ornamental candlesticks. There my in
quiry brought a response. "Yes," Horst said, "I have a reques
from Frau Lietschnitzer for the Erfurt Menorah, but only tha
one request in the last year. Two, three years ago, I received
other requests."

Since he seemed to be implying something, I asked, "Well, what does that mean?"

"I would think it means," he said, "that it is known that it is off the market."

"You mean someone has obtained it?"

"Possibly. One can't be sure with a missing object of that kind."

He referred, I knew, to potential claimants of property seized or looted by the Nazis. They had flocked to Vienna in the years following the end of the war.

"I can only tell you," he went on, "that it is fashionable these days to have Hebrew art objects in one's home."

"Why is that?"

"A fad, a fancy," he said with a nervous cough.

"But there must be a reason for it."

"You must understand, Herr—— Herr——"

"Becker."

"Yes, Herr Becker, you must understand that Vienna is a city that takes great pride in its theater, its music, its art. The Jewish citizens of Vienna contributed much in the old days. So the artistically inclined Viennese collect objects out of nostalgia, out of regret; they pay homage."

He gave me an anxious glance, as though hoping that the information had registered well.

"Very interesting," I said. "Can you give me the names of some of these artistically inclined people?"

"You would not go to them directly?"

"Why not?"

"Well, you see, the Erfurt Menorah is in that category of objects that are not, strictly speaking, on the open market."

"Because it was stolen?"

"Not by the Viennese," Horst said hastily. "It disappeared,

no one knows how, and then, after the war, it somehow becam
known as an object of great value. The collectors have th
information, they obtain it somehow, and it is in that way w
find out about such objects."

"You mean," I said, "that it probably landed in the colle
tion of some Nazi official, who felt it wise to dispose of it afte
the defeat, and it was passed on in that way."

"Possibly so, Herr Becker," Horst said, "but I think it mor
likely that it was looted, that the loot fell into the hands of th
Russians, and that it was exchanged by Russians for objects the
regarded as having more value. You must remember, the Ru
sians were here until ten years ago. I am sorry to say, ther
was an active black market during the period of Occupation

"How often have you been asked about the Erfurt Menorah?

"Oh, several times during the past ten years."

"Can you give me the names of those who asked about it?

"Not very easily. I can give you perhaps two names, but
would suggest that when seeking information you employ a
intermediary."

"Such as?"

"Someone in the theater, the art world, who would kno
these people."

"I'll agree to that," I said. "I'd appreciate having the nam
now, because I don't have much time to spend in Vienna."

Still Horst hesitated.

"Naturally, I'll pay a fee," I added.

That hurried him up. He consulted a ledger, gave me th
names and addresses of Helmut Schwanda and Otto Koeche
and I handed him two hundred-schilling notes in return. "I'
at the Imperial," I told him, "in case you have any further i
formation for me. Who are these people, by the way?"

"Schwanda," Horst said, "is an actor with the Burg Theat

—quite well known in Vienna. The other, Koechert, is a manufacturer—of sweaters, I believe."

I thanked him and left the shop. I was on the Ringstrasse and not far from my hotel on the Opern Ring. By the time I had got there the concierge had a message for me. No name. A gentleman had called and asked that I be delivered the information that the lady I wanted to contact was now named Christine and that she performed at a club called the Kit Kat.

"If you are seeking evening companionship," the concierge said, "I would suggest that you can do much better than the ladies at the Kit Kat."

I stared at him for a moment and then could not help breaking out into a broad smile that embarrassed him, and he apologized profusely.

"It's all right," I said. "But Christine has been recommended to me."

"Yes, of course, I understand," the concierge said, but of course he didn't.

Then I further confused him by asking if he could obtain me a seat at a performance at the Burg Theater that evening. Of all things, *Death of a Salesman* was being given there, and I saw that the cast included Helmut Schwanda in the role of the elder son.

The Burg Theater was one of the most beautiful in Europe and once had been more ornate. Damaged during the war, and now the Vienna National State Theater, it presented old and modern classics and maintained its own company. The boxes and balconies formed a semicircle that went vertically up to the high ceiling. The halls and lobbies were far more decorative than the interior of the theater itself, which had been restored with simplicity and had excellent acoustics. I sat in the third tier, and everyone's words reached me with startling clarity. The performance, though, even allowing for the language difference, was stodgy. The standards of the Burg Theater were not, at the moment, up to what they had once been.

Disregarding Horst's advice, I found my way to the dressing rooms after the performance was over and asked for Helmut Schwanda. "I am an old friend from America," I told an employee guarding the stage door, and this so impressed him that he let me through into the dressing-room area. I found Schwanda's room and knocked on the door and was immediately invited in.

"I must apologize for the intrusion," I said quickly, when I saw the smile of greeting fade from his face. "I am in Vienna on a commission for a client, and your name was given me as someone who might have some information."

"Your name, please?" he asked in English. He looked older than on stage.

I handed him my card, and then, with more courtesy, he shook my hand and asked if I would have a brandy.

"No, thank you," I said. "I'll only bother you a moment."

He had been in the process of wiping cold cream from his face, and now he continued, eyeing me meanwhile from his mirror. He was a large, handsome man of about forty, and I had the feeling at once that he did not have the Professor's candelabrum. For something was taking root in my mind, and it had to do with what Horst had told me earlier in the day.

I told him what I was searching for and that I had heard rumors to the effect the candelabrum might be in someone's possession here in Vienna. "I am of course prepared to offer a considerable sum for it, even though the Professor I represent does have a legitimate claim on it." I knew I was stretching a point, but I thought it best to mention both legality and money.

"You are a lawyer in America?"

"Yes."

"And you come all the way to Vienna for this candelabrum?"

"I have some other business here, too."

"I see. Well, I am sorry, but I cannot help you."

"But I was told you once inquired about that object yourself."

"I am sorry to say that you have been informed wrongly. I do not collect such objects. I like paintings, myself."

"You've never heard of the Erfurt Menorah?"

"No."

But I had caught just a flicker, the slightest of hesitations, before he gave his answer. I thought: *He does know about it.*

"I am staying at the Imperial Hotel," I told him. "If, by chance, you should hear anything of any kind that might give me a clue, I'd appreciate your calling me."

He shrugged. "If I have not heard about it until now I see no reason why I suddenly should——"

"I mean," I said, "that perhaps you might mention it to someone, and in that way you might come across some information. As I say, there's a considerable reward, that is, a fee."

Schwanda held out his hand, and I shook it. "I hope you enjoy yourself in Vienna," he said.

"Well, thank you. I enjoyed your performance, by the way, very much."

His face lit up. He was effusive with thanks as he showed me to the door.

In a taxi, on the way to the Kit Kat Club, I tried to remember what it was Horst had said in the antique shop that had just taken on significance for me. Yes, he had said: *they pay homage.* To Jews, I thought. In Vienna, where the Jews had been so numerous in the city's cultural life. Guilt, I thought. They were not paying homage, but acting out of guilt. Why I should think this small amount of reasoning could be considered grounds for encouragement was not fully clear to me. But it had struck me that the man who might want to possess such a thing as the Professor's menorah might also have a past of some embarrassment to him. I knew I'd have to see Silbermann again.

18: Somehow they are all alike, those strip places in European cities. The same doorman, shifty-eyed but insistent, invites you inside, where the show is "truly good," and you can "meet the girls." The same photographs are plastered behind glass enclosures, each with a gold star beside the name of the performer. In Vienna the poses were a little more discreet, perhaps, than in, say, Frankfurt, but enough flesh was revealed to make the point. At the Kit Kat, a poster advertised, in addition to the strippers, that *fröhliche Dame,* Christine, who sang songs of spice. The club was located on Mariastrasse, a side street that was reached from the busy Kärntnerstrasse within the ring of the old city. A red neon sign flashed the magic words STRIP-TEASE every second or so. "The show is just beginning," the man at the door said. "Ten girls. All beautiful." Fearful that I would hesitate, he added, "Everything. They show everything."

I had to pay an entrance fee of fifty schillings and another twenty-five schillings to check my coat. Once inside, the Kit Kat was, if anything, more dismal than the usual club: a drab room, with a bar at the rear, a dozen bare-topped tables, and a stage with a dingy curtain, closed at the moment. Along the sides of the rooms were booths that offered a certain amount of gloomy privacy. I told the headwaiter I would take a booth, and he led me, to the accompaniment of a recorded version of the *La Dolce Vita* theme music, to a booth close to the stage. At the bar, three girls sitting on stools turned their heads to watch my progress. Business wasn't very good this evening. There were several empty tables, and such customers as there were dawdled over their drinks; all were male. It was not the kind of place where nonprofessional women were overly welcomed.

The waiter, who appeared quickly, asked me if I would have champagne.

"No, Scotch," I told him.

He looked regretful.

"It is less expensive to have champagne," he said. "And you have a whole bottle for your pleasure."

"Scotch," I said.

"Here it costs one hundred schillings," he said.

With a hundred schillings the equivalent of four dollars, I could see that the Kit Kat made no bones about clipping its customers.

"All right," I said. "I'll still have Scotch."

The word must have been passed quickly to the girls at the bar, for hardly had my drink been brought, when a young woman, wearing a tight black dress, appeared at my table.

"May I join you?" she asked.

"No, thank you," I said.

"You would not like to buy me a drink?"

"I'm afraid not."

"Perhaps you would like to meet another girl?"

"No."

She looked displeased and went back to her position at the bar. I turned and saw three girls discussing this cranky American customer.

The Kit Kat did not even boast a master of ceremonies. A voice announced, over a P.A. system, that Fräulein Ilse Weber would do her famous *Wagon Lit* number. The curtain parted, a record played, and a girl came on stage. The setting was the minimum needed to suggest a train compartment with a berth. Fräulein Ilse Weber carried a suitcase with her, and she opened it and brought forth a filmy black nightgown. Moving in time to the music, she undressed, lay on the berth, removed her stockings lingeringly, kicked her leg up, kicked the other leg up, took off a garter belt, removed a brassiere, and got up to do her goodnight exercises, wearing only the skimpiest of panties. She fondled her breasts, worked herself into several athletic positions, and then put on the nightgown, which turned out to be transparent. The last part of her number was the removal of her panties. She displayed herself for a moment wearing only the nightgown, and the curtain closed. The applause was not thunderous.

Another stripper followed. Her act portrayed her as a typist, clattering away at her typewriter and growing warmer by the second. She had to remove her skirt, her sweater, and everything else in order to accomplish her work.

"Christine," the voice announced over the P.A. system. "She will sing for you."

Christine came out, buxom and cheerful. She wore a blond upswept hairdo and sang her songs, all of them suggestive, in a loud voice that showed some training. She danced around a bit on the stage, too, holding her hands to breasts that amply filled her tight red dress, fondling her hips, and making cooing sounds addressed to her audience. But she did not take off her clothes. She seemed to be an entr'acte for the strip numbers that followed. I put Christine somewhat past the age for stripping.

When the waiter hovered near me, eyeing my unfinished drink, I beckoned to him.

"Would it be possible to offer the singer, Christine, a drink?"

"Certainly, sir," he said.

A few minutes later he led Christine, still wearing the red dress in which she had performed, to my booth.

"It is good of you to ask me," she said, speaking English carefully, and she sat down beside me, making sure to move as close as possible.

"Yes, what would you like to drink?"

"Champagne?"

"Bring us a bottle," I told the waiter, and he went off happily.

"You like to see striptease?" she asked me.

"I came here to see you," I said.

"Me? You know me?"

"No, but I've heard of you."

"Yes? Who told you about me?"

"I'll explain," I said. "I'm here on business. I'd like to talk to you. Can I meet you somewhere tomorrow and talk?"

"Tomorrow?" she said dubiously. "I sleep all day, and I work all night. Why can't you talk to me here?"

"Do you have a little time?"

"Enough time to drink a bottle of champagne," she said. "You realize I must keep busy."

"I realize," I said.

There was little doubt that she received a commission for

each bottle of champagne she encouraged a customer to order. The waiter came and displayed a bottle of Austrian champagne for my approval. I told him it would be all right.

"You prefer French champagne?" Christine asked.

"This is fine," I said.

The waiter opened the bottle and filled two glasses. I didn't touch mine, but Christine disposed of half her glass in a single gulp. She knew her work well, but I had already guessed that from the fact that Silbermann had been able to locate her so easily. She was undoubtedly registered with the police.

"You have business with me?" Christine asked, curious, but nevertheless professional enough to press her thigh against mine.

"Your name is Christianne Macklenburg—is that correct?"

"How would you know that?"

"Because I found out," I said. "I'm not here to bother you. I'd like your help."

"For what?"

I examined her face, the eyes so heavily mascaraed, but large and gray, the lines extending from her lips that the makeup failed to hide, the creases in her forehead. She was floridly pretty but once had been more so, most likely. She was running a little to fat, but her large body was still firm.

"You would like to kiss me?" she asked.

"Look," I said, "I just want some information about a girl you might have known once. A little girl. Her name was Sarah Rembarsky. She was in the Reichenau concentration camp with you."

"Who told you I was in that camp?"

"It's my job to know about those things," I said. "You don't have to worry. There's nothing wrong. In fact, it was because you helped that girl that I'm here."

"Who is this girl?"

"I have been told that you gave some help to a little Jewish girl in the camp. Do you remember a girl named Sarah?"

"There were so many girls," she said.

"I have a picture of her," I said.

I took the snapshot from my wallet and showed it to Christine, who studied it.

"Yes," she admitted, "I recognize her. The crazy little girl."

"Do you remember what happened to her in the camp?"

"I remember what happened to everyone in the camp. It was all the same. We worked, we starved—some died. If I had not been such a fool I would not have been taken there. I'm lucky to be alive today, you know."

"I know."

"But this is the wrong place to talk. The manager will not like it. I am not supposed to do business here. I am supposed to entertain the customers."

"That is why I suggest we meet away from here tomorrow."

"But we could go upstairs."

"What's upstairs?"

"Private rooms. I can tell the manager that you wish to be alone with me upstairs. He will understand. But it will be necessary to purchase two more bottles of champagne."

"At four hundred schillings the bottle, that's a little expensive."

"For an American, that's not so expensive. Now, before we go upstairs, you must kiss me."

"Why?"

"So the manager will think we go to make love."

Without hesitation, she plastered her lips against mine and then giggled. "Now I must take off the lipstick," she said. With a paper napkin she wiped my lips and then hers. "For the manager," she said, with a wink.

I paid the bill I had accumulated, and we were led up a staircase in the rear by the headwaiter. He opened a door at the head of the stairs, and we seemed to be in another, but smaller nightclub. This one was empty, however. It also had booths, about six of them, each curtained off. We were led to one of these, and I saw that instead of a table it had a narrow couch, nothing else. The light came from a shaded bulb on the ceiling.

"The waiter will bring the two bottles of champagne," she said, "and they will leave us alone. Then we can talk. But first you must pay me something."

"Why?"

"Because you are using my time."

"How much?"

"Five hundred schillings."

I agreed, though I realized now that my talk with Christine had gotten rather costly.

The champagne was brought, one of the bottles was opened, and the waiter retired after I paid him.

"Now we are alone," she said. "What may I do for you?"

"Tell me what you remember about the little girl in the picture."

She pouted. "But you have *paid,*" she said. "You would not like to make love with me?"

"No," I said, "I'm not here for that."

"Perhaps you like a little show? You Americans require little things before you get passionate. I will show you myself. You will not be disappointed."

"It's not necessary," I insisted.

But with a practiced movement she had already unzipped her dress. She slipped out of it. She had nothing on beneath but a skimpy brassiere and black panties.

"Tell me when the show is over," I said.

She took off her brassiere, and cupped her hands beneath her large breasts. The nipples were big and brown.

"You like them?"

I didn't answer.

"I will show you more," she said.

She stepped out of the panties and displayed her body with her hands on her hips. Then she turned around and swayed her hips back and forth so that her large buttocks moved in a kind of rhythm.

"Now," she said, "we make love?"

"No," I said. "Get dressed."

She didn't put her clothes back on but sat beside me on the couch, evidently puzzled if not fully discouraged.

"Maybe you would like me to touch you," she suggested. "I feel like doing all kinds of crazy things to you."

"No good," I said, smiling at her efforts to do her job. "I'm just here to talk."

"Very strange," she murmured. "Perhaps you are not normal?"

"Normal enough," I said. "How long have you been doing this?"

"Doing what?"

"Entertaining customers this way?"

"I don't entertain anyone," she said, with a touch of pride. "I must like the gentleman. I like you. Otherwise I would not have come upstairs with you."

"But we came here to talk. You suggested it as a place to talk."

"I thought you needed an excuse. You Americans are some-times—how do you say it?—a little repressed. I have met many Americans, you know."

And Russians, too, I thought, if she had been at the business that long.

"I'd better explain," I said. "I'm a lawyer. I represent the woman who was once the little girl in the picture. She is not well. She is, to be truthful, mentally disturbed. But we need evidence to show she became that way in the camp."

"But I have already told you; she was a crazy little girl. Very sad. She had no one to look out for her. So I helped her. I was only sixteen myself."

"I know what happened in the camp," I said. "I'll have to be blunt: was she in the brothel with you?"

"The brothel?"

"The officers' barracks."

"You know about that, too?"

I nodded.

"You know everything, don't you? Or you think you do. But can you understand it was the only way I had of staying alive? Did you know I was a trained singer, that I was already on the stage, here in Vienna? And then I was taken away for something very foolish."

She took a champagne bottle by its neck and drank from it directly. Then she rested the bottle on her nude thigh. She was at a party, she said. Students and young actors were there, and, being so thoughtless and young, she had pasted on a black stage mustache and strutted around the room in an imitation of a ranting Adolf Hitler. Someone at the party had reported her, and she was seized at her home the next day. "Just like that," she said, snapping her fingers. She was questioned and beaten, then put in a transport bound for Reichenau. "It was not sup-

posed to be a death camp," she said, "but an internment camp
for laborers. Yet they died like flies there. Most were Jews and
Poles, but there were Austrians like me, and now and then a
German. The Jews, of course, had it worst. The men's camp, on
the other side of a long fence of barbed wire, had it really
terrible."

She described how one tall, husky guard in boots would
face a ragged line-up of men, shuddering in their thin issued
clothes, and would suddenly leap into a line, drag out a man,
and beat him with a club. Then he would walk around ten
minutes until he had located, through whim purely, another
victim. Each morning and evening he would do this, and there
was no doubt that he had killed his victims, because the bodies
would be tossed afterward on a growing pile in the yard. They
were left there, for days, these bodies, because it was winter
and they remained frozen.

It was not quite as bad in the women's compound, but it was
bad enough. Each morning at six the women would be piled
in trucks and taken to a factory some ten miles away. They
would work for twelve hours, with blows rained on them if they
slackened, and would then be returned to the camp, faint from
the lack of food. "How hungry," she said, almost moaning in
memory, "how hungry we were."

"And Sarah," I asked, "she was with you?"

"Yes, she worked too. I would take her with me, the frightened little girl, so terrified she could not say a word. I would
try to do the work for both of us, to save her from the beatings,
but sometimes she would receive the blows anyway, from the
female guards, from the men, it didn't matter. They all treated
us the same. At night, beside me, she would hold my hand, and
when I talked to her she would smile. That was all. She was

brought to the camp with her parents and separated from them. The father was probably killed in the other compound. The mother must have sickened and died. So many died. I'll tell you why I protected her. I knew she would be killed otherwise. They would have found out she was not fully normal. You know what I mean? The silence. She never talked. Always the frightened look."

"But something happened to cause that."

"Yes, those terrible experiences."

"In the brothel?"

"No, before that."

"Well, what happened to her before?"

"How would I know that? I only met her in the camp."

"I am talking about sexual abuse," I said. "She was a child."

"There was no sexual abuse. I saw to that."

"You're certain."

"Of course. No one touched her. There were grown women enough for that."

"Well, that's it," I said tiredly. "Suppose you put your clothes back on, and we'll go back downstairs."

"What you want," she said, her eyes shrewd, "is for me to say that things were done to her."

"I don't want you to say anything that is not true."

"But if it will help her, I will say it. What does it matter?"

I considered her offer. If Christine, as Christianne Macklenburg, would sign a statement saying that Sarah, a girl of twelve, had been sexually molested by the SS officers at Reichenau, I could arrange for the compensation, amounting to approximately two hundred and fifty dollars a month for the rest of her life. As simple as that. A lie would work, and the truth would be chancier.

"You will pay me a little something," Christine said, cupping her hands under her large breasts and wetting her lips with her tongue. "And I will make a statement for you."

"Are you collecting compensation yourself?"

"Me? Why should I? I am not a German. I am not Jewish. I am Austrian. Here they don't care about me."

"If you inquired, you'd probably find you were eligible."

"And tell everyone I was a whore for the SS? Are you crazy?"

I couldn't quite figure out her logic, so I didn't press the matter. But I did want to know more about those beatings she had spoken about. They had been administered with clubs, she said, thick round clubs cut from long poles. One of the female guards used a whip, and she enjoyed most cutting it across the most tender areas of women's breasts, and once Christine had witnessed her kick a woman with her boot in the genital region, and the woman had been so badly injured that shortly after she had died in what passed for the camp hospital. "Oh, I *love* Germans," Christine said. "Do you know that no matter what a German who comes here will offer me I will not make love with him?"

"But you saw Sarah being beaten?" I said.

"Yes, several times."

"And she was not given enough food?"

"Are you mad? Of course she didn't get enough food. No one did. *I* gave her food. I saved scraps for her, scraps of food that were earned with the sweat of my thighs. I took no chances. I tired those filthy brutes out with my movements, I assure you. The more I moved and sweated, the more I ate. Your little Sarah was saved by *this*." She patted her pubic region. "You don't want that in the statement, do you?"

"It's not necessary," I said. "I'll type out something for you to sign. It will be sent to you from New York. If you agree with the statement after reading it carefully, sign it, and return it to me after having a notary seal applied to your signature. You'll be paid a thousand schillings for your trouble."

She sniffed. "That's something, anyway. You would not like to make love with me now? I have a good body, yes?"

"Yes," I said. "But put your clothes on."

"For thirty-six, I'm not bad," she said with a show of pride. "I still have men who come to see me regularly. I am very good at making love. I know many tricks. Where do you stay in Vienna?"

"The Imperial."

"No, I am not allowed in there. You will have to take a room elsewhere if you want to make love to me."

"I want your address," I said, "but not for that."

"For the statement?"

I nodded.

"It will not get me in trouble?"

"No, I'll guarantee that."

She gave me her address, and I wrote it down in my notepad. "If you don't get dressed right away," I told her, "I'm going to have to leave you here."

"All right, all right," she muttered, sounding both peevish and disheartened. "What about the champagne? You haven't touched it."

I stood up. Hastily, she stepped into her panties, snapped her brassiere into place, and shrugged into the red dress. The odor of Chanel No. 5 mixed with underarm perspiration filled the little room.

"You will come back?" she asked. "You will bring me something to sign?"

"It won't be necessary. I told you, it will be done by mail."

"You don't like me," she said solemnly. "I am no good for you."

"Don't worry about it," I said, giving her a pat on her shoulder.

We went down the stairs, and in the entranceway of the club Christine gave me a gay little wave, as though we'd had a wonderful time together, and blew me a kiss with her fingers. I stepped outside and took a deep breath of the Viennese night air. Poor Sarah, I thought, poor Christine.

I got in touch with Silbermann again in the morning, after sleeping late. After the formality of putting in a call to his "wrong number" and being called back, I asked him if I could see him again.

"I have a busy day," he told me. "How long will you stay here?"

"I don't have much time. I'd like to get away as soon as possible."

"You're too impatient," he chided me. "When you're looking for someone or something you have to take your time, go up an alley, go down a street, think things over, and wait for the answer to come to you."

"You're absolutely right," I agreed. "But if I could see you today I'd be in a better position to go up alleys and down streets. And the lead you gave me yesterday worked out. I want to make out a little check for your organization."

"You found the lady? She was the right one?"

"The right one," I said. "I don't have to look any farther in that direction."

Silbermann agreed to meet me at one o'clock at the Rebhuhn, one of the city's oldest cafés, on Goldschmiedgasse, not far from St. Stephen's. The interior, when I arrived, was hazy with tobacco smoke, and those sitting at tables looked as though they were ensconced for the day. A few conversed; most were absorbed with their newspapers or magazines, which were attached to thin poles and taken from racks. Silbermann made his appearance within a few minutes of my sitting down. As he came toward me he glanced about with his heavy-lidded eyes, making sure there were no secret agents or sinister characters in the café—or so it seemed.

This time I followed his lead and ordered tea. The Vienna coffee, it was true, was strong and had disquieting effects on the digestion if drunk to excess. I hadn't bothered much about meals the day before and had substituted coffee instead.

"How did you find my lady?" I asked him after the waiter left. He sat across from me and leaned his elbows on the table.

"Everything should be so easy," he said. "I made one telephone call—to the police—and like that——" He snapped his fingers. "You can forget the little check you mentioned, unless, out of the kindness of your heart, you feel you should support what I am doing. You understand, the contributions I receive, I never use for myself."

"I knew that," I said.

"Now what else can I do for you? Is it the Professor's candlestick?"

I nodded. "An idea came to me. I'd like to check it with you." The waiter appeared. From his tray he placed before each of us a porcelain teapot, a water pitcher, a little silver tray containing slices of lemon, a small silver bowl containing the crystals of amber sugar. It made for a lot of clutter on the table merely for two cups of tea.

I told Silbermann about what I had come across the day

before, the remarks made to me by the antique dealer, and the certainty I had that Schwanda had known about the Erfurt Menorah. "If he owned it himself," I said, "I think he would have been curious about the *amount* of money I might have been willing to offer."

Silbermann made no sign of agreement or disagreement. He simply looked at me.

"Then let's examine what the dealer said, those words about regret and homage. Substitute for those the word 'guilt.' Does anything occur to you?"

"Nothing," Silbermann said bleakly.

"All right," I said. "Let us construct a picture of a man. Assume, for a minute, that he is a Viennese who works in some artistic field. Assume, too, that he is not Jewish, because if he were it would be relatively easy to ascertain that he had an item such as the Erfurt Menorah. What is his background? What would make him collect Jewish art objects? First of all, he is highly successful in his field, because he has the means to indulge his artistic tastes. Secondly, he has a past that bothers him, embarrasses him—maybe, at a guess, he functioned perfectly well while the Nazis were in control in Vienna. An artist who continued his career, like Feurchtwangler in Berlin. He still continues that career today, but he must prove something: that he loved his old Jewish associates, who have all disappeared. Narrow it down further: he is known to or is an associate of Schwanda. A theatrical personage, in other words. A very important man today."

I was suddenly aware that Silbermann had an odd little smile on his ordinarily stolid face.

"You are making a joke," he said.

"No. Why?"

"Because you have described someone."

"Who?"

"You have given a description of Anton Friedrich Wohl, a film and theater director who has given Helmut Schwanda many excellent roles in his productions."

"Is he a collector of Jewish art objects?"

"That," Silbermann said, "we will very quickly find out."

19: Silbermann sent me a memorandum, a kind of dossier, on Anton Friedrich Wohl the following morning. I learned that Wohl was Viennese-born to an actress mother and a musician father, that he had studied in Salzburg, Munich, and Berlin, and that his theatrical career had begun as a singer in Viennese light opera. "An undistinguished performer," Silbermann noted. But he soon turned to directing. In 1934, at the age of twenty-two, he was appointed director of a then popular operetta company that toured Austria and Germany. In 1935 he directed an Austrian film about the early life of Franz Lehár. In 1936 he staged a production, actually a cycle, of three Wedekind plays at the Akademietheater, to mixed acclaim. Nevertheless, he was at this time regarded as a brilliantly promising ornament to Vienna's theatrical scene.

But this was not the reason for his being in Silbermann's files. A letter he wrote to a Viennese newspaper in 1937 caused considerable comment and "marked agreement," in Silbermann's words. The gist of the letter was that while he, Wohl, had personally many fine Jewish friends and associates, it was nevertheless true that Jewish control of Viennese culture, and this included the field of journalism, had become extreme. Silbermann's memorandum had an actual quotation from this letter: "The Jewish percentage of the Viennese population comes to twenty percent. But one finds in the musical life, the theatrical life, the fields of publishing and journalism, that Jewish contributors far outnumber their percentage share, in terms of population. This is not only unfair, it hampers the growth of a more unified national culture."

Silbermann added a notation: "Wohl's figures are incorrect. At no time did the population of Vienna include more than eleven percent Jews, and this total included half-Jews. Secondly, while it is true that Jews flourished in the arts and journalism, these were fields that were more open to them than others, and at no time could they have been said to be in control."

Wohl, at any rate, may have published his letter out of prescience. There was no record of his activities between 1938 and 1941, but it was Silbermann's feeling that he had worked in minor capacities in Nazi cultural ministries in Austria. "In 1941," the memorandum continued, "a picture was published in the papers showing Wohl at a function given to honor Rainer Schloesser, who bore the Goebbels-bestowed title of Reich Dramatist. Wohl stood in a small group that had Schloesser in its middle. In the fall of the same year, significantly, Wohl received his first important appointment: assistant supervisor, in the office of the Administrator of Viennese Cultural Affairs. During the following years he became a supervisor and was responsible for overseeing productions at both the Burg and the Akademietheater and also at other theaters of the city."

Silbermann had, of course, not been in Vienna in those years. He was aware, however, he said in the memorandum, of talk and gossip about Wohl that continued even to the present day. It amounted to two schools of opinion about him. On the one hand, the theaters of Vienna had been made "Juden-frei" during Wohl's period of supervision; but on the other, high standards had been preserved all through the Nazi days, and a nucleus of talented professionalism had remained after the bombing destruction and the collapse. But Wohl went under a heavy cloud during the postwar period. He was interrogated rigorously by representatives of all four occupying powers, and his clearance did not come until 1949. In his favor was the fact that he had never become a member of the Austrian Nazi party.

According to Silbermann, Wohl had resumed his career in 1956, after the Russians had left Vienna, and Austria was free once more. The mood at that time was to forget the past as quickly as possible and to look toward the future. Wohl made a film about the life of Franz Schubert that proved locally popular, he directed a Tennessee Williams play at the Burg Theater, and in Munich he directed a German film about the dance and, incidentally, married one of the ballerinas in that production. Because of the relatively low state of the Austrian film industry, he worked more frequently in Germany, where Helmut Schwanda, who appeared often in his films, was almost as popular as at home.

"Wohl presently makes his home in Nussdorf, a suburb of Vienna," Silbermann's memorandum concluded, "and I have ascertained that his collection of art objects includes many Jewish examples."

I sat in the Imperial's café, mulling over Silbermann's facts about Wohl and considering how I might best attack the problem of meeting him, talking to him, perhaps even viewing his art collection. In the past, whenever I had made attempts to reclaim lost or confiscated possessions for clients I had run into strenuous opposition. All quite natural. Germans—and this included Austrians—tended toward extreme sensitivity over anything that had to do with their pasts. The direct approach was not always the best.

But I was in a hurry to leave Vienna. My case in behalf of Sarah had turned out to be insubstantial. I could do nothing more for her here, and the only reason I had for staying was the Professor's candelabrum. I wasn't so much worried about not making myself or my firm richer by dawdling—and Vienna was a pleasant city to dawdle in—but I had a queasy sense of time being misused. True, my curiosity as to whether the Professor's candelabrum was myth or reality had been aroused, but I couldn't carry on the search endlessly—it simply did not have enough overriding importance—and Wohl was going to have to be the last stop. Somehow I couldn't see myself walking up to his villa in Nussdorf and asking to see the master of the house. Yet, to claim a missing object, it had first to be seen on the premises.

I chose a less direct approach.

I had not seen Helga Thompson for years. Swiss by birth, she had married an Army friend of mine, Larry Thompson, who had met her while he was stationed in Vienna as a cultural affairs officer with the American military mission. Larry had fancied himself a serious composer and had gotten about a lot in Viennese musical circles for a few years after the war, helped less by his talent than by his American officer's uniform. Helga —then Helga Dreisinger—was a young and quite attractive violinist. She had performed with the reborn Vienna State Opera Orchestra and had given a few solo recitals. Larry, when he brought her back to New York, had notions of a brilliant concert career for his wife, but this had failed to materialize. I had seen quite a bit of the two of them through the early fifties. But the marriage broke up after Larry retreated to a New Hampshire college as an instructor in musical theory, perhaps because of the dull academic life Helga was subjected to. Or perhaps for other reasons. I never knew. I did know that Helga had returned to Vienna, where she taught the violin and performed occasionally with a quartet.

I had no idea of the kind of greeting I would get from Helga, but there was no harm in looking her up.

She was easily located. The concierge at the Imperial found two telephone numbers, one for her studio, one for her home. I tried the studio first and heard the shrieking of a violin in the background as Helga answered with impatience in her voice.

I told her who I was, and her tone changed at once. "Alfred," she exclaimed, "how wonderful that you are here. I am to see you, I hope."

I told her that I was indeed anxious to see her again.

"You shall come and have coffee with me, this very afternoon," she said. She had three more students to look after, and she would then be free to meet me at her flat at four o'clock. She gave me the directions. Did I know where the Schotten Ring was? Well, from there it was easy to find the Kolin Gasse, which led to the Schlicke Platz. She lived at Number 12 Schlicke Platz. I was to ring the outside bell, and when the door opened I would find a hallway that led to an elevator with a black iron grating. She was on the fifth floor, and I must make sure to close the elevator door after me when I got out.

"Four o'clock? *Gut!*"

Her directions were impeccable. The house, once a mansion but now converted to flats, had cracks in its white cement exterior, and its hall had to be lighted by a succession of buttons, which gave one fifteen seconds of illumination to find the next button. I made sure to close the squeaky elevator door behind me and barely managed to find Helga's door, which had her name on a card, before I was once more in darkness.

Helga opened the door and said, "Alfred!" as though this was her most dramatic reunion in years. She hugged me, and took me by the hand, and led me inside.

"I have these three rooms," she said, "which are pleasant and cheap, and soon I will move into my house, which I am terribly excited about. You see, my father, who has been saving money for me for years, has at last been persuaded to give me my inheritance in advance. And so I am building a house. It is almost finished."

After making sure that I was seated in the most comfortable chair in her sitting room, she fussed around filtering some coffee in a pot heated on an electric burner, filling a plate with small cakes.

"You look well, Alfred," she said. "Hardly a day older. Maybe one day, but that's all."

"Well, I'm older," I said.

"You Americans are wonderful," she said. "You never age."

Helga was now in her early forties and looked it. Her complexion had lost its youth, and lines showed clearly on her forehead. Her chin was beginning to double, too.

"Tell me," she said. "Do you ever see that poor former husband of mine?"

"Not for years," I said. "The last time I saw him, you were still with him."

"But anyway—that's so long ago. My life is so different now. What about yours? Are you still married to that nice Lottie?"

"Yes."

"But she's not here with you?"

"No, she's off on a trip of her own, to Israel."

"So, now tell me what you are doing here. But first the coffee. How do you take it?"

I told her, and over the coffee I explained the nature of my trip to Vienna. I told her about Sarah Stein and about the Professor.

"*Phantastisch,*" she murmured. "So you still do the same thing. That's very good, Alfred. I am very proud of you. But I think you come to me for some help. Is that true?"

"Well, yes, it's true," I said, with some embarrassment.

"It's all right, it's all right," she said soothingly. "Why else would you have remembered me? If I can help, I will be glad to."

I explained the circumstances that had led me to hope that Anton Friedrich Wohl might be harboring the candelabrum.

"But I know him!" she said. "No, that is not completely correct—I have met him. The person I know is his wife. Perhaps you've heard of her? Monika Felsmann? She was once a ballet dancer. Now she does nothing but stay at home and complain that her husband neglects her. I'll tell you something. I have been dying to see that house of theirs. They are supposed to have done wonderful things with it. You will provide me with a good reason. I'll telephone her and tell her I want to get some decorating ideas for my house, and that will certainly swell her head. Although I don't think I will get any decent ideas, because they are both—how do you say it in America?—a little phony."

"Pretentious?"

"To say the least. He is a film director who makes terrible films, but she makes him out to be a genius. I'll find out if I can pay a visit, and you will go with me as my dear old American friend."

"Perfect," I said.

"We shall do it. I will telephone her this evening and arrange it, perhaps for tomorrow, which is Saturday and a good day for visiting. And, since we will take my car I will show you my house, too. Now, tell me about life in New York. I hear they are tearing the whole city down and building it over. Is that true?"

Helga picked me up at the Imperial at one in the afternoon. Her house was on the outskirts of Grinzing. Houses were being renovated all through this relatively removed area of Vienna, solid and square, with traditional architecture. After Helga had proudly pointed out the new features of her house—the copper pipes, the wiring conduits, the insulation of the walls, and, joy of joys, the latest in oil heaters—we continued on our trip to Wohl's villa, stopping on the way for a light lunch with beer.

"This Anton Wohl," Helga told me as she drove with concentration and care over a hilly road on the western outskirts of Nussdorf, unaware that at every turn she was providing me with impressive views of the Danube, of the Vienna forests, and, once, of a castle sleeping peacefully on a low hill, "this Anton Friedrich Wohl, as he insists on calling himself, did not always smell so good. In the days when Larry was here he used to grovel around the cultural section of the military mission. No one would have anything to do with him for a time because of his record with the Nazis. But a man like that can be useful. The Russians made use of him for locating Viennese film technicians to make their news films, and after 1956 his hand seemed to be in everything. His line was that all along he had only tried to preserve Viennese artistic traditions. And, even if true, this was not so difficult, because the Nazis had a certain amount of respect for Viennese culture and the beauty of the city. It was to become a jewel of the great Third Reich, you see—though a provincial center, naturally, in comparison to what Berlin would be. Now he is accepted. He has money, though there are some who wonder where it came from. He will not be there at the moment, by the way. He will come later, but meanwhile Monika will show us the house. If we come across nothing, we can always make excuses and leave."

She parked her car on a downgrade before a villa of three stories that was guarded by an iron-spiked fence and gate. It was a handsome house with tall windows and yellow shutters, built in the period when the Strausses were writing their waltzes and there were emperors and archdukes. A piece of modern formless white stone sculpture in the garden struck an incongruous note.

"You see what I mean?" Helga said, with a nod of distaste toward the sculpture.

But once inside she was all enthusiasm and praise for the decor and the way the house had been redone and refurbished. This was after we had been admitted by a housekeeper, brought to a small entrance salon, and greeted by Frau Monika Wohl, a trim woman with a practiced smile.

Her manner was a mixture of formality and calculated casualness. She and Helga exchanged an embrace and the *"Gruss Gott"* of Viennese intimates, and Frau Wohl professed to be honored and flattered that Helga would want to see her house and more than that to show it to an American of such prominence—for Helga had been elaborate in her advertisement of me as we were introduced.

On the whole, though, Helga managed it very well, I thought. She knew I would be interested, she said, in the kind of art and objects that Anton Friedrich collected. As the two women gossiped, interspersing such remarks as "Truly?" "Can it be really so?" "I never for one moment would have imagined——" we were shown the ground floor first. In these formally furnished and uninteresting rooms there was not a sign of a candelabrum. The only real treasure was a small Picasso.

Another blank wall, I thought.

We took a spiraling staircase to the next floor. A music room with a piano and some high-fidelity components, a library, and the master bedroom. And it was in that room that Helga and I caught sight at the same moment of a candelabrum. But it was of silver and had the eight branches more characteristic of the Hanukkah celebration (the feast of dedication that lasted for eight days with the appropriate kindling of lights). She gave me a veiled but inquiring glance, and I shook my head in the negative. The candelabrum was not of this century and was curiously wrought, but it was not what the Professor wanted.

Helga asked about it anyway. "What is this?" she said, fingering a thin, curved branch with a vine-leaf design curling about it.

"That is Hebrew," Frau Wohl said. "Tony has a fondness for collecting Jewish folk art."

"Really? So interesting——" Helga said.

"Yes, he has grieved so for the Jewish friends he has lost in the past——" I felt the information was addressed more to me than to Helga. "This is his memorial to them."

"There are others?" Helga asked.

"Oh yes, on the floor above."

We were shown three more bedrooms on that floor, the top floor of the villa, and in each one of them was a candelabrum, displayed on either a mantel or the top of a cabinet. But they were not the Professor's either, for he had given me a sketch of the Erfurt Menorah before I had left New York, and I had Max Gerson's description to go on as well.

"The best room," Frau Wohl said, "I have saved for last. It is Tony's study, his workroom. He does not like it shown, for it is so personal, but he is not here yet, so I will show it to you."

The room, at first glance, with its eaves and a dormer window, struck me as the kind of room a scene designer would create as a setting inhabited by a successful man of rare talent. A large globe on a stand, a brass telescope, a deep leather arm-chair, a cabinet with dictionaries and encyclopedias, and the work desk, a large mahogany piece that had on it, in addition to its brass inkstand and a lamp with a green glass shade, a candelabrum of seven branches. So artfully, artlessly was it displayed that it seemed to have been put there as an after-thought. The base, I saw, was of brass, but the branches were of a deeper, more reddish metal, each laboriously hand-carved. The black candle-spikes had the shape of dagger blades. I wished Elizabeth were here.

"How beautiful," Helga said, almost as a gasp.

"I have been looking for one like that," I said.

"Oh yes?" Frau Wohl said. "That one is very rare. It is Tony's pride, which is why he keeps it in this room."

"The one I'm looking for bears the name of the Leschnit-zer-Erfurt Menorah."

Frau Wohl's eyes widened. "But that is the one!" she exclaimed. "It is called the Erfurt Menorah, I am quite sure."

"Oh, it couldn't be," I said.

The expression of my doubt was genuine. I could not see, I could not fully believe, that the naïve and simple faith of the Professor, of Max Gerson, and of Frau Lietschnitzer would have led me to the menorah.

I grasped the menorah by its base and lifted it. It took a

considerable effort. Gerson had spoken of it as weighing in the neighborhood of fifteen pounds. It weighed easily that much.

"Has your husband verified that this is the Erfurt Menorah?" I asked Frau Wohl.

"It is without question," she said. "He paid a very large sum for it, and he would not have done so unless it had great artistic importance."

"That is not Jewish folk art," Helga said. "It is a work of art."

"Oh, indeed so," Frau Wohl beamingly agreed. She had obviously not expected to make so great an impression on us with her husband's treasures.

She began ushering us from the room. Tony would be home soon, she said, and he would insist that we stay for a drink. I took a lingering last look at the menorah. The branches seemed to have taken on a darker shade, almost as black as the candle-spikes that pierced the emptiness, as though testifying to an anguished and still proud faith that the lights they had held would blaze again. Frau Wohl led us to the library on the floor beneath. Soon after, the housekeeper appeared, as if on cue, bearing a tray with coffee.

Within the half-hour, Anton Friedrich Wohl joined us. He was slim and sleek. Deep brown, melancholy eyes were set in an almost saturnine face. Above the eyes were arched black eyebrows, and from a receding brow his thinning black hair was combed smoothly back. Well into his fifties, he looked younger than his wife.

He was honored, he said, to greet us. Knowing that I was American, he assumed as a matter of course that I would like a martini. He was an excellent martini mixer, he said.

Helga stared at me, as though wondering how I would broach the subject of the menorah. Somewhat gingerly, she accepted the martini handed her by Wohl. She had not drunk these, she said, since leaving America. "Alfred was a friend of my husband's," she explained to Wohl. "They were in the same unit together in the Army."

"Yes, and what was that?" Wohl asked me.

I gave him a brief summary of my Occupation duties.

"And you are here in Vienna on business?" Wohl asked me.

I said I was. I was a lawyer representing clients whose business took me to Germany and Austria occasionally, I told him.

"So you are able to make use of your former Army experience," Wohl said.

"In a sense," I agreed.

I sipped the martini he had given me. It was cold, clear, and dry. "Excellent," I said.

He stood with his back to a fireplace that was stacked with logs but was unlit.

"Are you, by any chance, the American who went to see my friend, Helmut Schwanda, in connection with the Erfurt Menorah?" he asked me.

I saw Helga blush. Her subterfuge was about to be revealed. "Yes," I said.

Wohl gave me a half-smile.

"The same one who saw the antique dealer Horst?"

It was my turn to smile.

"You see," he said, "I am kept informed."

"I wonder, then," I said, "why I was not referred to you directly."

"Oh, I think that is very easily answered, that question," he said. "They wished to know, first, whether I was prepared to deal with you. I was considering contacting you, but as events have worked out, through this pleasant coincidence, I am spared the trouble. Would you care to take a look at the Erfurt Menorah?"

"He has seen it," Frau Wohl interjected.

"Oh? Very good. Then we must talk about it. I hope you will agree to be my guest for dinner tonight at the Sacher."

"Certainly," I said.

"We can discuss the matter there, just the two of us. Now tell me what you have been doing in Vienna. I would like your opinion on the atmosphere here. I would like to know how our artistic life compares with New York. Would you believe it—I have never been to New York?"

Helga and I exchanged glances. We didn't linger much longer. After a discussion that never broke the surface of generality, we decided we should leave, and neither Frau Wohl nor her husband pressed us to stay.

Helga drove me back to the Imperial, alternately serious and laughing on the way. "How can I ever face Monika again?" she asked me. "She will always speak of me as a spy in her home." But that thought amused her as much as it dismayed her. "She will feel like a fool," she assured me, "when she realizes we had no real interest in her house. What awful taste! Did you see those monstrous tile stoves stuck in corners? Useless. And what pretension. Do you think he will sell you the candelabrum?"

"I can't figure him out," I said.

"What nerve he has," she said, "a man with a record like his, parading that Jewish *folk art* all over his house. How his heart must bleed."

"You don't believe him?" I asked her.

"Do you?"

"I don't know him."

"You are much too kind," she said.

"Not kind, cautious," I said.

"I must tell you something about the Viennese," she said. "But thank God I am Swiss and so somewhat immune to the disease."

"Disease?"

"All of them," she said, "all of them who are old enough to have been through the Nazi mess and the war, bear wounds that have never healed. They never will. In Berlin, in spite of everything, a few Jews were saved. But not here. They were all of them taken away. Some lucky ones bought themselves free. But the Viennese never lifted a finger. And now that it is once more a beautiful city they know that deep down there is something missing. The people who helped so much to give life to the city will never come back. They have a wound, the older Viennese, and nothing can cure it. They know they are *little* because of the wound, and this only makes them feel worse. They go to the *heuerige* taverns, and drink the new wine, and talk and laugh, but it does no good. I tell you, Alfred, I make my music in a dead city, a city like a museum, full of tourists. Thank God, I can be happy making my music, and the young ones, they are all right. The city will come back to life only when the old ones have died, every last one of them."

"Did you know that some Viennese have this hobby of collecting Jewish remembrances?"

"Honestly," she said, "this is new to me. How did you hear about it?"

"From an old woman," I said, "and an antique dealer."

"It won't help," Helga said with a shake of her head. "When they try to fall asleep late at night they know themselves. Tell me, will Wohl ask a lot of money for the candelabrum?"

"Probably," I said, "if he'll sell it at all."

20: I'd have to get an idea of the monetary worth of the candelabrum from Max Gerson, I decided, and when Helga dropped me off at the Imperial I was about to head for my room to make the call to Berlin. But a distraction came when I stopped for my key at the desk in the lobby. The attendant at the desk handed me a telephone message slip. It *had* to be from Elizabeth, and I had been hoping, if not expecting, that she would call me. I would have been the one to break the silence if I had figured out some clear course to follow with her. The urge to be with her was strong enough—not much doubt about that. But there were, as is said, things to take into consideration; they were there, all lined in a row, daring me to knock them over. It took me a moment to absorb the information neatly scrawled on the message slip. Stupidly, I had been counting on Elizabeth to rescue me from indecision, but it was not she who had telephoned. What the slip said instead was, "Mrs. Becker telephoned you at 1450 hours. Call Tel Aviv Operator 22."

Next question: how had Lottie managed to reach me here? Through Gloria in the New York office, probably. A cable to

Gloria, and Gloria would have relayed my itinerary in an answering cable. But why the hurry on Lottie's part? Cables and telephone calls involving all that distance bespoke some kind of emergency, and I could think of only two possibilities, one being that Lottie wasn't well, and the other that she had decided to return home with me by way of Vienna and Berlin, after all. Both gave me a sinking sensation; both would certainly delay my seeing Elizabeth. *There* was something symptomatic, I thought, that I should be putting Elizabeth first.

But this could be my opportunity to get it all out in the open. I only had to allow hesitation and ill ease to creep into my voice. Lottie, in a flash, would be asking questions, for she knew it was not like me to be hesitant, and all I would have to do would be to answer truthfully. Was I trying to make it easy for myself? No, for Lottie. And for eighteen years I'd been trying to make it easy for her without ever making much headway. She'll have to hear the truth, I thought.

I got hold of the Vienna international operator and asked her to put through the call. Odd clattering noises came over the line, and I heard a jumble of distant voices speaking unrecognizable languages. Tel Aviv was nearly fifteen hundred miles away, and half a dozen countries lay between here and there. The Israeli operator came on the line speaking English, and then an operator at the Dan Hotel in Tel Aviv, that one speaking Hebrew. I remembered the Dan, a memory principally of an odor of freshly hardened concrete, for the hotel had been very new when I was there. A loud buzzing and I heard Lottie's voice. "Yes?"

"We have your husband in Vienna, Mrs. Becker," the Dan Hotel operator said, this time in English.

"Hello!" Lottie called, louder than was necessary. We had a good connection. "Is that you, Alfred?"

"It's Alfred," I said, putting the usual amount of warmth into my voice. I would have to seek out the right moment for telling her. "How are you, Lottie? Is everything all right?"

"Not too good, Alfred," she said. "I want you to come to Israel." The words were positive, but she didn't sound very sure of herself, or of me. "I want you to meet me in Tel Aviv. When can you come?"

"Aren't you well?" I asked. "Is something the matter?"

"You must come here," she said. "I can't discuss it over the telephone. I am not sick, but I assure you it's an emergency."

"I have some business to finish up here. I couldn't leave right away," I told her.

"When could you come?"

"Well, I have to go back to Berlin——"

"No, come here first. I've checked it out. A jet takes only three hours from Vienna."

"Well, what's it all about?" I was on the defensive, unwilling to make a trip even farther than I'd planned, and how could I tell her now about Elizabeth?"

"But I must talk to you as soon as possible," she said. "When can you come?"

"Monday, possibly."

"All right, Monday. On Monday I will be here at the Dan Hotel. Do you wish me to have a car for you at the airport? Your flight will take you to Lod."

"I'll know better tomorrow," I said. "I'll send you a cable."

"But remember, come. Are you well, Alfred?"

"Quite well."

"And your business?"

"So-so," I said. "I'll tell you about it when I see you."

"So you'll come?"

"Yes."

"Good. I'll see you on Monday."

"Or Tuesday," I said. "But I wish you'd———"

"Not now, Alfred. The telephone won't do. Besides, this call is costing a fortune."

A lot less, I thought, than a trip to Tel Aviv.

"Good-by," I said. "Lots of love." The words were automatic.

"Yes, lots of love." And the same for her. Sometimes she gave those words an ironic inflection, as though she were merely repeating mine. I wasn't sure this time. After she hung up I went over our conversation, seeking clues to what it was so important to talk to me about and also looking for loopholes in which I could have interjected what I had been absolutely sure I was about to tell her. Maybe when it comes to things like that I'm a coward, I thought. But I had been sure, when I called her, that I was going to tell her about Elizabeth. Not *Elizabeth,* exactly, but a more or less abstract woman with whom I'd fallen in love.

On impulse I got the Vienna operator back, and told her there were two Berlin numbers I wanted to reach. I wanted Elizabeth's number first.

"I have Fräulein Weisse in Berlin for you," the operator said.

"Is that you, Elizabeth?" I asked, sensing that she was already on the line.

"Yes, my darling." She sounded calm, almost cool. "You're returning to Berlin."

"Not yet," I said.

"I thought you would be ready to come back by now. How has everything gone?"

"I'm close to the Professor's candelabrum," I said.

"How wonderful for him," Elizabeth said.

"And how are you?" I asked, much too desperately. "Have you been thinking of me?"

"Of course. But what keeps you?"

"I'm going to Israel. Lottie called. She wants me there, so——"

"Oh, I see."

"No you don't. It's some kind of emergency. I don't know exactly what it is."

"But naturally you must go. She's your wife."

"I thought I would talk to her——"

"Don't be rash, my darling. There is no guarantee of anything."

Her voice was pleasant, but it held a rebuff for me. I had put it badly.

"Please don't misunderstand," I said.

"But I told you when we said good-by. I am remarkably understanding, and I intend to remain so. You will call me when you return to Berlin?"

"Yes, I think I can be there in another four or five days."

"When you return, my father would like to see you again."

"Why?" I asked stupidly.

"Your negotiations, naturally. I have been discharged. It seems I did not do such a good job."

"Listen," I said, "I want you to know that none of my feelings have——"

"Alfred," she said, "you must not speak like that. You are going to see your wife. Have a nice trip. I'm sorry I can't talk any longer, but I must make myself ready to go out."

I didn't ask her where she was going, or with whom. I merely said good-by and hung up, and, for a moment, I was confused when the operator rang me again and said she had my other call ready to Berlin. I spoke to Max Gerson and told him about the candelabrum, and he congratulated me in a way that implied he was also congratulating himself. He guessed the worth of the candelabrum to be somewhere around five thousand dollars, but he suggested that I offer no more than two thousand at first. "The Professor will make good whatever sum is required, I am sure," he said.

I wasn't so sure, but I knew that, if necessary, the sum could be raised from my own sources.

"How do I make certain it's the real thing?" I asked.

"Have you seen it?"

"Yes."

"And what is your feeling?"

"That it is genuine."

"Trust your feeling," he said. "But obtain a guarantee from Wohl. He must refund the purchase price if experts refuse to accept it as genuine."

"That's half the battle," I said.

"What do you mean?"

"I mean, first he has to agree to sell it."

"And that is why the Professor has asked you to represent him. You are a persuasive man, Herr Becker. We are in good hands."

"Thanks a lot," I said.

I bathed, I changed, and nothing lessened my uneasiness. First of all, I didn't want to make the trip to Israel. But that I could adjust to if only I were sure that Elizabeth was as understanding as she had professed to be. Damn it, I thought, she's thinking this is going to be my reunion with Lottie and why else would I go that damned distance? And by what reasoning had I expected that she would remain calmly in Berlin, waiting for me patiently while I battled it out with my conscience? Besides, she was beautiful, and there were others she knew, and with one of them she was going out this very evening, so soon that she hadn't had time to talk with me on the telephone. I took a deep breath. Get hold of yourself, I thought. You're here on business.

At eight I was at the Sacher. The lobby had a Saturday-evening bustle, and a large group was at the entrance to the restaurant, waiting for the elderly headwaiter, in tails, and a model of distant formality, to seat them. I gave him my name, and I was granted the privilege of being taken, ahead of the others, immediately to the table of Anton Friedrich Wohl. He had preceded me and was wearing a dinner jacket. I regretted that I had not thought to wear mine, having chosen my most sober dark suit instead.

Wohl seemed to gleam. His high forehead shone, his hair was brushed back with precision. His black tie was of satin; his studs were small diamonds. No doubt his slippers were of patent leather. (I discovered later that they were.)

"Please sit down, Mr. Becker," he said in precise English— British English. "It is very good of you to meet me here."

The kindness was all his for, not only did he have the candelabrum, he had chosen one of Vienna's best restaurants. The hotel had been restored to all its old charm, but the restaurant had a special elegance, and one felt special to be dining here. We were in the smaller of the two adjoining dining rooms, and most of the men, like Wohl, were in dinner jackets. Well, I'm a simple man, I thought, and no use hiding the fact. The women were in evening dress, too, and pleasant perfumes mingled with pleasant odors of tobacco.

"I have taken the liberty of ordering champagne," Wohl announced, "but if you prefer whisky——"

"No, champagne, by all means."

Since I was the visitor and he the host and native, he felt it incumbent upon him to point out some of those who were dining here. "That old gentleman," he said, "with the very pretty young lady, is perhaps the most prominent of Vienna's psychoanalysts. He is supposed to have studied with Freud. There is a rumor that he was once flown in great secrecy to China and there treated Mao, who is said to have suffered from a neurological disorder."

"Seriously?"

"I for one believe it, Mr. Becker. The gossip in Vienna has a reputation for being true."

"And the girl with him?"

"Beautiful, isn't she? A patient of his, no more than twenty, her father a German industrialist."

"But he must be at least eighty," I said.

"And a great comfort to the troubled young lady, I am sure. He always manages to be seen with a lovely young woman, and the gossip is that he is quite capable, still." Suddenly, strangely, one of Wohl's eyes closed in a wink, giving his face an even more saturnine look. "I think we should drink him a toast, don't you agree?"

He raised the glass of champagne the waiter had just filled for him, after filling my glass, and we clinked our glasses to the old psychoanalyst's bedroom prowess. In one sense, I thought, Vienna was not so dead, after all.

Wohl insisted that we make our way through the crowded menu and order (I chose a house specialty, *Tafelspitz*) before getting down to our discussion, and then there was the wine to choose (Wohl suggested a 1961 Gumpoldskirchner), and I began wondering if the purpose of all this was to soften me up in some way or merely a display of Wohl's practiced charm. But then, as though suddenly launching into an attack, he asked: "Mr. Becker, why did you not approach me directly?"

"Two reasons," I said, for I had prepared myself for something like that question. "There was no open acknowledgment on your part of the object's being in your possession, and before making a claim on it I had to know for sure that you had it. The second reason is that I wanted to meet you socially, in any case, so that I could discuss the matter with you."

His dark, almost melancholy eyes still fixed on me, he asked: "But how *did* you learn that it was I who owned the menorah?"

I chose to be vague. "The search has been intensive," I said, "and through a process of elimination it led to you. Even so, it was a guess—a lucky one, I hope."

"You intend to make a claim?"

I could have said yes, but I decided not to. "I doubt a claim would work legally," I told him. "I would prefer to make an offer."

"Kindly inform me," he said, "of who wishes to acquire the menorah and for what purpose."

"My client," I said, "is Professor Herman Marcus, formerly of the history faculty at the University of Weimar. His father was Rabbi Marcus of the Erfurt Synagogue, where the candelabrum we're talking about had reposed for one hundred and thirty-six years. Rabbi Marcus died of a heart attack after a savage beating during the Crystal Night rioting. The synagogue from which the candelabrum was taken was actually a custodian of the property—it belonged in a sense to the Erfurt Jewish community, which, of course, no longer exists. The Professor desires to present the menorah to a congregation that he has helped establish in New York and that is attended mainly by Jews of German descent. I should mention, too, that a surviving member of the Lietschnitzer family, which originally owned the candelabrum before it became known as the Erfurt Menorah, has also been seeking it, but Frau Lietschnitzer has relinquished her own possible claim in favor of the Professor's."

"I see," Wohl said, his finger rubbing the side of his chin. "Very odd. Very odd indeed. Now I shall make you my own explanation. Has it occurred to you why I myself made such efforts to obtain this object?"

"I've wondered about it."

"Involved as I have been," Wohl said, "with artistic concerns for much of my life, I have naturally known many Jews and have had dear friends among them. Very early, when I saw the Nazi spirit rise in Austria, I attempted to warn these friends of the danger for them here. There could be no doubt of it. An Austrian Nazi was as fanatic as a German Nazi, and soon enough they became the same thing. Nevertheless, many of my Jewish friends failed to take seriously my warnings, and they are members of a vast persecuted company of victims. I am not one of those who hide my gaze from what happened, Mr. Becker."

"You wrote a letter once," I said.

"Ah, you must know Silbermann. He makes a great deal of noise about that letter. It was my way of warning those fine Jewish artists of Austria that their time was growing short. In addition, it happened to fit me, in the eyes of the Nazis, for custodial duties—which I like to think were somewhat helpful in the long run. The Jews, by the way, were gone from those institutions I supervised long before I was put in charge. The day the Germans marched into Austria their tenure was over. You are aware of the circumstances, I hope?"

"Aware enough."

"Now, in the years following the end of the war, I became aware that a great many objects of historical value, looted objects mainly, were circulating around this city. Many were in the hands of individual Russians. Several collectors in Vienna made it a practice to acquire them, and I myself collected some of those candelabra you have seen in my home. Shortly before the Russians left Vienna, a major then staying in the very Imperial Hotel you are in now offered for sale the Erfurt Menorah. I could not afford the price he was asking. The major's claim was that this menorah had been found in the vault of a private banker in Leipzig. The banker had been put on trial by the East Germans—it seems he had illegally acquired some businesses formerly belonging to Jewish owners—and was shot. Some of his possessions were confiscated, and a few found their way to Vienna for sale on the antique market here. The major decided to sell the menorah himself. A few years ago I asked my friend Helmut Schwanda to make discreet inquiries about the menorah. One day, slightly more than a year ago, it was brought to my home wrapped in brown paper. A note with it told me to make out a bank draft for one hundred thousand schillings, four thousand dollars of your American money, payable to bearer. The bearer was a boy of eighteen or so who knew nothing but that he was to bring back a letter to a gentleman. No name. That is how I acquired the menorah. Helmut's story is that he merely went from antique dealer to antique dealer making inquiries, making it known that I wished to collect the menorah, and one day it simply came to me. You could have done as much, Mr. Becker, and I would have brought you the menorah."

"But all the secrecy——"

"Mr. Becker," he interrupted, "surely you are aware of the large and, I am afraid, subterranean market in art objects. First it was a black market. But with restitution claims being made in great numbers during the years following the war, one never

knew what legal difficulties he would face if he acquired anything of value. I must tell you frankly, Mr. Becker, that there
were those who insisted on what was known as the Auschwitz
guarantee. In other words, price to be repaid if a survivor insti-
tuted a property-restitution claim."

"I've been in restitution work for a long time," I said, "and
I've never heard anything about an Auschwitz guarantee."

"It is one of those black jokes of execrable taste one sometimes hears. You don't think this beautiful city is entirely free
of anti-Semitism, do you?"

The question didn't demand an answer.

"To go on," he said, "I must admit that I have the custodian mentality, and I had determined that if ever anyone appeared with a rightful claim on any piece of mine, he would
have it. I am not selling the Erfurt Menorah, Mr. Becker."

"Are you saying that the Professor's claim is not rightful?"
I asked.

"No, Mr. Becker, what I am saying is that the Professor
shall have the Erfurt Menorah. I agree with you—it is right-
fully his."

"And how will this be arranged?"

"With a handshake, between two gentlemen. The honor
will be entirely mine. And I shall consider it a token, a
memorial, to the memory of my Jewish associates who were
lost in the holocaust."

That was enough to make me mistrust his sincerity. He was
too smooth, too slick. His use of the word "holocaust" was a
word that someone Jewish and intimately involved with past
atrocities would have used, but not a cultivated Viennese. He
wanted something.

"I should tell you," I said, "that I'm well prepared to make
a monetary offer."

"No, I insist, it must be a gift."

"But certainly you'd want something. You went to a lot of trouble to acquire the object."

"Oh, perhaps," he said, with a negligent wave of his hand, "if you wished to announce me as the donor, to make it public, that would be sufficient payment for me."

As indeed it would be. The gift of the menorah to the Professor would amount to a clearance for him. Jews themselves would honor him.

"I'm afraid," I said, "that any announcements would have to come from Professor Marcus. I act as his agent only, you see."

His dark eyes grew more melancholy. He sensed now that I did not trust him, and he professed to be wounded. "But you would certainly explain to him the circumstances."

"I'll explain them exactly," I said.

He studied me. I wondered if he was about to withdraw his offer, and I was already turning over in my mind ways of instituting a claim for the menorah.

"Your hand, then," he said.

I extended my hand halfway across the table, and he reached out and grasped it.

"The gift is accepted?" he asked.

"Accepted," I said. "And I will put you in touch with Professor Marcus."

I rather doubted that the Professor, upon hearing the circumstances, would want to attribute the recovery of the Menorah to Anton Friedrich Wohl. I got through the details of the shipment of the piece to the United States as speedily as I could, trying not to give the impression that I was in a hurry. The best arrangement, Wohl agreed, was to have it delivered to my hotel, and I could then arrange for its shipment to the Professor by air express. I would of course provide him with a receipt. He was not entirely happy with the result of our consultation, I could see, for I had not promised him much of anything in return for his so-called gift. But with Silbermann on my side in the background, he was shrewd enough to know that he was on unsure ground.

I remembered, later that evening, to remove Eva Lietschnitzer's check from my wallet. I tore the check into four pieces and put them with a letter I wrote to her.

21: The Caravelle landed me at Lod Airport just as daylight was fading, and lights were winking on in Tel Aviv, several miles away. I had cabled my arrival time to Lottie, but I hardly expected her to meet me, for she was not the kind of woman who delighted in running out to airports to meet her husband. I should have checked the temperatures in Israel, for as soon as I stepped from the plane I was met by a heat that seemed to be flowing insistently from the desert regions to the southeast. My collar wilted as I made my way toward Immigration and Customs. I realized I was wearing much too heavy a suit.

The Israeli official was uncertain as to whether to classify me as a tourist or a businessman. I told him I would be in the country only two or three days.

"What is the purpose of your trip?"

"I am here to meet my wife," I explained patiently, "who is here on a pleasure trip with an American Hadassah group."

"She will return with you to Vienna?" he asked, as he examined my ticket.

"We will discuss it," I said.

"And that is what you do here—meet your wife and discuss your return?"

"I want to see a little something of the country, too."

"A tourist, then," he said, with a measure of triumph in his voice, and he proceeded to stamp in my passport with energy a visa good for three months and then another stamp specifying that I would not accept a job in the country during that period. At Customs, too, I was held up. The transistor radio I carried with me caught the inspector's eye, and he felt it necessary to write in my passport that the radio I carried must be with me when I left the country.

Well, it's a new country, I told myself. I saw no porters in my vicinity and carried my bags to the bus platform outside, where I spotted a few taxis waiting. The one I got into was an old De Soto, which looked and smelled well beyond the age of retirement. "Twenty-five Israeli pounds," the driver informed me, after I had given him my Tel Aviv destination. "Price fixed. That is eight dollars and thirty-three cents American. You wish to share? I can wait."

"It's all right," I said.

He was old enough to have been a concentration-camp victim, and that I learned he was, although he seemed unaware of the statistics against his having survived. He groused about the housing situation, grumbled at the high prices of goods, and thought the country needed a new premier. He also drove with a cheerful disregard for rules of the road and other cars, and I found myself clutching the arm rests from time to time as we miraculously avoided crashes.

At the Dan Hotel, in the busy lobby, I gave my name to the desk clerk, who consulted his files and came up with the information that a single room had been booked for me.

"A single?"

"Yes, we have no doubles available for at least two weeks."

"I'll take it," I said, thinking that Lottie had probably switched us to another hotel for the next day.

The Dan, I was glad to find, was air-conditioned. In my room, a small one that looked out on the sea, I took off my damp shirt, put a towel around my shoulders against the chill of the air conditioning, and used the telephone to ask for Mrs. Becker's room. No answer to my ring. Then, while I was showering, the telephone buzzed, and I got to it, dripping. "Hello, Lottie?"

"Alfred," she said calmly, "you are here. Good. The evening has been arranged. We will have dinner at the Fontainebleu on Dizengoff Street. You know where that is?"

"I'll find it. Where are you now?"

"On my way to the hotel to change."

"Why don't I pick you up at your room?"

"It won't be necessary," she said. "And I must do an errand. After dinner we will go and meet Simon."

"Who's he?"

"My old, dear friend from the camp at Sodesheim. You remember him?"

"Yes, but not too well."

"Did you have a good flight?"

"Yes, fine," I said. "Are you feeling all right?"

I had it in my mind that Lottie had some kind of indisposition, but her voice sounded firm and confident. I wanted to ask her exactly what it was I was supposed to be doing here, but with a "see you in an hour" she rang off.

After dressing, I went down in a crowded lift to the bar of the Dan and ordered myself a Scotch. I was among a lot of Americans, I saw, who were preponderantly female. They were older women, mostly, members of touring groups and

Jewish charitable organizations. After finishing my drink I went outside and stood on the esplanade. The darkness was complete by now, and I sensed rather than saw the Mediterranean. There was something tacky about Tel Aviv for me; it was not my favorite city. A group of dark young men passed by in animated conversation. They looked Arab, but they spoke Hebrew.

I walked to Dizengoff Street, only a few blocks from the Dan, and found the restaurant, which was not unlike one I might have expected to see in Miami, with its brass hanging lamps, little bowls of flowers, and uncomfortable-looking, red-jacketed waiters. It was occupied mainly by tour groups of women, and I threaded my way toward Lottie, who was already seated at a table.

She gave me her cheek instead of her lips to kiss. She looked very well, I saw. Her face had more animation than when I'd left, her dark eyes shone, and her dark hair threaded with streaks of gray had been ministered to by a hairdresser. She was still a handsome woman.

Sooner or later, I was sure, she would want to know about what I had been doing, and I would tell her. I would tell her about Weisse and the daughter he had sent to be a go-between, and then I would describe the progression of events after that. I had tentatively worked it out on the plane, much like preparing myself for an appearance in court (an irony, that), and as I talked, it would all come out. But, unlike a court appearance, I would be the witness, and Lottie would be the interrogator. She would ask the questions, and I would not dodge the answers. She was well, at least, and for that I was thankful. I had left myself only the one contingency: if she had been ill I would have waited for a more proper time.

But, no sooner was I seated beside her, when habit gripped

ne again. This was no phantom Lottie but the woman who was
a solid part of my existence. Now she was the one who was
real, and Elizabeth seemed like someone I had met vividly in
a dream. Almost desperately I clung to the image of Elizabeth;
made myself recall our most intimate moments.

"You look tired, Alfred," Lottie said, with an examining
glance. "Have you been working hard?"

Was that the question that would give me my lead? I
heard myself answering, "Just this damned going from one
place to another. I was expecting to be in Berlin today, finishing up."

"I know," she said, almost contritely. "But I thought it bet-
er that I should see you."

"About what? You still haven't told me."

"Why don't you have a drink, Alfred?" she suggested. "I
don't think you're in a good mood. You're a little nervous. It's
important that we both be very calm and reasonable."

With a grim smile, I said, "Yes, that's always important."
Lottie had a favor to ask of me, I guessed, something she assumed would displease me. She couldn't have picked a better
time to ask something of me, of course. "I'm fine," I assured
her. "The change of climate is bothering me, that's all. This
suit I'm wearing is too heavy. You see, it was cold in Vienna
when I left, and here it's in the eighties. I got hold of the
Professor's candelabrum, by the way. Sent it off to him by air
express this morning."

"That's nice," Lottie said.

A little annoyed by her response, I said, "I went to quite a
bit of trouble to get it."

"You'll tell me about it later," she said. "Here's a waiter.
Tell him what you'd like to drink."

I asked for Scotch and soda, and Lottie said she wanted a

sweet sherry, if they had any here. When the waiter said he would find out, she told him to bring any kind of sherry he had. "Madeira, maybe?" the waiter asked.

"Yes," she said, "all right."

"What have you been doing here?" I asked, anxious to get on to what I had been doing. It was as though I must not keep Elizabeth waiting.

"I left the tour," Lottie said.

"Yes, I assumed you had."

"I just didn't feel at home with all those fine ladies," Lottie explained, "and finally I said to myself, 'I'm not a Hadassah lady, I am basically a Jewish woman from Europe who had planned to make her life here in Israel, and now that I have the chance I will look around by myself and see what I missed.' I was in Caesarea when I told them I was leaving the tour. I took a bus here to Tel Aviv and looked up my old friend Simon, who lives here."

"I see," I said, but I didn't—yet.

"Simon took me around and showed me the Israel I had never managed to see before."

"Wonderful," I said perfunctorily.

"He's a wonderful man, Simon. He came here in 1948, in time to fight the Arabs and nearly got killed himself. Then he joined the Histadrut and became a quite important official, and about ten years ago he took up painting. Would you believe it, Alfred? Simon is regarded as a very important painter here, and they will show some of his work when the new museum opens in Jerusalem."

"Had he painted before?"

"Oh, he used to dabble at it in the DP camp, but I never took it seriously. It's a wonderful thing to discover your real talent."

The waiter brought our drinks.

Lottie held her glass by the stem, and said, with a sudden little throb in her voice. "Drink to us, Alfred, please."

"Yes," I said, automatically touching her glass with mine.

"To me and Simon," Lottie said.

And her eyes filled with tears. I suppose they were for me.

I met Simon, Simon Ben Arkan, as he called himself now, later in the evening at his apartment in the Ramat Gan section of Tel Aviv. By then I had absorbed the news that Lottie had given me, and, while my knees had a certain weakness to them and my voice to my own ears seemed thin and strange, I was able to assume a reasonably cheerful manner. But I had hardly been able to touch the food served to me as Lottie carefully, even logically, attempted to explain what had happened and why.

"I knew that our marriage was not as it should have been," she said, "and I knew, also, that you regarded me—well, not as a mental case, exactly, but as a neurotic woman whose complaints came from some past experiences. Yes, Alfred, I have sometimes had nightmares about those experiences, but I also know that I am basically a strong person and that I was unhappy for other reasons. You understand what I am trying to say to you?"

"Yes, I think so," I said.

"It is not that I have not felt love for you, Alfred. I shall always feel it. In your way you have been quite wonderful to me, and I am not implying that it has been a selfish way. But all those years I did feel useless. You could have gotten along quite well without me. I was no help to your success in your work. What I seemed to be was some kind of advertisement to you."

"No, that's not true, Lottie," I protested.

"Yes, kindly admit it. Having seen and been overwhelmed by what you saw, having come so late, too late really, you had this great impulse to rescue. So you made me your wife. This proved that you cared—not so much about me—but about what happened to people like me. You could not stand the innocence of those who were punished for simply being what they were— Jews. You were afraid you had lost your own Jewishness, but through me you would have it again. A gesture, Alfred, that was all it was. And all these years you have tried to make it into more. By taking on my suffering you thought you could cross the bridge to the mass of suffering. But it was never possible. It was possible for none of you. I have thought about this a lot, Alfred, and it is true what I am saying."

"Are you saying it was the suffering, the concentration camps, that you had in common with Simon?"

"Partly that, but it is more. We both were charged with the crime of being Jewish. Oh, how it was burned into us. So, we criminals must stick together. Simon came here, where he knew he belonged, and he was right, and I took the easier way that you offered, going with you to America. I made a mistake, Alfred. You attracted me so. You seemed so sure. I kept trying to find myself in this country you brought me to, but it never happened. After a time I resented you—I'll admit it. Alfred, the truth is, I should have come here. It wouldn't have been a hardship for me. They could have sent me to the desert to fight with a gun, and I would never have complained. And, with you, all I did was complain."

"You exaggerate," I said.

"No, I wasn't a good wife to you. Like the women I despise, I punished you the way those women do. You know what I'm talking about."

"You did that to punish me?"

"Please, Alfred, realize that I didn't know what I was doing. Not then. It was Simon who made this clear to me."

"Why hasn't he married?"

"He did marry. She died two years ago. The poor woman was never well. She had suffered too much in a camp. He kept her alive as long as he could. But I must tell you this, Alfred—Simon and I understand each other more with our little fingers than you and I do with our minds. We don't have to talk about it. We know. It is only right that we should spend the rest of our years together. And that is what I ask of you, Alfred, that you divorce me, for in Israel that is what is necessary before I can marry again. You don't have to do it here. I will arrange for it to be done before some rabbis in New York. An hour of your time is all it will take. But I cannot tell you how necessary it is that you do this for me. Will you give me your consent?"

I sat at the table with her, feeling quite numb for a long moment. Then I felt a surge of warmth for her. She was a brave woman, I now knew. Her fierce pride had not allowed her to keep from me any longer than necessary a decision she had made. And, though it was only an empty gesture on my part, a kind of protocol demanded that I give every chance to those years that had cemented us together until this moment.

"Have you thought about this enough?" I asked, my mouth strangely dry.

"I have done nothing else but think about it," she assured me, fervency in her voice. "Give me credit for that, Alfred. And you should think about something, too: Have you truly needed me?"

Her dark eyes, leveled straight at me, had a look of solemn

wisdom. So much wisdom, that I wouldn't have been very sur
prised to have her tell me she already knew about Elizabeth
or someone like Elizabeth.

"Yes, I have needed you," I said. "I'm sure of that."

"We both have needed love," she said. "But do we need i
from each other? Be honest, Alfred."

"Love is a commitment," I said. There I was, being a close
mouthed lawyer-type again, while she was squarely facing the
truth.

"That is a little different," Lottie said, "from the kind o
love I am talking about."

"You mean, making love."

"Yes," she said. "I am able to make love with Simon." She
bit her lip, because that was the hardest thing of all for her to
say to me.

Maybe, with that admission from her, I should have made
my own admission, but what purpose to it now? She might have
taken it as my way of striking back at her. I was as little
ashamed of sleeping with Elizabeth as she was of sleeping
with Simon, but she had found her pride, and I wanted her
to keep it. She was a woman in love. Why sour it for her
A useless confession it would make now, I thought.

"We will always be the closest of friends," Lottie said. "
hope you will allow that."

"Oh, hell," I said, "what else could we be?"

And Lottie took a deep breath, as though filled with relief

When I met Simon he wore an embarrassed smile, welcom
ing us into his apartment in a building that couldn't have been
finished more than a few months before. "It is all right
Simon," Lottie told him forthrightly. "Alfred knows and un
derstands."

Immediately Simon grasped my hand warmly. "Wonderful

wonderful," he said. "You are the man I knew you would be."

Simon was short, not much taller than Lottie, and his head had grown almost entirely bald, and he had a moon face and a slightly twisted nose. He was not the handsomest man in the world, but I could see how women would find him highly likable, and I liked the paintings I saw on his wall, too—large paintings of abstracted figures, done in bold strokes and vivid colors, with reds and blacks predominating.

"I seem to be the stranger in the house," I said, and we all laughed, a little nervously, but it helped to lighten the atmosphere.

Then Simon insisted on making us Lebanese coffee, which he knew how to make, he claimed, with absolute authenticity. The three-room flat was spacious and contained a kitchen of the utmost modernity. The floors of pale wood were polished to a high shine and were covered here and there with small rugs of vivid patterns and colors. This was where Lottie would make her next home, and I could see she would be happy in it—far happier than in the large apartment she was co-owner of in New York.

Simon served us the rich black coffee ceremoniously, brought out a bottle of brandy, apologizing for its being of a local nature, and then insisted that I tell him what my trip to Europe was about. He must have heard about it before from Lottie, but he behaved as though it was all new to him. Maybe it was because of an underlying feeling of being slighted that I also brought in a reference to Elizabeth, as Oskar Weisse's courier. When I mentioned how attractive she was, I saw Lottie's eyes glance at me shrewdly for a moment. But I said nothing further about her.

"And you go back to Berlin now? Do you think you will win your case?"

"I'm going to try hard," I said. "I may have to settle fc
less, but I think we'll get something."

"Yes," Simon said, nodding, "and a few more residents c
Tel Aviv will be able to do some extra shopping on Allenb
Road. It's a big and not very funny joke here about these pay
ments that come from Germany. Some think the whole econom
will collapse when they stop."

"You don't think that, Simon," Lottie said.

"No, I don't. Forgive me. I didn't mean to cast doubt o
what you are doing. But I am not inclined to look on the Ge
mans as my long-lost friends. I would be quite happy if we di
without them. But that's my opinion, and all I have are th
scars to back it up. Arab *and* German scars, I might add."

"Some of Alfred's best friends are Germans," Lottie saic
She meant it as a joke, but Simon didn't appreciate it.

"How do you find them?" he asked me.

"They're mostly business friends," I said. "I deal witl
them. I find them honest, on the whole."

"Fair is fair, Simon," Lottie said.

Simon shook his head. "Someday there will be a final solu
tion to the German problem," he said, "but don't ask me whe
and how. Well—some more brandy, yes?"

"I'd better be getting back to the hotel," I said. "A long
hard day." I looked at Lottie, to see if she would be goin
back too.

"I'll stay here for a little while," she said. "I have thing
to talk about with Simon."

She came with me to the door, and Simon was discree
enough to leave us alone. "Are you all right, Alfred?" sh
asked. "Do you feel this is the right thing for all of us?"

"Let's talk again in the morning," I said. "There'll be som
arrangements you'll want to make."

"I'm not asking for anything, Alfred."

"No, but it's for your own good."

She nodded and told me to wait at the entrance of the building for the taxi that would come along. Simon was telephoning for one now. We kissed each other's cheeks, and hers were wet.

In my hotel bed my own eyes smarted with tears for awhile. All that time, I thought, all that time.

In the morning I woke up, still tired, my back aching. Probably a physical reaction to shock. I had lost my wife, after all, and losing a wife was a different thing from losing a lover. And there were legalities. I hadn't thought about them too much when planning to tell Lottie about Elizabeth, for I wasn't certain of how she would react. Nor did I know how adamant I would have been if Lottie had begged me to stay with her. I would never have that knowledge, now. I could only speculate about the ugliness of the scene that might have transpired, *if* there had been no Simon. But I rather suspected that I had misjudged Lottie all along. I was the one who had held on to the marriage, not she. I had invested Lottie with my own guilts, worried about protecting her, and all she had been asking was that I be honest with her. What she didn't know wouldn't hurt her, I thought, but it was what she knew that had hurt her. She had been waiting for me to make the admission, if not Elizabeth, then whoever. I felt rather like a damned fool.

My telephone buzzed—it was one of those modern Scandinavian telephones, combining mouthpiece, receiver, and dial stand all in one—and the reservations clerk greeted me with a good-morning and, like a bad joke, an announcement that he, happily, now had a double room for the Beckers. I told him it wouldn't be necessary to change us, because I'd be leaving today.

"I went to a lot of trouble for you," he chided me.

"I'm much obliged," I said.

Breakfast was set up in the grill room, and Lottie joined me there. She looked fresh and well satisfied with herself, and it was a fairly new experience to see her so.

"You look younger," I said.

"I'm starting a new life," she told me solemnly.

We worked it out. I said I wanted to settle ten thousand dollars on her, and I would further send her monthly payments for the next two years that would add up to another ten thousand. Again her eyes filled with tears, because she thought I was being generous.

"Look, I'm a lawyer," I said unnecessarily. "You'd get that easily enough, if you had the sense to ask for it."

"I came to you with nothing——" she began.

"And you've devoted eighteen years to me. Let's not talk about it. If I couldn't afford the money, it would be a different thing."

"You're leaving today?" she asked.

"If I can get a connection. I have a call to put in to Jerusalem first."

"Your case in Berlin?"

I nodded. "While I'm here I might as well check out a couple of details."

It helped to talk about business.

"Simon was very impressed with you," she said. "He thinks you're a fine man."

"I was impressed with him," I said. "Remarkable talent. I only know what I like, of course, but I like his work."

My forty-six-year-old former wife blushed like a schoolgirl to hear my praise. And it was sobering to me to realize that she was more excited over Simon than she had ever been over me.

"Simon made an interesting remark about that Weisse you talked about last night. He said if he had come across a man like that he would have been tempted to shoot him."

"Does he have a gun?"

"No, of course not."

"Then he oughtn't to talk like that. You don't take things into your own hands. I don't, anyway. Tell him to forget about it. He'll be handled."

The thought had occurred to me that some crazy Israeli kid might get some wild idea of that kind.

"In fact," I said, "I shouldn't have mentioned his name. We're only going on supposition."

"Yes," she said submissively, "you're right."

I asked Lottie if she'd be returning to New York to claim her clothes and personal possessions. She choked up at that, and I said that if we didn't talk about it now it would be a lot better for both of us, and besides we could handle it all by letter.

"What will you do?" she asked.

"I'll work," I said, "and remember all the good things about our marriage."

"You're nice to say that," she said. "But you're an attractive man, and lots of women will be after you."

"Or me after them, maybe."

"You've had some practice already, haven't you?"

That sounded a little like the old Lottie—but with a difference. No jealousy, just simple interest and curiosity. And if I mentioned Elizabeth to her, in this context, it would merely seem to her like a conquest, a proof of my masculinity.

I escaped by saying, "Look who's talking about practice."

That made her blush like any schoolgirl.

"But you understand, don't you?"

"Now that I have had a chance to know Simon, I understand," I said.

She squeezed my hand. "Alfred, I want you to be happy. Please remember that."

"I'll try," I said carefully. "I'll certainly try."

We finished our coffee and went out to the lobby together, and there we said our good-by. I saw her take out a handkerchief as she walked away, and my eyes, it must be admitted, were again a little blurry. Turning away, I went out to the hotel terrace and blinked from the dazzle of the bright morning sun on the sea. A ship was anchored not far off. Something was bothering me, trying to edge its way into my mind. I should have been thinking of Lottie and Elizabeth, but it was Hilde's face I saw—that moment, long years past, when I had told her it was over between us. I hadn't given her any reason, not the real reason, and it was because she, being German, would, I feared, be deeply wounded that I had selected a Jewish woman for my wife. At this moment, I became aware of the real reason why I hadn't told Lottie of Elizabeth. In a way, it was the same thing, I thought, and my cowardice had to do less with them than with myself.

A little later, in my room, I put through a call to Leon Fridman at the Yad Vashem in Jerusalem. Fridman was one of those who had helped locate the former Zeller-Bricken slaves now residing in Israel. He was a deputy director of the institute, in charge of archives relating to crimes against Jews. We had done our work of collaboration by letter, and although we had never met, he knew my name well enough.

It took ten minutes to get through to him, and after he had gotten over his surprise at hearing from me, he wanted to know to what he owed the honor of the call. I reminded him of the

Zeller-Bricken case and told him that some information had
come to me about former and present directors of the company
and that I wondered if his archives might be able to throw any
additional light on the matter.

"You are now in Tel Aviv?" he asked.

"Yes."

"I suggest, then, that you come here to the institute."

"I am leaving today. I had hoped that you would be able
to consult your files——"

"Impossible, my good friend, to do that over the telephone.
You see, for such matters certain clearances would be required."

"Then what good would it do for me to come there?"

"You are a good friend, and we might be able to have a
confidential chat."

"What's the quickest way to get there?"

"From Tel Aviv," Fridman said, "there are trains, buses,
and taxis. Of these the taxi is the fastest, but it will depend
on the road traffic. With luck—an hour and a half."

"I'll be there," I said.

I had one of the concierges round up a car and driver for
me—"Not an old rattle trap," I warned him—and then checked
at a travel agency (one of the lobby shops) for flight information. El Al had a plane that left at ten minutes to six for Rome
and Frankfurt: Frankfurt arrival at 9:45 P.M., local time. That
would give me time enough to catch a late plane for Berlin.

Somehow, keeping myself busy dissipated my tiredness.

Shortly after ten, my bags were in the trunk of the hired
car, and I was on the road—which is to say my driver was
threading his way through Tel Aviv's maze of streets, crowded
with traffic. He took the long way, through Jaffa, to get on the
Jerusalem Road finally, and, once on it, he risked his car and
two lives cutting in and out to get around the trucks that

clogged the highway. Many of them were lorries, carrying young Army men wearing brown uniforms of heavy British Army-type cloth and brown berets. It was understandable that this road should have a constant flow of military traffic, for this was the narrowest stretch in all of Israel, and here an Arab armored column could cut the country in two with a thrust of a dozen miles or so. "This car belongs to the Army," my driver told me rather proudly. He was stocky, round-faced, and in his middle forties. "War comes, and like that," he snapped his fingers, "I put on my uniform and take this car to my reserve unit."

"What's your unit?" I asked.

"Personnel carrier," he said, "attached to an armored brigade."

"You're not expecting war, though."

"I always expect war," he said. "You're a Jew, you expect war. This time it's the Arabs who hate us. Next time, who knows?" He shrugged, hardly seeming disturbed.

We had time to talk, for the highway, four lanes in some sections, three lanes in others, had a way of narrowing down inexplicably to two lanes, with a resulting hold-up of traffic. I couldn't see how we would make the trip in less than three hours, and that meant I'd have to spend the night in Jerusalem, for I wouldn't be able to get to Lod Airport in time for the flight.

Traffic ran smoother after we reached Ramee, a midpoint and also the gateway to the Jerusalem corridor. I glimpsed minarets glistening in the hot bright sun, and, nearer to me, chickens squawked as they skittered across the road. Out of the town, we were on open road, the traffic thinner but still held up often enough by big produce trucks, groaning on the inclines. My driver demonstrated a high degree of skill as he dove in and out, calculating the distances between us and approaching vehicles with precision. No wonder he'd been classified as an Army driver. One truck that passed was filled with a female Army unit. They too wore the brown drab and berets, and the sweet girlish voices were lifted in song. This is not a country, I thought; it's an army. The drivers of military lorries would make way for us on the hills, keeping to the very edge of the road, but not the buses. Their drivers took it as effrontery that we should want to pass and after keeping us behind them on the downgrades, barreling at a dangerous speed, they would use the momentum gained to negotiate the upgrades.

I found myself enjoying the ride after awhile and was surprised, when we had climbed high in the Judean range and were making a winding descent toward Jerusalem, that we had used up only eighty-five minutes. The Yad Vashem was on a hillside on the way into the city. I caught a glimpse of the white spaceship-like dome of the Shrine of the Scrolls of the new museum, just before we turned into the road leading to the Yad Vashem's own museum and administrative building.

"Get some lunch," I told my driver, "and be back here in about two hours."

All this riding for two hours, his look seemed to say. But he was being paid well, and he promised to be back. "You may have to wait," I said, and he shrugged.

Fridman was cordial. He was a small, intense man of about forty, with an aquiline face made longer by a small goatee. His habitat was a compact office in a row of similar offices along a narrow corridor on the first floor of the institute. He had an impeccable knowledge of his files, and he was known to have done important work, for those files had proved immensely useful during the Eichmann trial.

"Ludwigsburg has been in touch with me," he said, after he had beckoned me into a chair beside his desk, "about a Zeller-Bricken director whose name is Weisse. Does this concern your case?"

"It could," I said, "and perhaps tip it either way. If Ludwigsburg picks him up and holds him for trial—not too likely at the moment, by the way—his company might dump him, laying all the responsibility at his door. They'd get rid of Roehling at the same time. Then we would have a much poorer case. It's more to our interest to keep him there for the time being."

"I assumed so when I sent the two names to Elihu Grossman's committee in New York. We have little interest in them here; they seemed to operate only as functionaries."

"How does Silbermann of Vienna come into this?" I asked.

"You know him?" He gave an amused shrug. "He claims to be doing much of our work. We send him copies of our files, on request—those that are not privileged. I assume he requires the publicity to continue his career."

"He was useful to me in Vienna," I said.

"Good. Most of the time he is useful only as an irritant. He makes noise, and people react. Naturally, as an institute for archives and research purely, we can't make regular announcements of what we discover. So Silbermann makes the announcements. You know, of course, who does the real work."

"Who?"

"Oh, sorry. I thought you knew. I am not permitted to say."

I assumed he referred to Israeli intelligence and let it go.

"Well, now," Fridman said, "I suggest we pay a visit to the files. Follow me, please."

On the way to the basement rooms, where the archives were stored, he said: "You understand that I cannot release any of our documents to you. That would require government permission and would take some time to accomplish. Any notes you wish to take are your own responsibility. I do not intend to watch what you write."

In a cool room, filled from floor to ceiling with files and neat stacks of microfilm rolls in labeled cardboard boxes, Fridman went directly to a section at one end of a long row of shelves and drew out a roll. "Let us examine this," he said, leading me to a viewing machine. Through the lens of the machine, as he slowly unwound the roll of microfilm, I was able to view, magnified, a series of SS documents that appeared to have emanated from RHSA, Berlin, in 1943. Each document bore the signature of O. Weisse, Hauptmann, and most seemed to be requisitions—paper supplies, Luger side-arms. I saw, also, microfilmed copies of the letters from Weisse to Roehling that I had been shown at Ludwigsburg.

"That's it?" I asked

"It was on the basis of these documents," Fridman said, "that I furnished the names of the two gentlemen to Mr. Grossman."

"If that were all there were to it," I said, "my case would be simpler."

"What else is there, Mr. Becker?"

"Zhitomir," I said.

"The Himmler conference? How would a man like Weisse enter into that? He was young at the time."

"An anonymous informant has placed him as being present."

"And, if so?"

"Then it would show, legally speaking, his foreknowledge

of the fate of the Jews he helped arrange to have shipped to Hanover."

"That would make him a murderer?"

"What do you think?"

Fridman's eyes seemed to take on a somber glow. "I think it would make," he said softly, "a most interesting case for a German court to have to decide. There have been no such cases as yet. Are you anxious to open up this particular can of sardines?"

"If I can inform myself, I would like to do that much—for the next round of negotiations, if nothing else."

"Then," he said, "the thing to do is for us to look at the Zhitomir file. Will you wait here, please? I will not be long."

He returned a few minutes later with another roll of microfilm. He threaded it into the machine and peered through the viewer.

"The summary of the conference," he said, "is to be found in the American War Crimes file in your archives at Alexandria and is classified 'Secret.' An accompanying report lists those present; among them Himmler, Thierack, Rothenberger, Streckenbach, and Dieckhoff. They are all deceased, so they will not help us."

"What else?" I asked.

"There is a listing of several references that contain information about the conference and its instigation."

"Anything else?"

"A curious little item. The Zhitomir conference is referred to in the diaries of Mordecai Goldfarb, who perished at Chelmno in December, 1943. Goldfarb was a rabbi who managed to keep a voluminous diary of all that happened to the Jews during the extermination phase. The diary was preserved, after being given

for safekeeping into the hands of a Polish labor supervisor. He
was promised a good deal of money if he would see to it that the
diary found its way either to responsible members of American
Jewry, or to Eretz Israel, as our country was then known."

"Did it?"

"Yes. The diary is presently at Kibbutz Lohamei Haghettaot,
in their museum known as the Ghetto Fighters' House. A most
interesting story in itself, of how it came to rest there. Mordecai
Goldfarb is a revered martyr at Lohamei Haghettaot. You
know where it is?"

"Yes," I said, drawing a deep breath, "fifteen miles north
of Haifa—way the hell at the other end of this country. The
kibbutz also got us some of our affidavits for the Zeller-Bricken
case."

"Quite a case," Fridman said with a melancholy smile. "Will
you go to the kibbutz?"

"How accurate was Goldfarb?"

"Amazingly so, I am told. He was an assiduous collector
of information on every detail and phase of the holocaust. He
never doubted the German intention to massacre every last Jew
in Europe, and although he doubted his own survival he had no
doubt that the Germans would one day pay for their crimes. I
suggest you look at his diary."

"Okay," I said, nodding.

"I will give you a letter to the director," he offered, leading
me from the room and then carefully locking the door behind
us. "Why not have lunch with me? It is a long drive to the
kibbutz. You will probably want to stay overnight in Haifa,
before going there, and I suggest that I make you a reservation
at the Dan Carmel. They will probably be booked full, and
I can be helpful."

I remembered that I would have to cancel my reservation for the flight that evening.

The drive to Haifa required five hours, after which I released the driver from further bondage to me, plunged myself into a tub of cool water, and planned for a recuperative evening at the hotel. There would be dinner. There was a movie the management was showing for its guests to help fill the long, empty evening. A sense of loneliness gripped me, as though I were wandering a no-man's land and did not know how to find my way to safety. I made sure to have two warming, dizzying martinis at the bar before going in to dinner, where Hadassah ladies, with hair of blue and lavender-dyed-silver, all perfumed, all corseted, chatted noisily of bridge, children, and charities at most of the tables.

The kibbutz was near the seashore, not far off the main road that ran between the old city of Acre and the new city of Naharia. The management of the Dan Carmel had procured for me a hired Renault, small, snappy, and quite new, and in the cooler air of western Galilee, in dazzling sunlight, I pulled into a parking area beside the stark concrete of the Ghetto Fighters' House, which stood on a rise and overlooked the cultivated fields below. I was the first visitor of the day, and the director, Itzak Bernstein, made me welcome and offered me a small research room in which to look through the diary of Mordecai Goldfarb. The manuscript, translated into English, French, and Hebrew from its original Yiddish, had been typed, duplicated, and bound looseleaf between heavy boards of leather and was simply titled *Chelmno Diary*. I was given the English version.

The style of Goldfarb's writing ranged from a tone of

J'Accuse! to a jeremiad; the more than one hundred pages were suffused with an intense emotion that had obviously sustained him through the always dangerous and arduous work, done in secret, and protected by his companions in suffering. Although I was looking for only one reference, I found myself reading from its beginning—"I am now in Chelmno. . . ."—to its last words—"I tell of the torture, the foul murder of four hundred thousand Jews in this place alone and yes, of six million all told, and I will recount all until . . ." And there it ended. The last recorded date was the tenth of October, 1943.

The room was bare, its walls whitewashed, except for the wooden table and the chair on which I sat. Sun streamed in through one small opened window, and the odor of ripening fruits, of fertile fields, was strong. Mordecai Goldfarb wrote of his conscience, which would not let him rest unless he recorded what otherwise would be buried forever, for his fear was not only of his own death but of not a single Jew remaining alive, so that the horrors experienced by all would be lost in oblivion.

"Thus I gather, thus I write. . . . I know all. I have seen it with my own eyes. I have heard it all from others. I was one of the few always on the watch, but my brethren would not listen. Now we are but shadows of Jews, benumbed, bereft of hope. Not one of us is whole, not one is possessed of a whole mind, and people after us will wonder how it was that so many millions were led so docilely to the slaughter. Because hidden will be the vile deceit of the murderous tricksters, they will cover up their traces, their boots that kicked will be washed clean, their hands that wielded the guns, the clubs, the whips will be white again, and no one will know the woe that befell an entire people. Did we not resist? Oh, we resisted, and many are the acts of martyrdom. But we faced a great machinery, and I will tell of its miserable clatter."

Goldfarb traced in his own overwrought language the preparation of "the insensate, vile-hearted nation" for slaughter, the plans of the leaders, and how the "most stupid, the most evil, the most criminal of other nations" were recruited to share the task of extermination. What surprised me was the accuracy of his knowledge, to the very names of the perpetrators: Philip Bouhler, Goebbels, Himmler, Globocnik. And on the seventy-first page I came to his account of the Zhitomir conference, where it had been decided, for the greater welfare of the glorious Reich, that certain Jews be selected for labor, to be made available to industrial firms engaged in the war effort, and to "extract value from the slower deaths granted to them."

"At Zhitomir," Goldfarb wrote, "were the following, and I swear to the truth of these names, for they come from one who was there and who observed and who engraved their presences in his memory. The Reichsführer Himmler himself was there, and with him were Otto Thierack, Kurt Rothenberger, Bruno Streckenbach, a certain Colonel Bender, a Sturmbannführer by name of Karl Dieckhoff, and a Hauptmann O. Weisse, who accompanied Streckenbach as an aide. This infamous gathering made charts and calculations, and proposed that 250,000 of the healthiest Jews be selected from their places of internment and shipped to factories where labor needs were most critical. I tell you this is the truth, and I swear to the date of the meeting, which occurred on September 14 of last year."

I stayed in the small room, reading, for the better part of two hours, and before leaving I copied out the section that dealt with the Zhitomir conference.

I did not linger at this kibbutz named after the Polish

martyrs, the fighters who had perished in the Warsaw Ghetto, and back at the Dan Carmel an hour later I quickly drafted a cable to Elihu, which I gave to the desk clerk to send off. REPORT ON OUR FRIEND IS POSITIVE. CHECK THROUGH GRAHAM. CONTACT ME KEMPINSKI. The case was hardly legal, but it was a case, and I did not want the dead rabbi's words to have been written entirely in vain.

22: It was well past midnight when my BEA flight skimmed into Tempelhof; I had taken one of the last planes from Frankfurt, the El Al 707 having been delayed in its departure from Rome. At this hour, with the streets of West Berlin all but deserted, the traffic was nothing at all, and my taxi swung into the Kurfürstendamm hardly ten minutes after leaving the air terminal. The pavement cafés had their glass sides closed tight, and many were dark inside. A few dawdlers sat at tables at the Am Zoo Café, waiters hanging grimly near as a reminder for them to leave. The lobby of the Kempinski was not so deserted. A late party had been held in one of its public rooms, and women in furs and men in dinner jackets still chatted while waiting for their cars to pick them up. Something to do with politics, I gathered from the animated snatches of conversation I overheard.

A political gathering in Berlin usually meant a scarcity of hotel rooms; but one had been held for me, and I was accommodated with a good-sized room. It faced the hotel's parking lot, but that was all right because it would mean less noise from outside. I was truly tired, but to make sure I would sleep I took a mild chloralhydrate pill, not bothering to look at the small pile of telephone messages and letters the hotel porter had handed me. Call Elizabeth? No, send her flowers first.

In the morning I opened a letter from Bob Pryor, one of my partners in the firm, and his message was to the effect that he hoped I would clean up the Berlin business as soon as possible, because a new client, a theatrical producer who was about to go into television production and was setting himself up as a corporation, had specifically asked for me to handle the matter. The account looked lucrative. Between the lines I got another message: the restitution cases were petering out and were all but gratuitous anyway. I was to head into other areas. Change was the order of the day. One must push ahead.

So be it. I next read Elihu's letter, which had been sent air mail special delivery and had arrived the day before. No luck on the document I had asked about. He had contacted Graham Heckler, as I had suggested, and Heckler had made an inquiry. Nothing on Weisse, nor on Zhitomir. "On the other hand," Elihu went on to suggest, "why not throw a scare into Z-B with what you have? As for your own involvement with Ludwigsburg, there are other people who can do that kind of thing better. Don't mean to downgrade you, Alfred, but stick to what you do best. That half-million-dollar figure may have to go down somewhat. Heckler told me that the deal with Z-B was about to go through any day, so it would be advisable to act fast."

But the letter had been sent, of course, before my cable to Elihu from Lod Airport.

So, fast action being demanded of me, I made my first call

of the day to Karl Steglitz. "I'd like another meeting with the directorate of Zeller-Bricken," I told him. "And, as soon as possible, please."

"I am not sure that can be arranged so easily," he said, his voice even more dubious than his words.

"Yes, it can," I assured him. "My people in New York are pushing me in this matter, I have some new facts to present, and I strongly suggest you do your best to arrange the meeting. I won't be in Berlin for long. And I don't see how I can keep this from the press much longer."

"I will call you back," he said curtly.

The next action of what I regarded as my two-pronged attack was to telephone Weisse at his office. He was in conference, I was told, and his secretary seemed surprised that someone should call and expect to find him available, just like that. I asked her to give him a message to the effect that I would appreciate hearing from him at his earliest convenience.

That done, I went down to the lobby and ordered flowers—dark red roses—and had them sent to Elizabeth's flat. I wrote on the card simply: "Love—Alfred." Maybe it was nagging shyness, maybe it was because of the screws I was about to twist on her father, that I wanted her to call me. Besides, I had no right to assume anything.

At the newsstand, as I was picking up the previous day's editions of the Paris *Times* and *Tribune,* I heard myself being paged. I took the call in one of the lobby booths.

"This is Weisse," I heard through the receiver after I said hello.

"Yes, Herr Weisse. I understand you would like to speak to me, and I would like to speak to you. When can we arrange it?"

"How long will you be in Berlin?"

"Not long. I'm free most of today."

"Where would you like to talk?"

"That limousine would be a good place," I said.

"Very good," he said. "I will be outside your hotel in one hour."

He hung up without another word.

I went back to my room and looked through my telephone messages. One from Herr Langsehn in Ludwigsburg, one from Liz, and one from Max Gerson. I telephoned Gerson and told him the news about the candelabrum, that it would arrive in New York in a day or so, and that my and the Professor's appreciation would be expressed in the form of a check.

"Not necessary," he said.

I telephoned Liz at her office and told her the news about Sarah Stein.

"Does that mean you can't claim compensation for her?" Liz asked.

"Not necessarily," I said. "I'll speak to Justice Kimmel about it before I leave, and it's possible that without proof of psychic trauma having been inflicted in the camp we can still prove some kind of claim. I can get testimony from two former inmates of the degrading conditions, plus the fact that these conditions could only have worsened her obvious state of shock. I can also tell Sarah's psychiatrist more of the facts he needs for treating her. So, it's not a total loss. I'm not giving up."

"Anything else I can do?"

"That's about it for now," I said. "You've done enough."

"Will I see you before you leave?"

"I hope so. I'm not staying for long. They want me back at the office."

"Well, be sure to call. I know how busy you are. Anything new on that other very important person?"

"A couple of things not well suited to telephone conversation."

"My, my," she said, "you sound like a true Berliner. I'm dying to hear when you get the chance."

I studied the message from Langsehn, then decided he would have to wait for awhile. I hadn't finished my unpacking, so I put away some suits and shirts in the closet and, while doing so, came across the package that contained the blouse I had bought for Gloria. It had not been so long ago that I had shopped with Elizabeth, but it seemed like months. I left the package at the bottom of the bag, because I had a habit of forgetting things placed in hotel-room drawers.

Back in the lobby, I waited behind the glass doors of the hotel entrance until I saw the long black Mercedes limousine glide to the curb. The same chauffeur I had seen once before was driving. I went outside and came to an abrupt halt. For, sitting in the rear with Weisse, I saw Elizabeth. It occurred to me at first that I was mistaken, that Weisse had brought a secretary with him, but the tight-faced nod of recognition that Elizabeth gave me was all the proof I needed. They were together, and I felt almost physically sick.

Weisse gave a peremptory beckoning gesture of his hand, and by that time the chauffeur had left his seat and gone around the hood of the car to open the rear door for me. I got in, next to Elizabeth, who sat in the middle of the seat. Weisse did not offer me his hand, which I interpreted as a significant lapse.

"Why are you here?" I asked Elizabeth.

"I have asked her to be with us, Herr Becker," Weisse answered for her from his corner. His tone was cold. "I think it important that she understand the kind of blackmailer you are."

Elizabeth turned to me and gave me an intense stare. There was pain in it and warning, and a plea for understanding.

Weisse leaned forward and tapped sharply on the glass separating us from the chauffeur's seat. Obediently, the chauffeur shifted into gear, and we moved forward to the corner, then turned right on the Kurfürstendamm away from the busier section.

"I don't quite understand you," I said to Weisse.

"I will make myself clear," he said. "I happen to know that you have taken advantage of my politeness and generosity to ingratiate yourself with my daughter and to use her in your efforts to obtain information about me."

"That is not true, Papa," Elizabeth said.

"Be quiet," he commanded her.

I felt Elizabeth's body freeze next to mine.

"You are not to talk to me like that," she said to him evenly.

"Why did you come?" I asked her.

"We have nothing to hide from each other, Alfred," she said simply. "Speak freely."

"You see," Weisse said angrily. "You have estranged me from my own daughter. What right do you have to interfere with my personal life?"

"You're quite right," I told him. "None. I had no intention of doing so. So, suppose we get down to the business we're here for."

"My own daughter regards me as a monster," Weisse complained.

"I can't help that," I said.

"Nevertheless, you are the one who has put doubts about me in her mind."

"I would prefer if we only discussed our business together."

Weisse stared at me through lowered lids. He gave an abrupt shrug of his wide shoulders and asked, "What do you want now?"

"You also wanted to see me," I pointed out.

"Well, we are together. I merely wished to tell you how wrong you are concerning me. I also wished my daughter to hear this. Any activities of mine you may have learned about were in the best interests of the very people you represent. The fact that you are in a position to represent them today is, in itself, proof enough of my good intentions. In addition to that, I have proof that I was fully cleared—De-Nazified, if you will —by both your American authorities and the present German government. Now you wish to tear me down. Why?"

"It is not my business or purpose to tear you down," I told him. "The reason I wished to see you was to hear your final offer. I have no more time to spend here on this case. If you prefer, I'll go to the directorate instead. I have no intention of blackmailing you. Your daughter knows my position on that. I have something else to tell you, but I'd prefer if your daughter were not here for that."

"Speak, Alfred," Elizabeth said tiredly. "My father and I have had a long talk. I know more than you think."

"You realize," Weisse said to her, "that this man you sit next to and defend is a married man whose wife was a Jewess from a concentration camp and who was imprisoned not because of her race—for that was not known—but for criminal activities."

"Yes, I know," Elizabeth answered him wearily.

"You've been looking into my record, too," I said, genuinely surprised. "You put an odd interpretation on my former wife's behavior."

"Former?" Elizabeth said, turning toward me.

"I'll explain that, too, if you give me a chance," I said. "But not now."

"Well, what is it you have to tell me?" Weisse asked.

We had gone along the Kurfürstendamm, as far as Rathenau Platz, and now, turning into the Königs Allee we were in the

Grunewald residential section, with its weathered houses and secluded villas. The Königs Allee led into a wooded park-like area of the Grunewald, and this was the direction the chauffeur was now taking. The houses thinned out, a hush seemed to descend over us, and I could clearly hear the hissing of the limousine's air-conditioning system.

"First of all, those criminal activities of my wife's you mention are a joke, and in extremely bad taste. But we'll overlook that remark. Secondly, your own record has some serious criminal possibilities. That is what I wanted to tell you, that I know something of your record. Do you still wish me to proceed in the presence of Fräulein Weisse."

Weisse gave a scoffing laugh. "Go ahead."

"The record I speak of shows certain SS activities prior to your employment by Zeller-Bricken. It also reveals your very close connection with the transport of slave Jewish labor to the same firm, your own proposal of the use of this labor, the charges specified for its use, your knowledge that, in effect, these laborers would be worked to death. It's quite well documented, I'm sorry to say."

"You see, Lise," Weisse said to his daughter, "this gentleman proposes to blackmail me."

"You know what he says is quite true, Papa," Elizabeth said quietly.

Weisse's face took on a decidedly pink color.

"I wanted to tell you," I went on, "that I propose to present this information to the directorate of your firm, so as to establish conclusively Zeller-Bricken's responsibility for the mistreatment of the Jewish workers. I intend, also, to bring the same information to the attention of the appropriate agency of the American government."

"And, if money is paid, you won't do this," Weisse said.

"The claim stands, regardless."

"And you leave me with what?"

"You'll have to look out for yourself. I am not your accuser."
Weisse studied my face, his eyes screwed up calculatingly.
The driver had returned to the Königs Allee, and as we headed
back in the direction we had come from I could see the wounded
façade of the Kaiser Wilhelm Memorial Church stretching
upward in the distance, stark against rows of glassy new buildings.

"One million marks," Weisse said.

"Not enough."

"What will you accept?"

"One and a half million. Just today I received a letter auth-
orizing that amount as acceptable."

"I will propose it," Weisse said, "and let you know."

"When?"

"Tomorrow or the following day."

"I'll be at the Kempinski," I told him.

"You talked about documents," Weisse said. "What documents?"

"The Zhitomir list, for one."

Weisse collapsed slowly against the backrest of the seat
"You are in very deep waters, Herr Becker."

"So are you."

"We'll see," he said.

"What is the Zhitomir list?" Elizabeth asked me.

"You'll have to ask him," I said.

"Papa?"

"It's all nonsense," he said gruffly and turned away from her
to look out the window.

"You can drop me anywhere along here," I said. "I'm near
enough to the hotel."

Weisse tapped on the glass partition and indicated to the

chauffeur to stop the car. We drew in to the curb, and I asked Elizabeth before stepping out, "Will I see you?"

She didn't answer. She was staring straight ahead. Weisse didn't glance at me either. But I heard the word he muttered, as though to himself. "Jew," was the word. Elizabeth had also heard, for a look of anguish came to her face, and she turned to her father but then caught herself and remained silent.

The door was opened for me by the chauffeur, and I stepped out. I wasn't sure, but I could have sworn that I saw tears in Elizabeth's eyes. The car drew away from me. I may never see her again, I thought dully.

At first I waited in my room, hoping for a call from Elizabeth, but none came. I read through yesterday's copy of the weekly *Zeit,* through the morning edition of the *Frankfurter Allgemeine,* which had several columns devoted to the debate in Bonn on the extension of the statute of limitations on "crimes against humanity," and, thoroughly maddened that there should even be a debate on such a matter, I left the hotel room to walk off my ire. I made the Tiergarten Zoo my destination, as had a great many others, I found when I got there. The balmy weather had brought out the animal-loving Berliners, and I thought: Their love for humans may be suspect, at times, but never for animals. But the thought came from some residual bitterness I felt, a bad taste left over from the encounter that morning with Weisse. Returning to the hotel I passed the Bahnhof am Zoo: not so long ago I had entered that station on an exploration with Elizabeth, a dream it now seemed.

In my room again, I telephoned Judge Kimmel.

"I'm happy to hear from you," he said. "I would like to take up with you a clarification of Appendix II, Chapter 7, of the Federal Compensation Law. We have had several misunderstandings at the American end. A problem of language, I suspect."

I made an appointment to see him the following day.

The evening came with no word from Elizabeth. Fearful that she might call and that I would miss hearing from her, I ordered dinner brought to my room. Berlin became a lonely, barren place as the evening dragged on. I went through my briefcase, getting Sarah Stein's documents in order for my visit to the judge the next day. Kimmel was a stickler for accuracy. My travels had not disarranged the Zeller-Bricken papers I had brought with me, but I went through them anyway, particularly the same contract I had drawn up before leaving. I could make the wording of the preamble more positive, I saw, and I changed the term "indirect connection between" to "direct connection between," and added "inasmuch as." We had a case now, no doubt of that at all, and if Weisse was in communication with his fellow members on the board of directors they would all certainly see the dangers in their former position. Feeling confident, I sent off a cable to Elihu, informing him that I was hopeful of an imminent settlement along the lines of his most recent instructions.

By concentrating on those matters I was able to stave off calling Elizabeth until ten in the evening. If we are to meet again, I kept telling myself, she must be the one to call. Fearful I might not follow my own instructions, I left my room and got into a waiting taxi outside the hotel. "The Alabama Saloon," I told the driver on a whim. A four-piece rock-'n'-roll combination produced deafening reverberations in the low-ceilinged main room. I sat at the bar and watched the twisting, undulating dancers. The girls moved with abandon, while their faces remained vacant. The young males perspired in their efforts to keep up.

Behind me a vaguely familiar voice cried, "You are back! Such a pleasant surprise!"

I turned to my left and saw Annemarie Kolisch, perched on the stool next to mine. Her yellow hair was piled high on her head, and her lips glistened from a heavy application of lip rouge. She wore a pink satin dress that outlined her large breasts and revealed a generous amount of cleavage.

"Well," she said, "certainly you will buy your lover's sister a drink!"

"What would you like?"

"Something sweet, rich, and creamy, please. I have had very little dinner, you see."

The something sweet, rich, and creamy turned out to be a Brandy Alexander, which, on demand, I ordered for her.

"What are you doing back here now?" she asked. "I thought you had left."

"I had, I'm back, I'm still working here."

"And when am I to go to America?"

"When do you want to go?"

"Any day, after you have found me the job."

"I'll have to be back in New York for that," I told her.

"You really mean to do it?"

"Certainly. It's not a hard thing to do."

It wasn't. She could be placed easily enough with an import-export firm that needed bilingual secretaries. Whether or not she remained in the job would be up to her. But I knew from past experience that most German girls liked America and stayed on.

"And when do you return to New York?"

"A few days, probably."

"Did you know that your lover—your *former* lover I speak of, of course—is going to be married?"

"Hilde?"

"You have other lovers in Berlin? You Americans!" She shook a finger at me in mock chastisement.

"Who is she marrying?"

"The old boy friend, the one who has been hanging about for years. Suddenly she accepted him. One day she said no, the next day she said yes. My own opinion is that it will be a dull life for her."

"Then why is she doing it?"

"You were her last hope, maybe."

"I doubt it," I said.

"You'll buy me another drink?" Annemarie asked.

"Of course."

She reminded me suddenly of Christine at the Kit Kat in Vienna. She was much younger, but it wouldn't take long until she was as practiced and professional.

She ordered Scotch, but I doubted that it was Scotch the barmaid put in her glass.

I lifted my glass. "Please send your sister my congratulations."

"You gave her a beautiful gift," Annemarie said. "She is very proud of it."

"I'm pleased."

"What kind of work do you think would be best for me in America?" Annemarie asked.

"What do you do best?"

"Not very much. Some typing. I can do translations."

"What I suggest," I said, "is that you take a course right away in shorthand, an American system, and improve your typing. That way you'll be able to get a job right away."

"And where do I put this nice hair of mine at night?" she asked, fluffing her hair delicately.

"We can find a way for you to share an apartment with another girl. Rents are expensive, and that would be the best and cheapest way."

"You'll do all that for me?"

"Why not?"

"But why do you do this?"

"Maybe for Hilde. She seems to want it."

"I know what she wants," Annemarie said discontentedly. "She wants me not to come to this place all the time. She thinks I do something wrong here, but I don't."

"Well, maybe she's right, anyway," I said.

"Would you like to take me out somewhere else tonight? Since you don't seem to like this place."

"Do you have a suggestion?"

"Have you been to the Chez Nous?"

"No."

"Shall we go there?"

"All right."

I was free, I thought, really free for the first time in many years, and why not Annemarie?

The Chez Nous featured a cast of transvestites, remarkably feminine, most of them. The cabaret acts were reminiscent of a former Berlin of the twenties. Annemarie assured me that every one of the performers, including Dany Dollar, Striptease Number One, as "she" was billed, was male, too.

"Well, he certainly doesn't look it," I commented.

That made Annemarie giggle. We'd ordered a bottle of champagne, and she was doing a good job of downing it.

"I like you," she said. "I like you very much." She put her arm through mine and tossed back her head. An amorous look came into her eyes.

I began to feel uncomfortable. I was a little worried about what was coming. It came.

"You could sneak me into your hotel room," she said with an arch wink, "if you were very, very careful."

"I don't think that would be a good idea," I said.

"No? Why not? You prefer one of those?" She indicated the "girls" seated now at the bar.

"No."

Annemarie shrugged. "They say that America is the land of opportunity. So is Berlin, you know."

"I don't go around looking for opportunities," I said.

"You have one sitting here right with you."

"Thank you," I said. "You're very nice to flirt with an old fellow like me."

"You're not old," she said. "I know a man when I see one. Maybe in America, eh?"

"Who knows?" I said uncomfortably, suddenly feeling an urgency to leave. "Meanwhile, we won't complicate things."

"So, to you, I am just a favor to Hilde."

"You're a friend, too."

How to get away from her? I wondered. I had the fearsome notion that Elizabeth would come into this cabaret with friends and find me with this flaccid girl, whose arm was twined so familiarly through mine. I gave a very significant glance at my watch.

"You must go?" she asked, responding to the hint.

"I'm afraid so."

"Well, escort me back to the Alabama, and I will allow you to go to your lonely rest." She made a kissing sound with her pink lips.

I paid the bill and had the doorman get her a taxi. I gave the driver a five-mark note and told him to deliver the fräulein to the Alabama Saloon. Annemarie shook a mocking fist at me as she was driven off. I walked for awhile in the night air to

clear my head of the cigarette fumes of the cabaret. Then I
hailed a cruising taxi and got myself taken back to the hotel.
I checked at the desk: Still no telephone call from Elizabeth.
What the hell was going on, I asked myself. Was she on her
father's side, after all? In my room, I came close to wishing
that I had brought Annemarie with me.

I was awakened from sleep by the ringing of the telephone.
I couldn't find the instrument at first in the dark, but finally I
clutched it and asked who was waking me up at this hour.

"Alfred," Elizabeth's voice said solemnly.

"What time is it?" I asked stupidly.

"Four. I have not been able to sleep."

"Why didn't you call earlier?"

"I didn't know what to say to you. Those lovely flowers are
sitting on my table, and I have been drinking champagne. Do
you mind?"

"No."

I found a lamp switch and let some light into the room. I
sat up in bed crosslegged.

"That was terrible today with my father, wasn't it?"

"Why did you come?"

"He asked me, as a last favor. You see, we had words."

"What was it all about?"

"I'll tell you later. But why these flowers? Are you trying to
seduce me again?"

"Quite likely," I said.

"Have you no shame?"

"None," I said. "As a man free and unattached, I feel I
have the right to send flowers to anyone I want to."

"Now you worry me," she said. "You haven't done anything drastic, have you?"

"I'll tell you later," I said.

"At this moment there is half a bottle of champagne left. Would you like some?"

"Now?"

"I can't sleep, Alfred."

"I'm sure I can't anymore, either. Is it too late to pay a call?"

"Perhaps not," she said. "But I might be just a little bit drunk. You don't mind?"

"Considering the circumstances, not at all."

"Come soon, Alfred."

After hanging up the telephone, I went into the bathroom and dashed cold water over my face. My eyes smarted from lack of sleep. If I had let Annemarie come here, it would have been all over, I thought. Somebody up there still seemed to like me.

I was clearer-headed by the time I had walked to Elizabeth's apartment house. She met me at the door, wearing a red silk dressing gown. When she was in my arms, I soon realized she was wearing nothing beneath it. "First, drink your champagne," she commanded. She had poured it into a large kitchen glass. "It will not be fair if we are not both a little drunk," she said. "You will have an advantage over me."

We didn't bother to go into her bedroom. We made love on the sofa instead. I was filled with a vast sense of freedom and completeness. I could make love to her without pangs of conscience or guilt, and I had had to wait until my forty-fifth year for that to happen.

We slept a few hours. I was awakened by Elizabeth's getting out of bed. I heard her running a bath. I got up and opened the bathroom door. She was in the tub, in the midst of foamy bubbles that gave off an odor of fresh seaweed.

"*Voyeur,*" she said accusingly.

"It's not every day I get the chance to look at you."

"My hair looks terrible. You shouldn't see me like this."

"You're beautiful," I said.

"You should have told me that before you seduced me."

"I get better at it as I go along."

As the morning sun streamed into her sitting room, we had strong freshly brewed coffee and buttered rolls together, and we talked. I told her about what had happened between Lottie and me in Tel Aviv. She wanted to know just how that had made me feel and I tried to describe my reactions as exactly as I could. "Then you were the rejected one," she said with a totally concerned expression. "Of course that will make you more attractive to women. They will want to comfort and mother you. And I also think we should be careful not to see too much of each other."

"I don't understand," I said.

"You are not fully aware of it yet, Alfred, but you are in much too mixed up a state, and to leap from one woman to another would be wrong for you right now. But there are other reasons, too."

"What reasons?"

"After I left you at the Vienna airport I began having many thoughts. I felt you were beginning to be very serious about me, and so I began to look at the future. And I also looked at the past—your past, my past. For that reason I went to my father and told him much of the truth, that I had gotten to know you well, and to be very fond of you, and that therefore it was necessary for me to know how justified you were in seeking information about him. I asked him about this case you are on, and if it endangered him. And I asked him to tell me the truth about the transport of those Jews to Hanover."

"You don't have to tell me what he answered."

"But I will, because it is senseless to avoid it any longer. He said that there were things he could not tell even me, because they were secret. He said he had always been a patriotic German, and this was true during the time of Hitler, too. If a policy was decided on, he followed it. He had nothing particularly against Jews, he said, but it was also clear that they were being eliminated from the German state. It was not up to him to decide any differently. What he did, anyone else would have done in his position. After the collapse, he said, it was recognized even by the Americans that he had abilities that should be employed in the reconstruction of the country. Therefore, he was never blamed for anything. He also told me not to trust you; you were out after money, and you would get it any way you could. So it became a question for me of believing in either you or him. And then I saw my father with your eyes, that you could not help but despise him, even though you were careful not to say this to me. 'Did you mean to help the Jews you sent to Hanover?' I asked him, and he said, 'Naturally not. And lucky for you, because I would have been sent to a camp myself, and there would have been no one to look after you and your mother. The Jews were all to die, anyway.' I could hardly believe what I was hearing, but I asked him had he thought what might happen to him if I told you what he had said. He answered that nothing would happen, he would see to that. 'One must decide,' he said, 'who is to be preferred, a true German or a Jew.' I told him I had decided, and I would not see him anymore."

"But you saw him yesterday."

"For the last time," she said. "He thought, I am sure, that by facing you with him I would see you quite differently. But, what happened was that I saw him more clearly. You heard what he called you at the end."

"Yes."

"Then you left the car and were gone. It was quite unpleasant."

"Why not tell me," I suggested gently.

"It was hard for me," she said. "I am not used to it—speaking to my father in that manner. But I was revolted."

She had shot out the words, spitting them almost. He was not her father, she told him, not a father she could acknowledge. "You sicken me," she said to him. "You, and everyone like you."

Weisse had hunched himself in his corner of the rear seat, and at first he had merely gazed at her with a thin, quite superior smile, as though she were only a wicked child having a tantrum.

"I am proud to tell you," she said to him, "that I love that man." And here she was referring to me.

Her face became flushed as she recalled the moment. "Perhaps I only told him that to hurt him all the more, and perhaps you will dislike me for it?"

"Did you mean it?" I asked.

"Yes, I meant it. I meant everything I said. I told him more: that he had bestowed on me the handicap of being German, his kind of German, and I would have to live it down somehow. And do you know what he did then?"

"What?"

"He disowned me. He said it exactly like that: 'I disown you, for always.' For some strange reason, it made me laugh. Then I opened my door, and said, 'Thank God. It is a great relief to be disowned by you.' I was still shaking a little after I was out on the street and walking away. I thought of other things I could have said to him, that he had given me a shameful badge to wear, even though I had done nothing wrong. But, do you see? With that badge how could I possibly face your friends and your family in America?"

"Some of my best friends are not Jewish," I said.

"And those too I could not convince I was not like my father."

"In New York," I said, "there is no one more convincing than a beautiful woman."

"I do not joke, Alfred. I feel this."

"And is that why you practically cut me to pieces when I called you from Vienna?"

"I think so, and also, I will admit, out of annoyance that you were going to travel so far to see your wife. I assumed you would have a fond reconciliation, and just the thought made me jealous. I couldn't help it. I thought: What is the use? You would always make me feel jealous and miserable, and it would be best to avoid all that."

"I don't think so," I said. "I think I could make you feel pretty good."

"You had a German girl friend once," Elizabeth said, "and you didn't make her feel so good."

"I'm beginning to get some ideas of my own about badges and labels. They can work both ways. Hilde accepted the identity I imposed on her. Would you, if I were to act the same way?"

"Alfred," she said, "you still don't know very much about women. My better sense tells me that if you marry again it should be to a woman who is Jewish. It would be easier and safer for you."

"Does that mean you should marry a German man?"

"I don't know," she said. "To be frank, I do not care much for German men. And, if I should see signs of my father in them, I will like them even less."

"Well," I said, not too seriously, "then you might be safer with someone Jewish, like me."

But she didn't react lightly. "Your Jewishness," she said. "What is it? I only like you for what you are and what you stand for! But is it because you are Jewish?"

"Not according to Lottie," I answered. "She doesn't regard me as much of a Jew. I am beginning to think that under ideal conditions, it doesn't matter a damn. Do you understand?"

"No, not really."

"One fears what happened to so many others might one day happen to you. To become Jewish is a way of putting yourself on guard. So that you won't be taken by surprise, so that you can go down fighting if necessary. When I saw for the first time the Professor's candelabrum——"

"You found it," Elizabeth said excitedly. "But why didn't you tell me?"

"You didn't ask me."

"Do you only speak when spoken to?" she said. "Tell me about it."

"But I was about to make an important point."

"I want to know about the candelabrum," she said almost childishly.

I told her about the leads I'd followed, and the help I'd had, and about Wohl's surprising act of generosity.

"That will make *him* feel very good, I'm sure," she said caustically. "Anyway, it's wonderful. I wish I had been there. I would like to see the Professor's face when you give it to him."

"He has it already," I said.

"And what did it look like?"

I described it to her as best I could, the fierce strength I had seen in it. "That was the sense of Jewishness that counted," I said. "I was going to try to explain it to you. The persistence of tradition and of what that tradition means. Those seven branches go back a long, long time."

"But what do they mean?" she asked.

"I can tell you what they mean to me." I explained what I knew, that the menorah of seven branches could be traced back directly to the seven-branched candelabrum that was set alight each day in the Holy Temple of Jerusalem, known as the Second Temple. The branches then contained cups for oil, each cup filled daily with the same amount of oil. "There was a miracle connected with it," I said.

"Yes? Tell me."

"One branch continued to flame until the following day, after the others went out."

"Do you believe it?"

"Well, some of our more realistic scholars think there was nothing supernatural about it. It was simply a way of conserving the very expensive oil that was used. Even so, there was a symbolism involved. The light that remained burning symbolized many things—God's presence, peace, knowledge, understanding, life itself."

"How beautiful," Elizabeth said. "How very beautiful. Everyone should know about it."

"But the light that burned was not regarded as exclusively Jewish."

"Yes," she said softly, "that is very important. But, even so, what you tell me makes me want to become Jewish."

"Better think about it," I said. "You'll run into a lot of prejudice."

23: At the lobby desk of the Kempinski I was handed a message. Sanford Johnson of the American military mission in Dahlem had telephoned and wished me to return the call at my earliest convenience. I didn't know a Sanford Johnson, but I called him back. Johnson's voice had a soft Virginia tang; he was polite and almost off-hand. "I'd like to see you, Mr. Becker, if it would be at all possible for you to call here."

"What's it about?"

"Oh, just a little chat. Your name has come up in conversation here, and I think we should meet. We have similar interests, in a manner of speaking."

I was fairly sure our similar interests involved the Zeller-Bricken matter and my closest guess was that Elihu had caused some flurry in an office at the State Department, with consequent teletype clattering at the military mission in Dahlem. I agreed to see Johnson in his office at two-thirty.

I called on Judge Kimmel before going to see Johnson. The Main Restitution Court was a restored mansion of some grandness in an area of official buildings not far from the Berlin

Hilton. I knew my way to the judge's office, and walked in without ceremony. His desk, as usual, was littered with files of problem cases.

"You look well," he said. "Shall we have a social conversation first?"

The social conversation took up hardly a minute. The judge, while not brusque, liked to deal only with business in his office.

"We have a problem on this Appendix II, Chapter 7, I mentioned to you," he said, abandoning the personal note. He handed me a copy of the most recent appendices to the restitution and compensation legislation and directed my attention to the clauses in Chapter 7, explaining to me the interpretations he gave to them. The trouble, I saw, came from an imprecise English translation of the clauses, and between us we decided that a clarification would be a good idea. "I will have inserts printed and sent to the concerned parties," he said.

That question resolved, he leaned back in his chair and asked how the Zeller-Bricken matter was proceeding.

"It should be coming to a head in a day or so," I told him.

"If you get the money, I'll be surprised," he said sagely, but didn't amplify.

I then broached the Sarah Stein case to him. "Physical injury beyond the usual malnutrition can't be established," I explained, and I further explained that I had been looking into the possibility of sexual assault, at the suggestion of the psychiatrist handling her case. "That can't be established either," I said. "But here is a case where compensation is absolutely necessary, and yet, frankly, I can't figure out which grounds would best be used to justify it. Practically every loophole is closed except for that relating to proven mental injury."

"What has happened in the lower courts?" Judge Kimmel asked.

"Rejection all along the line."

"Has the appeal reached this court?"

"Not yet. The thing has been dragging on for years. Frankly, if I had handled her case originally, I would have used other grounds. But time has run out on those."

Judge Kimmel made a tent with the fingers of both his hands. "What are you asking of me?"

"Advice," I said.

"Her parents are dead, I presume. What about a claim relating to inheritability for damage to liberty relating to her parents?"

"That's the one I would have tried earlier, but it's too late now."

"The girl's mental illness is permanent?"

"Looks like it. There's a chance, but not much."

"You have testimony about mistreatment?"

"Yes, I think I can prove that. I'll make the assumption, anyway."

"Interestingly enough," the judge said, "several of your American psychiatrists have formed a group to clarify those cases relating to mental damages suffered during confinement in concentration camps. But, if we were to accept their viewpoint, almost every victim would be entitled to some form of compensation. I'm inclined toward a liberal recommendation, and I will make one in my report to Bonn and the Landtag, but your case is still going to be a difficult one to resolve. Were there no others who knew the girl before she was sent to a camp?"

"They've disappeared from the face of the earth," I said.

"Yes, literally," the judge added dryly. "What I suggest is this: that you continue the claim along the lines you are following now, that the psychiatrist's report be made as full and

detailed as possible. You, as her lawyer, should assume the following: her parents were seized in front of her eyes and taken
away, following which she was also seized and sent to the
Reichenau KZ. This terror-stricken little girl was then put into
primitive, disgusting surroundings. List the brutalities she witnessed. List her condition when found. Supply also a judgment
by both a psychiatrist and a medical doctor as to the effects such
experiences would have on the mind of an immature girl. Supply also records of the circumstances of the demise of her
parents. Then cite Chapter II, Paragraph 2(b), relating to
groups of 'Special Eligibility,' and add to this the 1959 amendments to the Second Edition of the Compensation Laws, published in 1956. Show cause as to why 'Special Eligibility' should
apply in the girl's case."

"And," I added, "send the brief directly to you."

"Upon which," he said, "I will take the matter up directly
with the Land court involved."

"That means six more months," I said.

"Six months is better than two years," he pointed out.

I had only pretended annoyance. The judge had made a
major concession, I knew, for one known to exemplify German
judicial correctness, which he stressed all the more because of
some Jewish elements in his own lineage.

As though to avoid any gratitude on my part, he quickly
changed the subject. "One of our translators," he said, "a
quite attractive woman, told me she was an acquaintance of
yours years ago when you were in the Army. I took the liberty
of giving her your New York address." He squinted at me
inquiringly.

"Yes, she wrote me," I told him. "We had a reunion here
recently."

"No paternity claims or anything like that, I hope," he said slyly.

"No, just talk about old times. As a matter of fact, she's about to marry again."

"Again?"

"She was married once before."

"I see, I see," Judge Kimmel said.

His curiosity satisfied, he rose and offered me his hand. I left the courtly little man to ponder over his file folders, each one representing some claim for past sufferings, past indignities, irretrievable losses, endless grief.

The United States military mission occupied a group of buildings on Clayallee, all—with the exception of Truman Hall, now a shopping center for Americans—constructed for Goering's proud Luftwaffe and possessing no architectural distinction whatsoever. The largest of the gray concrete structures was occupied by a headquarters that provided mainly consular services. Seated behind a desk near the entrance was an MP, in uniform and wearing a red-and-white-striped helmet liner. He directed me to Johnson's office, which was down a long corridor on the main floor. A small card on his door read: *Political Affairs, American Sector, Berlin.* The door opened into a small reception office. I gave my name to the sole occupant, a sharp-featured young secretary, who nodded and indicated the door to the inner office. "Just go in," she said, and went back to typing. Johnson, when I opened his door, stubbed out a cigarette on his desk, empty except for an ashtray and a telephone, and got to his feet. He was gangling, in his mid-thirties, and looked slightly pained, an expression, I discovered, that was not due to my presence but was seemingly perpetual. "Good of you to visit us, Mr. Becker," he said. "Please sit down." I wondered about the "us."

Two hard-backed steel chairs were on the opposite side from where he sat at his desk. I took one. The room was otherwise bare, except for two steel filing cabinets. Apparently not very much went on in this office, and for all I knew it was only used for a conference such as this. I already sensed something that involved security.

"Cigarette, Mr. Becker?"

"No thanks."

"I don't know exactly how to approach this," he said tentatively.

I didn't answer, because he probably knew very well how to approach whatever it was he was going to approach.

"But, you'll agree, won't you, that whatever is said won't go farther than this office."

"If you feel it necessary."

"I do, Mr. Becker. We seemed to have stepped into an area of some delicacy."

"We?"

"I suppose I should tell you that I'm not exactly speaking to you in my usual capacity, but on behalf of another agency of the government."

That meant the CIA, I knew. He was either an agent or doing the work for an agent who preferred to stay in the background.

"You might as well get right into it," I said. "The routine is not unfamiliar to me."

"Yes," he said, "well, uh, Mr. Becker, as I understand it you represent some parties in a negotiation with the West German firm of Zeller-Bricken."

"Quite true."

"Electronics systems, that sort of thing."

"My case hasn't anything to do with what they manufacture."

"I realize that, yes." A furrowed brow now accompanied the pained look. "I also understand," he went on, "that some of your dealings have been with a gentleman by the name of——" He looked upward, as though to refresh his memory. "Oskar Weisse?"

"Yes."

"Correct me if I stray from the line," he said, "but you or your associates profess to have certain information about the background of this gentleman—his pre-Federal Republic activities, shall we say?"

"He was a Nazi," I said, "party member, SS administrative, and some evidence of his involvement in the extermination apparatus."

"Really, that bad?" Johnson looked genuinely surprised. "Was this the sort of thing you were planning to make public?"

"Not planning," I said. "A recourse, if necessary."

"Then it's a good idea we're having this little talk. You see, Mr. Becker, I have been asked to advise you that any such publicity might prove severely embarrassing to our government."

"Because of the Defense contract?"

"Only partly that, actually. Perhaps not that at all." He paused to light a cigarette and inhaled deeply. After exhaling he coughed and cleared his throat. "That's not our worry. By that I mean it's not the worry of this other agency of the government I mentioned before. Let Defense do its own worrying. Right?"

He smiled at me broadly as though he had said something very funny. Then his face grew suddenly solemn, and he said, leaning forward, his elbows firm on the desk. "No, the embarrassment goes a little deeper than a bit of fuss in the newspapers."

"Are you going to tell me why?" I asked.

"I might be able to," he said, "but it would require taking you into our confidence. The information would be privileged, eyes-only type stuff, if you know what I mean. It's this other agency of the government that's actually concerned."

"I don't want to play guessing games," I said. "You'll have to make yourself clearer if we're going to get anywhere. As a matter of fact, I don't know where we're supposed to get. Do you want my agreement that I won't make my information public?"

He leaned back in his chair, with his cigarette between his lips and, squinting against the smoke that spiraled toward his eyes, studied me carefully.

"Yes," he said, scratching the back of his neck, "and no. What I'm trying to suggest is, Mr. Becker, that a little more is at stake here than even someone as astute as you might realize. Do you have time for a little explanation?"

"At your service," I said.

"Well, just to refresh your memory," he said, his voice becoming brisk all at once, even the trace of Virginia accent disappearing, "there once operated in the Federal Republic an organization known as the Gehlen Bureau. Does that suggest anything to you?"

I nodded.

"You know, in that case, that the Gehlen Bureau operated for several years as an intelligence apparatus. But what else do you know about the organization, Mr. Becker? I'd be interested in hearing."

"All right," I said. "Gehlen was a spy chief for the Wehrmacht and, after capture by our forces, was said to have been flown to Washington, where he entered into negotiations with Army G-2. Simply put, he offered us his intelligence staff, his apparatus of agents, and his files. According to well-founded rumor, this offer was gratefully accepted. After the German collapse he was set up by us, supplied liberally with funds that were said to have come first from OSS and then CIA, and allowed to operate freely in all four zones of Germany. His data came mainly to us, although the fiction was maintained that the Gehlen group was strictly a West German operation. His staff grew so large and his operations so complex that the whole thing was eventually quartered in a compound near Munich. I believe Gehlen and associates operated there under the name of the South German Industrial Development Corporation."

Johnson shook his head slowly, as though to say, "I'll be damned."

"Who supplied you with all that?" he asked.

"*Der Spiegel*," I said. "They published it in their articles."

"Really? That much?"

"And more," I said.

"Well, they've saved us some time, anyway. Because I can now offer a further fact to add to your collection. This Mr. Weisse we have been talking about was once an important staff member of the South German Industrial Development Corporation."

I sat back in my own chair.

"You see, Mr. Becker," Johnson said, allowing himself the bare wisp of a smile, "Weisse was one of ours."

"An agent," I said.

"A possible, even a likely supposition."

A great deal that had puzzled me up to now began to come clear. I started putting it together, not feeling anything at the moment. "I would expect that he was granted immunity from any potential prosecution for any activities of his during the war."

"You're onto it now," he said, nodding with approval. "He was indeed."

"No matter what that policy might have been condoning."

"Well, I don't go into those aspects in my capacity, Mr. Becker. All that was well before my time. My briefing was only to the extent that this fellow Weisse performed quote invaluable services unquote for an agency of our government. His contacts in the Eastern Zone, particularly in Poland and Czechoslovakia, were regarded as unique, and as you might well imagine these services were performed at considerable risk to his own person."

"That means we were employing a war criminal, however," I said. "At Ludwigsburg, for your own information, they're building a case against him."

"Will that amount to much, do you think? Just between us, of course."

"They seem pretty serious about it."

"Well, we may have to look into that aspect. You see, this could have some ramifications along international lines. By that I mean to say, the kind of information Weisse got hold of sometimes came from friendly as well as unfriendly sources. Naturally, our government wouldn't want that known. You understand the embarrassment any public exposure of any, let us say, damaging facts about Weisse could cause our government. Not that he doesn't check out very well these days."

"By checking out well, I suppose you mean that you don't hold him responsible for the transport of three thousand Jewish slaves to the Hanover plant of his present firm."

"An administrative matter, surely. Like others, he was just a cog in a great big wheel."

"That's your *position*, Mr. Johnson, and a very similar one to his."

"Our government's position, Mr. Becker. The books are closed on Weisse. We couldn't open them, you realize, without great damage to very sensitive lines of connection."

"The Zeller-Bricken contract wouldn't be part of a payoff to him, would it?"

"Oh, hardly. No, we're not concerned about that. Wouldn't matter too much one way or another. An American firm manufactures much the same sort of equipment, and I suppose that contract has more to do with relations between Bonn and Washington. However, I do have one more piece of information for you. I've been given to understand that the Zeller-Bricken company wants to make your group an offer of one million five hundred thousand marks as a sort of indemnity for hardships imposed on non-German workers at the Hanover plant during the war years. I believe a certain Karl Steglitz, a legal representative for the firm, will contact you on this matter in a day or so. It is hoped by the agency of the government I mentioned to you before that the offer will prove acceptable to you and your group."

"I think I get the whole picture," I said.

"That about does it," he said. "I knew we'd be able to clarify things by having this little chat. A pleasure to meet you, and I hope you're enjoying your stay in Berlin. The weather is good, for a change."

He got to his feet, and we shook hands.

"You know something," he said, "I'll be damned if I can remember a word of what we talked about."

He opened the door for me, made a painful effort to smile, and ushered me through his outer office. It only occurred to me when I was outside the gates of the military mission and hoping to spot a taxi that I had finished my work in Berlin. It had all been arranged so neatly. I hadn't negotiated a damn thing, I realized. I had merely made myself enough of a troublemaker to get attention higher up—all the way up. Weisse had not, for one moment, a thing to fear from me or anyone else. The sacrificial victims had been decided on, and they did not include him.

I made the call to Ludwigsburg that same afternoon. I told Langsehn, without elaborating, that I could not see my way clear to assist him on the case we had discussed, and that, in any event, I was leaving Germany shortly, because my negotiations had been concluded.

"I understand, Herr Becker," Langsehn said, matter-of-factly. "But I hope it has been made clear to you the difficulty of our task here. The problem is always the same—the lack of cooperation from those who could help us."

Because suddenly the burden had been shifted to me, and people like me, I answered him sharply. "We both of us know, Herr Langsehn, that you don't always have to obtain a conviction to do something constructive. You have plenty to go on as it is, it would seem to me."

"I am a prosecutor, Herr Becker," he said. "Under Federal laws, my area is strictly defined. I hope that groups you represent in the United States will appreciate the work we do in spite of the obstacles we encounter. Sometimes, unavoidably, we must drop certain cases."

And that, I thought, was why he had wanted to see me. He had wanted to check out his own assessment of Weisse's invulnerability. He had been tipped off. Was I? And, if so, would I proceed? I gave him his answer.

"Such as the one we're talking about," I said.

"Good day, Herr Becker," Langsehn said.

I told Elizabeth at dinner that evening that my work was finished. We had met at the same small Italian restaurant where we had talked with Ulrich on a day that now seemed far in the past. "Another couple of days and there'll only be one reason for staying."

"Me?"

"That's right. You."

"Then you should not stay. I don't believe in it. I do not mind sharing your life while you have reason to be here, but we would both become discontented if we were only to drift because it was pleasant."

"It's a lot more than pleasant."

"Perhaps only because we do not face the truth."

"And what truth is that?" I asked.

"I explained it all to you," she said tiredly. "We do not have to go over it again. We ask a lot of each other, and neither of us has decided if we are capable of giving it. The sleeping together is easy, certainly, but it has made me feel much more of a woman, and as a woman I need much more."

"If I can give it, you've got it," I said.

"No," she said. "I don't want those offers, not here, and not for awhile. But I don't understand what you just said. Your work is finished? Has my father met your terms?"

"Not your father," I said. And I decided that I was going to have to breach Sanford Johnson's security. There was nothing Elizabeth could tell her father, if she were ever to see him again, that Weisse didn't know already. I told her I had been contacted by an American government official and had discovered that all had now been neatly arranged.

"So," Elizabeth said, "you found out about the intelligence work my father did."

"You knew about it?"

"Strangely enough, from Ulrich. He once told me that East German friends of his were convinced my father was working for the Americans. That could only mean one thing. I knew enough not to ask my father, but he indirectly admitted it. And it seems you forced him to go directly to his friends in your government."

"But who forced him to meet our terms?"

I knew the answer, but I wanted to find out if she saw it the same way.

"I think it was quite simple, really," she said. "That is how these things are often done. His American friends agree to pressure you into silence, and he agrees to get the firm to pay the money."

"So it's a payoff," I said.

"Why not? It's done all the time. Germans have been forced into paying for nearly twenty years now. It's all part of the recovery and the new image. Now the question for you becomes: Do you want to take the money?"

I stared at her, not knowing quite what to say because her last words had struck directly at my own doubts.

"You're not happy about it," she said. "I can see that. You came to those people, saying to them that they must face up to what they had done and that their money must be regarded as a token of their shame and guilt. Isn't that so?"

"It's a way of putting it."

"And instead you find that they give you the money because you have become an embarrassment to them. Is that what you hoped to do? Cause embarrassment?"

"I came to get compensation for clients," I said.

"And is that what you are getting?"

"Yes, I'm getting the money for them."

"And you consider that your job is done?"

"I have to," I said. "When you come right down to it, my loyalty has to go to my own country, my government. An official ruling has been made. There's a larger thing at stake now. I could talk my head off, and it would be denied. The only thing that would happen is that I'd make a bigger mess of things."

"It seems to me very simple," she said. "The money means nothing anymore."

"To my clients, it does."

"But not to the people paying it," she said.

Yes, she had made it very simple. I remembered what Joseph Mittelman had said to me at the Wiener Group meeting before I left New York. "Blood money," he had called what I was hoping to get, and I had thought his view stark to the extreme. But this was worse. Meaningless money. It was a deal, that was all, and a favorable one for Zeller-Bricken. Here was a company with a heart, the money would say, and now totally cleansed of anything shameful in its organizational past. And, meanwhile, the truth was that it was linked to its past as solidly as ever. Expediency still ruled, not the flame of humanity. And I would be made a collaborator.

"I'm beginning to feel like a fool," I admitted to Elizabeth.

"Yes," she said, "I will tell you honestly that I think that they have been cleverer than you. It doesn't make me love you less, because I do not admire people who are that smart. But I know how my father will think of you."

"I know what he thinks of me."

"And," Elizabeth said, "this is his way of killing you, isn't it?"

My face must have gone white, for I saw Elizabeth's eyes fill with a look of profound concern. I didn't realize it at first, but my fingers were pressed hard against the edge of the table.

"Alfred," she said almost pleadingly, "believe me, I am on *your* side. I will always defend you."

"Against what? Killers?"

"Alfred," she said. "Don't let him. It's you he worries about. No one else. It is because you are more than a businessman that he was forced to do what he did. If you had been less than you are, he would have known how to handle you. You forced him to play his last card."

"God damn it," I cried out, and other diners turned to look at us. "Why did you have to see it, and not me?"

"I perhaps understand Germans a little better than you."

"But it's not up to me," I said, still staving off some kind of confrontation. "I represent, I don't decide."

"I think, Alfred," she said, "that it is going to have to be up to you to decide."

"Well, I'll think about it," I said, and doggedly attacked the sauce-covered veal scallopini on my plate.

In the morning two days later, Elizabeth drove me to Tempelhof in her Porsche. I had come to no firm decision; but I had at least temporarily avoided the issue by stalling Steglitz when he called. I told him I would have to return to New York and confer with my associates before giving him a final word. "But it can so easily be wound up while you are here," he said, his manner too eager for comfort. "Couldn't you telephone or cable? It has taken some work to get agreement from the board, and in my view the offer is remarkably generous." I told him to send a letter to my hotel with the firm's stipulations, and I would take it to New York with me. When I received it, I doubt that I had ever read a more unctuous statement of intent. It had come to the attention of the Zeller-Bricken directorate that some shocking incidents had occurred during World War

II at the Hanover plant, and the directors were of one mind in insisting that compensation be paid to anyone who might have been the victim of certain misguided employees of the firm, which, of course, had been entirely reconstituted after the war. And so on. I didn't read to the end.

But, as for ourselves, Elizabeth and I did not yet know what to do. In her apartment earlier that morning we made use of the last opportunity to share her soft bed. "I must tell you something," she said, her head cradled on my shoulder. "I am going to do much thinking—about us. Then, perhaps, some day soon, I will pay a visit to New York. Wouldn't it be nice to just run into one another on the street? If you consider me, and, after looking at me honestly, you decide that we might be able to like each other for a long, long time, you will let me know. You will find a way to let me know. But we must not enter into something like enthusiastic children."

"I feel very grown up right now," I said.

"Be serious," she said. "Go home first, and see how you feel after some time has passed. Suppose we were to have a child? Do you think such a child would approve of his mother's family? You see? I could become a great problem to you."

"A great, big, beautiful problem."

"We are not going to make up our minds," she insisted, "here, now, and in this bed."

Elizabeth went with me as far as Customs, and, just before I passed through, she flung herself against me, and tears streamed down her cheeks. "Oh, I will miss you," she sobbed. "Do write. Be sure to write."

I managed to tell her over the huge lump in my throat that I would write, that I would telephone, that she would hear from me very soon. Then she turned abruptly and walked away. I had a lonely trip ahead of me, and a lot of loneliness after that.

A little later, I was fastening my seat belt. Then the motors of the DC-6 caught and throbbed into life. By the time I reached Frankfurt and changed to the jet, I knew what I was going to tell Elihu.

And in New York I told him. We lunched, the day after I returned, at Barbetta's, his favorite restaurant. I had filled him in on the whole course of the Zeller-Bricken discussions, and I simply announced to him that I was resigning from the case. "Anyone can handle it now," I said. "You can decide to accept the offer or reject it, as you think best."

"And what do you think, Alfred?" He regarded me shrewdly. No one took advantage easily of Elihu. "What do you advise?"

"My advice? That we reject the offer and withdraw from all negotiations with them."

"And why, Alfred?"

"Because now it's become a simple matter of a payoff."

"And that isn't what we want?"

"Do we?"

"There are sixty people who can use the money."

"I know. But if they don't get it, are they going to starve?"

"No. So what you're saying is that we blow the whole deal, to put it nicely."

"Why not? By taking the money we join them in the cover-up."

"And how would I explain this to our people?"

"Tell them the truth, that what we wanted was an admission of complicity, and that we're not getting it, so the money is valueless and meaningless. Frankly, it was someone else who pointed this factor out to me."

"Who?"

"A friend of mine in Berlin."

"A good friend?"

"Yes, a very good friend."

"Well, it's certainly a point," Elihu said. "I don't know what the hell to do. But, for the moment, I'm inclined to agree with you. With no money, who would reimburse your expenses?"

"We'll forget about that."

"So you wasted you time in Berlin."

"No, I don't think so," I said.

"And you've lost a wife," he said. "That was quite a trip you had."

"Yes," I said. "Yes, that's true."

"I hate to forget about it," he said. "Do you know the trouble I've gone to? And now you come back and hit me in the stomach this way. I'll take it up with the Lodge."

"And consider me resigned as of now," I said.

"Even so," Elihu said, "you've done a good job."

One morning some ten days following my return I picked up the *New York Times* left outside my door and read it over the breakfast I had prepared for myself. I was beginning to settle into a new routine. On waking, I would stack several records on the changer and let music boom through the speakers. It was company of a sort. I had arranged for a maid to come three times a week, but, after the first time she had come I had yet to see her again, for she would arrive at ten and leave at two. A few days before, I had packed up Lottie's clothes, and there were several cartons piled up, waiting for shipment to Tel Aviv. There were other signs of her presence left, however— her perfumes, a medicine chest filled with pill bottles. The apartment was too large for me and gave me a feeling of emptiness. Twice already, I had written to Elizabeth, but I had avoided making any concrete suggestions to her.

While reading the paper, I heard the telephone and took the call on the kitchen extension. "Have you the *Times?*" The voice belonged to Professor Marcus.

"I'm reading it now."

"Turn to the page with wedding announcements," he ordered. "You'll see something that will interest you. I didn't want you to miss it."

When he hung up I found the page he had referred to and looked for familiar names among announcements of weddings and engagements. While doing so I came across what the Professor had called about, a headline in small type that read: SPECIAL CONGREGATION SERVICE. "The Congregation Beth Hillel in Kew Gardens," the story read, "announces a special Friday evening service on May 23rd, during which the recently discovered Erfurt Menorah will be lighted for the first time in this country. The Menorah was located several weeks ago in Vienna, after having disappeared from the Erfurt Synagogue during the Crystal Night anti-Semitic riots of 1938. Members and friends of the Synagogue are cordially invited to attend."

I was among those present, of course. And so were several faces familiar to me from my attendance at the monthly Lern Tags, among them Mark Abromovitz and the elderly Mrs. Arenstein and even Joseph Mittelman, who could hardly be accused of sentimentality. "We are thinking of proposing you for the new chairmanship of the Weiner Group," he said to me portentously. "I couldn't spare the time," I told him. "I really couldn't." Mittelman said snappishly: "That's the trouble these days. No one has the time for anything anymore."

Elihu was there, too, and I sat in the second pew, with him on my left and the Professor on my right. The candelabrum, having made a safe journey from Vienna, stood on the raised platform, the Bimah, in the sacred center of the synagogue, and Rabbi Goldstein made much ceremony—improvised, to a degree —of lighting a small candle from the flame of the Ner Tomid, the ever-burning light that was said to be symbolic of the candelabrum in the Temple of Jerusalem, and then, one by one, lighting the thick white candles impaled solidly on the seven spearlike spikes of the Erfurt Menorah. I felt a smarting sensation in my eyes and was completely surprised to find my eyelids, when I touched them, wet with tears. I blinked, and beside me I heard Elihu clear his throat. "A very moving sight," he murmured to me.

The rabbi next recited a Kaddish for the martyred rabbi of Erfurt, who had perished on the Night of Crystal, and, following that, addressed us briefly. "We must all feel pride on this evening," he said, "an occasion of great meaning for those of us assembled here and, I might be so bold as to add, for Jewry everywhere." He went on in that vein, and I knew heads were turned in the direction of me and the Professor. I almost wished I hadn't come. "We owe this profoundly generous gift to the Beth Hillel Synagogue," the rabbi finished, "to Professor Herman Marcus, who is known to and beloved by all of you. We praise him and thank him."

I took the Professor's hand and pressed it. "You see," he muttered to me gruffly, "I always told you such things do not disappear."

When the service was over, I left with Elihu, who had driven to the synagogue in his car and who had offered me a ride back to Manhattan. "Well," he said, in the car, "that was very nice, really very nice. The menorah is a beautiful object, quite striking. I wish we had something like it for my own congregation."

"All it takes is a little looking around," I said.

"I know the truth about that," he said, with a pat on my shoulder. "I suppose you won't be going back to Germany for awhile?"

"Not for awhile."

"Well, maybe you could do something for me from your New York office."

"I'm not your lawyer anymore."

"Yes, but maybe just one more thing. My Lodge met in executive session, and it was decided to accept your recommendation. We would like you to inform the Zeller-Bricken Company that we are rejecting their offer and that we are dropping our claim on behalf of the Jewish laborers."

"Sure," I said. "I'll be glad to do that, and I won't charge a fee."

"And could you maybe suggest politely that they go to hell?"

"How about a phrase to the effect that you don't feel their offer has been made in good faith and for reasons that have a bearing on the original claim?"

"However you lawyers want to say it," Elihu agreed. "Tell me, are you keeping that large apartment? Seems like a lot of space for a single man to rattle around in."

"Oh, you never know," I said. We stopped at a traffic light on Queens Boulevard. It was the kind of rare, clear night in which the towers of Manhattan could be seen outlined and shining.

"You've already found a nice Jewish woman?" he asked in a needling tone.

"Not necessarily," I said.

"You lawyers—you never come right out and say something."

"What do you want me to say?"

"Am I asking you anything?" He was all innocence. "You're a single man now. We old married fellows like to know what you bachelors are up to."

"Nothing," I said, "for the moment."

"But something must have happened while you were over there."

"You know what happened."

"Everything?" Elihu kept his eyes on the traffic, as we headed toward the Queensboro bridge, but he was waiting expectantly, I knew.

"Okay," I said, "but this has to be just between us, Elihu."

"Naturally."

"Weisse's daughter," I said. "You'll remember I mentioned her to you?"

Elihu nodded. "What about her?"

"I'm thinking of asking her to marry me." Now that I had spoken the words aloud, I knew I had been thinking of nothing else since I had arrived back in New York, and that there was no other possible choice for me.

"This is not a joke, Alfred?"

"No, it's not a joke."

"Forgive me, Alfred, for saying this, but you must know she doesn't have exactly the proper background for you."

"I'm tired of all that," I said. "If I feel a certain way, I have to do something about it."

We had begun to rattle over the bridge toward the towering buildings of Manhattan.

"Well," Elihu said, with a sigh, "speaking as your good friend, and as a fairly tolerant individual, I must nevertheless tell you that I think you are slightly out of your mind. So you had an affair. That doesn't mean——"

I interrupted him. "I didn't say I had an affair."

"What does she look like?" Elihu asked.

"She's beautiful," I said.

"And you didn't have an affair?"

"Let's not go into that," I said.

"Is she intelligent?"

"Of course," I said. "What's all this got to do with it?"

"I guess I'm waiting for you to tell me something else," Elihu said.

"All right. She was in the middle at first, helping her father to negotiate, but, I assure you, she came over to our side."

"She's a good person, you mean."

"A very good person."

"And what about your intended father-in-law?"

"She told him to go to hell."

"Not much of an in-law problem," Elihu said. "That's a plus."

"No jokes, Elihu."

"So you're really interested in what I think?"

"I wouldn't have mentioned it, otherwise."

"What I think is you'll cause a lot of gossip if you go through with this, they'll say it's an insult to your former wife, and they'll all line up out of curiosity to meet the woman. Would you allow me to be the first to extend you a dinner invitation?"

"Many thanks," I said.

"Don't worry," he said. "We'll all treat her like a person."

"I'm not worried." And I wasn't.

"No, you bastard," Elihu said, "you were all ready to cut your friends dead, weren't you?"

"The thought had crossed my mind," I admitted, "depending on their behavior."

We had left the bridge, and were headed crosstown. Elihu turned up Park Avenue.

"You'll keep all this to yourself for the time being," I said. "You never know."

"Of course I'll keep it to myself," Elihu said. "You want people to think I'm crazy too?"

But, when he stopped in front of my building, he smiled and said, "Good luck, Alfred."

"Thanks," I said. The doorman had appeared to open my door for me, and before getting out I asked Elihu if he wanted to come up for a drink.

"No, it's a little late."

He drove off, and I glanced at my watch and saw that it was twenty minutes past eleven. Would it be so terrible to wake her at this hour? At twenty minutes past five in the morning, Berlin time, light would be breaking over the city. I'd give her another hour to sleep, I thought.

About the Author

Born in Herkimer, New York, Hollis Alpert grew up in Philadelphia. During World War II, he served in the European Theater of Operations as combat historian. Today he is well known as film critic and contributing editor for *Saturday Review.* Mr. Alpert's previous books include three novels, *The Summer Lovers, Some Other Time* and *For Immediate Release;* a book of essays on the film, *The Dreams and the Dreamers;* and *The Barrymores.* His articles, reviews and short stories have appeared in *Esquire, The New Yorker, Partisan Review, Playboy, Mademoiselle, Harper's Bazaar* and numerous other publications. Mr. Alpert is married and now lives in New York City.